The Spanish Note

A NOVEL

ROSEMARY DOYLE

Dedicated to my husband, a constant source of love and support over more than four and a half decades of marriage, and to our four wonderful children who have enriched our lives immeasurably.

"Let me not to the marriage of true minds
Admit impediments."

"Love's not Time's fool..."

~ Sonnet 116, William Shakespeare

"The world is a book and those who do not travel read only one page."

~ Saint Augustine

Author's Note

The completion of *The Spanish Note* is the culmination of a wish that I had long cherished to create a love story inspired by the country which has fascinated me since my childhood days. Attracted to historical novels that interweave the past with the present, I yearned to trace the life journeys of three generations of two families separated by time and distance as they embraced the joys of love, friendship, family, travel and new cultures.

Describing the development of St. Boniface Hospital from its inception in 1871 to the period during which one of my main characters, Maggie, studied and worked at that institution would not have been possible without the valuable information I gleaned from the publication entitled *Tradition, Innovation & Inspiration since 1871: A Brief History of St. Boniface General Hospital* co-written by Carole Barnabé, Michel Verette and Luc Côté. I also wish to thank Mrs. Shirley Delaquis, former Chair, Archives Committee, St. Boniface Registered Nurses' Alumni Association, for answering my questions about the nursing program offered by the hospital during the first decades of the 20th century and for providing me with certain documents relating to that period.

Creating the atmosphere that Maggie knew in Winnipeg and the specific places that she visited from 1913 to 1919 was made possible by consulting several documents produced by the Manitoba Historical Society in Winnipeg, in particular its 2012 summer publication entitled *Manitoba History: Titanic – The Manitoba Story* by Michael Dupuis, its autumn 1988 publication *Manitoba History: History and Live Theatre in Winnipeg* by

Barry McCarten and its 2002 spring/summer publication *Manitoba History on Stage: Theatre and Theatres in Early Winnipeg* by James B. Hartman. Jim Blanchard's book *Winnipeg 1912* also provides an informative look at the fast-paced life of the capital city in the early years of the 20th century.

Dale Barbour's excellent study of the turn-of-the-century resort of Winnipeg Beach, *Winnipeg Beach: Leisure and Courtship in a Resort Town, 1900-1967*, allowed me to paint the special setting for Maggie's and Eduardo's memorable day in that community. Wally Johannson's *Those Were the Days: A Pictorial History of Winnipeg Beach* was also a valuable reference in developing my portrait of the resort at its sunniest.

Anne Renaud's look *Into the Mist: The Story of The Empress of Ireland* presents an informative account of this luxury ship that, like the *Titanic*, is forever associated with tragedy. The http://ssmaritime.com/Empress-of-Ireland-1906.htm website was another source of interesting details about the ship.

I also consulted Barbara Chisholm's *Castles of the North: Canada's Grand Hotels* for details about our country's majestic railway hotels and Carol Ferguson's and Margaret Fraser's study of *A Century of Canadian Home Cooking (1900 Through The '90s)* for its tour of Canadian culinary history. The August 2020 edition of *National Geographic Magazine* was a source of valuable information about the deadly routes taken by disease over the centuries and the Manitoba Historical Society's spring 2011 publication on *Manitoba History: From Nose Sprays to Nursing Shortages: Managing Epidemic Polio in Manitoba, 1928-1953* offered a good overview of the polio situation in the Keystone Province.

While my own many trips to Spain over the years provided me with a rich storehouse of memories from which to draw in describing my experiences in that country, I found the following travel books to be not only interesting but very helpful in confirming the accuracy of certain dates and events that I mention in my novel: the 2015 edition of *Frommer's Spain*, Frances Mayer's *A Year in the World: Journeys of a Passionate Traveller;* James A. Michener's *Iberia*: *Spanish Travels and Reflections*; Jan Morris's *Spain* and Rick Steves's *Best of Spain.*

Finally, I wish to acknowledge the role that my parents played in fostering my love of travel by organizing an annual family trip to a variety of appealing locations in North America throughout my youth and, later, by inviting my husband and me to join them on their trips to beautiful Hawaii. My wanderlust was undoubtedly born during these early trips and developed over the years into a deep love of travel, which first found its expression in a work experience in France, a study program in Spain and then in numerous trips to foreign lands enjoyed with my husband. Today, a chance look at a recipe for tapas or the seductive sound of flamenco music and the clack-clack of castanets instantly take me to Seville; a few bars of *Parlez-moi d'amour* and the heady yeast smell of freshly baked baguettes will transport me to Paris; the sticky feel of honey and the taste of a savoury phyllo pastry redolent with salty feta cheese, pungent rosemary and sweet figs can sweep me on a magic carpet ride to Santorini; the enchanting sound of the harp and a few lines of lilting Irish poetry or even of gentle blarney can cause me to rhapsodize about a misty Dublin: the warm kiss of the sun reaching through a palm tree swaying gracefully by the ocean and a slice of banana bread studded with macadamia nuts can have me dreaming instantly of Maui and, yes, a cerulean blue sky on a sunny but frigid day with the snow crunching beneath my feet can even carry me back to Winnipeg where my story begins…

Rosemary Doyle

Prologue

Arnaud, Manitoba—January 1, 1905

"Wake up, Maggie! Your mother and baby brother aren't well and need your help now. Hurry!"

Awakened by her father's plea, the young woman quickly transferred the creased letter under her pillow to the pocket of her bathrobe and rushed down the stairs. While she had read the letter so often that she could recite its contents from memory, she could not bear the thought of witnessing the deflation of her hopes once exposed to the inquisitive eyes and scrutiny of her family. Reaching the large kitchen of the old farmhouse., Maggie was greeted by chaos. The twin girls, Beth and Winnifred, were making a valiant effort to prepare the special New Year's Day breakfast that had been promised to the large family but the smell of burnt pancakes and blackened sausage quickly explained the disappointment of the hungry children clamouring for their meal. Maggie's mother, soon to give birth to her 10th child, lay exhausted on the couch attended by her worried husband. The youngest of the children, eighteen-month-old Anthony, lay strangely quiet in the arms of his favourite sister Molly, his red cheeks and glazed eyes as well as the listlessness that had replaced his usual bright spirits signaling that he was ill.

Where to start? Maggie walked over to her mother, noting her swollen ankles and the enlarged varicose veins running angrily down her legs, as well as her complete lack of energy. While she smiled bravely at her daughter, she couldn't mask the total fatigue that had overtaken her worn body. Maggie asked her father for two pillows and placed them under her mother's legs. "Please ask the boys to fetch me some ice to bring down Mom's swelling. And bring her a cup of sweetened tea and a piece of toast."

Maggie took her mother's pulse and was reassured that it was only slightly above normal despite the tremendous amount of work she had undertaken lately, even in the final stages of her pregnancy. She reassured her father that her mother was stable for the moment but warned him to ensure that she stay off her feet and rest as the consequences of failing to do so could be serious for her and the unborn baby.

Maggie then turned her attention to her little brother. She placed her hand on his warm forehead, confirming that he had a fever and noted his lack of appetite. "Molly, please make your brother drink a glass of water or of lemonade and then give him a tepid bath afterwards to help lower his temperature. I'll check on him later but let me know if you see any rash or spots on his skin."

"Do you think Anthony may have chickenpox?" asked her father. Your cousins were here just before Christmas and one of them apparently had red spots on his back and chest which later turned into blisters."

"We'll know soon as the rash appears a day or two after a fever but it's quite possible that Anthony has developed chickenpox as he was in close contact with the sick child. At least, all of my siblings have already contracted chickenpox and Mother had it as well as a young girl. It's important to keep Anthony well hydrated and to ensure that he rest. If he develops a rash, I'll rub some calamine lotion on his skin to provide him with some relief from the itchiness."

Maggie surveyed the kitchen, checking Beth's and Winnifred's unsuccessful attempts to make breakfast. "I'll take over now but see that the younger children wash their hands and brush their teeth." She turned to her brother Joseph who, at just ten years old, was always willing to help his older sister. "Would you take some of this fresh hot coffee to your brothers who are milking the cows in the barn on this frigid morning? Tell them that pancakes and sausages will be waiting for them when they have finished their chores."

Two hours later, Anthony's fever was down and he was sleeping soundly in his crib. Maggie's mother was more comfortable and the famished children had all eaten their fill of pancakes with maple syrup and were drawing images of the snow falling over the snowmen they had made in the backyard the previous day. Maggie's father, having checked on the animals in the barn, strode about the kitchen with a pipe in his mouth and worry etched on his brow. He placed his hand on his eldest daughter's shoulder and remarked, "Maggie, how would we manage without you? With all these children, your mother and I rely so much on you and you seem to know instinctively what to do. You are truly a treasure, my dear!"

While appreciating her father's warm words of praise, Maggie began to feel once again the faint stirrings of resentment that had taken hold of her over the past few weeks despite her devotion to her parents and siblings. She didn't begrudge helping them but she wondered when she would finally be able to lead her own life. At twenty, she only foresaw much of the same daily routine that characterized her current life loom before her for years, especially with the birth of each new child into the family. However, with the arrival of her Winnipeg cousin's letter a few weeks before Christmas, the dreams that she had allowed herself to entertain during her few precious moments of leisure had suddenly taken shape. She wanted to become a nurse, maybe even travel a little and have some money to purchase a few select items of her own such as the occasional book that had attracted her attention.

Maggie reached for the letter in her pocket to convince herself that there were other options in life. Her cousin Clara had mentioned a friend of hers who had enrolled in the Grey Nuns' School of Nursing, which had officially opened a few years earlier. Clara wrote that the school's first three graduates completed their studies in 1899 and that new applicants were enrolling in the program every year. Would Maggie with her instinctive nursing skills not be interested in this possibility? Also, would she not enjoy living in the city and experiencing some of its amenities rather than being isolated on the farm where chores consumed most of her days?

Maggie, as a loving and devoted daughter, was very conflicted by her new thinking and felt guilty about her desire to flee her current life with her large family to concentrate on her own aspirations. She had tried over the past few weeks to broach the topic with her parents. However, every potential opportunity to speak with them had vanished as there were too many activities at Christmas, too many visitors on Boxing Day, too many preparations for the New Year's Eve celebration at home and finally, today, despite the words of support from her father, too many worries about her mother and baby brother.

Later, that day, with the younger children in bed and the older ones reading or playing cards, Maggie decided that there would never be a perfect time to discuss the subject of her choice of career with her parents and she might as well raise it now. After one last check on little Anthony and with her mother improving after some much-needed rest, she mentioned the nursing program to her parents and her wish to enroll in it.

"Why, Maggie, I understand why this program would interest you, but is it really necessary? You already know a great deal about nursing and besides, what would I do without you?" queried her mother.

"And, what's more, dear Maggie, how would we pay for this program? While we would be proud to see you graduate as a registered nurse and become a professional, you would have to devote two and a half years to this schooling and would need some money of your own to live in the city," added her father.

"We would miss you so much, Maggie, if you left for Winnipeg and so would your siblings. We would rarely see you during your training," stated her mother as she rubbed her swollen belly.

"Maggie, wouldn't you want a fellow of your own? Bobby on the next farm would make a good husband and provider. You must have noticed that he follows you with moonstruck eyes," teased her father.

"Yes, but I don't love Bobby and there are few prospects here for me. I'd like to choose my own husband, one whom I would love deeply for the rest of my life. Moreover, I wish to become a nurse, given that I have long been interested in medicine, as you know," declared Maggie.

"Life doesn't always present us with many choices, my dear," replied her mother carefully. "It's best to be happy with what you have instead of seeking to follow bright stars that quickly disappear under the light of day."

Sensing his daughter's disappointment, Maggie's father attempted to soften his decision by adding, "While it might not be for now, perhaps in a few years, we could reconsider your wishes and help you become a nurse."

Maggie's fingers reached for the letter in her pocket, crushing it into a ball between her fingers. Was she asking for too much? Would she really be able to achieve her dreams in a few years or would they slowly fade into oblivion as life's exigencies and the passage of time gradually removed them from her grasp?

Chapter 1

Winnipeg, June 1970

With a heavy heart and a slow step, I walked down the sidewalk to the old but welcoming house in Winnipeg that my siblings, cousins and I had known for most of our lives as "the ship" due to the sloping floor that characterized its kitchen. The house was situated on a tidy street with well-maintained shrubs and flowers welcoming visitors and residents alike. While the dilapidated canvas screens on the front veranda where we had occasionally enjoyed sleepovers as children were now bleached by the sun and were only a pale stroke of their original vivid orange and green hues, the rich purple irises, deep pink peonies and sunny yellow marigolds still provided a bright splash of colour against the faded paint of the ageing residence. It was a familiar sight to me as my siblings and I had frequently visited both my Aunt Maureen and my grandmother over the years on those Saturdays when my parents escaped on a "date night" or when we met for large family gatherings at Christmas and Easter or on birthdays. This time, however, circumstances were very different as my beloved grandmother had died a few months earlier and my aunt had asked me if I would help her sort out the many items that had accumulated over the years, especially those her mother had stored in the attic as her "souvenirs".

In preparation for my aunt's forthcoming move to an apartment, I, of course, agreed, willing to help her in a time of need but, if truth be told, especially because I wished to take one more trip down memory lane.

My grandmother's attic had always been a source of great delight to me: as a child, it was an Aladdin's cave full of undiscovered albeit questionable treasures. A prolific reader of children's fantasy books, I sometimes imagined that I would find a burnished lamp, thus summoning a genie who could grant me the most exotic of wishes. Later, the attic became a source of curiosity and family history as I opened old boxes full of relics from the past and pondered the wisdom of keeping antiquated toys, outdated clothing, sepia-coloured photographs and spine-damaged books in their dusty refuge. Today, however, the attic would whisper of nostalgia as, for the last time, I would move from box to chest to trunk to examine what my grandmother had left behind …

It had been several years since my last foray into the attic but I remembered its eclectic collections well. The boxes to the extreme right contained the old family photos that had provided me with so many moments of pleasure and even hilarity as a child. How I had laughed indiscriminately at the baby photos of my father and uncles who, as toddlers in the fashion of the time, had been dressed more like girls than boys! Fortunately, as they grew older, the sartorial choices improved and I noted with approval several photos of them in the classic sailor outfits so popular over the years. As my grandmother had given me carte blanche to take home the photos that I wanted, my childhood album included some of these baby photos, as well as a few of my father as an intern, surrounded by several pretty nurses in their starched white uniforms and caps. Of course, my mother was not very fond of these gifts from the ancestral attic! I was, however, entitled to keep my father's graduation photo from medical school to add to my burgeoning photo album which also contained a picture of my aunt Maeve's (Maureen's sister) graduation from the St. Boniface School of Nursing. Oh, and here was a photo of my grandmother's graduation from the same School of Nursing! Intrigued, I checked the back of the image and was surprised to read that it was dated 1913. Difficult to believe that it was so long ago… Twelve young women, dressed in long uniforms covered by white aprons, and proudly wearing their nurse's cap and pin, smiled at me over the decades. There was also a wedding photo of my grandparents dated 1915, which I set aside, along with the graduation photo, hoping that my aunt would allow me to keep them. Noting that time was advancing fast, I rushed to label the boxes of yellowing photos, most of which I did not recognize, with the approximate range of years covered in order to facilitate my aunt's inspection of their contents and, most probably, eventual disposal.

The next few boxes were filled with old newspaper clippings and magazines. As I disturbed their dusty slumber, filling yet another garbage bag with crumbling, moth-eaten pages, several headlines caught my attention: the front page of the April 15, 1912 edition of *The Manitoba Free Press* screamed, "TITANIC SINKS AT SEA—LOSS OF LIFE MAY REACH 1,800" while, only two years later, in referring to the *Empress of Ireland*, *The Winnipeg Tribune* reported that "HUNDREDS DROWN WHEN LINER SINKS". A yellowed copy of *The National Post* described the tragedy as "CANADA'S TITANIC: THE SINKING OF THE EMPRESS OF IRELAND". I once asked my grandmother why she kept these mouldering reminders of the past but her response was enigmatic. "When I was young, I dreamt of travelling in luxury ships to distant foreign lands such as Spain and Greece but, of course, I never did. Then, one day, I actually met a woman and her brother from Spain who had travelled to Canada on the *Empress of Ireland.* They became very close to me but then I lost them both." When I asked my grandmother if they had perished on the ship's final voyage in May 1914, she replied, "No, but there are many other less dramatic but equally painful ways of losing someone special." No matter how hard I pressed her for more information, my usually loquacious grandmother remained mute on the subject.

As I continued to add old magazines and newspapers to the garbage bags, I was struck by another headline referring to the increasing casualties caused by the Spanish Flu that plagued the world from 1918 to 1920. Had my grandmother nursed any patients suffering from this deadly influenza pandemic? In the way of children who live in an eternal present, I had never thought to ask my kindly, rosy-cheeked grandmother about her own life as a vibrant young woman seeking to realize her dreams, a life undoubtedly very different from the much later one that I had witnessed of a doting grandma devoted to pleasing those around her. Who had she been beyond the white-haired, rather portly, elderly woman wearing old-fashioned floral print dresses and sensible black oxfords? Now, of course, it was too late to ask her... Was it not my mother who had once observed how youth dismisses old age until it is almost upon them?

In the area of the attic devoted to what could euphemistically be called "vintage" clothing, I searched for the colour sketches of the latest fashions of the 1940s that my father had drawn for Eaton's as a way of augmenting his income while attending the University of Manitoba; at that time, it appeared that drawings were used in the store's newspaper advertisements. "Victory Suits", those tailored knee-length skirts and nipped-in jackets that created an hourglass silhouette, were very much in style, given that not only were they flattering to the female form, but they also promoted the rationing of fabric required to satisfy the demands of the Second World War during this decade. My father's talent in rendering the fashions of the time on a sketch board was evident as I studied his detailed drawings. I gathered my favourite ones and added them to my bag of potential souvenirs before sighing as I moved to the old moth-eaten and outdated clothing that I soon uprooted from its hiding spot and added to the ever-increasing pile of material to be discarded.

I then started the more difficult task of culling books, many of which my grandmother had read to my siblings and me as children. I quickly placed all the Bobbsey Twin books, Enid Blyton's adventure tales about islands, castles and ships, as well as several classics, in one pile destined for the local library and consigned all the heavily damaged books into another relegated to the garbage heap. After years of happy reading, the spine of Lucy Maud Montgomery's popular *Anne of Green Gables* was, unfortunately, falling apart and I bade it a reluctant farewell. Had it held a special meaning for my grandmother? I tried to picture her as the young bride in her wedding photo but, as she had had her children late in life and I had only known her as a sweet, old woman with a cane who loved to entertain her grandchildren with her many stories and desserts, this image was very difficult to summon. I noted a copy of Mark Twain's travel book, *The Innocents Abroad*, which described the author's journey to Europe and the Holy Land aboard a steamship and wondered if my grandmother had ever imagined herself in such exotic locations... Why not read about Twain's travels myself? I added the book to the items that I wished to keep.

In sorting the books, I fell upon one I remembered very well from my childhood: an old Spanish grammar book that my aunt Maeve had lent me when she heard how I had pleaded with my parents to learn the Castilian language, which had attracted me for so long. Perhaps the book would be of some use to me in the fall when I resumed my Spanish courses at the university. I pulled it from the other books and placed it in my bag of souvenirs, along with the photos that I wished to keep, subject to my Aunt Maureen's approval.

The melancholy gathering of old toys was next on my list and I cast a wistful eye upon the blinded doll minus an arm, the old doll carriage with its missing wheel, and the once treasured but now damaged wooden train set built for my father by the grandfather that I had never known. While these were not my toys, they represented those enjoyed by my father and his four siblings and I found it rather sad to cast them in the trash. A box remained in the corner and I pulled it out, eager now to finish the task at hand. I lifted the decorated lid and discovered, carefully wrapped among layers of silk paper, the much-loved children's china tea set that my grandmother and Aunt Maureen had used so often to serve tea and cake for the "candlelight parties" they had held for my siblings and me when they sat us for an evening. How those delicate cups and saucers with their matching teapot, creamer and sugar bowl had fascinated us as children playing grown-ups! The image on the inside of the cup of young children playing with their toys including a teddy bear and the vivid colours worn by the children portrayed on the china were imprinted in my memory. I checked a saucer and was surprised to see *Santa Clara* stamped on it. Was this not a Spanish dinnerware company? I quickly closed the ornate box, determined to ask my aunt if she wished to part with the special tea set that was such an important part of my childhood memories.

Finally, I opened the trunk that I had reserved for last as it contained my grandmother's ivory-coloured satin wedding dress, the now missing veil with orange blossoms covering the cap, as well as the delicate gloves and cream leather boots fastened with tiny satin-covered buttons. How, as a child, I had enjoyed trying on her wedding regalia until I reached out for the veil which disintegrated between my very fingers… I was so afraid that my grandmother would scold me for destroying her veil and so relieved when, between fits of tears, I confessed my misdeed only to hear her reassure me that it wasn't my fault as the veil was over half a century old. "Why don't we go downstairs and have a piece of Wacky Cake (a cocoa-based cake created as a result of rationing during World War II when eggs and milk were scarce but one which she continued to make with her grandchildren and to serve many years after rationing had ended) and a cup of tea?" she had suggested. I knew that my grandmother had always had great faith in the restorative power of food and drink not only to energize the body, but also to improve one's spirits. "Are you hungry?" had always been her words of welcome no matter what time of day it was when we arrived at the home she had shared with my aunt Maureen after Maeve's marriage.

In the dim light of the attic, I almost missed seeing at the bottom of the trunk an elaborate Spanish fan made of ivory with hand-painted pink roses ornately framed with black lace sprinkled with pearls. I couldn't recall having seen the fan before and wondered if it had been a special gift my grandmother had acquired in her youth. The fan was tied by a purple satin ribbon to a bundle of old envelopes bearing Spanish stamps and addressed to my grandmother, both in her maiden and married names. With whom in Spain had she exchanged such correspondence? It was all very strange as, except for one trip to Ireland, I had never heard about my grandmother having travelled outside the country nor had she ever spoken about the Maria Cristina who had apparently been such a good friend of hers, so loved that fifty years later her letters were still preserved in the trunk next to my grandmother's wedding dress. Was this the Spanish woman, accompanied by her brother, whom she had mentioned in connection with *The Empress of Ireland*? If so, why had she kept their relationship so secret?

Two old studio photographs lay beneath the letters: the first one was of a lovely young woman wearing a mantilla and holding a fan while the second was of an extremely handsome young man with the most engaging smile. There was also a velvet jewelry case sitting next to the letters which immediately captured my attention. However, upon opening it, I only found two ticket stubs: one for a July 1913 performance of *Carmen* at Winnipeg's former Walker Theatre and the other was for a return trip on the "Moonlight Special" travelling from Winnipeg to Winnipeg Beach a month later. With whom had my grandmother travelled on the "Moonlight Special"? She obviously had considered it to be a special train trip to have conserved the ticket stub for all these years. I was about to add the jewelry case and its cobwebs to the rest of the trash that I had collected when I noticed a tiny card peeking out from beneath the area where the missing piece of jewelry would have been placed. I carefully pulled it out and was surprised to note that it was a message in Spanish. It read: "*A mi preciosa Margarita, un recuerdo de un verano que nunca olvidaré y una promesa de un futuro feliz a tu lado. Con todo mi amor, Eduardo.*" ("To my precious Margarita,—a play on my grandmother's third given name, Margaret, and the Spanish word for daisy?—a souvenir of a summer that I will never forget and a promise of a happy future by your side. With all my love, Eduardo.") Who could this man have been? My grandma's lover? Surely not! The Spanish brother of whom she had spoken in relation to the newspaper coverage of the sinking of *The Empress*? Perhaps…

I knew that my grandmother, who had been baptized Fiona Deirdre Margaret, had been known as Maggie throughout her life, thanks to her godmother who had disliked her first two given names, choosing instead to call her Maggie from her christening day onwards. The name had caught on and, gradually, even her parents began to call her Maggie except, of course, on very formal or serious occasions when they reverted to Fiona.

I was interrupted in my thoughts when I heard my aunt Maureen call out, "Sophie, are you almost finished up there? Dinner will be ready in just a few minutes." It was time to leave the attic and all its many memories and return to the present.

I carefully gathered the letters, photos and the jewelry box, along with the other items which were my last treasures from the attic, grabbed the bags of garbage to be thrown away and made my way to the kitchen, determined to question my aunt about the mysterious Eduardo who had piqued my curiosity. On second thought, I concluded that it might be better to rein in my curiosity and to keep my grandmother's carefully guarded secret to myself for the time being. I placed the photos and the jewelry box with its intriguing message in my purse but handed over the fan and Maria Cristina's letters to my aunt, hoping that she would return them to me as soon as possible as they might reveal more about Eduardo and his apparent special presence in my grandmother's life...

As I gently closed the door to the old attic for the last time, it suddenly occurred to me that this chaotic family library of both my grandmother's lost dreams and her recorded achievements, a collection which had breathed life into many of my childhood memories, was now itself part of those memories.

Chapter 2

WINNIPEG, EARLY JUNE 1913

Beep, beep, beep… Despite the shrill ring of her alarm clock, Maggie awoke from the fog of sleep with a smile on her lips and the strong feeling that she would be welcoming a special day in her life. She rose from her narrow bed, crossed her small, austere room on the third floor of the nurses' residence adjoining the hospital and smiled as she looked out her window at the rustling elm trees and the placid river below. Robins were chirping cheerfully, the sun shone brightly and, in her elated mood, she was reminded of Wordsworth's enthusiastic words: "Bliss was it in that dawn to be alive\But to be young was very heaven!"

Maggie's long-held dream was to be realized today. After two and a half years of dedicated studies and long, full days on the wards, she was about to graduate from the St. Boniface Hospital's School of Nursing. She was very proud of her achievement as she reminisced over the long path that had seen her become a registered nurse despite the obstacles that she had faced. The first daughter born into a family of eleven children, she had worked hard on her parents' farm in addition to acting as a second mother to her many younger siblings before she was finally able to enter Nursing School in 1911—no small accomplishment in a world that witnessed few women adopt a professional career. Yes, there were the Nellie McClungs, the Susanna Moodies, the Lucy Maud Montgomerys, the Emily Carrs in Canada but other than a few teachers, writers and artists, the number of women with professional training was very limited. The first trained nurses in Canada had mostly been members of religious orders and schools of nursing had only just started to welcome lay students. Maggie glanced at the copy of Florence Nightingale's book, *Notes on Nursing*, first published in England in 1859, which she proudly displayed in the bookcase that held her Bible and a few literary classics, as well as textbooks on gynecology, communicable diseases, surgery, anatomy, physiology, obstetrics and pediatrics. She thought of the brave woman dubbed "the lady with the lamp" who had devoted her life to nursing the sick at a time when hospitals were not only unsanitary but frequently a source of infection and nurses were considered to be little more than uneducated help performing menial tasks.

It was only in 1897 that the Sisters of Charity (the Grey Nuns) officially inaugurated their School of Nursing under the auspices of Western Canada's first hospital, St. Boniface General, which had opened in 1871. The success of this undertaking was mainly due to the untiring work of four intrepid nuns from Montreal who answered Archbishop Provencher's plea for assistance by undertaking a perilous two-month journey by canoe in 1844 to reach the Red River Settlement where they would help educate the children and provide care to the sick. By 1870, the Grey Nuns realized that they could no longer adequately tend to their many patients in the convent they had built shortly after their arrival in Manitoba and they sought to build a new structure separate from their residence in order to pursue the work of their mission.

As she put on her uniform, Maggie pondered the many changes that had occurred at the hospital in the four decades of its existence. By the turn of the century, the original four-bed structure had been expanded several times and could now accommodate 125 beds as well as two operating rooms, a sterilization room and a pharmacy. Only two years before she began her training, the hospital had organized a fundraising drive to purchase an X-ray machine; Maggie could not even begin to imagine how useful this acquisition would be in determining whether a patient had suffered a sprain or a fracture.

Only fourteen years had elapsed since the first class of three women had graduated from the Nursing School and Maggie looked forward to joining her eleven peers in a few hours as the school's current graduating class of nurses received their diplomas. She adjusted her cap with its black ribbon and checked to see that her full-length blue dress with its stiff collar, long removable sleeves and floor-length white apron gathered at the waist and extending in pleats to the floor was sparkling clean and that her black shoes were well polished. She touched the spot below her left shoulder where her new gold graduation nursing pin would be placed during the brief ceremony on the Youville Ward later that day. The pin with the motto chosen by the school, *Estote fideles*, that is "Be Faithful", would be a symbol of her steadfast efforts and studies, as well as of her dedication to her profession. While she would be working long twelve-hour shifts, she would finally receive a salary, the first money that she would ever earn herself and be able to spend as she chose.

After receiving their pin and diploma, Maggie and her fellow nurses would have their photograph taken: twelve smiling faces captured for all eternity as they proudly displayed their new diplomas conferred by *Les Soeurs de la Charité de l'Hôpital Général de St-Boniface*, attesting to the fact that they had "passed with credit all the required examinations conducted by the Board of Examiners of said Hospital, and that (their) conduct had been in all respects exemplary..." After tea and sweets in the spacious study and recreation room in the student nurses' residence, the twelve graduates would be given the weekend off before embarking on their first day of work as full-fledged nurses the following week.

Maggie looked forward to spending this time with her extended family. Not only would her parents and siblings be present for the big family picnic to take place on Saturday under the oak trees of their large property, but her parents had also invited aunts, uncles, cousins and a few friends to join in the festivities. After the simple fare at the hospital, Maggie's mouth watered at the thought of all the special food that her mother and sisters would be preparing: she could already taste the savoury veal and pork pie in its flaky crust, which would be served cold with mustard relish and rhubarb chutney made from the many plants that grew on the farm. There might even be a little rhubarb wine to accompany the meal if she was fortunate. Dessert would undoubtedly include a cobbler featuring the best of the blueberries or saskatoons from the woods in the surrounding area and possibly a gingerbread cake with lemon sauce. Dare she hope that her mother would mark this special occasion by serving ice cream enhanced with the addition of strawberry jam, the highlight of family picnics and a very special treat before the advent of refrigeration?

The celebration had been perfect. Maggie had so enjoyed seeing her family and close friends who had travelled by horse and buggy to reach her parents' farm in order to share in the joy of her accomplishment. Her hardworking parents had ensured that the picnic tables were laden with delicious food and her younger siblings had even offered to take on the laborious task of turning the crank on the ice-cream machine to make the delicious treat of which their eldest sister was so fond. The day had ended with the presentation of an uncommon gift from her parents: a lovely shawl made of the finest silk and brightly decorated with red and yellow roses, as well as delicate white, pink and magenta flowers which, she was told, were apparently ubiquitous in tropical countries where they were known as bougainvillea. Where had they ever found such a magnificent gift and why had her normally frugal parents decided to splurge on such a purchase? A homemade woolen wrap would have been a typical gift but not such a costly and exotic item. The shawl had an attached tag which read *Hecho en España* (Made in Spain) and Maggie learned that her parents had made a special trip to the new Eaton's store in Winnipeg to buy something very special for the daughter of whom they were so proud, the first child of theirs to embark on a professional career.

As she tried on the shawl, preening in front of the mirror, Maggie allowed herself to dream that perhaps, one day, she would be able to visit the far-away lands that Twain had described in his book, *The Innocents Abroad*, a copy of which she had just purchased from a second-hand bookseller to celebrate her success. She reflected with pleasure that, now that her studies had ended, she would have more time to pursue her love of reading and a little more money to spend on the books that she so enjoyed.

Chapter 3

JUNE 1913—ON BOARD *THE EMPRESS OF IRELAND*

With the brisk sea air whipping her dark hair over her face, Maria Cristina strolled on the first-class promenade deck of the luxury ocean liner that was transporting her to Canada. She had never imagined that her parents would consent to their only daughter's travel from Madrid all the way to Liverpool, England by train and then across the Atlantic in this beautiful ship to Quebec City and then by train once again to Winnipeg. Moreover, it was almost as if she were undertaking this exciting voyage on her own as travelling with her elder brother Eduardo left her free to explore her surroundings without the irritating presence of a *duenna*. Not that she planned to do anything improper but it was just so much easier to enjoy life without the constant restrictions imposed by a chaperone. Eduardo would always be there to protect his little sister but not to suffocate her with regular admonishments and advice. She could see him further away chatting with a pretty blond girl who obviously didn't mind his warm, Latin attentions. Maria Cristina was content just to admire the huge waves with their frothy lace borders lapping against the side of the ship and to smell the salty sea air as she daydreamed of the days ahead.

Launched in 1906, the *Empress of Ireland* was operated by the Canadian Pacific Railway (CPR) that had secured the profitable contract for the delivery of mail from England across the Atlantic Ocean in addition to the one it had already been awarded for mail delivery across the Pacific to Asia, a feat made possible by its vast railway network across Canada. As well, the company's new, faster steamships were transporting international passengers and European immigrants to Canada who were responding to the Canadian Government's invitation to help settle the vast lands of the Canadian West.

Carrying some 1500 passengers travelling in three classes, the *Empress of Ireland* offered luxurious first-class accommodation for those wealthy enough to afford a most comfortable ocean journey. Among the distinguished passengers who would board the *Empress* during her short career were Dr. John McCrae, the Canadian physician who would later compose the stirring war poem "In Flanders Fields" in the back of a field ambulance at Ypres, as well as two of Canada's governors general, Lord Grey and the Duke of Connaught, and William Lyon Mackenzie King who would become Canada's tenth prime minister.

With access to the open boat deck and two enclosed promenade decks, first-class passengers could enjoy the sun and the sea breezes as they strolled or relaxed in a teak lounge chair with a good book and a cup of Earl Grey tea. Maria Cristina, tired after her long journey across Europe and the excitement of her first sea voyage, succumbed to the effects of sun, wind and fatigue and was soon fast asleep in her comfortable deck chair.

"*Maria Cristina, Maria Cristina, ¡despertate!* Wake up!" Eduardo sought to rouse his sister from her deep sleep. "It's late and we must change for dinner, which will be served in 45 minutes." Maria Cristina glanced at her watch, surprised that she had slept so long and promised to be ready in time for her brother to escort her to the ornate Dining Room, photos of which she had admired in the CPR's promotional material for its twin ships *The Empress of Ireland* and *The Empress of Britain*. "*Te veo pronto. I'll see you soon,*" she called out as she rushed to her stateroom.

Forty-five minutes later, after descending the grand staircase which led past two lower decks to the entrance to the dining room, Maria Cristina and her brother, attired in evening dress, walked into the Edwardian setting of the three-story high room with its finely detailed doors with intricately decorated panels, its plush leather banquette seating, delicate mahogany and teak woodwork, sculpted ceilings, generously-sized portholes and striking glass fixtures. In the middle of the dining room was a glass atrium which rose two levels to reach the music room. Along with fine crystal and sterling silver silverware, the tables were set with Minton china featuring delicate garlands of purple flowers, as well as a central medallion enclosing the CPR logo. "*¡Qué bonito!* How beautiful!" exclaimed Maria Cristina as she admired the splendour of the dining room. Enhancing the elegant atmosphere, a five-piece orchestra softly played Strauss waltzes in the background. Shades of *The Titanic* thought the young woman as she struggled to suppress the image of the celebrated but doomed ship that had sunk just over a year earlier in the cold waters of the very ocean that they were crossing on this voyage.

Maria Cristina and Eduardo approached their table where a couple was already seated with a young woman who appeared to be their daughter and a distinguished looking gentleman with impressive sideburns. The two men rose from their seats immediately and introduced themselves. Eduardo was happy to note that the pretty blonde to whom he had been speaking earlier on the promenade deck was to be one of their dinner companions for the duration of the week-long crossing.

"I am Timothy Flanagan and this is my wife Emily and our daughter Grace from Winnipeg, Manitoba."

The single gentleman at the table introduced himself with a noticeable brogue, "I am Alexander MacTavish from Glasgow, Scotland."

"And I am Eduardo Martínez travelling with my sister Maria Cristina Martínez from Madrid, Spain. *Encantado de concercerlos*. Sorry, I forgot my English for a moment. We are pleased to meet you all. Mr. Flanagan, may I ask you what is the motivation for your trip on *The Empress of Ireland*?"

"Certainly, Señor Martínez. I am a senior representative of R. J. Whitla and Company in Winnipeg, which is a dry goods store featuring a wide range of foreign and domestic fabrics which are sold both on the premises and to retailers as far west as the Rocky Mountains by means of a network of travelling salesmen and the production of an annual catalogue." Mr. Flanagan explained that he had just concluded a visit to Ireland, his homeland, as well as to Scotland and England where he purchased some fine textiles and woolens. He added, "I hope they will sell well in our store. They should prove to be popular during our frigid Winnipeg winters. I was fortunate enough to have my wife accompany me for this combination business and pleasure trip. Our daughter who will be beginning a new study program this fall wished to join us as well and, as Mrs. Flanagan and I thought that this might be the last time that we could travel together as a family and in such luxurious fashion, we readily agreed. "

"Indeed, Mr. Flanagan, I am sure that your daughter was most grateful to accompany you and your wife on this great voyage," replied Eduardo as he smiled charmingly at Grace. "May I ask, is Winnipeg a city known for its, how do you say, clothing industry?"

"Yes, the garment industry has a lengthy history in Winnipeg, given the city's important transportation links with the rest of North America. Its first clothing factories such as the Winnipeg Shirt and Overall Company were established at the end of the 19th century, producing clothes for railway and farm workers. However, there are still many tailors, dressmakers and milliners who require fine textiles to produce more elegant clothing for their patrons."

"And you, Miss Martínez, what prompted you to travel to Canada?" asked Mrs. Flanagan.

"I am a language teacher who is qualified to teach Spanish, French and English, but my real dream is to travel. Although I have visited several countries in Europe and Northern Africa, this is my first trip across the Atlantic. Canada with its French and English heritage and its vast spaces appealed to me and I was fortunate enough to secure a short teaching contract with St. Mary's Academy in Winnipeg after I complete an initial period of adjustment in the capital. My parents agreed to this proposal and suggested that my brother Eduardo accompany me for the beginning of the trip. Why don't you explain to our fellow diners what your business interests are in Canada, Eduardo?"

"Please forgive my English, which is not as good as my sister's. Our father is a wine merchant and he has asked me to investigate the possibilities of selling *Jerez,* I mean sherry, Spain's well-known fortified wine, to Canada's famous network of railway hotels while I am in the country. The British are great *aficionados* of this wine already and my father hopes to expand his wine export business overseas. I have a large supply of sherry with me in order to introduce this product to Canadian hoteliers when I visit Winnipeg, Toronto, Ottawa, Montreal and Quebec City. I will also be introducing a new sparkling wine from the Catalonian region of Spain. Cava tastes like Champagne but costs much less. If anyone would like to try some, I will bring a bottle to our table tomorrow."

"Indeed, Señor Martínez, I would like to try your sparkling wine as I am a great aficionado of Champagne but, unfortunately, without the purse to afford it", stated Mr. MacTavish. "Could you tell me more about Cava's history?"

"Of course, Mr. MacTavish. Using the *méthode champenoise,* Josep Raventós Fetjó uncorked his first bottle of Cava in 1872 on the Codorníu estate located in Catalonia and was so pleased with the results that he had a cool cellar (*cava*) created to provide suitable conditions for the fermentation of this sparkling wine. His son continued to perfect the new beverage, eventually supplying the Royal Household in Madrid with Cava, the designation given to the sparkling wine produced in the Penedès region close to Barcelona to distinguish it from the sparkling wine made in the Champagne district of France."

Eduardo added, "You may be interested to know that the first bottles of sparkling wine produced by spontaneous fermentation in France were cast aside as they were considered to be the *vin du diable* (devil's wine). However, times have changed and, today, Cava is increasingly popular in Spain and, I hope, eventually in the world. But, as the British say, the proof of the pudding is in its tasting and tomorrow you will have the opportunity to try Cava for yourself at dinner. On another topic, if you don't mind my asking, why did you choose this splendid ship for your travels?"

"Well, I was recently offered a position at the new Winnipeg School of Art, where I begin teaching in two weeks. My fiancée, Jane, is currently teaching at a girls' school in Scotland following her studies at the University of Glasgow but will be joining me next year in Winnipeg. I hope that she will enjoy her move there but I am somewhat apprehensive about her tolerance for life on the prairies. Time will tell."

"May I ask how you met your fiancée?" asked Miss Flanagan who had not yet spoken.

"Well, as a matter of fact, I was one of her teachers", admitted Mr. MacTavish who blushed as he revealed this fact. "And you, Miss Flanagan, what program will you begin this fall?"

"I have been playing the piano with the Winnipeg Theatre Orchestra for some time, but, this fall, I will be studying at the Conservatory of Music in order to pursue a career as a pianist. I hope eventually to play some of Chopin's lovely music at the new Walker Theatre in Winnipeg if I am successful."

"How lovely, Miss Flanagan. May I say that Chopin is my favourite composer for the piano. Perhaps you would be kind enough to interpret one of his nocturnes, the music of moonlight, for me in the ship's music room?" suggested Eduardo.

"I would be delighted to play for you and your sister tomorrow afternoon," replied Grace but, while her words included Maria Cristina, her shining eyes were fixed on Eduardo…

The next afternoon, Maria Cristina and Eduardo made their way to the ship's striking music room with its rounded sofas encircling the glass dome overlooking the first-class dining room. A grand piano held pride of place in the room and could be played by any first-class passenger who wished to do so. At the appointed time, Grace entered the music room, smiled at Eduardo and Maria Cristina and sat down at the piano. She announced to those gathered there that she would be playing four works by Chopin, two nocturnes, one *polonaise* and one sonata and soon began to fill the room with the composer's graceful and elegant music. At the conclusion of her performance, the audience included many more passengers from the deck who had been drawn to the salon by her masterful interpretation of Chopin's music. "Such talent!" "An amazing performance!" "Bravo!" were among the accolades that followed her last chords on the piano. As Eduardo and Maria Cristina thanked Grace for her performance, the Spaniard whispered, "We will celebrate your success with a glass of Cava tonight in the dining room."

A few hours later, Eduardo poured a glass of Cava for each of his fellow diners at the table. "As you will see, this sparkling wine has many of the properties of Champagne but without the disadvantage of its cost," noted Eduardo. Mr. MacTavish tasted the golden elixir in his glass and declared it to be a fine substitute for Champagne although it lacked the latter's complexity.

"I am sure that you are right, Mr. MacTavish, but do you not appreciate its fine taste and effervescence?" questioned Grace, not wishing to have anyone offend Eduardo.

The Spaniard then proposed a toast to Grace, declaring her virtuosity at the piano to be quite outstanding. "Would you care to dance now, Miss Flanagan? The orchestra is playing Franz Lehár's beautiful *Merry Widow Waltz.*"

As the couple danced away, Maria Cristina wondered how long it would take for the gentle Grace to fall completely under her brother's magic spell…

"Eduardo, would you like to accompany me to the library today?" asked Maria Cristina when her brother knocked at her stateroom door the next day.

"No, unfortunately, I will be unable to join you as I will be meeting Grace for high tea and a walk on the deck."

"Brother, be careful, as I fear that Grace is a kind spirit whose wings can easily be clipped."

"*No te preocupes, cariña,* don't worry, my dear, we will enjoy ourselves on the ship for the six-day passage and then we will say *adios* without regrets."

"But Eduardo, Grace lives in Winnipeg and may expect to see you again after the crossing as you will be staying in the capital for some time to introduce your wines to several merchants there."

"My sweet sister, who knows what life will have in store for me by then?

"Eduardo, you are incorrigible!"

"That is what makes me so attractive to women!"

"If I didn't love you so much, I would report you to Mamá and Papá."

"I will see you at dinner. Enjoy your afternoon in the library while I enjoy other pursuits," Eduardo responded teasingly.

Maria Cristina spent the afternoon in the ship's well stocked library, penning a long letter to her parents in which she described the Empress' many amenities, as well as the long journey by train from Madrid to Liverpool. Knowing that her parents would be interested in her activities aboard the ship, she also wrote about the passengers with whom they shared meals in the resplendent dining room before ordering a cup of coffee at the Italian Café where, unbeknown to her, Eduardo and Grace sat at a distance, chatting with great enthusiasm.

Each lovely day at sea followed another in seemingly quick succession and in twenty-four hours they would already be in the historic walled city of Quebec after a scenic journey on the St. Lawrence where Eduardo and Maria Cristina, along with their fellow passengers, were excited to observe different species of cetaceans cavorting in the water, including blue whales and the impressive humpbacks swimming into the mouth of the Saguenay Fjord to feed near Tadoussac. It was difficult to believe that this would be their last night aboard the ship and they looked forward to a celebratory meal featuring such epicurean Canadian products as smoked salmon and lobster served with delicate fiddlehead greens. What a gastronomical feast that would be!

Earlier in the day, near Rimouski, a small steamboat met the *Empress* to collect the mail for Canada while various officials boarded the ship. As it travelled on the St. Lawrence River, CPR agents provided passengers with train tickets for their journey across Canada, including sleeping car reservations to their ultimate destinations, while doctors examined passengers for any illnesses that would require them to be quarantined at Grosse Île, an immigration depot and lazaretto (maritime quarantine station) located on an island in the Gulf of Saint Lawrence. Customs personnel inspected luggage while immigration officials ensured that all passengers were in possession of the appropriate documents required for entry into Canada.

At dinner that evening, the mood was quite elated as passengers recalled the many interesting stops that they had made in Europe before boarding the *Empress*, as well as described their plans upon arrival at their Canadian destination. Many of the tourists on board were curious to learn more about the Canadian dishes on the menu that evening. Maria Cristina asked the chef for more details about the fiddleheads, an accompaniment that she had never tasted before. The chef explained that the indigenous population of Canada had been harvesting them for years. The ferns earned their name due to the fact that they resembled the curled ornamentation or scroll at the end of a fiddle. They were also known as croziers after the curved staff used by bishops, which had its origins in the shepherd's crook. Eduardo wished to find out more about the maple syrup used to make the dessert that had been served that evening and was surprised to learn that so much sap was required to produce one gallon of syrup. He turned to his dinner companions and asked them if they had ever tasted maple syrup toffee. "Why yes, Mr. Martínez," replied Grace, "it is a spring treat made when maple syrup is poured over clean snow and hardens into a candy that adults, as well as children, enjoy. In Quebec and Ontario, many of the sugaring-off facilities offer fiddle music, dancing and hearty food at that time of the year."

The next day, the *Empress of Ireland* docked in Quebec City and its passengers bade farewell to their ship companions. Mr. MacTavish and the Flanagan family left immediately on a train destined for Winnipeg, wishing Eduardo and Maria Cristina an enjoyable stay in the capital. "When you reach Winnipeg, be sure to contact us," added Mr. Flanagan. "Perhaps you would like to visit our store?" Eduardo and Maria Cristina thanked him with the assurance that they would be in touch soon after their arrival in Winnipeg. As they waved goodbye, Maria Cristina noticed that Grace blew a kiss in Eduardo's direction. "I told you, *hermano mío,* that you would be breaking hearts once again! One day, it will be your turn to suffer, my dear brother, if you are not careful."

Eduardo then hailed a horse-drawn buggy and helped Maria Cristina into it. They crossed the narrow, cobblestone streets of the Old City excitedly pointing out the sights to each other. Maria Cristina exclaimed in wonder when she noticed the beautiful building in a French château style with copper roofing and enough turrets, cornices and towers for it to be included among the castles of Europe. It was undoubtedly the Château Frontenac, part of the chain of grand hotels that linked Canada along the rail line. What a dramatic location it had, towering over the old section of the city with its commanding position on the cliff! Maria Cristina knew that its opulence rivalled that of European hotels and was eager to explore the hotel's rich interiors including its elegant Palm Court where afternoon tea was served, as well as its magnificent ballroom inspired by the Hall of Mirrors at Versailles. She looked forward to the brief stay that Eduardo and she would enjoy at the hotel while they visited the highlights of the Old Capital before taking the train to Winnipeg, her future home for several months. What a wonderful new experience awaited her!

Chapter 4

Winnipeg, June 1913

As she walked silently down the hospital's corridor, Maggie reflected upon her first month as a registered nurse with its many diverse experiences as she adjusted to her new, demanding career. It was certainly hard work, but she was not afraid of that challenge, having worked energetically throughout her life on her parents' farm. She was also exposed to many new situations that required her to maintain her composure while never forgetting to provide the necessary compassion to the patients under her care. She smiled as she recalled an incident that had just taken place at the hospital.

Maggie was tending to a patient when another nurse rushed into the room, asking her if she spoke any French. She replied that she had a basic knowledge of the language only. "That will be good enough," declared the other nurse and grabbed her by the hand, guiding her down the hall to the new x-ray department. When they entered, Maggie realized that the patient, a young Frenchman, was terrified as he stood before the hospital's proud acquisition, an x-ray machine. The patient's doctor told Maggie that the Frenchman had been involved in a car accident in St. Boniface, a rather rare occurrence in 1913 and the physician, suspecting a leg fracture, had ordered an X-ray of his patient's limb. However, as the Frenchman didn't understand any English and was worried that they were going to amputate his leg, he was creating quite a fuss. Given that most of the staff on duty that day didn't speak much French, they sought the assistance of Nurse Sullivan who did have a rudimentary knowledge of the language. She stopped the patient's cries with her comforting but elementary words, "*Pas couper, seulement une photo!*" (No cutting—only a photograph). Maggie was amazed to note how her ability to speak some French had obviously increased her stature with the hospital staff, if only briefly.

Maggie was looking forward to the next weekend when she would enjoy a few days of leave. She and her sister Beth had agreed to meet at Winnipeg's new Assiniboine Park and to take advantage of its many amenities. They would stroll through the park, explore the colourful flower displays in the Formal Garden, visit the Conservatory and possibly the zoo before enjoying tea in the Pavilion.

Near the Pavilion, Maggie noticed a pretty olive-skinned young woman accompanied by the handsomest man upon whom she had ever set eyes. Who was this Adonis dressed in the latest fashion with thick wavy black hair, striking brown eyes framed by long, sweeping eyelashes, a warm smile and a charming demeanor? Beth nudged her, telling her it was time to move on. It was at that moment that the young woman accompanying the man who had claimed Maggie's attention tripped over a broken bottle and fell on several pieces of glass that had carelessly been left on the path to the Pavilion. Maggie noticed blood running from the woman's right hand and forearm and rushed to her aid. "I am Maggie, a nurse. May I assist you, Miss?"

"Thank you so much, nurse," she responded with the same wide smile as Maggie had noticed on the man bending so solicitously over her. "I am Maria Cristina and this is my brother, Eduardo."

"Let's move to the First Aid Station where I will be able to clean your wound and remove any glass or debris that has penetrated it."

After cleaning, disinfecting and dressing the wound, Maggie gave her patient instructions for caring for her injury and advised her to take aspirin for the pain if required.

"Nurse Maggie, would you and your sister join us for tea tomorrow at the Royal Alexandra Hotel so that we may thank you properly?" suggested the handsome Eduardo. Maggie had to resist from shouting a resounding "Yes" a little too eagerly but Beth quickly took control of the situation by answering on her behalf, "I would enjoy that very much but I am afraid that I have already promised to see a movie with my fiancé tomorrow afternoon. However, I am sure that Maggie would be delighted to join you and your sister."

"Then, it is settled. We will pick you up, Maggie, tomorrow at 3:00 and take you to the Royal Alexandra for tea."

Tea at the Royal Alexandra! Maggie had not yet had the good fortune to walk into that grand hotel and to do so with Eduardo and Maria Cristina seemed like a golden opportunity that she could not miss.

As Maggie approached the hotel, she was excited about the opportunity she had to visit the first truly impressive hotel on the Prairies, which was named after Queen Alexandra, wife of King Edward VII of England. For the Royal Alexandra, unlike its previous hotels, the CPR chose a more contemporary style rather than the château-like design of its earlier buildings. The Royal Alex's elegant Gold Drawing Room with its walnut furniture adorned in gold silk brocade was indeed a lovely venue for afternoon tea. Maggie, on Eduardo's right arm with Maria Cristina on his left, was somewhat intimidated by the circumstances, both the great luxury of the venue but especially the unexpected pleasure of being so close to the handsome man to whom she was so attracted. Unreasonably so, she told herself as she did not know him well and furthermore, she was a trained nurse well into her late twenties who should be better able to control her emotions. Surely it took more than good looks and a measure of charm to cause her pulse to race and her usual loquaciousness to lapse into taciturnity!

"Maggie, may I ask you about your name? Is it a nickname?" asked Maria Cristina as they sat down at their table in the Gold Drawing Room.

"Actually, my given names are Fiona Deirdre Margaret but I am known as Maggie."

"Ah, so Maggie is short for Margaret, is it not? It means a daisy in Spanish," observed Eduardo.

"Does it really? It is pleasant to think that my name is associated with a flower."

"Are you comfortable?" asked Maria Cristina, concerned that her new friend was ill at ease.

"Yes, Maria Cristina, I'm just a little awed by this tea room and its luxurious appointments. It is very different from tea at the hospital poured from a tin pot into heavy earthenware mugs!"

"Maggie, perhaps you could describe some of the pastries on the tray for us. We are not familiar with them as they do not resemble those we have in Spain."

"Of course. I would be very pleased to do so. In the centre of the tray, you have butter tarts, the quintessential Canadian dainty. The essential ingredients are butter, eggs and a sweetener but opinions differ as to whether sugar or syrup or both should be used or whether currants or raisins are a necessary ingredient in butter tarts. In any case, I am sure that you will enjoy them. Beside the tarts are shortbread, a classic treat brought to Canada by our Scottish ancestors, which consists of sugar, butter and flour. There are also some meringue-based cookies called coconut macaroons and, my favourite, Empire Tarts, which have a very tender dough filled with a cake-like mix with raspberry jam and iced with almond paste. Delicious!"

"Maggie, now that you have described these sweets so well, I can't wait to try them all, especially the Empire Tarts that are your favourite. Do you know that, in Spain, we are famous for our marzipan which is made with almond paste? It is a tradition started in the 13th century by nuns who wished to conserve eggs in periods of war. Today, the sweets are made in the shape of various fruits and vegetables and are as lovely to look at as to eat," concluded Maria Cristina.

"How I would enjoy visiting Spain! What do you like doing in Madrid where you live?"

"Madrid lives for the night and *madrileños* are called *trasnochadores* for their habit of spending the night eating, drinking, singing, dancing, etc. Here, I notice that it is very quiet at night, so very different from what we experience at home. If you were to travel to Madrid, Maggie, I would take you to the Plaza Mayor where you would enjoy the very heartbeat of Spain in a square that has witnessed so much history over the years. Today, you can admire its architecture while drinking a glass of wine or eating tapas, little mouthfuls of delicious shrimp or of ham or olives." Eduardo then described the numerous *mesones*, informal café-bars found along the streets radiating from the Plaza Mayor. "If you go there, you might even end up dancing on the table while patrons drink a toast to your health! Or you can walk down one of the main streets in Madrid and admire the beautiful fountain of *Cibeles,* the lovely goddess of agriculture who sits in a chariot pulled by lions in front of our main post office. The play of lights on the fountains at night makes *Cibeles* one of my favourite sights in the capital. But I have talked too much," concluded Eduardo.

"Oh no, hearing you speak of Madrid makes me wish to visit it, too. However, I must admit that I have never travelled outside of my home province of Manitoba and even then, only to a few towns. Living in Winnipeg has been my only experience of a large city."

"Maggie," said Maria Cristina, "I hope that we can welcome you to our parents' home in Madrid one day and show you all the sights. However, you know that, while Madrid is very exciting, Eduardo and I are happy to be here in Winnipeg which is very different from the other cities that we have known to date. We would be so pleased to visit the city or even some of the countryside outside Winnipeg with you if this were possible."

"If you would to like to visit a real-life Canadian farm, perhaps you could spend a day or two at my parents' home. However, I warn you that your rooms will not be luxurious and that you will probably have to share them with my siblings. However, the food will be good and plentiful and there will be acres of trees, crops and wheat fields to see and, if you like, you will be able to go for a boat ride on the small river adjoining our property."

"That would be delightful, Maggie!" exclaimed Maria Cristina.

"I would enjoy that, too!" added Eduardo. "However, in the meantime, could you direct us to a shop where we could have some lighter clothing made? I must confess that we thought that it would be much colder in Winnipeg than the hot days that we have experienced to date and that we are most uncomfortable in our heavy attire."

"Yes, I, too, would enjoy having a lighter dress or two for these warmer days. Eduardo and I must have been thinking of snow when we packed such heavy clothing for our stay here," giggled Maria Cristina.

"You should not see snow until late October or November but, in the meantime, I would be delighted to accompany you to a suitable store," replied Maggie.

"Why not visit Mr. Flanagan's store?" suggested Maria Cristina. "Eduardo, you do remember the gentleman who worked at R. J. Whitla and Company whom we met on board *The Empress*? I am sure that he would be very helpful."

"That is an excellent idea. Perhaps if you wouldn't mind, Maggie, we could go together. Mr. Flanagan did invite us to visit his store and I am certain that he would be pleased to assist us. Moreover, we would appreciate your advice on the type of fabrics that would be appropriate for the summer and early fall," concluded Eduardo.

"I would be pleased to accompany you. How about 3:00 on Wednesday afternoon before I start my shift at the hospital? If you are free then, that would give us enough time to shop before I begin working."

"Next Wednesday, I only have a meeting in the late morning with the future manager of the Hotel Fort Garry, which I understand will be completed later this year," replied Eduardo.

"And I have a meeting in the morning at our hotel with the principal of St. Mary's Academy but am free in the afternoon," added Maria Cristina.

"So, it's all set for Wednesday. I will see you both at the store," said Maggie.

Business was brisk at the R. J. Whitla and Company in Winnipeg's Exchange District as Maggie and her two new friends entered the large, well supplied store. Mr. Flanagan recognized Eduardo and Maria Cristina immediately as his former shipmates and rushed to welcome them and their companion to his store. "How lovely to see you again, Maria Cristina and Eduardo, and to meet your friend! May I be of assistance to you?"

Maggie explained that her companions were looking for lighter fabrics for summer clothing. Mr. Flanagan asked his daughter Grace, who was in the store, to help Maria Cristina select the appropriate style and texture for the season while he attended to Eduardo's requirements. Soon, cooler fabrics had been chosen and the requisite measurements taken for Eduardo's new linen suit and Maria Cristina's summer dresses. Maggie could not help but notice that young Grace's initial happiness upon seeing Eduardo enter the store was very much muted by her own presence. Had there been a shipboard romance between the two? Before the trio left the store, Grace seized the opportunity to walk up to Eduardo to tell him about a very special performance that would be presented in Winnipeg the next week, the popular opera *Carmen*. "Perhaps you would be interested in attending, Eduardo, given your interest in music and your Spanish background? Are you familiar with this great work by Bizet? The music and scenes will take you right back to Spain!"

Eduardo, with his charming smile, replied that, indeed, he would be most interested in attending the performance as would his sister and possibly Maggie. With these last words, Grace's enthusiasm faltered but her good manners never failed her. "Well, of course, you're all welcome to attend *Carmen*, which will be held in the spectacular Walker Theatre. It's quite a coup for Winnipeg to be presenting this very special opera. I hope that you all enjoy it."

Chapter 5

WINNIPEG, JULY 1913

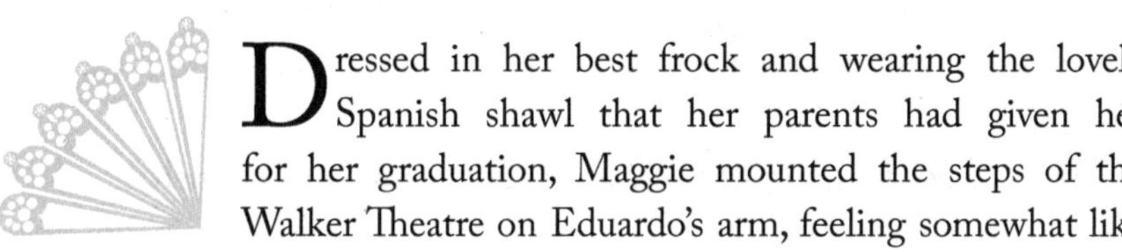

Dressed in her best frock and wearing the lovely Spanish shawl that her parents had given her for her graduation, Maggie mounted the steps of the Walker Theatre on Eduardo's arm, feeling somewhat like the heroine of a fairy tale. How Eduardo had changed her life with his winning ways and attentive manners! Was he only being polite or was he truly interested in her? Was this just a summer romance for the handsome Spaniard who had already found a place in her heart? Time would tell as her mother was fond of saying.

As they walked into the foyer, Maggie provided her friends with a description of the new Walker Theatre. "Eduardo and Maria Cristina, although I am sure that you have many outstanding theatres in Madrid, you might be interested in knowing that Winnipeg is recognized as one of North America's most important theatre centres, given its location in the middle of the continent. The Walker Theatre opened just a few years ago, easily surpassing any other cultural venue in Western Canada with the richness of its décor which boasts of Italian marble, intricate plasterwork, gilt trim, velvet carpets, silk tapestries, murals and crystal chandeliers."

"What type of program does the theatre present?' asked Eduardo.

"It offers plays, opera, pantomime, orchestral concerts and musicals. This theatre has welcomed notable Shakespearean actors, as well as other famous artists from the English-speaking world. It has also presented *Uncle Tom's Cabin* and even an epic performance of *Ben Hur* with twelve horses pulling three chariots in a memorable race! Moreover, the theatre hosted a debate last year on the voting rights of women featuring Manitoba's teacher, author and suffragist Nellie McClung on stage with the province's Premier! However, tonight, with its presentation of *Carmen*, the theatre is returning to its prime calling. I have never seen *Carmen* but so look forward to it and, for you both, it will be reminder of your home country of Spain with all its colour and passion."

"Thank you for all this information, Maggie. It seems that we Spaniards are not the only ones to speak with 'colour and passion,'" observed Eduardo with a mischievous grin.

"May I ask you about the lovely silk shawl that you are wearing tonight?" questioned Maria Cristina. "It reminds me of Spain and instantly caught my attention with its bright roses and bougainvillea. Where did you purchase it?"

"It was a graduation gift from my parents, one that I cherish."

"It suits you very well, Maggie," added Eduardo with a smile that made her blush. "Are you familiar with the bougainvillea bracts that are part of the shawl's pattern?"

"I only just learned about them when I received the shawl but they instantly appealed to me, being so delicate, almost like silk or paper flowers although I have never seen them in person. Do bougainvillea grow in Spain?"

"Do bougainvillea grow in Spain? Do matadors fight bulls? In Andalusia, they embellish practically every city and town with their pink, magenta, purple and orange splashes of colour against castle walls, churches, villas and modest homes. If you saw them in Sevilla, you would be truly amazed by their striking beauty against the white walls of the buildings."

"And you, Maria Cristina, what a lovely piece of jewelry you are wearing, a delicate pendant with an intricate design of gold doves and flowers against a dark background!" commented Maggie.

"It's damascene art, one that is famous in the Spanish city of Toledo. Goldsmiths hammer 14 karat gold threads into steel, creating magnificent pieces of art, as well as jewelry and even the swords used by matadors."

"What unique jewelry!" exclaimed Maggie.

Once seated, Maggie also remarked on Maria Cristina's elegant ivory fan, hand painted with pink roses. "Yes, Spanish women consider fans to be an important accessory to their dress and select them carefully. They are practical as well, given that they provide a little breath of coolness on hot days and nights."

"But Maria Cristina, you haven't even mentioned the secret language of love associated with fans," Eduardo reproved. "I am sure that Maggie would enjoy hearing about this. Here, let me show you how it is done with Maria Cristina's fan. This is the way you would hold your fan if you were trying to attract a man's attention. Waving a fan rapidly in the direction of a man indicates your wish to develop a relationship with him while waving it slowly means a lack of interest. Now, would you like to practice your skills in using a fan with me?"

"Sshhh. The opera is about to begin," cautioned Maria Cristina. The curtain rose, the lights dimmed and the audience sat in rapt attention as the first act began. The sterile hospital wards where Maggie had been working just a few hours earlier were suddenly transformed into a vibrant square in Seville next to the Tobacco Factory. The highly starched nurse's uniform that she had been wearing was now a colourful and provocative skirt with layers of flounces rustling with every movement. The moans and cries of patients became the fiery Carmen's haunting habanera on the rebellious nature of love (*L'amour est un oiseau rebelle*). The magic, punctuated by the clicking sound of castanets, was complete, especially with the presence of the man who had so quickly won her heart sitting so close to her that she could hear him breathe, smell the spicy cologne that he was wearing, sense the warmth of his skin beneath his tuxedo jacket and even feel his shirt cuffs with damascene links scratch against her shawl when he raised his hands to applaud.

When the curtain descended after the first act, Eduardo asked Maggie if she wished to have a glass of Champagne during the intermission. Why not? It was a night to throw caution to the winds!

In the ornate foyer, Maggie saw the Flanagan family and waved hello as she sipped her Champagne. She had never tasted such good wine before and found it to be exhilarating like the opera. Eduardo thanked Grace for having recommended *Carmen* to him and complimented her on her lovely silken green dress. "I do hope that you are enjoying the opera as much as we are," he added kindly before turning to Maggie and escorting her back to the main hall for the second part of the opera. In the darkened theatre, Maggie sensed Eduardo's fingers gradually moving closer to hers until their fingers touched and he reached for her hand and held it firmly in his. Intoxicated by both the Champagne and her happiness in being with him, Maggie wished that the evening would never end.

Arriving at the nurses' residence after a pleasant moon-lit ride in a horse-drawn carriage in the warm July night, Eduardo helped Maggie descend from the conveyance and then escorted her to the main door of the building. He moved away from the streetlight and asked Maggie if she had enjoyed her evening. "I have rarely enjoyed an evening so much," she replied sincerely, her eyes shining in the moonlight as she smiled at Eduardo.

"It was a very special evening for me, too, and not only because the opera reminded me of Spain. You, Maggie, made it so. You make me think of the love poetry of the great Spanish writer of the Romantic Era, Gustavo Adolfo Bécquer. I shall have to quote some of his poetry to you one day."

Eduardo then raised her chin, looked into her eyes and gathered her in his arms, kissing her gently for the first time before bidding her goodnight. Maggie rushed to her room and quickly fell asleep, dreaming of Spanish fans, shawls and operas but especially of one Spaniard…

Winnipeg, July 1913

Queridos mamá y papá,

How I wish I could capture for you, in a few words, a description of the life I am currently leading in Winnipeg! I am so grateful to you both for having provided me with this opportunity. Life in Madrid is so far removed from what I am experiencing here that I can readily understand that it is difficult for you to picture my daily experience in Canada, thousands of kilometres away from you.

I am very fortunate to have met a nurse from Winnipeg, Maggie, who has become a very close friend of mine since that very first day when I fell at Assiniboine Park and she attended to my wounds. She has accompanied Eduardo and me to see Carmen *at the opera, assisted with our shopping for new, lighter clothing to wear during the hot summer here (almost like Madrid's "three months of hell"), answered our questions about living in Winnipeg, served as our guide here and introduced us to Canadian traditions and food. However, I am reserving the best part for last as I describe the wonderful weekend that Eduardo and I spent at the farm with Maggie and her family last week.*

It was such a novel experience for Eduardo and me, having always lived in the city. Due to the friendly relations that my dear brother has cultivated with the concierge at our hotel (thanks in part to donations of papá's sherry and Cava!), he was able to secure a motor car for the weekend, thus enabling the three of us to travel easily to the large property that Maggie's parents own in the country. And what an impression the car made on her siblings who rarely have the opportunity to ride in such a vehicle! Maggie's brothers, in particular, lined up by the car just for the privilege of cleaning and polishing it. When Eduardo offered them a ride, they eagerly jumped into the Model T, excited to be going to the nearest town for ice cream and happily waving to any neighbour who could spot them in the car, rather than the usual horse and buggy.

Maggie's parents could not have been kinder to us, welcoming us as special guests to their home. Although I had to share a room with Maggie and her younger sisters, it was no hardship as we giggled and talked together throughout the night while, across the hall, Eduardo entertained his new followers, Maggie's brothers, with stories of his many adventures in Spain.

On the day that we arrived at the farm, there was so much food being prepared that we thought we must be walking through a hotel kitchen getting ready for a banquet. But no! It was July 1, Dominion Day, when Canada celebrates its birthday and a huge outdoor picnic was being prepared. Can you believe that the country is only 46 years old! Apparently, large picnics are very popular on Dominion Day and people from miles around travel by horse and buggy to enjoy this social event with family and friends. On this particular day, Maggie's parents were the hosts and were expecting many guests to make their way to their farm for the occasion. Maggie told Eduardo and me that, as a child, she could even remember hearing the scraping sounds of a few old Red River Carts from miles away as visitors travelled to their farm. It was a particularly irritating noise caused by the friction of the dry wood of the wheel turning on the axle. Apparently, it can be compared to the sound of an untuned fiddle or perhaps to that of a chalk squeaking on a blackboard. I have learned that these wooden carts were originally used for the fur trade but, today, there are only a few settlers travelling westward in these cumbersome but reliable conveyances. In the winter, I am told that the wheels of these carts can even be removed, enabling them to glide across the ice.

But to return to the food: huge spreads of cold baked ham, fried chicken, potato salad, coleslaw, chutney, bread, jelly rolls, date cookies and rhubarb pie (a rather tart fruit but delicious in pies), accompanied by lemonade, are the mainstay of these picnics. After eating, there are wheelbarrow races, softball games and even some dancing. Later in the day, we witnessed a very different custom here, totally unfamiliar to us. Fancy lunches prepared by marriageable women were packed in pretty, well decorated boxes and auctioned to the highest male bidder. Maggie tells me that, after a short courtship, one of her cousins actually married the man who bet on her lunch box. I am surprised that Eduardo didn't bid on one of these boxes!

Maggie and some of her siblings took us for a boat ride later in the day when most of the guests had left. The atmosphere was very tranquil after the boisterousness we had experienced earlier and we were content to listen to the sound of the birds in the trees and to spot the occasional beaver and muskrat along the river banks. When we returned to the house, we enjoyed a light supper with the family and Eduardo served some of papá's sherry. The women, unaccustomed to alcohol, were a little tipsy afterwards but happily cleaned up the many dirty dishes used for the picnic, eagerly anticipating the last treat of the day: a splendid fireworks show on the large property. How exciting it was to witness the Roman Candles light up the inky blue night sky!

It was very hot here today; I am certain that the temperature reached over 30 degrees Celsius. We Europeans always imagine Canada to be in the grip of a frigid winter but I can assure you that it experiences hot summers as well. Maggie's younger siblings threatened to throw me into the water as we paddled down the river and I confess that the thought of being refreshed in the cold water did not displease me although it would not have been very ladylike.

I hope that I have been able to sketch a portrait of our life here in Manitoba, one of Canada's prairie provinces, and to give you a capsule view of our days here.

I think of you often and hope that you are both well.

Con cariño,
Maria Cristina

P.S. Eduardo sends you his love and says that he will write soon to describe how well his wine transactions are progressing here in Canada.

As Maggie was working a late shift and Eduardo was busy, she planned a lovely day with Maria Cristina, having been fortunate enough to receive two tickets to the Lieutenant Governor's Annual Garden Party from a kind woman who had been her patient at the hospital.

The day dawned bright and sunny as the two friends arrived on the grounds of Government House, dressed in their best Sunday frocks and hats. It was a pleasure to meet the Lieutenant Governor, Sir Douglas Cameron, and his wife, Mrs. Margaret Cameron, who graciously took the time to greet their many guests as they strolled along the manicured grounds and beautiful flowers of their imposing residence. Tea, sandwiches and dainties were served as the guests listened to the music of a small orchestra playing classical as well as popular selections. Maggie explained the role of the Lieutenant Governor to Maria Cristina who was somewhat confused by the number of vice-regal members serving as His Majesty The King's representatives in the various provinces of Canada.

As the two women walked through the grounds, Maggie pointed out a few important local figures who were attending the Garden Party. Her companion, who was much more accustomed to gatherings of high society than Maggie was, appeared to be delighted to have the opportunity to socialize and certainly the unusual mantilla and shawl that she wore to compliment her striking dress, as well as her exotic fan, attracted a great deal of comment. She, of course, was pleased to talk about her native Spain and her experiences in Canada.

After speaking to the Lieutenant Governor and Mrs. Cameron, the two friends retired to a quieter part of the large property and caught up on their news. Maria Cristina spoke with enthusiasm about her new position at St. Mary's Academy but confessed that she was somewhat worried about how she would be received. Would students mock her accent? Would they doubt her ability to teach? How would they accept a foreigner as their teacher? Maggie assured Maria Cristina that her future colleagues and students would undoubtedly be as pleased to be in her company as Maggie's own large family and friends had been.

Maria Cristina then shyly asked Maggie about her relationship with Eduardo, not certain how she would react to her questioning. "Amiga querida, my dear friend, I hope that my questions do not make you uncomfortable but I so wish to see both you and my brother happy."

"As to being happy, I have never been happier since the day that I met Eduardo. He is such a thoughtful and caring person and, of course, I cannot deny that he is the best-looking man that I have ever seen. Despite that, he has always behaved like a perfect gentleman."

"Maggie, *me alegro tanto*. I am delighted to learn that Eduardo is such a good companion to you. Although he is my brother, I have to say that his fine features and winning ways have always made him so successful with women that he is considered, rightfully or not, to be somewhat of a Don Juan and I was concerned that you might be hurt. Do you remember Grace? I fear that she, too, found Eduardo most attractive and is now sadly nursing her wounds."

"I understand, Maria Cristina. However, Eduardo explained to me how young and impressionable Grace is and how sorry he was that he was the unintended source of her disappointment. Truly, I can't believe my good fortune that he is attracted to me. I keep thinking that I will wake up from this wonderful dream and see it turn to dust."

"Maggie, if Eduardo cares for you and you care for him, that is wonderful and I wish you both every happiness."

"Thank you, Maria Cristina, for sharing your thoughts with me. I am fortunate not only to have met such a wonderful man, but also to have you as my close friend. Well, we had better be off as we promised to meet Eduardo in half an hour for refreshments."

After walking down Broadway Avenue, Maggie and Maria Cristina met Eduardo at a café where they ordered lemonade. "What is that large, castle-like building that we see down the street?" asked Maria Cristina.

Maggie, relishing her role as guide, explained, "Ah, that is the future Hotel Fort Garry, a hotel that is being constructed in the elegant château-style of French medieval castles. Charles Melville Hays, former President of the Grand Trunk Railway, had plans to establish a chain of luxury railway hotels across Canada built in the same manner as the Château Laurier in Ottawa, another one of his hotels. Did Eduardo not tell you about this hotel, Maria Cristina?"

"Yes, he did mention that the manager told him that the hotel is being built on land that once welcomed Western Canada's most important trading post, Upper Fort Garry, and that the hotel of the same name is scheduled to be completed later this year."

"And did not the unfortunate Mr. Hays perish aboard the *Titanic* just last year on his way to Ottawa for the official opening of the Château Laurier?" asked Eduardo.

"Yes, indeed, Eduardo, you are right. The sinking of the ship caused ripple effects for so many around the world. To think of all the families who lost loved ones as the result of that tragedy!" reflected Maggie. "But look at the time: I must be headed back to the hospital now."

"May we accompany you there?" asked Eduardo. "We can't have one of the hospital's best nurses arrive late for her shift, *verdad*?"

"I would not wish to be late although I'm not sure that I would be described in the same glowing terms you have used, Eduardo. We can take the streetcar back to the hospital; it should take us there in time."

At the main door to the hospital, Eduardo paused and asked if he might have supper with Maggie the next day before her shift began at 7:00. "Perhaps we could go for a walk before supper and you could point out some interesting facts about St. Boniface history or perhaps just talk about yourself? Maria Cristina will be unable to join us, however. I hope that will be all right?" he asked with a teasing smile.

"I will risk a few hours alone with you," laughed Maggie, ecstatic at the prospect of spending time alone in Eduardo's company for the first time…

"Eduardo, would you like to visit St. Boniface Cathedral, which you must have noticed from the streetcar?" asked Maggie the next day. "I attend mass there every week as it is very close to the hospital and the nurses' residence."

"Yes, I would enjoy visiting the cathedral. Do you know anything about its history?"

"Well, I can tell you that the Roman Catholic mission founded by Bishop Provencher in the early 19th century was an instrumental one in the religious and cultural life of St. Boniface, as well as the centre of missionary work in the Red River Settlement. There were several earlier versions of the cathedral but this one was only constructed a few years ago. It is considered to be the largest and most impressive cathedral in Western Canada. I'm sure, Eduardo, that you have more imposing cathedrals in Spain but this one is very grand for us. Let's hope that it lasts longer than its predecessors!"

"Well, of course, as our history is much older than yours, we have had experience building cathedrals for much longer than Canadians. My favourite Spanish cathedral is the one in Seville whose construction started at the dawn of the 15th century but which took more than one hundred years to complete. Those entrusted with its planning expressed their wish to build a church so magnificent that those who came after them would think that they were madmen. To please Maggie, he repeated the statement in Spanish: *"Hagamos una Iglesia tan hermosa y tan grandiosa que los que la vieren labrada nos tengan por locos."*

"Oh Eduardo, I could listen to you speak Spanish forever but I suppose that we should visit the cathedral now."

After touring the majestic cathedral, Eduardo remarked, "Maggie, I have the impression that the Cathedral's cemetery is quite historic as well. Who is this Louis Riel whose tombstone is so prominent?"

"He was a Métis leader, born in St. Boniface, who fought to secure favourable terms for Manitoba's entry into Confederation in 1870, not even two decades before I was born. In seeking to protect the Métis people and their rights, he led a rebellion and was hanged for treason. His role in Canadian history has been very controversial with some considering him to be a hero while others think he was a traitor. Who knows how history will treat him? Perhaps one day, we will pay tribute to him as the founder of Manitoba and even issue a stamp in his honour. If you are interested in history, there is the grave of Marie-Anne Gaboury, Louis Riel's grandmother and the first woman of European descent to settle in Western Canada."

As the couple walked in the direction of the hospital, Eduardo asked about the long building built with white oak logs and boasting dormers and green-shuttered casement windows. "Ah, that is the oldest building in Winnipeg, the convent where the first Grey Nuns who travelled to the Red River Colony lived, beginning in 1847. It also served as a school, an orphanage and even as an infirmary, eventually leading to the establishment of St. Boniface Hospital where I currently work."

"And how is it, Margarita, that you know so much about the history of this area?" asked Eduardo.

"My parents always felt that their children should learn as much as they could about the area where they lived and the new province that had welcomed them as Irish emigrants. I always enjoyed history and in my few free hours would read about those who contributed to the life and legacy of Manitoba."

"I'm constantly amazed by the things that you know, Maggie. Tell me why you became a nurse as I'm sure that it could not have been easy to choose such a profession in a world where women are usually expected to marry young and have a family."

"When I was a child, I used to tend to the animals, milking the cows, feeding the chickens and grooming the horses. Whenever I would see an animal with an injury or that appeared to be sick, I would try to take care of it. Moreover, as my mother had so many babies and I was the eldest daughter of the family, I frequently had to look after the younger children when they fell sick. With each passing year, I learned what medicines and herbs to use for various ailments and how to dress a wound and cure a stomach ache. As I grew older, I also learned more about pregnancies and deliveries as there were so many women around me including my mother and aunts who were giving birth. I loved to handle the babies and give them their baths and soon I began thinking about becoming a nurse. My parents initially were not overly supportive as they needed my help on the farm but, eventually, they recognized that I, too, had dreams that I wished to pursue and they gave me their blessing to enroll in a nursing program."

"I'm very proud of you, Margarita. You're a very determined woman but also a very gentle one. I can see why you are such a good nurse and so popular with your patients," declared Eduardo.

After eating a light meal at a little café, the couple began walking back to the hospital, arm in arm. "Ah, my precious little Margarita, do you realize that I will be leaving for Spain in just two weeks? I am already sad, knowing that I will have to say goodbye to you so soon. I think that I will have to practice my goodbyes with longer kisses, that is, if you have no objection."

"Oh Eduardo, how could I ever object to your kisses!" exclaimed Maggie as she raised her lips to meet his in a passionate kiss, amazed at her own ardour.

The next day, Eduardo arrived early in the afternoon, along with a picnic basket. "Let's walk by the river today, Maggie, and then we can have a picnic before your shift begins."

As the couple sat comfortably enjoying their meal, Eduardo reached for Maggie's hand. "Do you remember my referring to the poet Gustavo Adolfo Bécquer, my sweet? He was a Romantic poet of the nineteenth century who wrote very touching poetry and there is a beautiful statue in Seville that pays tribute to him. One of his most famous poems is included in the collection known as *Rimas y Leyendas* in which Bécquer answers his lover's question as to what constitutes poetry."

> *¿Qué es poesía? ¿Y tú me lo preguntas?*
> *Poesía... eres tú.*

"The words sound lovely, but what do they mean?"

"Bécquer is telling his beloved, who is looking at him with her beautiful blue eyes and asking 'What is poetry?', that the answer to her question is that she herself is *poetry*."

"My dear Eduardo, you are such a romantic. I have never heard poetry recited with such feeling as when you quote it. What will I do when you leave?" asked Maggie, her eyes bright with nascent tears.

"*Te amo Maggie, con todo mi corazón*. I love you, Maggie, with all my heart."

"I love you, too, Eduardo *con todo mi corazón* as you say. Love poetry sounds so much sweeter in Spanish."

"A kiss is even more convincing than words of poetry," declared Eduardo as he pressed Maggie against his chest, kissing her until she felt a warm wave of desire sweep over her body.

"To ensure that you will remember me after I leave for Spain, I had a photograph taken at a Winnipeg studio; I hope that you like it."

"It is a wonderful likeness, Eduardo, and I shall treasure it forever. It is quite a coincidence that you had a photo taken for me as I also took the liberty of having a studio portrait taken so that you could remember the girl from Winnipeg whose heart you stole."

"I never planned to fall in love with you Maggie but it happened. Would it be too immodest of me to tell you that, while women generally flirt with me, using their wiles to great advantage, in this case Cupid's arrow reached its target when I first met you and has stubbornly refused to detach itself from my heart?"

"When I first saw that there was an attraction, between us, I couldn't believe my good fortune. Please kiss me, Eduardo, once again before I leave for work."

"With great pleasure, my Margarita."

A somewhat disheveled Maggie with flushed cheeks, a rapid heartbeat and an unspoken but sudden comprehension of human passion raced up the steps to the nurses' residence, knowing that she had just experienced the type of desire that would be increasingly difficult to ignore. As she reflected upon this discovery, she was seized with the brutal realization that in two weeks her Eduardo would be leaving for Spain and that she would never see him again…

Chapter 6

WINNIPEG, AUGUST 1913

"Eduardo, what surprise have you planned for Maggie and me today? I see that you have managed to borrow the hotel car once more. Did you offer the concierge another bottle of Father's sherry?" teased Maria Cristina.

"One of sherry as well as one of Cava! But it will be worth it, my dear sister, as I have a special day planned."

After picking up Maggie at the nurses' residence, Eduardo announced that he would be driving down Wellington Crescent, a wide street lined with lovely mansions set well back from the sidewalk. "Maggie, as I only remember a little of what the concierge related to me, I am relying on you to be our guide in this fashionable district. What can you tell us about it and its inhabitants?"

"This whole area boasts of large, sprawling properties framed by greenery and landscaped lawns. With its striking homes partially hidden from the street, people can stroll along and appreciate the beauty and ambience of the neighbourhood and its great profusion of elm trees. Eduardo, you might wish to stop the car here."

"Is this grand home of particular importance, Maggie?" asked Maria Cristina.

"Yes, this property at 393 Wellington Crescent was built in 1911 for the unhappily named Fortune family. Mark Fortune, his wife Mary, son Charles and three daughters were all travelling on the *Titanic* on its ill-fated maiden voyage in April 1912; both the father and son perished and the remaining family members are now living in this large Tudor-style home completed just a short time before they left on an extended journey to Egypt, Greece, Italy and France. Ironically, I remember reading about their plans in the paper's society column and wishing that I, too, could travel to such distant, exotic lands," Maggie concluded wistfully.

"What a sad story!" exclaimed Maria Cristina.

"Yes, but they were not the only ones to know tragedy. Thomas McCaffry, John Hugo Ross and Thomson Beattie, three prosperous bachelors with a Winnipeg connection, were accompanying the Fortune Family as they sailed home on the *Titanic*, having canceled their passage on another ocean liner to experience the White Star's new, "unsinkable ship". Unfortunately, the three friends perished with the sinking of the *Titanic.* Ironically, Beattie's body was buried at sea on his mother's birthday, close to the area in the Atlantic where she had been born 82 years earlier on a ship travelling to Canada."

"I didn't realize that there was such a Manitoba connection with the *Titanic,*" whispered Maria Cristina, much moved by Maggie's account.

"Yes, indeed, but sadder yet was the story of the Allison family, also from Winnipeg," declared Maggie. "Hudson Allison, his wife Bess and their young daughter and son were also travelling on the *Titanic,* along with their children's two nursemaids. One of the nursemaids rescued the baby boy and was safely in a lifeboat while Mrs. Allison and her daughter were placed in another. When Mrs. Allison heard that her husband was in a third lifeboat, she rushed out with her daughter to find him and their infant son. The three perished as the parents looked inconsolably for their son who, unbeknown to them, had already been rescued."

"What a tragic story, Maggie!" exclaimed Maria Cristina and Eduardo in unison. "Tell us something more cheerful."

"Look! There is St. Mary's Academy where you will be teaching in September. See that building with its Second Empire features including peaked dormers. The nuns selected this site when the Academy outgrew its previous facilities in the crowded commercial core of the city. Some 200 students study there, both boarders and day students. I think that you will be happy in such beautiful surroundings."

"Ah, Maria Cristina, you must recognize the next landmark: Assiniboine Park where you had your accident shortly after our arrival from Madrid and where Maggie came to your rescue. We will have lunch here at the Pavilion," added Eduardo.

The trio walked into the Pavilion where they saw Mr. MacTavish dining by himself. After inviting him to join them at their table and introducing him to Maggie, Eduardo queried him on his new life in Winnipeg. "Are you enjoying your new position here? Will your fiancée be arriving soon?"

"Thank you for asking. Yes, indeed, I am very much enjoying my new position with the Winnipeg Art Gallery. My fiancée will be arriving in Winnipeg next spring and, of course, I am looking forward to seeing her after such a long absence. Señor Martínez and Miss Martínez, how have you found your stay here so far?"

After answering Mr. MacTavish's questions, Maria Cristina asked him about his former life in Scotland and whether he had travelled frequently before moving to Canada.

"Quite honestly, most of my travels prior to leaving Scotland were to the United Kingdom but it is possible that my fiancée and I will travel to the continent next year for our honeymoon. However, I understand that you and your brother have travelled extensively in Europe if I'm not mistaken."

"Indeed, we have been most fortunate. We have enjoyed many trips to France, Italy, Greece and England and, last year, we visited Egypt to see the treasures of the Nile."

"And you, Miss Sullivan, have you also travelled extensively overseas?" asked Mr. MacTavish.

"I'm afraid that I have never ventured more than forty miles away from my home. How I would love to visit Spain and France! Eduardo has described his country's many attractions to me," added Maggie. "As a child, I used to read travel writers such as Mark Twain and dream of exotic lands. However, this passion of mine was not encouraged by my family who thought that I was aspiring to things beyond my reach."

"Margarita, Maria Cristina and I would so love to show you our country. Perhaps you might consider a trip to Spain next year?" suggested Eduardo.

Throughout the meal, Maggie pondered Eduardo's words. Was he really serious about seeing her again or merely being polite? Dare she even hope that he might wish her to travel to Spain? And what would happen then?

After a delicious meal, the three friends returned to the car and Eduardo announced that they would be travelling through the countryside to enjoy the sights and smells of summer.

"Eduardo, where are we headed on this fine day?"

"Well, Maggie, I thought that you might enjoy spending a few hours with your family, especially as we have the means today to make our way to their farm, thanks to the generosity of the hotel's concierge."

"Not to mention Papa's unrecognized generosity with his spirits!" added Maria Cristina.

An hour later, they arrived at their destination to the excited whoops of Maggie's younger siblings who immediately begged Eduardo for a ride in his car. "Of course, climb in the car and we will try to find a place where we can buy ice-cream."

"Yippie, that would be great!" they exclaimed in unison.

"Maggie, why don't you stay and have a little chat with your parents while Maria Cristina and I spend some time with the younger children?"

"How thoughtful of you, Eduardo! Thank you."

Maggie was soon seated in the kitchen with her parents who were eager to find out more about her nursing career, life in Winnipeg and her new friends Maria Cristina and Eduardo.

She quickly told them about life at the hospital and her various outings with her Spanish companions and how wonderful life had been since she first met Eduardo and how sad she would be when he left in two weeks.

"Fiona," her father began to remonstrate, preparing Maggie for an opinion that she would likely not appreciate, "I know that it will be difficult but it is probably better for you that he should leave."

"Why do you say that, Papa? Eduardo is so kind and considerate towards me and, well, I care for him very much."

"That is precisely the problem. Where will all of this lead? You would just become fonder and fonder of Eduardo and then... If he asked you to marry him, what would you do? Leave for Spain and abandon the life you have always known here, your family and friends, your new career, your traditions and even your language? In Spain, you would be an outsider, never truly accepted and always judged by different standards. It is best to marry one's own kind. Why not consider a good Irishman like me?" he concluded with a smile. "Have you not met any Irishmen in Winnipeg?"

"But. Papa, I have met a good Spaniard!"

"Who will soon leave you in tears... I admit, Fiona, that Eduardo is a fine gentleman but he is not for you. He comes from a different level of society with a prosperous, upper-class background far different from your own."

Maggie's mother added, "Just think of your relationship as a special moment in time, one to remember fondly but not to nurture for your future. Once he leaves, you can forget him and concentrate on meeting the man you will eventually marry. Time is fleeting and you are not getting any younger, I dare say." Her mother's rather harsh words jarred Maggie and she looked up to see sympathy in her father's eyes.

At this point, the conversation ended abruptly with the return of Eduardo, Maria Cristina and the children.

"Eduardo, Maria Cristina, would you care for a piece of rhubarb pie before you leave? I baked several pies this morning with the rhubarb that the children gathered for me."

"Thank you, Mrs. Sullivan. That would be lovely. I fear, however, that the children have eaten so much ice-cream that they may not be hungry for pie."

"Then, there will be more for the rest of us!"

On the way back to Winnipeg, Eduardo noticed that Maggie was not her usual loquacious self. "Why so quiet, my sweet?" he asked her. As she did not wish to share her parents' comments with him, at least at that moment, she replied that she was tired and just wished to rest for the return trip to

Winnipeg. She closed her eyes but her thoughts were disquieting: what had she thought the future would hold for her? A handsome Spaniard who would whisk her away to his country and marry her? Eduardo was leaving Canada; he had never promised her the gold ring which glistened in her imagination but not on her finger… For all she knew, he might already be engaged to a lovely *señorita* from a distinguished Spanish family who was planning their wedding at this very moment. Maggie tried to dispel her negative thoughts and concentrate on the remaining time she had to enjoy Eduardo's company before his departure for Madrid.

Chapter 7

Winnipeg Beach, late August 1913

During Eduardo's last week in Winnipeg, his courtship of Maggie proceeded at a feverish pace. After her day shift, he would be at the hospital daily to see her, sometimes inviting Maggie to join him for a picnic while at other times suggesting a movie or simply a romantic walk by the river, his arm tightly embracing her. He whispered loving words into her ear and occasionally more risqué suggestions which caused her to blush. His kisses became increasingly passionate, causing Maggie to feel the warmth of desire rising as their lips met and she felt his firm, muscular chest against her soft, full breasts. On the Friday before his departure, Eduardo informed Maggie that he had a surprise in store for her on his final weekend in Winnipeg.

"Have you ever heard of the Moonlight Train to Winnipeg Beach, *cariña?*"

"Yes, I have heard about it many times. How do you know about it?"

"My trusty concierge, Pierre, has suggested that we take it as part of a romantic experience for our last weekend together. We will travel by train to the beach, have a picnic there, swim, go for a boat ride, walk through the midway area, have dinner at a hotel and then return to Winnipeg in the early hours of the morning on the Moonlight Train. What do you think of my plans?"

"It sounds like a delightful day and so exciting for someone like me who has only ever travelled a few miles away from her home but perhaps also a little naughty."

"It is only as naughty as you wish to make it, my sweet. Have I not always been a gentleman with you?" he asked.

"Yes, Eduardo, that is true but…"

"But what, Maggie?"

"Perhaps on the Moonlight Train, I might start wishing that you were slightly less of a gentleman…", she admitted with a measure of guilt, having always behaved in a manner judged to be appropriate for a young Irish-Canadian Catholic woman of her time. Eduardo's good looks, his confidence and his charm were undisputedly seductive and she was very conscious that the space between them was closing each time that they met.

"Ah, I am very willing to try, my darling! But seriously, we will have a lovely day together and, if I stray from my usual gentlemanly conduct, you can always remind me that I am to behave."

Maggie found herself daydreaming about their upcoming day at Winnipeg Beach where Eduardo and she would enjoy the picturesque lakeside setting. It was Manitoba's version of Coney Island in New York or Brighton Beach in Britain: a three-mile stretch of sandy beach beckoning to Winnipeggers who wished to benefit from a day's outing by the water, as well as the many amenities offered by this new resort. Day trippers could enjoy a promenade on the boardwalk skirting the lake before heading to the beach for a leisurely picnic on the soft sand or to relax after a strenuous swim in the lake. An amusement park containing one of the largest wooden roller coasters in Canada guaranteed thrills for the more daring while a penny arcade, bowling alley and bumper cars entertained those of a more timorous disposition. A dance pavilion where the top Manitoba bands of the time played was a popular source of entertainment for young couples seeking a venue for dancing, socializing and courting. Winnipeg's elite stayed at The Empress Hotel, making the most of its modern amenities, tennis courts, bowling greens, sailing yacht, beach bonfires and special evening concerts, as well as of its smoking room, magnificent dining room with fireplace and its legendary lavish bar.

As Maggie and Eduardo stepped off the train, they could see the sparkling lake burst into view, matching their ebullient spirits.

"Eduardo, this is so beautiful. I have often wished to visit Winnipeg Beach but have never had the opportunity. Do you know that Manitoba has three great lakes, Lake Winnipeg, Lake Winnipegosis and Lake Manitoba, all of which are very impressive bodies of water? This lake, Lake Winnipeg, has miles of sandy beaches reminiscent of those surrounding an ocean, I am told."

"Si, *querida*, let's walk down the boardwalk by the water and enjoy the fresh breezes off the lake as well as the sight of so many people picnicking or sunning on the beach, swimming in the lake, riding a sailboat or a steamer or just strolling about on the boardwalk. What a lovely day to enjoy together!"

Arm in arm, the couple strolled about, content to take in the ambiance of the lakeside resort. They could hear the whistle of the many excursion trains as they arrived at their destination at various times throughout the day. There were the picnic trains carrying church, social and ethnic groups to Winnipeg Beach in order to foster good relations and bring these communities together. "Daddy Trains" brought fathers and husbands who worked in Winnipeg during the week back to their families for weekends at the cottage. Finally, the "Moonlight Trains" enabled young adults to reach the resort for a fun day and a return journey to Winnipeg late at night where they could romance their date under the cover of darkness.

A carnival atmosphere created by the tinkling sounds of the penny arcade, the music of the calliope (mechanical steam organ), the tinny melodies from the merry-go-round, the shots from the shooting gallery, the billiard balls knocking against each other, the shouting of the circus barker announcing the midway's many attractions, coupled with the screams emanating from the giant roller coaster as its passengers careened over dips all added to the thrill of exploring the town and walking down its boardwalk. Observing how enchanted Maggie was, just like a child at the circus, Eduardo proposed a ride on the roller coaster that promised a heart-stopping experience, as well as the opportunity to hold one's companion tightly as the cars tilted on their downward journey across the tracks. Before she could say no, Eduardo had purchased the tickets and they were soon seated on the roller coaster. As the cars began their wobbly ascent, Maggie screamed so hard that her companion held her tightly to silence her fears.

After disembarking from the roller coaster, Eduardo asked, "Well, my sweet Margarita, would you like to have lunch now to calm your nerves?"

"Eduardo, I still can't believe that I actually was brave enough to ride the roller coaster. See what an effect you have on me! I am starving now and would really like to eat. What have you brought for lunch?"

"Let's find a good spot on the sand where we can spread our blanket and then we can discover what my trusty concierge has arranged for us."

The two settled on a shady area and opened their wicker basket, happy to find ham sandwiches, cheese, cookies and oranges, as well as some freshly made lemonade. They ate with gusto, admiring the sailboats, motorboats and canoes plying the lake as they finished their lunch. "Maggie, why don't we rent bathing suits and swim?"

Shyly, Maggie confessed that, outside her immediate family, she had never worn a bathing suit in public.

"Then, I will be the first lucky boyfriend to see you in a bathing suit."

Off they went to rent their outfits and to change into the clumsy bathing suits of that period which covered most of the body and were highly impractical for swimming. Maggie chose a navy and white striped, knee-length, puffed-sleeve wool dress with a sailor collar, worn over bloomers trimmed with ribbons. To ensure decency according to the standards of the early 20th century, she wore long navy stockings, bathing slippers and a cap for her hair. She was pleased with her appearance but, despite the modesty of her bathing suit, she had never displayed so much flesh to a man before with almost bare arms and a hint of neck and upper chest showing and felt somewhat awkward before him.

"Why, my Margarita, you are so pretty in your bathing suit that you are tempting me to be less of a gentleman right now which, I am sure, would disappoint you.... or not?"

"Really, Eduardo, you are being naughty!" she replied but deep down she was feeling a new exciting but uncomfortable wish to feel his hands touch her where she had never been touched before. To hide her embarrassment, she challenged Eduardo to race her to the water.

Eduardo rushed into the water but was unprepared for its cold temperature. "Maggie, I forgot, that the waters here are not as warm as they are in Spain. I am shivering."

Maggie, who was accustomed to swimming in the cool water of the river next to her parents' property, held him in her arms to warm him, playfully telling him, "As your nurse, I worry about hypothermia and must ensure that you do not suffer from the cold."

"Thank you. I am feeling very warm now," he assured her.

A few minutes later, Maggie chided him, "Your hands, Eduardo!"

He teasingly replied, "Yes, where would you like them?" before swimming to shore as Maggie, blushing, decided to cool off a little more in the lake.

Later, as they sunbathed under the hot sun, Eduardo began writing in the sand with his finger. Maggie understood his message, "*Te amo mucho*" (I love you very much) and traced her own in the sand: "*Yo también*" (I do, too).

Eduardo asked Maggie if Maria Cristina had taught her some Spanish and when she indicated that indeed she had, he wrote another message, "*¿Puedo darte un beso?*" (May I kiss you?).

Carefully, Maggie wrote, "*Si, me gustaría un beso.*" (Yes, I would like a kiss).

Eduardo kissed Maggie and then informed her that he had purchased tickets for a one-hour ride on the steamer that provided passengers with a scenic view of the shoreline and cottages, as well as of the town. "We must change now to be at the pier in time for our boat ride."

As they left the beach, Maggie noticed that the incoming waves from the lake had already obliterated some of their love letters in the sand. She wondered if their romance would disappear as quickly as those ephemeral words, now that Eduardo was leaving the country. Would he remember her in another month? She thought that she would never forget him, no matter what happened.

On the steamer, Eduardo found a quiet corner, put his arm around Maggie's waist and told her how she had transformed his life. "As I look into your deep blue eyes and contemplate your kind, generous personality, I realize that I never wish to let you go. Please believe me, Maggie, when I tell you that I have fallen in love with you, my darling. Yes, I who always found it difficult to be satisfied with one woman, now find that my heart has been struck with Cupid's arrow so deeply that I find the thought of leaving you behind unbearable."

On bended knee and with Maggie's hand in his, Eduardo said, "I know that this is very sudden, but will you marry me and follow me to Spain as my wife?"

Maggie felt more emotions in that instant than she had ever known: love for the man who had so quickly won her heart, wonder that he wished to marry her, relief that she would not lose him with his departure for Spain, sorrow at the prospect of leaving her dear family behind, worry about adopting a new country as her home, but also happiness and excitement at the prospect of finally experiencing the world as it beckoned full of the promise of love, a different life and new adventures.

"Yes, Eduardo, I will marry you and follow you to Spain," she declared after a few seconds.

They sealed their commitment with a long, passionate kiss and were surprised to note when they released each other that several passengers who had quietly overheard the proposal were applauding Maggie's answer. The couple, slightly embarrassed, slipped away to another part of the deck, delighting in the glow of their happiness.

"Well, Maggie, as this is a very special day in our lives, I have arranged for us to enjoy a splendid dinner at the Empress Hotel in celebration."

"And what would you have done had I refused your proposal?" teased Maggie.

"I would have done my best to change your mind during our romantic dinner, being extra charming so that you could not resist me. Perhaps I would even have quoted Bécquer to you in Spanish since, apparently, you enjoy hearing this language very much. Do you remember my telling you about the monument in Seville erected in honour of this poet which includes a statue of Cupid taking aim with his arrow? We will have to visit it on our honeymoon, *mi amor*."

"Oh Eduardo, this is a dream and I fear I will wake up and be Cinderella by her pumpkin, having lost her prince and fancy carriage."

"Margarita, you will wake up in my arms and the dream will never end for us."

"You are a hopeless romantic, Eduardo, but it is one of the reasons why I love you so. To think that this morning, I was determined to enjoy this final day with you as, once over, I believed that you would be gone from my life forever. And now, not only will I accompany you to Spain as your wife but I will also live in a country that I have longed to visit for most of my life."

As the couple walked into the graceful Empress Hotel, the maître d' greeted Eduardo by name, saying, "Mr. Martínez, a table is ready for you and your lovely companion."

As Maggie walked into the dining room, she exclaimed over its magnificent amenities including a fireplace. "Eduardo, what a beautiful place you have selected to celebrate our engagement!"

The couple was escorted to a lovely window table and given a menu with the evening choices for dinner. "Let's have Winnipeg Goldeye, Eduardo," said Maggie who had always wanted to try this popular delicacy fished from Lake Winnipeg. "Did you know that, some years ago, a fishmonger selling goldeye miscalculated the heat of his smoker and accidentally developed a method of hot smoking this fish after soaking it in a solution of brine, brown sugar and spices? The attractive bright red or orange colour of the smoked fish and its appealing taste have contributed towards the establishment of goldeye as a fashionable gourmet dish in Winnipeg and its surrounding area."

"What an excellent choice, Maggie! I raise my glass to you and to our future life together. As I look into your beautiful blue eyes shining against the last rays of this glorious sunset, I am reminded of a stanza from Bécquer's *Rimas y Leyendas* in which the poet pays tribute to the woman he loves, imagining that he can see a lost star in the azure depths of her eyes that inspires him.

"And do I inspire you in the same way?" asked Maggie playfully.

"Indeed, you are the source of my inspiration," declared Eduardo.

"Ah then, let me quote a few lines of poetry to you as well. They are from the *Sonnets from the Portuguese* by Elizabeth Barrett Browning, a nineteenth-century English poet who described the love that she felt for her husband Robert Browning, also a poet, in the following manner:

> *"How do I love thee? Let me count the ways."*

She then elaborates:

> *I love thee to the depth and breadth and height*
> *My soul can reach, I love thee to the level of everyday's*
> *Most quiet need, by sun and candlelight…*
>
> *—I love thee with the breath,*
> *Smiles, tears, of all my life!"*

"How very beautiful! Perhaps, one day, I will study English literature and quote some love poetry to you in the language of Shakespeare. In the meantime, you can teach me."

"I would be pleased to do so, dearest Eduardo. It seems so incredible that we are talking of marriage when I was ready to bid you a sad farewell. However, I am worried about your parents' reaction: how will they feel about our marriage? My own parents, who very much appreciate you, spoke to me when we were last at their place about the difficulties of marrying someone from a different society and culture."

"Now, I understand why you were so sad upon our return trip to Winnipeg the last time that you saw your parents. I am sure that we will be able to solve any problems, my sweet. Would you like to know what I am planning if you agree?"

"Of course, dearest heart."

"As you know, I leave Winnipeg the day after tomorrow and plan to return to Madrid as soon as possible. I will advise my parents of our engagement and make arrangements to return to Canada next May when we will be married in your local church if you choose. We will set out for Spain as a married couple a few weeks later and, if you wish, spend our honeymoon in magnificent Seville, Ronda and Malaga where we will be able to appreciate the beauty, culture and rich history of Andalusia, the southern part of Spain."

"It sounds so wonderful, Eduardo. And to think that Maria Cristina, whom I love almost as much as you, will become my sister-in-law!"

"May I suggest that we keep our plans secret until Christmas in order to complete all our arrangements before we announce our engagement. However, we could share our happy news with Maria Cristina as it will be difficult to keep our plans secret from her."

"Yes, Eduardo, I think that would be wise and, in any case, I could not keep this wonderful news a secret from her as we are so close."

"May I propose a toast to you, Maggie? I have ordered a bottle of *Veuve Cliquot* Champagne for tonight as we are celebrating our engagement. *Amor, salud, dinero y tiempo para gozarles!* (Love, health, money and the time to enjoy them!) This is a common toast in Spain. However, I wish to propose a more romantic toast to you, as well: may each day of our marriage be happier than the day before!"

"What a lovely wish, Eduardo. I will drink to our ever stronger and deeper love!"

As the meal was concluding, Eduardo reached into his pocket for a box, which he presented to Maggie. "As I will obviously not have time to buy you an engagement ring, I have a gift for you which will represent our commitment to each other. I hope that you like it. When I return to Canada next May, I will give you a very special engagement ring that has been in the Martínez family for several generations and which I will have restyled especially for you. My grandmother willed the ring to me in the hope that I would present it to my future fiancée. In the meantime, you will have this piece of jewelry to remind you of my love."

Maggie first read the note that accompanied the gift which said:

"A mi preciosa Margarita, un recuerdo de un verano que nunca olvidaré y una promesa de un futuro feliz a tu lado. Con todo mi amor, Eduardo." ("To my precious Margarita, a souvenir of a summer that I will never forget and

a promise for a happy future by your side. With all my love, Eduardo.")

Greatly moved by Eduardo's romantic words, Maggie opened the box, discovering a lovely diamond and amethyst pendant, a bouquet of precious stones on a gold locket. Inside was a miniature photograph of Eduardo and on the back of the locket were their intertwined initials. "How lovely, Eduardo. I will wear you close to my heart every time that I can. And I have a special gift for you as I know how well dressed you like to be." Maggie gave him a small box that contained her gift, along with a short message as well: "*To the man of my dreams: I will never forget you.* Of course, when I wrote the note, I didn't know that I would be giving you an engagement gift!"

"Why Maggie, *mi corazón*, how thoughtful! A tie pin with a black pearl from Tahiti which will be perfect on my silk cravats! Thank you so much. I, too, will be able to wear this piece of jewelry close to my heart."

As the happy couple left the dining room of the Empress Hotel, the maître d' informed Eduardo that he and his fiancée were welcome to enjoy the huge bonfire that would take place on the beach by the hotel during the next hour.

"What is this bonfire, Maggie?"

"It is a large, contained fire on the beach for the enjoyment of guests. It is the great rage at beach resorts such as Coney Island right now. People often toast marshmallows on the beach, using a long stick. It is one of the newest diversions in summer activities."

"But what is a marshmallow?"

"It is a confectionary sweet made with sugar, egg whites, and marshmallow sap. The marshmallows, when slowly roasted, will swell up to more than their normal size and are delicious if somewhat difficult to eat as they are so sticky."

"Yes, it sounds like fun, Margarita. Or would you prefer to go dancing at the pavilion?"

"I think that I would prefer another hour on the beach with you, dear fiancé."

The couple settled on the beach, allowing the still warm sand to drift through their fingers. A luminous moon shone overhead as Maggie pointed out the various constellations embellishing the evening sky. A huge bonfire was prepared on the beach and the couple was given some sticks on which to spear their marshmallows. "Be careful, Eduardo, not to over grill your marshmallow or it will become a charred mess. The outside colour should be golden and the interior should be gooey."

"I fear that I have lost my first marshmallow," commented Eduardo as the flames consumed his treat.

"Don't worry: why don't you share mine?" offered Maggie. "Let's each eat half of the marshmallow on the stick." After eating most of it, the couple's lips met in a sugary kiss. "My strategy worked!" observed Maggie.

"And I will see if mine will work later tonight," whispered Eduardo. "Now, here on this beach in the shadow of the moonlight with the stars overhead, we can dream of our future happiness."

As the couple walked by the shimmering lake in the moonlight, Maggie asked Eduardo if he knew when she had first fallen in love with him. When he signified that he wasn't sure, she declared, "It was when I first met you and I noticed how caring you were of Maria Cristina when she injured herself at Assiniboine Park. I thought that any man who was so solicitous of his sister would make a good husband."

"Really? And do you know when I first fell in love with you? It was during our trip to the opera to see *Carmen.* Your interest in the opera and your enthusiasm for life won me over almost immediately. I wasn't at all sure how you felt about me but, as I witnessed your generous spirit, your love for your family, your interest in life and your kindness towards Maria Cristina, I knew that I wanted to win your heart. I fell in love with you and wished to have you by my side forever."

"Thank you, Eduardo; I am very touched. Look! Do you see the young men with banjos and mandolins and the young girls in canoes singing close to the beach? Is this part of the entertainment provided by the Empress Hotel?"

'Yes, I was told that there would be entertainment later in the evening," confirmed Eduardo.

What an incredible evening thought Maggie! Later, the couple strolled to the town pier where in the secluded darkness, they whispered of their undying love for each other and of their hopes for the future. In tandem with the rhythmic waves kissing the shore, Maggie could hear Eduardo's heart beating against hers, feel the warmth of his arms drawing her to him, see the passion in his eyes, smell the faint traces of the cologne he had applied in the morning and taste both the saltiness and sweetness of his lips.

Ah, the Moonlight Train! It was the culmination of the Winnipeg Beach experience that brought young men and women to a destination where pleasure reigned on the boardwalk, the beach, at the midway or in the Dance Pavilion. Stimulated by alcohol and ardour after several drinks and many hours under the hot sun with their girlfriends, the young male passengers would struggle with the conductors, turning off the lights in the cars repeatedly until the frustrated train workers recognized the futility of their efforts and retreated with the cars unlit. Under the more auspicious cover of darkness, the young men would then begin romancing their dates as the darkened train rumbled along the tracks to Winnipeg. It was all part of the lore of the Moonlight Train which seduced Eduardo and Maggie after the magic of a perfect day together and the promise of a charmed life for the future.

Chapter 8

WINNIPEG, SEPTEMBER 1913

Maria Cristina reflected over the past three weeks of her life in Winnipeg. Despite her initial apprehension about her new teaching position at St. Mary's Academy, all had worked out well. Her students were eager to learn French and Spanish and her colleagues had welcomed her with open arms. While her room at the institution was far from equaling the luxury of her earlier hotel accommodations, she was, nevertheless, comfortable and did not have to worry about her daily transportation to the school. Moreover, she continued to see her good friend Maggie and to explore Winnipeg's attractions. The two women had returned to Mr. Flanagan's store where Maria Cristina had purchased several outfits suitable for teaching during the autumnal season.

The only sad note in Maria Cristina's life was Eduardo's return to Spain. She and her brother shared a special bond and she missed him a great deal. She had been overjoyed to learn of his and Maggie's engagement, thus acquiring the "sister" she had never had in childhood. However, she was worried that Eduardo had underestimated their parents' reaction to his future marriage to Maggie. He had told her not to worry, that, of course, they would be overjoyed to receive her into the family. Was this really so? Surely, they would object to the fact that she wasn't Spanish, that she didn't even speak the language and that she came from a far more modest background than their own, a privileged one that included a large estate, a generous financial situation and servants. How would Maggie compare in her parents' eyes to Victoria, the lovely, intelligent daughter of a very rich Madrid family that had been friends of theirs ever since she could remember? She thought of the many times and ways that Victoria had sought to win over Eduardo for the past two years, how she had communicated her interest in him using the language of fans (Maria Cristina laughed to herself when she remembered how he had taught Maggie the very wiles that Victoria herself had used in her attempt to win him over) and how seductively Victoria had moved in his presence. Might there have been a secret understanding between them?

Maria Cristina shook her head and told herself that she was subjecting herself to futile worries, that, of course, Eduardo was right and that soon he and Maggie would be married and that she would be rejoicing with them when they returned to Spain. Yes, indeed, all would be well…

What was Eduardo doing at this very minute? Maggie had been mentally following his activities ever since his last day in Winnipeg and subsequent departure for Spain. She had received a letter from him, written on *The SS France,* which described his return journey to Liverpool and how he missed her. One declaration, in particular, she had committed to memory: *Each morning, when I wake up, I dream of the day when you will be beside me again and, every evening as I fall asleep, I imagine that I am holding you in my arms, never to let you go.*

Eduardo had also described his journey on the *SS France* whose amenities were so magnificent that the ship was known as "The Versailles of the Atlantic". He had written enthusiastically about his voyage from New York to Le Havre: *While* The Empress *offers excellent suites, the* SS France *is truly opulent. If only you were here with me to see its lavish appointments, including the grand staircase which leads to the elegant Louis XIV Salon with its full-length portrait of the Sun King himself! On board the ship, one can even find a hair salon, a gym, and an elevator! Moreover, the French cuisine meets the highest standards of gastronomy.* Eduardo finished his letter by asking: *Dearest Maggie, how would you like to travel on the SS France for our honeymoon journey to Europe?*

The Sunday after their unforgettable day at Winnipeg Beach, Maggie and Eduardo had joined Maria Cristina for dinner at the Royal Alexandra Hotel where they had first enjoyed tea together. During the course of their meal there, Eduardo and Maggie had shared the news of their engagement with Maria Cristina who was absolutely delighted. "Now, my two favourite people will be together. What wonderful news!" The trio had talked of the couple's wedding plans throughout dinner, trying to forget Eduardo's scheduled departure the next day. Maggie, who was proudly wearing her new amethyst and diamond pendant, was happy to show Maria Cristina her engagement present as was Eduardo whose new black pearl tie pin was prominently displayed against a blue tie.

All too soon, Monday dawned and it was time to leave for the station where Eduardo would board a train headed for Montreal and then New York City. After Maria Cristina bade farewell to her brother, she discreetly left the platform and the newly engaged couple was free to indulge in one last kiss before the train whistle blew and the conductor called, "All aboard!" From his window, Eduardo waved goodbye, mouthing "I love you, Margarita" as the train slowly left the station.

A tearful Maggie and a sad Maria Cristina comforted each other as they walked away from the station to prepare for their next day at work. Maggie tried to reassure her friend that she would do well as a teacher and Maria Cristina tried to console Maggie, repeating that an eight-month absence wasn't really so long and that soon Eduardo would be back to marry her.

Maggie returned to the hospital and to her busy life as a nurse. The opening of a new obstetrical ward scheduled to take place in a few months would certainly keep her busy and she hoped that she would be assigned to look after the tiny newborns who would be welcomed into the world by hospital staff. How wonderful it would be to hold the babies and be responsible for their care and that of their happy mothers! A smile returned to Maggie's lips as she thought of what the future held in store for her...

Chapter 9

Winnipeg, September—November 1971

In the introduction to her book *Spain,* Karen Brown's description of the magical spell cast on travellers to that sun-kissed land proved to be prophetic for me.

As the Beach Boys sang about the waning days of summer, I began to prepare for my next year of university classes and my more advanced oral and written Spanish courses that would allow me to fully appreciate the country I planned to visit very soon.

It was also during this period that my aunt Maureen informed me that my grandmother had bequeathed to me two items that she thought I would treasure. The first was the old Spanish tea set that had been used for our many tea parties when I was a child and the second was her lovely amethyst and diamond pendant. I was thrilled to receive it as I had long admired that piece of jewelry. Moreover, I now believed that it was another missing piece of the puzzle that I had first uncovered in her attic: was it not the pendant that the mysterious Eduardo had given her years earlier? The locket was empty but I traced the initials M and E with my fingers and wondered how my grandmother had explained that to her family and friends... I rushed to find the old jewelry case with its note and placed the locket in the groove where I thought it had initially lain; as the piece of jewelry was a perfect fit, I was quite certain that it was Eduardo who had given it to my grandmother many years earlier and that he had held a special place in her heart.

I asked my aunt if she had finished reading the letters from Maria Cristina but was disappointed to learn that she had passed them on to my aunt Maeve who now lived in the Yukon and probably would not return to Manitoba for some time. How much longer would I have to wait to learn more about my grandmother's presumed old flame? On the other hand, there was no guarantee that the mystery of Eduardo would be solved by reading the letters as my aunt Maureen had made no mention of their contents. When I asked her to what the initials "M" and "E" referred, she answered rather vaguely that her mother had told her that they were the initials of a distant relative who had given her the pendant when she graduated as a nurse…

When did my love affair with Spain begin? And why? I often asked myself why I was so fascinated by Spain. Growing up in a small village in Manitoba, I had no contact whatsoever as a child with the language, music, food or culture of the country which had seized my imagination for so long other than the old-fashioned paper doll cut-outs of fiery flamenco dancers attired in their colourful polka-dot dresses, of imperious *duquesas* (duchesses) wearing lace mantillas supported by ornamental combs and of dashing grandees in their elegant regalia. Why then was I so drawn to Spain, a country that I associated with the exotic and the magic of travel?

There is no Frigate like a Book / To take us Lands away… declared Emily Dickinson and, indeed, the first stirrings of curiosity I felt for the land of Cervantes were fanned into major interest by reading as I searched my school library's limited collection of books for stories of crenelated castles and radiant *señoritas* in their fiesta finery, riding side-saddle on horses led by *caballeros* dressed in the traditional "traje corto" (short suit) consisting of fitted trousers and an elegant short jacket worn with leather boots and a wide-brimmed hat.

I also remembered a rather striking moment in Quebec City when I was about five or six and my holidaying parents took me to a supper club on St. Jean Street in the Old Quarter as there was nobody to look after me for the evening. I was very impressed by the three Spanish-speaking sisters in matching gold dresses who sang "Besame Mucho" and then walked over to our table and kissed my father's forehead. How brazen of them I thought and complained to my mother who smiled indulgently at me! My father remarked that it was a Mexican song of which his mother was particularly fond although he couldn't fathom why she was so attracted to it, given that she had little knowledge of Spanish and, as far as he knew, had never even met someone with a Latin background. Thinking back to my childhood now, I couldn't remember any hint whatsoever of a Spanish connection in my grandmother's life any more than in mine.

When I was ten, my aunt Maeve lent me her grammar book after finishing a Spanish course, given my interest in learning the language. (This was the same grammar book that I had rediscovered in my grandmother's attic shortly after her death.) I made a valiant attempt to use it but, of course, at such a young age, learning a new language on my own was extremely difficult and I eventually returned the volume to my aunt. I began to plead with my parents to enroll me in a Spanish course but, alas for me, no such course was taught in our school. My parents attempted to console me by promising that, one day, when I would attend university, I could register for a Spanish class. I am sure that, at the time, they felt that my desire to learn Spanish was but a passing fancy. However, my quiescent dream remained with me and the day that I registered for my first-year university courses was also the same day that I enrolled with great excitement in my first Spanish course!

Just before beginning university, my school division selected another grade twelve student and me to represent our two schools at an international conference for youth held in Brandon, Manitoba as part of the province's centennial celebrations. Although we had never met before the conference, Stella and I soon became great friends and were enthusiastic about learning as much as we could from the over one hundred international student delegates attending the conference. Of course, I was immediately attracted to the first Spaniard that I had ever met and enjoyed hearing about his country and culture. I was also happy to learn that my new friend Stella shared my interest in learning Spanish and was enrolled in the same Spanish course that I would be taking at university.

Soon after the conference, Stella and I plunged into our Spanish studies at the university. The first few weeks were challenging as practically all of our classmates had taken four years of secondary-school Spanish while we had never had the opportunity to study the language. However, we did have the advantage of being fluent in French, a language that had similar grammatical rules and constructions as Spanish. Our unbridled enthusiasm to learn a language that we believed to be both grandiose and musical incited us to spend long hours reviewing the material covered in the class. Our tenacity eventually paid off as, within a few months, we had surpassed most of our classmates' knowledge of Castilian and began to dream of visiting Spain.

As the Spanish course progressed, Stella and I eagerly started planning our participation in a summer program of intensive Spanish studies in Madrid. How many wonderful hours we spent imagining our anticipated time in Spain as we soldiered on in the language laboratory and practiced what we had learned in class together!

Chapter 10

Winnipeg, October—December 1913

The vivid, abundant colours of autumn mirrored the fullness in Maggie's heart as she read Eduardo's second letter over and over on a warm fall day, committing his words to memory. He wrote to her about finalizing the various details of their travel to Spain once their marriage in Manitoba had taken place in mid-May 1914. He would arrive at the end of April on the *Empress*, thus allowing them sufficient time to marry as well as to say their goodbyes to family and friends before departing for Spain. Could Maggie handle all the wedding arrangements in Canada? After the church wedding and reception and a couple of weeks visiting family and friends, the newlyweds would take the train from Winnipeg to New York City where they would see the sights and then board the *SS France* sailing to Le Havre, France. From there, they would travel to Paris, the City of Light, where they would spend a week before taking the train to Madrid to meet Eduardo's family and then on again to Andalusia where they would explore *La Ruta de los pueblos blancos* (The Route of White Villages) with stops in Ronda, Sevilla and Malaga before returning to Madrid. Maggie could barely believe it! If only she could share the news with her own family now! Eduardo had asked her to wait until Christmas and, of course, she would comply. However, she was free to discuss all her plans with her close friend, Maria Cristina, whom she would be seeing soon. They had arranged to meet for tea at the pavilion in Assiniboine Park.

Later, that week, as the two friends chatted excitedly over tea, Maria Cristina commented on the beauty of the fall season. The changing colours of the leaves with their rich bronzes and scarlets on display throughout the city amazed her as autumn was more muted in Spain than in Canada. While they were talking, the Flanagan family suddenly appeared, greeting them with enthusiasm. Also accompanying them was Mr. MacTavish who was eager to update them on his fiancée's visit to Winnipeg; she was seeking to become familiar with the city during the spring before permanently establishing herself there. "How I hope she will like it here as much as I do!", wished Mr. MacTavish. Grace Flanagan asked Maria Cristina how her brother was faring and was disappointed to learn that he had sailed for Madrid. "How sad for you, Maggie," she commented, unaware, of course, of the engagement. "I do hope that he will return to Winnipeg soon for your sake." Maggie reflected on Grace's generous wish, knowing full well that the young girl had herself once hoped to win Eduardo's heart and thanked her for her thoughtfulness.

As autumn's falling leaves were replaced by winter's snowflakes, Maria Cristina found it difficult to believe that in only another week, she would be boarding the train to Halifax prior to sailing on the *Empress* for Liverpool. She was pleased that she would be able to have a glimpse of another Canadian city before returning home to Spain, given that the ship sailed from Halifax rather than Quebec City from October to May to avoid the icy waters of the St. Lawrence.

She hoped that all was well for her good friend Maggie who had appeared to be rather discouraged during her last few visits. Perhaps she was working too hard or Eduardo, after an initial burst of fervour, had not been quite so constant in writing to her. Nevertheless, she was so pleased to hear that he had already made all the necessary arrangements for Maggie's and his travel after their May wedding in Manitoba. How he had changed! She reflected on his earlier amorous adventures, thinking how his love for Maggie had truly transformed him. Maggie would be so relieved to be able to share the news of their engagement with her family at Christmas. What a special day it would be for her! She prayed that Mr. and Mrs. Sullivan would welcome the news despite the fact that it could very well mean that they might not ever see their daughter again…

Before Maria Cristina's departure from Winnipeg, Maggie had insisted that the two of them visit the Christmas lights and decorations on Portage Avenue, particularly the window displays at Eaton's which were truly spectacular. How exciting it would be, Maria Cristina thought, to walk down the festive street with all its holiday lights peeking beneath a light dusting of snow!

Under the softly falling December snow, Maggie and Maria Cristina strolled down Portage's wide avenue, intent on enjoying one of their last evenings together in Winnipeg. Maggie was nostalgic as she thought about leaving her home province the next year but so excited about her new life in Spain! She licked the snow that had fallen onto her lips, saying, "Just think, Maria Cristina, next year, you and I will be welcoming the New Year in Plaza del Sol, eating one grape for each month of the year and listening to the crowd roar as the clock strikes twelve. It will be warmer and so different from here although right now with my hands in a cozy muff, my feet warm and toasty in long leather boots and the rest of me wrapped in a heavy wool coat, I don't feel the cold."

"It is so lovely and peaceful here, Maggie, with the snowflakes twirling about in the sky as they make their slow descent to the pavement. Sipping a cup of hot chocolate, listening to the carolers sing "O Holy Night" and admiring the festive lights and store windows with their Christmas scenes, I feel that I am in a winter fairyland like the one in The *Nutcracker Suite* which Clara visits in a magnificent sleigh. By the way, how did you know about our tradition of eating grapes on New Year's Eve? Was this one of Eduardo's lessons?"

"Yes, dear friend, he did describe this custom to me. Now that we have seen the holiday windows, let's visit the fairytale vignettes on Eaton's ninth-floor annex. It will be fun to see the moving papier-mâché and fabric fairytale figures with painted backdrops inspired by such tales as *Cinderella, Hansel and Gretel, Little Red Riding Hood, Rumpelstiltskin* and *Sleeping Beauty*. Let's be children again for a few minutes!"

There would be one last treat for the friends before Maria Cristina's departure for Spain. Maggie and she would have high tea in the just-opened Fort Garry Hotel where Maria Cristina would be spending the night before boarding the train to Halifax the next day. Seated in the elegant Palm Room, a curved lounge with a high domed ceiling and tall windows admitting streams of light, they listened to the music drifting down from the Musicians' Gallery above them. The two friends reflected over their momentous summer and the life ahead of them. "Maggie, I have a small gift for you, before I leave," said Maria Cristina as she gave her friend the ornate fan that Maggie remembered so well from the evening that they had enjoyed at the opera when Eduardo had used that very fan to teach Maggie the silent language of love.

"Thank you so much, Maria Cristina. I shall treasure this lovely fan forever," declared Maggie as she fingered the locket that Eduardo had given her just a few months earlier. "And here is something for you, Maria Cristina! It is a quilt that I made especially for you. On the plain squares, you will see that I embroidered little drawings representing the many outings that we enjoyed together including tea at Assiniboine Park where we first met, a trip to the clothing store, the Cathedral in St. Boniface, the picnic at my parents' farm and the spectacular performance of *Carmen* at the Walker Theatre."

"Ah, Maggie, this is an exquisite piece of work and so much effort and thought were put into it. I don't know what to say except that this quilt will always remind me of your kindness and generosity."

With that, the two friends embraced and bid each other a fond farewell, promising to write to each other frequently until Maggie moved to Madrid.

These violent delights have violent ends
And in their triumph die, like fire and powder,
Which, as they kiss, consume.
Shakespeare, *Romeo and Juliet*

Just a few days before Christmas, Maggie was elated to note that she had received a letter from Eduardo. Given her busy schedule at the hospital, she decided to save it for later that day and savour its contents when she had a quiet moment just before her trip home for the holidays.

Many hours later, her feet heavy with fatigue but her spirits buoyant at the prospect of reading her fiancé's letter, Maggie made herself a cup of tea, turned on the lamp and sat down by the window with the envelope that she had retrieved from under her pillow. She smiled in anticipation as there were only four and a half months to wait before Eduardo's return to Manitoba and their wedding. In three days, she would share the happy news with all her family as they gathered for their Christmas dinner! Maggie used a letter opener to carefully slit the envelope flap and began reading…

Tears slowly filled her eyes as she realized that there would be no Eduardo returning to Manitoba, no wedding and no fantasy trip to Spain. It was all over. She recalled a few words from Keats's "Ode on Melancholy": "And Joy whose hand is ever at his lips bidding adieu" and wondered if she would ever enjoy life again, having lost her one true love.

The next day, Maggie received another letter, this time from Maria Cristina who had written it while she was on the last leg of her voyage on the *Empress of Ireland.* The contrast between the emotions expressed in the two letters could not have been greater…

My dearest friend,

I know that I should start this letter with all the customary niceties but I am so excited that I know you will forgive me for delving immediately into my news. I am in love! I met a wonderful man on board the Empress, *a Spanish doctor who was attending an international conference on epidemiology in New York City and who then travelled to Montreal to attend another meeting on the same subject. In any case, we met on the pier in Halifax, dined together that first evening and have been almost inseparable since then. And wonder of wonders: Felipe lives in Madrid! The New Year seems so promising now. I can't wait to share all the details of our meeting when I see you in Madrid. Well, I must be off as Felipe and I will be selecting our train seats for the long journey to the Spanish capital: we hope to be seated together. The future looks so bright, Maggie, that I dare to hope that I will be as happy as you and Eduardo....*

With great affection,
Your friend, Maria Cristina

Maggie was very happy for her dear friend but, as her own heart was shattered, she could not, at least for the moment, bear to write back to Maria Cristina to wish her well. How would she even reveal the sad truth of the end of her own love affair? After knowing such great happiness with Eduardo, the pain she now felt was unbearable. She should have known that the wonderful plans she had made to marry Eduardo, bear his children and grow old together were fashioned from a dream born of a summer romance rather than reality. Tears streamed down her cheeks as she thought of what could have been but now would never be...

Chapter 11

WINNIPEG, SEPTEMBER 1972

I am back in Canada now, ready to begin my studies towards a master's degree in English literature after a most memorable summer in Spain. This was the beginning of my letter to my aunt Maeve a few weeks after my return from Europe. I reminded my aunt about my wish to read the apparently long-forgotten letters from Maria Cristina that I continued to hope would reveal a few clues about Eduardo, the man who had given my grandmother the locket that I wore frequently in her memory. Unfortunately, in her reply, my aunt told me that she no longer had the letters, having passed them on to her daughter who had expressed a wish to read them. I made a mental note to write to my cousin who lived in Halifax to ask her to forward them to me and began to pack my suitcases for the next chapter in my life: a move away from home to Montreal where I would begin my post-graduate studies. As I considered what to take with me, I reflected on the wonderful experience that Stella and I had enjoyed in Spain over the summer months.

Before leaving on my trip, my parents had warned me about the possibility of not finding Spain to be the country of my dreams, saying, "Sophie, we know how excited you are about finally visiting Spain but we hope that you are not disappointed as you have such high expectations." Alas, lending truth to my parents' comment, Stella's and my first stop at Madrid's international airport in May did not summon the expected images of the country that had fed our imagination for so long. Under Franco's last years as *Caudillo* of Spain, we witnessed members of the Guardia Civil armed with machine guns patrolling the airport, creating apprehension in Canadians like us used to the peaceful parades of RCMP officers in their red serge and of our ceremonial guards in bearskin hats marching in front of Parliament Hill. However, our experiences in Spain improved very quickly as we settled into our new life in Madrid.

Despite our busy schedule of studies, we did have enough time to explore the capital. Unlike her flamboyant Andalusian sisters, Seville, Cordoba and Granada, or Paris, her coquettish and romantic French cousin, Madrid reveals her charms gradually. While her attractions are not immediately apparent, the patient visitor will eventually discover and appreciate them as Stella and I did.

In a letter which I wrote to my parents in July, I described a typical day in our lives as students:

> *After morning classes in grammar and literature, we have a late lunch at 2:00, followed by a siesta for the less ambitious and studies for the more driven and then a return to classes in Spanish culture from 5:00 to 7:00 p.m. Dinner is served at 8:30 p.m. (early by Spanish standards) which enables students to better sample the lifestyle in Madrid later in the evening.*
>
> *We are all very familiar with the subway system by now and make our way almost daily to Plaza Mayor where much of the action in the city takes place. Stella and I have learned that Spanish men along our way who wish to attract our attention almost invariably whistle and then ask,* "¿Pss.. chica, guapa, quieres bailar esta noche?" *(*"Hey, pretty girl, would you like to dance tonight?"*) Having heard this question quite often, we have concluded that dancing is a very important aspect of their life and one that is apparently rather successful in appealing to the opposite sex. However, don't worry: we haven't fallen for it.... yet (just a "yoke" as the Spanish say, given their difficulty in pronouncing the English "j" in much the same way encountered*

by Anglophones attempting to replicate the sound of the Spanish "j" or jota).

The weather in Madrid has been hot and sunny but not the three months of "hell" decried in the familiar saying here about the capital's climate: "Nueve meses de invierno y tres meses de infierno" (Nine months of winter and three months of hell). *While it has been hot with the thermometer climbing from 30 to 35 degrees Celsius most days, it is sunny and dry which means that, on any walk, the shade provided by trees is instantly refreshing.*

Stella and I have become very familiar with the landmarks of the city through our frequent walks from our school to Puerta del Sol (Gate of the Sun), a lively square at the geographical centre of Madrid which attracts large crowds and which features the famous clock whose chimes mark the beginning of the New Year with the traditional eating of twelve grapes for happiness and prosperity, one for each of the following twelve months.

Plaza de España is an attractive square at the end of the Gran Vía, a grand boulevard conceived in the early twentieth century to replicate the famous boulevards of the world such as les Champs-Élysées in Paris and Fifth Avenue in New York and well known for its upscale shops, hotels and movie theatres. The plaza provides residents and tourists alike with a relaxing urban landscape featuring a large fountain, seating areas and trees. A statue of Cervantes with his literary characters, Sancho Panza and Don Quixote, presides over the square where olive trees have been planted to remind passersby of the vast and arid La Mancha fields where these two once wandered. Stella and I frequently stop for a short rest at the plaza on our walks to Madrid's Old Quarter.

One of my favourite landmarks in the city is Cibeles, the city's main post office, which is brilliantly lit at night, transforming its grandiose fountain of a goddess in a lion-drawn chariot into something quite magical. (Today, Cibeles is a municipal centre with a concert hall and galleries but it retains its superb fountain.) *Our reward for all this healthy walking at the end of the day is the ice-cream treat so*

> *popular here and available at all hours at practically every major street intersection in Madrid: a slice of Neapolitan ice cream sandwiched between two graham wafers.*

Of course, while in Spain, Stella and I felt that we owed it to ourselves to purchase tickets to witness what we considered to be an essential Spanish experience: bullfighting. Having both read Hemingway's novel, *The Sun Also Rises,* with its vivid descriptions of bullfighting, we felt that it was important to witness this archetypal Spanish activity. We purchased *sombra y sol* (shade and sun) tickets for a corrida with some trepidation but, nevertheless, with a willingness to understand the Spanish passion for bullfights. In a letter to my parents, I candidly described our striking naivety:

> *The corrida began well with all its ceremonial aspects including the proud entrance of the matador in his "traje de luces" (suit of lights), an elaborate, tightly-fitted costume embroidered with gold or silver thread and adorned with sequins. Accompanied by six assistants, the matador begins the highly ritualized corrida by running his cape over the bull's head and assessing its attitude and abilities. Of course, in Stella's and my highly sanitized version of a bullfight, there were no picadors on horseback stabbing the bull's neck and no banderilleros plunging barbed sticks into its shoulders. Finally, after waving his red cape to attract the attention of the weakened animal, the matador uses his sword to kill it. Did Stella and I choose to forget that the bull was doomed to die? In our fascination with things Spanish, we seemed to have conveniently overlooked this intractable truth. However, after witnessing a corrida, we are now ready to counter the cries of "Olé" from the onlookers to "Shame!" To add insult to injury in our estimation, a particularly courageous matador is awarded the dead bull's ears and tail, bloody trophies rather than the red roses we had imagined…*

To mitigate our disappointment with the corrida, Stella and I visited the *Museo Romántico* (now the *Museo de Romanticismo*) that provides a snapshot of nineteenth-century middle-class life in Spain through its collection of typical household items. I especially remember a red velvet lovers' settee (also known as a tête-à-tête) that I renamed the "seduction sofa", given that its two attached seats are configured in an S shape to allow lovers to remain in close contact with each other while maintaining a nominal physical barrier. Famous writers used to gather in this elegant building for literary evenings.

During my studies in Madrid, I met a medical student studying at a nearby campus where courses extended into the summer. In addition to becoming a good friend, Diego, who liked to call himself Iago (He was a great fan of Shakespeare), was interested in enhancing my education in Spanish culture and would frequently introduce me to the traditional foods, art and traditions of his country. As such, I had the advantage of visiting truly authentic corners of Old Madrid, rather than the more usual tourist fare. Here is how I described some of our evening activities to my parents:

> *We frequently enjoy sangria at mesones, which are rather appealing taverns despite their basic wooden furniture and rustic decor. Serving drinks, tapas and light meals, they are especially known for their lively atmosphere which encourages enthusiastic patrons to sing and even dance on the tables. It is in Madrid's mesones that I learned two famous Spanish drinking toasts:* "¡Arriba, abajo, al centro y al dentro!" *(*"Up, down, to the centre and inside!"*) and* "¡Salud, amor, dinero y tiempo para gozarles!" ("Health, love, money and the time to enjoy them!"*). As most mesones, restaurants and clubs operate until the early hours of the morning, the Spanish have deservedly acquired a reputation for being night owls (transnochadores).*
>
> *I am also learning about contemporary Spanish music, listening to the very popular songs of Joan Manual Serrat, a famous artist who sings in both Spanish and Catalan. Many of his songs have been critically acclaimed. A native of Barcelona, Serrat is strongly influenced by the Mediterranean in the writing of his songs. (*In 1974, Serrat was exiled to Mexico due to his condemnation of capital punishment under Franco's regime and it wasn't until a year later when Franco died, that he was allowed to return to his homeland.) *I have purchased*

his Mediterráneo *album and I fear that my old Beatles records may face some competition when I return home!*

*The Arco de Cucharillos (*The Cutlers' Arch*) is the prominent archway leading to Plaza Mayor from the narrow, cobblestone streets where workshops supplying knives to butchers* were once *located. Plaza Mayor, the historic heart of Madrid, provides a lively backdrop to impromptu musical performances with its many outdoor restaurants for hungry patrons or for those seeking late-night libations under star-lit skies in the company of good friends. The plaza also offers the opportunity to shop at one of the square's many arcaded boutiques.*

Dating back as far as the fifteenth century but rebuilt over subsequent centuries as the result of the vagaries of fate and fashion, Plaza Mayor has witnessed gruesome executions, the tortures of the Inquisition, passionate bullfights, boisterous soccer games and royal pageantry over its long life but, today, it is the centre of peaceful activity in Old Madrid. Some 200 balconies overlook the lively square from the three-storied buildings enclosing it. At night, it is easy to imagine the ghosts of the past returning to haunt the ancient square that witnessed so much history including the activities that once bloodied its cobblestones or, conversely, inspired pride and joy in the hearts of its citizens.

I'm not sure what my parents thought of the following anecdote about an incident which I experienced one evening at Plaza Mayor but I hope that they forgave Iago's entertaining peccadillo:

I have already described the atmosphere at Plaza Mayor to you in previous letters. However, I was not expecting to play a minor role in a little drama created by my friend, Iago. One evening, he decided to have a little fun at my expense and that of a patrolling police officer and pointed to the large equestrian statue of Felipe III in the middle of the square. Iago told the police officer that he had a Canadian girlfriend who desperately wanted to have her photo taken with the silent Felipe on his horse and that he hoped to realize my wish, no matter how difficult. (I, of course, was to pretend that I understood nothing of the conversation…) The policeman made the usual comments about silly tourists and was ready to bid a firm "Buenas noches" to Iago when the latter tenaciously protested that the officer could at least try to help him please his girlfriend. Of course, this was all to no avail and, finally, in feigned desperation, Iago asked him to produce a ladder so that I could climb it and have my photo taken on the statue. The police officer, by then tired of hearing Iago's entreaties, told him that he had wasted enough time on this matter. At that point, unable to control my laughter anymore, I told the officer that it was all a joke that my Spanish friend wished to play on me. Fortunately, the police officer had a sense of humour and the evening ended well.

Of course, a favourite topic for any student is the food that is served whatever the location and living in residence provided a good reason to fondly contemplate my mother's excellent culinary skills. Here is an extract of another letter to my parents in which I comment on the food that was served to students in the residence:

While I am enjoying the weather, the ambiance and my studies here, residence food certainly does not compare with your cooking. There is a very strong reliance on eggs, which, as you know, are not one of my favourite foods, and many meals consist of the ubiquitous Spanish tortilla (not to be confused with the Mexican one) that can be described as a potato omelette. The cured ham and chorizo bocadillos (sandwiches) are tasty but I wish they were served on French bread rather than the very crusty and hard rolls offered here. However, we do enjoy refreshing gazpacho soup and salads regularly. Dessert is usually very simple: ice cream or fresh fruit; unfortunately, pastries are rarely served. How I long for your delicious roast beef dinners with Yorkshire puddings or your coq au vin and apple cobblers! A highlight of our weekly meal, however, is the delicious churros prepared every Sunday for the students after church. They are fried-dough pastries which are elongated and twisted and frequently sprinkled with cinnamon sugar and served with hot chocolate. They are always a treat!

Perhaps my reflections on home cooking inspired my parents to call me (overseas calls were very expensive at the time) but they soon discovered that the institute where I was studying, which had no nocturnal curfew, was rather particular about waking up its students. One day, my parents waited until the early hours of the morning in Manitoba to call me at what they considered to be an appropriate time for a student taking morning classes in Madrid. Despite their good intentions, they were informed that 8:15 a.m. was too early to disturb the students! They called me again two hours later, and an announcement was made on the public address system asking me to report to Administration. When I arrived, worried that an emergency had occurred at home, I spoke to my parents who were somewhat bemused by the school's respect for its international students' morning schedules!

While enjoying sangria at various *mesones* in Old Madrid, Iago and his friends ordered a number of simple tapas. These included slices of the ubiquitous cold potato tortilla, *patatas bravas* (fried potato cubes covered in a spicy tomato sauce), olives of all types, almonds, thick chorizo and paper-thin serrano ham, sardines and grilled garlic shrimp. These hors-d'oeuvres reputedly acquired their name (tapas) from the small saucers filled with finger foods that were placed over glasses to prevent flying insects from inspecting their liquid contents. I sometimes wonder how this practice evolved as it suggests that Spaniards are more concerned about protecting their drinks than the food sitting on top of them! Nevertheless, the tapas were always delicious and a welcome addition to the basic food served at the student residence.

As I enjoy writing and as my parents had supplied me with postage money to help ensure that I would mail letters home during my stay in Spain, I wrote to them regularly about my life in Madrid. Of course, my letters also served as a journal to record my experiences. I remembered some of the letters that my parents had sent to me during their vacations when I was a young child and smiled to myself. My father always sent missives full of emotion, describing how much he loved me and my siblings or recalling fond moments such as how he and my mother had danced "like honeymooners" at the Château Frontenac during one of their holidays.

The next day, I would receive a letter from my mother typically beginning with "Now that your father has written to you, let me give you the news!" Of course, I also received the usual notes from my siblings such as the one from my younger sister gleefully announcing that she had temporarily moved into my room at home and was enjoying my books, records, decorations, posters and even some of my clothing during my absence!

To balance my descriptions of nocturnal life in Madrid, I also provided my parents with my impressions of the capital's cultural offerings:

> *This week, Iago and I visited the Prado Museum and he pointed out some of the most recognized paintings by the trinity of classic Spanish artists. Velázquez was the leading artist of the Spanish Golden Age (seventeenth century). Like the* "Mona Lisa" *in the Louvre, his* "Las Meninas" *is on the list of everyone's must-see paintings. This work depicts several figures from the Spanish court, notably the young Infanta Margarita Teresa surrounded by her entourage of maids of honour including some of the royal dwarves. The artist has even portrayed himself working on this large canvas by adding a mirror in the painting reflecting his image.*
>
> *El Greco's religious paintings with his signature elongated figures and his characteristic division of the celestial and the terrestrial on the same canvas also hang in the Prado.* "The Annunciation" *is one of the many such paintings for which he was acclaimed although his best-known canvas* "The Burial of the Conde de Orgaz" *is displayed in the church of Santo Tomé in Toledo, the very venue for which it was originally intended.*
>
> *Francisco Goya was a Spanish Romantic painter from the nineteenth century who was very successful in his lifetime. A great portraitist, he painted members of the Spanish Royal Family and it is rumored that the Duchess of Alba provided the inspiration for his* "La Maja Vestida" *(*The Clothed Maja*) as well as* "La Maja Desnuda" *(*The Nude Maja*)*, the latter *a risqué painting for its time. Goya, a political liberal, also recorded tragic moments in the history of Spain. His* "El 2 de mayo, 1808" *and* "El 3 de mayo, 1808" *captured on canvas the cruelty of the French occupation of Spain under Napoleon.*

Of course, Picasso is the best-known Spanish painter of the modern era and his "Guernica" (formerly displayed in the Prado but now hanging in the Museo Nacional Centro de Arte Reina Sofía) *is considered to be one of the most powerful anti-war paintings in history, depicting the destruction of a small Basque town during the Spanish Civil War. Painted in black, gray and white, the large mural illustrates the horror of war and the suffering of its victims. After hearing about the attack on Guernica, Picasso vowed never to return to Spain during Franco's dictatorship and remained in France for the rest of his life.* (He died in 1973, two years before Franco.)

The magnificent Palacio Real (Royal Palace) was built by Felipe V of the Spanish Bourbon dynasty in the eighteenth century and is reminiscent of Versailles, his French cousins' residence. The dimensions of the building (2800 rooms) and its ornate, gilded interior have made it one of the grandest palaces in Europe. The splendor of the Dining Hall elicits exclamations of wonder even from the most jaded of tourists as they contemplate the opulence of the china, crystal and silverware embellishing the banquet table set for a special event.

When we grew tired of museums, Iago and I would stop at el Parque de Buen Retiro, Madrid's largest park, formerly owned by the Royal Family. Today, many madrileños stroll through this pleasant park, row down its waterways, cycle on its trails or simply enjoy a picnic under the shade of its trees.

While in Madrid, I noticed that many women would use hand fans to cool themselves under the hot sun or as accessories to an outfit. In a letter to my parents, I described the many uses of fans as related to me by Iago:

He explained that the cooling breeze emitted by fans was not their only use as they were also employed to express the secret language of love. Waving a fan rapidly in the direction of a man indicated a woman's wish to develop a relationship while waving it slowly meant a lack of interest. Covering one's nose with a fan also suggested a woman's interest while closing the fan rapidly against her hand meant the opposite. There were many intricacies to this art, no doubt created at a time when "duennas" (chaperones) supervised most outings and visual messages had to avoid their close inspection. Iago *also showed me how to quickly open and close a fan, and I was amazed at how much practice was required to master the quick, economic movements involved.*

Not surprisingly, my parents did not question me on my newly acquired skills with fans! Of course, as a student, I could not afford the finer ones made of silk but many everyday fans were inexpensive and made me feel very Spanish as I waved them in class or on outings. In any case, fans were a lovely accessory that Stella and I used regularly for more than one reason…

While on the topic of conventions, I noted that most madrileños dressed rather formally and I was happy that I had packed more sundresses than shorts and t-shirts for my stay in Madrid as the latter were as much a dead give-away of one's tourist status as a camera and guidebook. Most Spanish girls my age tended to wear sundresses, along with an accompanying shawl during brisker evenings.

To further advance my education in Spanish culture, Iago introduced me to the writings of Gustavo Bécquer, a Spanish Romantic poet and writer. When Iago learned that, upon my return to Canada, I planned to begin studies towards a post-graduate degree focusing on nineteenth-century Romantic literature, he gave me a dedicated copy of Bécquer's *Rimas y Leyendas*, poems and tales which are common reading for secondary school students in Spanish-speaking countries. I still have this copy today to remind me of the kind, sensitive friend who helped me understand Spanish history and traditions.

While completing our summer course in the capital, Stella and I would frequently take advantage of the weekends to explore other parts of Spain, particularly those in close proximity to Madrid. One Saturday, we took the "El Rapido" train (ironically one of the slowest trains in Spain in the 1970s) to Segovia, the city long associated with its impressive Roman aqueduct and its Alcázar reputed to have inspired the creation of Disneyland's Sleeping Beauty Castle. The Alcázar was also featured in the 1967 movie *Camelot,* serving as the backdrop for Sir Lancelot's musings prior to his departure for England where he would join King Arthur and the Knights of the Round Table. After a refreshing lunch of gazpacho on ice and a salad, we spent the day touring the sights under a hot sun. When our interest in the structural marvels of the aqueduct and the many lovely churches in the city had waned, we decided to enjoy a picnic supper under the beautifully illuminated gaze of the city's storybook castle. While we were there, we met two Spaniards, Carlos and Jesús, who serenaded us with their guitars, singing traditional flamenco songs. We took the last train back to Madrid that evening, inebriated less by the sangria we had been drinking than by the heady essence of romance generated by the fabled castle under a sky full of bright stars and the Spaniards by our side!

We also visited Avila with its two kilometres of preserved Roman walls. While we were there, we even climbed onto a donkey and went for a short ride down one of the old streets, thanks to the animal's gracious owner who thought that tourists should experience a ride on a burro! *¡Muy típico!*

Aranjuez, a UNESCO cultural site, was another fascinating city that we visited one weekend and I described it in detail to my parents.

> *As we had read that Aranjuez was famous for its asparagus and strawberries, Stella and I decided to savour these specialties at a local restaurant prior to visiting the city. The Royal Palace with its many beautiful gardens was truly a joy to discover. It is a more feminine version of the Royal Palace in Madrid, being a summer residence built in the eighteenth century for the relaxation and comfort of its royal inhabitants rather than for ceremonial purposes. A unique feature of the palace is a striking room lined with white porcelain decorated with oriental motifs such as vases, samurais, birds and dragons. However, despite the beauty of the Palace itself, it is the magnificent gardens which capture the interest of most visitors.*
>
> *A small bridge over a canal leads to the Jardín de la Isla (the Garden Isle), a garden built on an island with its enchanting world filled with marble statues, fountains and lofty trees from the Americas. Magnificent fountains are scattered throughout the island such as the one of Bacchus drinking as he sits on a barrel of wine, another of a little boy removing a thorn from his foot (El Spinario) and a unique Clock Fountain whose water jet casts a shadow, thus enabling the visitor to*

tell the time. Walking through this garden is like taking a magic carpet ride through a sylvan site inhabited by nymphs and cherubs.

The Prince's Garden (Jardín del Principe) is distinguished by its plethora of different plants, as well as by several architectural features such as its division of different sections of the landscaped area into various sections featuring a delicate Chinese Temple, gazebos and, of course, magnificent fountains. Live peacocks strut down the paths amidst the lovely classical statuary, spreading the feathers of their colourful emerald and turquoise tail like a Spanish fan. In the midst of this botanical paradise is found the Royal Barges Museum which houses the very ornate longboats and gondolas used by Spanish sovereigns to navigate the Tagus River, as well as the Casita del Labrador (Farmer's Cottage) whose design was inspired by the Trianon at Versailles.

These enchanting gardens inspired the blind Spanish composer Joaquin Rodrigo to create the Concierto de Aranjuez (1939*), possibly the most famous guitar concerto ever written. While listening to his evocative work, one can hear the soothing sounds of the cascading fountains and of the singing birds, as well as the melancholy notes that are interwoven into the music. His wife revealed that Rodrigo wrote this masterpiece as he recalled both the happy memories of their honeymoon and the grief they felt when she miscarried their first child. (In 1991, the artist was raised to the nobility of Spain by King Juan Carlos with the impressive title of* "Marqués de los Jardínes de Aranjuez".)

In one of my final letters from Madrid, I wrote to my parents about Toledo, a city that remains firmly embraced by the past:

What could differ more from the realization of the bucolic dream that is Aranjuez and its magical gardens than the city of Toledo so firmly rooted in its medieval history? In contrast to the placid sounds of water and the coolness provided by acres of landscaped gardens, Toledo is perched on a hill overlooking deep gorges and the arid plains of La Mancha. Moorish, Jewish and Christian influences have all added their threads of history to the tapestry woven by the Romans and Visigoths who first settled in the area.

Michener described Toledo as the "spiritual home" of Spain, given its strategic location, its ancient Alcazar and military past, its devotion to history as the former capital of Spain, its role as the seat of Catholicism in Spain and its important influence on the arts. It is a majestic but brooding city without the liveliness of Madrid or the seductiveness of Seville. Stella and I visited its massive Gothic Cathedral hemmed into a maze of dark, narrow streets where women dressed entirely in black and carrying large wicker baskets made their way through a labyrinth of dizzying paths that were tiring to climb and difficult to locate (at least for us). However, we soon discovered that the same narrow space between the buildings on either side of the streets that obscured the sun also led to welcome relief from its powerful summer rays.

After visiting the rather sombre confines of the cathedral and the Santo Tomé chapel with El Greco's famous painting "The Burial of the Conde de Orgaz", *Stella and I were happy to sit in a café on the lively Plaza de Zocodover and savour a marzipan (known as mazapán in Spain) pastry, a sugar and ground almond local specialty first made by nuns in the thirteenth century. Exquisite marzipan sculptures in miniature ranging from various fruit to animal shapes delight visitors after a day of sightseeing and fuel them with more energy for the evening.*

For our last weekend trip before saying "adios" to Madrid and our studies, Stella and I decided to travel to Majorca, the largest of the Balearic Islands and a major tourist centre. This is how I described our journey in a long letter to my parents:

We took the slow Rapido from Madrid to Valencia, spending a long day in the hot, overcrowded train which barely seemed to move. One child, perhaps even less patient than we were to reach our destination, asked his father regularly when they would arrive. Quarter hour after quarter hour, the answer was the same: "le falta menos" (sooner than before)! In one village, a group of English-speaking tourists armed with a map was delighted to locate a familiar sounding word at a blisteringly hot and desolate train station and tried to find it on their map. "Urinarios" they cried out with great enthusiasm, not realizing that they had just seen the sign indicating the station's urinals!

From Valencia, Stella and I took the ferry to Palma, the capital of Majorca. What a journey that was! Unable to purchase any class of ticket above fourth due to the complete sale of all spaces on the overnight ferry, we were forced to buy the cheapest ticket of all or forfeit our trip altogether. Our only choices were 4A, a lounge chair on the deck with a cushion or 4B, a lounge chair without a cushion! Upon arrival on the deck, we were far from reassured by the unsavoury looks of the cast of male characters who embarked (mainly drunken sailors it appeared) and who leered at us, the only two females on the dark deck. We were so uncomfortable that we decided that we would take shifts, guarding each other from unwanted attentions and our bags from theft. We looked forward to the late hour dining as an opportunity to leave the deck and join other passengers. Unfortunately for us, we tried all the dining room venues but were soundly rebuffed as we only had 4th class tickets. Our protests about having the necessary money to pay for a good meal fell on deaf ears. Upon asking, "But where will we eat?", we were told that 4th class passengers ate in the galley! Hungry but apprehensive, we set foot in the crew's galley where we were served a stew of dubious origin that was casually slopped onto our plates, much to the amusement of the rather rough group of men who were gathered there for the simple meal washed down by many glasses of beer or crude wine…

We finally did make it to Palma the next day where we immediately headed for a hotel and then the beach! To our great disappointment, there were few Spaniards on the golden sands that we considered to be overrun with mostly German and English tourists. As we only had two days to explore the island before returning to Madrid, we had a quick look at the cathedral and then took a local bus to Valldemossa in order to explore the former Carthusian Monastery where the nineteenth-century Romantic musician, Frédéric Chopin, spent the winter of 1838-39 with his mistress, the French writer George Sand.

> *While this was a productive period for the couple artistically, they were unhappy with their stay there, given that the cold and damp climate that Chopin had hoped to leave behind in Paris followed him to the Balearic Island and led to his contracting tuberculosis. Nevertheless, he completed the last of his* 24 Preludes *during his period in Valldemossa while George Sand wrote* A Winter in Majorca *detailing her unhappiness with its inhabitants who frowned upon the fact that the couple, accompanied by Sand's two children, was not married to each other and that she wore pants and smoked cigars. Although many of their possessions were burnt by the proprietor who was afraid of contracting tuberculosis himself, Chopin's piano and various letters were spared and are on display in the small museum located there. Visitors can also stroll through a garden redolent with the smell of lemon trees.*

Stella and I returned to Madrid where we packed our belongings, including a few souvenirs (I purchased the first of many Spanish dolls wearing the regional costumes of the country's various provinces, as well as an unusual double doll representing a madriñelo couple attired for a special evening). We were both pleased that we had learned so much not only from our excellent courses and assignments, but also and most importantly from our experiences with the Spanish people whom we had met in the capital. Our language skills were much improved and we had acquired a great deal of knowledge about Spain and its denizens, traditions, history, art and cuisine.

We left Madrid with the rest of the students and embarked on a scheduled tour of several well-known Spanish cities including Barcelona, Salamanca (We were impressed that its university, founded in 1213, was still in existence), Pamplona (Our tour of the narrow Estafeta Street, site of the Running of the Bulls, was of much less interest to us after our day at the corrida in Madrid!) and San Sebastian. In this seaside city which was only a few kilometres from the French border, I met a tall, attractive Spaniard at a discotheque; we danced the night away and, the next day, after my class outing, he drove me to Biarritz, France where we spent a few hours admiring the wild Atlantic Ocean and enjoying pastries (I had complained about the lack of good pastries in Spain). As the sun set over the seaside promenade, the temperature cooled and my friend gallantly offered me his leather jacket although I could tell that he was cold. Not feeling the cold that easily, I turned his offer down and I could sense his relief: he had maintained his machismo without depriving himself of his jacket as I had become in his mind the Canadian "hija de las nieves" (the daughter of the snows). The next day, to my great surprise, José arrived in the parking lot of the hotel in San Sebastian where my classmates and I were staying just in time for our departure for Madrid Airport. I have to add that my *novio guapo* (handsome boyfriend) certainly impressed my new friends as he kissed me *adios* on the steps of the bus... Ah, those memories of Spain!

Chapter 12

WINNIPEG, MAY—AUGUST 1914

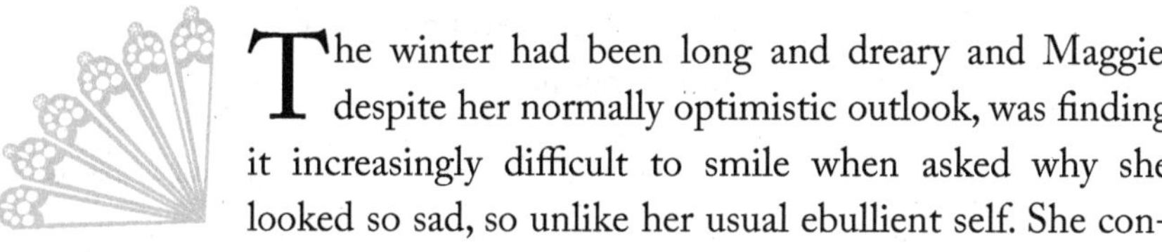

The winter had been long and dreary and Maggie, despite her normally optimistic outlook, was finding it increasingly difficult to smile when asked why she looked so sad, so unlike her usual ebullient self. She continued to provide the same caring service to her patients despite the fact that her heart was broken. Although she tried not to dwell on it, May was the month when she and Eduardo would have married. Her Christmas visit home, which took place so soon after receipt of Eduardo's letter, had lacked the joy of previous celebrations and, while her parents were careful not to mention her beloved, she sensed that they knew something promised had not been fulfilled. She had received another longer, gentler letter from Eduardo after the shock of the first one which sought to explain the situation but every time that she held it in her hands ready to consign it to the flames, she could not help but read it once again, stimulating the flow of tears:

> Dear as remembered kisses after death,
> And sweet as those by hopeless fancy feign'd
> On lips that are for others; deep as love,

Deep as first love, and wild with all regret;
O Death in Life, the days that are no more.

Tears, Idle Tears by Alfred, Lord Tennyson

Also, in a cruel twist of fate, Maggie read of the sinking of the *Empress of Ireland* in the Gulf of St. Lawrence as the ship left Quebec City for Liverpool. On board the ship was Jane MacPherson, Mr. MacTavish's former fiancée who had come to Winnipeg to join him but who was returning to Scotland as she had not been able to adjust to life on the prairies. How utterly sad for Mr. MacTavish who had not only been rejected by his fiancée but who had also truly lost his love in the frigid waters of the St. Lawrence!

The only positive note in the entire month of May was a letter from Maria Cristina which advised Maggie of her engagement to Dr. Felipe Gomez y Garcia; the two were to be married in early July. A few months after receiving this letter, she received another happy one from the new bride who was now on her honeymoon.

July 17, 1914
Ronda, Spain

Querida Maggie,

My heart is bursting with happiness! Felipe and I were married a week ago in a beautiful church ceremony attended by some 300 guests. Unfortunately, you were the only person I really wished to see who wasn't there but, of course, circumstances dictated your absence.

I felt like a princess in my beautiful satin and lace wedding dress with its cathedral train, especially as I looked into the eyes of my beloved husband. Who would have expected this great romance born on a ship to blossom into such love?

Yesterday, we arrived at the luxurious Hotel Reina Victoria in Ronda. The hotel has an exceptional location overlooking the gorge and its striking gardens provide guests with the opportunity to enjoy a stroll through an amazing variety of heavenly fragranced flowers. It is the perfect place for a honeymoon!

I hope that you are feeling better and are once again smiling at the world. I also pray that you will forgive me for making this such a short missive. After all, I am on my honeymoon...

Tu amiga,
Maria Cristina

Maggie smiled as she thought of Maria Cristina's words as she proceeded to check on her next patient.

"If it isn't Nurse Sullivan looking very happy today. Top of the morning to you!" was the greeting she received from her patient, Thomas O'Toole. "You should be wearing that special smile all the time as it lights up your face and makes me think of an angel."

"Well, well, Mr. O'Toole, it appears that you've been kissing the Blarney Stone. I fear that once I draw a sample of your blood you won't be comparing me to an angel anymore!"

"It's just that you have been looking rather forlorn ever since I arrived at the hospital and, today, your demeanor has changed. Have you been blessed with the luck of the Irish or possibly just found a four-leafed shamrock presaging good fortune? Or may I be bold enough to think that you have finally been overcome by my sunny presence and handsome countenance?"

"Mr. O'Toole, I'll have you remember that I am here to take care of you as my patient. However, if you must know, I have been rejoicing in the good news sent to me by my very good friend Maria Cristina from Spain. She was just married this month to a fine young doctor whom she loves very much and they are now on their honeymoon."

"Isn't it grand to have good friends to brighten up our lives? I'm glad that Maria Cristina's happiness is so important to you. As a matter of fact, your happiness is important to me too," commented Mr. O'Toole. "Having a pretty, good-humored nurse makes me think that life is special even when part of it is spent in traction in a hospital. If only I had the use of my legs now, I would be chasing you down the corridors here!"

"You're incorrigible," commented Maggie.

"But mind you, still loveable!" added the irrepressible Mr. O'Toole.

"How did you end up in our fine hospital?" asked Maggie.

"After arriving in Winnipeg after a long journey to Canada from the fair city of Galway, I decided that I would take myself to church to thank the Almighty for my safe travels (You heard what happened to the *Empress of Ireland*, didn't you?) when, as I crossed the street, this eejit driver of a streetcar hit me. They brought me here for x-rays and treatment and, as you can see, I am now in traction, having fractured both my legs. I don't know what I will do when I am discharged from the hospital as I arrived here planning to work long and hard to send home as much money as I could to my parents to help them raise the rest of their large brood. I don't have a job or even my own accommodation once I leave the hospital, which may not be for another four to six weeks. Fortunately, my friend Declan has offered me a room in his apartment until I get settled."

"And what type of employment are you seeking, Mr. O'Toole?" asked Maggie.

"I'm a professional tailor and was planning to find work with a reputable haberdashery in Winnipeg. I even brought a number of fabrics with me from Ireland but they are sitting in Declan's apartment for the time being. If only I could move these legs of mine!"

"I'll keep you in mind if I hear of any opportunities, Mr. O'Toole. In the meantime, please concentrate on getting better. Try to use the trapeze bar above you to move, rather than your elbows. I will be back in a few hours to check up on you."

"Thank you, Nurse Sullivan, and please keep that pretty smile on your face."

As Maggie left her patient's room, she reflected on the fact that, for the first time since she had received that fateful letter from Eduardo in mid-December, she had actually felt a measure of happiness once again. The good news from Maria Cristina, the sense of being of value to her patients, the love of her family, her recent move away from the Nurses' Residence to new, more private accommodations and even the promise of an enjoyable walk with her sister on a sunny day had all contributed to her more positive state of mind. She resolved that she would pay a visit to Mr.

Flanagan to see if he could offer her latest patient, Thomas O'Toole, some assistance in his attempt to work as a tailor. For that matter, she might even buy herself a new outfit to wear to her sister's wedding in September.

A week later, Maggie made her way to Mr. Flanagan's store where she spoke to Grace who was assisting her father with the family business during the summer months. She informed Maggie that Mrs. Flanagan had invited Mr. MacTavish over for dinner after *the Empress* tragedy and had tried to console him as a result of his loss of Jane. He had been quite devastated when his fiancée told him that she could not adjust to life in Winnipeg and would return to Scotland and then, just a few weeks later, to learn that she had perished on board the ship was a very hard burden for him to bear. Maggie suspected that Grace's feelings for Mr. MacTavish were deeper than she cared to admit but said nothing, knowing how difficult this time must be for her. Instead, she shared Maria Cristina's good news with Grace and revealed that she had not heard further from Eduardo in order to forestall any questions about him.

Mr. Flanagan came over to greet Maggie who explained her mission on behalf of her patient. "Well, I may very well be in need of his services as our business is fast expanding. Do you know, Miss Sullivan, that Winnipeg is becoming known as the "Chicago of the North", given that it is one of the fastest growing cities in North America? I will give this matter some serious thought and will contact you with my decision soon. On second thought, why don't you join Mrs. Flanagan, Grace and me for dinner next Wednesday? I should have an answer for you by then. Moreover, both my wife and I would be delighted to welcome you to our home."

After Grace showed her some of the latest materials and patterns available for the fall season, Maggie decided to have a new dress made to wear to Beth's wedding. Grace took her measurements and wished her well. She left the store, feeling the warm sense of satisfaction that accompanies the completion of a selfless act on behalf of someone else. Perhaps Mr. O'Toole would find employment after all…

Chapter 13

Montreal/Toronto, September 1972 to May 1976

I was now comfortably settled in Montreal, enjoying my course work at university, as well as my life and friends in a new city. I joined the university's Spanish Club where I spoke Spanish regularly with its enthusiastic supporters. During my studies, I also frequently visited my friend Stella with whom I continued to speak Spanish. One year, on my birthday, she invited me to accompany her to a Mexican nightclub where lively traditional and modern Spanish music was played. It was on this occasion that Stella met her future husband, a Mexican, as she was crossing the dance floor to tell me that she was leaving the club. Apparently, Ricardo had been eying her for a good part of the evening but hadn't summoned the necessary courage to ask Stella to dance until he noticed that she was on the verge of leaving. It was the beginning of yet another Hispanic connection!

Once I completed my university studies, I moved to Toronto where I accepted a position as an editor for a small publishing company. My first few months in Toronto were somewhat lonely as I didn't know anyone in the city but eventually my circle of friends grew as did my confidence and satisfaction with my new life there. Maria, one of my colleagues at work, became a close friend and, several months later, she invited me to her wedding, an event that promised to be a most elegant one with a reception at one of the vineyards in the Niagara Region. I hesitated, given that I had no escort to accompany me but my friend assured me that there would be a number of singles attending and that I would not feel out of place.

Before dinner, guests were invited to stroll through the vineyard and enjoy not only a glass of wine but also the music played by a trio of classical musicians. As I was listening to them play the "Anniversary Waltz", I heard someone ask me, "Isn't the music lovely, especially in such a setting with a glass of wine in our hands?" I turned towards the sonorous voice and there was its charming owner, smiling at me. "Hi, I'm David and I notice that your glass is empty; would you like me to get you a refill?"

"And I am Sophie and, yes, I would enjoy another glass of sparkling." When David returned with a fresh glass of sparkling wine, his eyes were mischievous as he said, "And here are your 'beaded bubbles winking at the brim'", a line from Keats's "Ode to a Nightingale" that I instantly recognized.

"Are you a Keats's scholar or a wine aficionado?" I asked.

"Neither. I am a professor of history but it was a lucky hunch on my part that you are obviously one if not both", was his reply. It was an auspicious beginning to a lovely evening. We danced the evening away under the stars to the sound of soft ballads whispering of gentle love, sweet kisses and happy tomorrows until it was all too soon time to leave.

Before saying good-bye to me that evening, David mentioned that he hoped to see me again and mentioned, "There will be a concert of classical guitar music next Saturday at the university. I was wondering if you would like to attend this event with me."

"Why I would love to attend the concert with you, David," I replied.

"And so, this is merely au revoir until next time," he said, taking me into his arms and kissing me gently on the cheek.

The next week, as we sat in the hall waiting for the concert to begin, I asked David about his musical preferences. He answered my question by saying, "I come from a large musical family from Newfoundland where we all played an instrument as soon as our fingers could stretch from key to key or from string to string. My parents and siblings were proficient at the piano, violin and accordion and I chose the guitar. Actually,

I am a professionally trained musician and supported my university studies by playing at various venues. I particularly enjoy the music of the Mediterranean and often play Spanish music."

"Really? Did you know that I am a fan of all things Spanish and particularly enjoy flamenco music? Do you think that you could play a few selections for me?"

"Of course, Sophie, if you would like that."

"Then, why don't you join me for dinner next Saturday at my apartment? The price of admission will be a few flamenco and other Spanish pieces," I joked.

"It's a deal. I look forward to seeing you next weekend," David replied.

A week later, I was transported to the beautiful gardens of Aranjuez as David played Rodrigo's famous guitar concerto.

"David, your music takes me back to those wondrous gardens which inspired Rodrigo's music. I travelled there a few years ago as a student studying Spanish in Madrid."

"I'm so glad that you enjoyed my playing and I can't tell you enough how much I enjoyed your gazpacho soup, paella and almond cake. Next time, if I'm invited again, I will play a selection of famous French songs for you."

"And I will prepare *Coquilles Saint-Jacques, coq au vin* and *baba au rhum* if you play "La vie en rose" and Aznavour's "La Bohème".

"Agreed."

Thus, began a new romance that was fostered with long walks by the lake, evening concerts, Mediterranean music and gourmet meals. As I enjoyed cooking and David appeared to appreciate my meals, I began to invite him to join me regularly for candlelit dinners on Saturdays. As he finished one of my meals, he confirmed with satisfaction, "The way to a man's heart is through his stomach." It appeared that I had won his heart and, when I playfully presented him several months later with a pretend bill after a dinner which he had particularly enjoyed, he looked at the total charge ("one gold ring") and commented that, while it was rather high, he was willing to pay it!

A month later, during a long, romantic dinner in a quiet corner of a French restaurant, David proposed to me on bended knee. He ordered a bottle of Champagne to celebrate the occasion and asked me if I remembered the line from Keats about "beaded bubbles winking at the brim" that he had quoted to me when we first met. When I told him that indeed I did, he added, "But, thinking it would have been too bold at the time, I didn't quote the next lines which reflect the way that I feel now with you beside me. Let's have a toast, compliments of Keats: 'That I might drink, and leave the world unseen/And with thee fade away into the forest dim.'"

"What a fanciful thought!" I exclaimed before we began to make plans for our future, including our wedding and honeymoon. David and I agreed that we would spend two weeks in Spain and two weeks in France, ending our wedding trip most appropriately in incomparable Paris, not only the City of Light but also the City of Love. In an age that had not yet embraced the use of computers, our friend, Sandra, a travel agent, spent hours deciphering complicated train schedules to enable us to travel to all the areas that we wished to visit. Those many hours of detailed preparation led to many happy moments exploring the fabled cities of the continent.

Chapter 14

WINNIPEG, OCTOBER-DECEMBER 1914

Maggie had dinner at the Flanagan residence where she enjoyed the opportunity to be with the close-knit family. She was also happy to note the presence of Mr. MacTavish who seemed to have eyes only for Grace.

"Maggie," reflected Mrs. Flanagan, "we haven't seen you lately and were wondering how life was treating you. Are Mr. and Miss Martínez back in Spain now? What are they doing there?

"Yes, indeed, they are both living in Spain, having thoroughly enjoyed their stay here in Winnipeg," she replied, not wishing to divulge more about her friends.

"Did you know, Mama, that while Mr. Martínez left over a year ago, his sister was actually here a few months longer, teaching at St. Mary's Academy? Indeed, Maggie and Maria Cristina actually visited the new Fort Garry Hotel before Miss Martínez's departure for Madrid," confirmed Grace, thus tactfully diverting attention away from Eduardo to the Fort Garry Hotel.

Maggie smiled gratefully at Grace before beginning her description of the charms of the Fort Garry Hotel, thus causing Mrs. Flanagan to forget to pursue her original questions about the Martínez family.

"And now, I understand, Maggie, that you are hoping to help one of your patients at the hospital by finding him suitable employment at our store," observed Mrs. Flanagan.

"Indeed, it would be wonderful if Mr. O'Toole could find gainful employment upon his release from the hospital as he, unfortunately, was struck by a streetcar only a few days after his arrival in Winnipeg and, due to his injuries, has already been hospitalized for a month. However, he is doing very well and his doctor expects to discharge him in another two weeks."

"Well, I would certainly like to help a fellow Irishman in need and, as things turn out, I will be requiring the services of another competent tailor in the very near future, given that business has grown substantially over the past year. Please tell Mr. O'Toole that I will visit him at the hospital next week and, if all goes well, I'll be prepared to discuss the necessary arrangements for his employment with us."

"Thank you so much, Mr. Flanagan; I'll be pleased to convey your message to Mr. O'Toole on my next shift. On another topic, may I ask, Grace, how your musical studies are progressing?"

"Very well, indeed. I am very happy to finally be able to study at the Conservatory where the professors are most talented. Speaking of talent, were you aware, Maggie, that the celebrated Irish tenor John McCormack will be singing at the Walker Theatre in mid-December? I do hope to be able to attend this concert."

"It will undoubtedly be a fine concert, Grace, and if I'm not working nights at that time, I'll definitely buy a ticket."

"And how are you enjoying your position at the Winnipeg Art School, Mr. MacTavish?" asked Maggie.

"I'm very happy to have accepted this position and pleased to live in Winnipeg. You may have heard, Miss Sullivan, that, unlike me, my late fiancée did not find the city to her liking and sadly was on her way home to Scotland when she perished on *The Empress of Ireland*."

"I'm very sorry for your loss, Mr. MacTavish, but pleased that you have adjusted so well to your current circumstances."

"Fortunately for me, the Flanagans have welcomed me with open arms and have been my refuge in troubled times. I shall forever be in their debt."

"Come, come, you are our friend and shall always be welcome in our home. I believe that my wife is signaling that it's time to move to the dining room for dinner before the food gets cold," added Mr. Flanagan.

Maggie spent a most enjoyable evening at the Flanagan household and the next day was happy to share with her patient, Mr. O'Toole, the good news she had received about his potential employment at the haberdashery.

"Tis a grand day indeed when I hear such positive news from such a pretty messenger," was his comment.

"Away with you now. Have you been busy kissing the Blarney Stone again while I was working, Mr. O'Toole?"

"I'm only stating the obvious, Miss Sullivan, and would dance a jig right now with you if only my poor legs would cooperate."

"I believe that you will soon make good use of your legs as your doctor told me this morning that you will be released from the hospital in two weeks. Therefore, he has asked me to help you walk a little every day until then to ensure that you have sufficient strength and mobility to move on your own by the time that you leave. Shall we start now? You will have to lean on me a little the first few times."

"Well, sure and away, it will be a pleasure to do so against the fine figure of such a charming colleen, Miss Sullivan."

After a week of walking her patient down the hospital corridor in his ward, Maggie suggested that he might wish to walk outside in the bright fall sunshine and take in some fresh air. As they walked along the hospital path, Mr. O'Toole mentioned that he had seen Mr. Flanagan earlier in the day. "And, Maggie, he offered me the position! I have to thank you so much for making all of this possible. When I leave the hospital, would you do me the honour of accompanying me to dinner? I owe you at least a meal for facilitating my life here."

"Thank you. I'm pleased to accept, Mr. O'Toole. And don't forget to address me as Nurse Sullivan while you are still in the hospital!"

Three weeks later, Maggie enjoyed a delightful evening with Thomas O'Toole whom she found to be quite charming with a great sense of humour. She realized during their conversation that they shared a great deal in common: their Irish background, their Catholic religion, their love of music and of literature, the great importance that they attached to family, etc. Soon, the couple began to see each other regularly, going for long walks in the crisp autumn weather and enjoying band concerts in Assiniboine Park amid the falling leaves. As the weather cooled, they began to attend church teas, as well as the occasional movie at the Dominion Theatre on Portage Avenue, one of Winnipeg's busy movie venues. They could even be seen occasionally at the Winnipeg Skating Rink where they attempted to try the new sport of roller skating, joining other enthusiasts who, in addition to the sport, also enjoyed the music which the band played as they glided about the rink.

"Maggie, would you care to accompany me to the Walker Theatre where John McCormick will be singing some of his most famous songs? I have two complimentary tickets given to me by Mr. Flanagan as a Christmas bonus and feel truly blessed to have this opportunity to hear my celebrated countryman sing here. If truth were told, I am suffering a little from homesickness as I think back of home in the old country and of my family gathered together at Christmas without me."

"Thomas, thank you so much for your generous offer. I'm very happy to accept your invitation. How wonderful it will be to hear such a famous and successful tenor from Ireland sing here in Winnipeg! As you know, my family is Irish as well. My grandparents arrived in Canada just after the Potato Famine to start a new life here and eventually became rather prosperous farmers."

In the opulent theatre, Maggie remembered her last visit there with Eduardo and Maria Cristina. What a magical moment that had been! However, she suddenly realized how special her second visit to the Walker Theatre was as well. No, she was not consumed by the same passion that had burned deep inside her at Eduardo's side but, nevertheless, she suddenly understood the extent of her feelings for Thomas and looked forward to each of his visits with increasing enthusiasm, enjoying their close communion of thought and similarity of interests. He could make her laugh so easily and truly exuded the proverbial charm associated with the Emerald Isle.

At the end of the performance, Maggie thanked Thomas for the lovely evening, telling him how wonderful it was to feel that close kinship with her Irish countrymen. "I'm most happy that you enjoyed the concert but I hope that you also feel a certain warmth towards the Irishman by your side at this moment, Maggie. I feel so fortunate to have met you and to have shared so many good moments together."

"Indeed, Thomas, I'm also very happy to have accompanied you here tonight, not only for the music but also for the pleasure of your company."

At that moment, he held her in his arms and bent down to kiss her very gently. "Ah, my beautiful colleen, you are a treasure, the pot of gold that the leprechauns hide at the end of the rainbow."

"And what would you do upon finding that pot of gold, Thomas?"

"I would treasure it for the rest of my life, dearest Maggie."

Not quite sure of where their conversation was heading, Maggie suddenly asked, "Thomas, what will you be doing for Christmas?"

"I'm afraid that I will be alone as my good friend Declan is planning to spend the festive season with his fiancée's family. I don't suppose there's a chance that you would have the time to brighten my Christmas a little?"

"How would you feel about spending the holiday with my family and me in the country? I'm warning you that it will be somewhat boisterous but it will also be fun and an opportunity for you to experience Christmas the way we celebrate it here in Canada," added Maggie.

"Ah, to be sure, that would be grand if your family doesn't mind including me. And might that Canadian experience include a little mistletoe under which a lucky Irishman can properly kiss a pretty colleen who is a member of the family?" was Thomas's enthusiastic reply.

Chapter 15

Winnipeg, January 1915

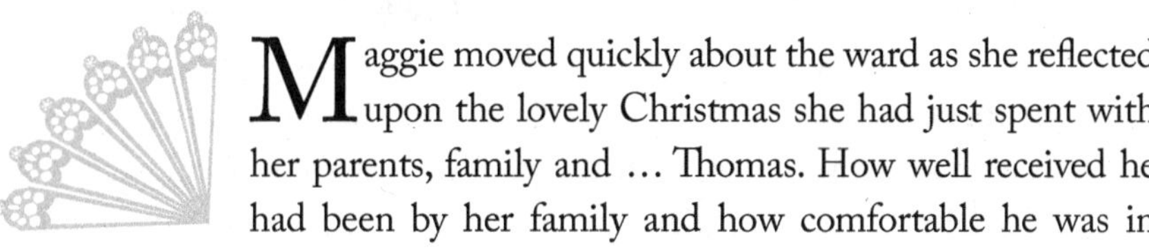

Maggie moved quickly about the ward as she reflected upon the lovely Christmas she had just spent with her parents, family and … Thomas. How well received he had been by her family and how comfortable he was in the company of all those who were dear to her! She remembered how, on Christmas Eve, while she and her sisters helped their mother to prepare the Yuletide feast, Thomas had spent the afternoon sledding with her younger brothers, sending them into peals of laughter as their toboggans veered off course and ended their trajectory prematurely in front of a huge mound of fluffy snow. "Again!" "Once more!" cried her brothers as they bounced down the uneven, icy hill near their home, impervious to the pommeling they received or to the strenuous climb up after an exuberant ride.

Later that night, Maggie's father hitched a wagon to two horses and the family climbed aboard for the short ride to the local church where they attended midnight mass. As they approached the building, the melodious sound of Christmas carols greeted them through the frosty air. With red cheeks and glistening noses, they trudged through the snow to the church, hearing the crunch-crunch of their feet against the crusty snow. After mass, they walked to their wagon, feeling the soft kiss of fresh snowflakes against their face. "How lovely to experience this winter wonderland with you by my side!" whispered Thomas to Maggie before stealing a clandestine kiss under the moonlit sky.

Christmas Day dawned, a bright sunny and crisp day full of the promise of good food and warm company. The fragrant smells emanating from the kitchen, the turkey crackling in the oven, the heady aroma of the rum-soaked plum pudding in its steam bath, the small bowls of chutney releasing their spicy flavours teased guests and family alike long before they were called to the table for the special Yuletide feast. Simple gifts of oranges, nuts, hard candy, books and homemade aprons and handkerchiefs, as well as a few prized store-bought dolls and games were exchanged as a flurry of bows and silk paper cascaded to the floor. Under the archway leading to the dining room was a mistletoe that Thomas was quick to spot and, as he made his way to the table, he reached for Maggie, kissing her soundly on the lips before her surprised parents...

The next day, during a quiet moment as Maggie was enjoying a leisurely cup of tea, her mother commented on the happy Christmas that they had all spent together, adding that she and Maggie's father had thought that Thomas blended in very well with the family. "You know, Maggie, that in the garden of life, there are many flowers that brighten our days. While a rose is usually the prima donna attracting the most attention, resplendent in its one brief moment of glory, it is also among the most fragile and shortest-lived of the flowers. The petunias, geraniums and marigolds in the garden, while not quite so showy, are still very colourful and have the advantage of blooming all summer and even into the fall due to their hardiness. You might give that some thought, my dear."

Maggie reflected on her mother's words, knowing that, while she may have deeply loved the flamboyant rose, it was time to set those memories aside and enjoy the beauty of other, longer lasting flowers...

A few days later, Thomas and Maggie went ice skating on the Assiniboine River, enjoying a cup of hot chocolate afterwards to warm up on the blustery, frigid winter day. "I was wondering, Maggie, if you would enjoy a sleigh ride with me next weekend. I have always wished to travel in a horse-drawn sleigh mounted on runners as pictured in the winter photos of Canada that we see in Ireland. I have found a farm on the outskirts of Winnipeg where one can rent sleighs for two passengers with a driver and enjoy a ride across the snow-covered fields. Would that appeal to you to celebrate the arrival of the New Year?"

"Why, Thomas, it's a splendid idea and I look forward to it very much," replied Maggie.

The next weekend, dressed in a long, woolen coat with a thick tuque, heavy scarf and lined mittens and carrying a fashionable rabbit fur muff to keep her hands warm, Maggie sat comfortably beside an equally warmly clad Thomas in a decorated sleigh with bells, a blanket and a thermos of hot chocolate that had been spiked with what she suspected was a generous quantity of Irish whiskey!

Under a full moon with a sky scattered with diamond-like stars, Thomas and Maggie were enjoying their ride in the horse-drawn sleigh that raced across the fields. They could see the twinkling lights of Winnipeg in the distance and hear a train roar through the otherwise silent countryside. Thomas put his arm around Maggie and told her how content he was with his new life in Winnipeg. She asked him if the sleigh ride with her was as good as he had hoped it would be. "Is it better than a toboggan ride with my brothers?" she teased him.

"It may be but it is still a tad early to say," he answered before kissing Maggie more passionately than ever before. Then, he gazed very deeply into her eyes and confided, "You know, my dear colleen, that I've fallen in love with you. Would you do me the honour of marrying me?"

"Yes, I will, Thomas, for I've fallen in love with you, too."

"And to answer your earlier question, Maggie, this sleigh ride has indeed been much better than my toboggan rides with your brothers!"

Chapter 16

MADRID, JANUARY 1915

Querida amiga,

My first Christmas with Felipe was marvellous! In our new home in Madrid, we displayed a lovely Nativity Scene called a Bélen *which is very typical here and includes the Holy Family as well as the Three Wise Men figures set against the background of village life in Bethlehem. We enjoyed our Christmas Eve (*Nochebuena*) dinner at my parents' home, savouring the traditional meal of prawns, turkey stuffed with truffles and a variety of sweets including* marzipan *and turrón, a nougat made of honey, sugar, egg whites and toasted almonds. Of course, Cava was served to accompany the meal. We then attended midnight mass which, in Spain, is frequently accompanied by the music of guitars, drums and tambourines. As you may know, we open our gifts on the Feast of the Epiphany rather than on Christmas Day, which we spent with Felipe's family. So much eating and celebrating with those we love!*

On New Year's Eve, we ate the traditional twelve grapes as the twelve bells of midnight chimed, ensuring good fortune for the rest of the year. However, Felipe and I have started early on our good luck as we are to become parents in May. We are so very happy!

Eduardo is moving to Barcelona next month as he has a new opportunity to develop a vineyard in the region and will be cultivating, among others, the Xarel-lo grapes used in the production of Cava. I do hope that he is successful in this new enterprise as it will be quite a challenge for him after his more stable employment as a wine merchant. However, given his strong motivation and knowledge of the field, I have every confidence that he will succeed.

I also hope that you enjoyed a lovely Christmas with your family. I think of you often and wish that you were here with me to share in all my good fortune.

With all my love,
Maria Cristina

Chapter 17

Our Lady of Hope Church, August 1915

"A very pretty but quiet wedding was solemnized at Our Lady of Hope Church on Saturday, August 28th when Miss Fiona (Maggie) Sullivan, eldest daughter of Mr. and Mrs. John Sullivan, was married to Mr. Thomas O'Toole, formerly of Ireland, in the presence of relatives and a few invited guests. Miss Irene, sister of the bride, presided at the organ.

The bride, who was given away by her father, was beautifully attired in a gown of ivory satin with an overdress of embroidered net. Her veil was prettily arranged in the Dutch cap effect, caught up with orange blossoms. She was assisted by her sister Beth, who was daintily gowned in corn colored silk with a bolero and ruffles of shimmering lace. Mr. Declan O'Shaughnessy supported the bridegroom.

After the marriage ceremony the bridal party returned to the home of the bride where a few friends and relatives partook of a sumptuous repast. Mr. and Mrs. O'Toole will make their home in Winnipeg after a wedding trip to Prince Edward Island.

The bride's travelling suit was of navy-blue serge, the smart tailored coat opening over a blouse of white silk net. Her hat was of white satin with a facing of black velvet. A band of plumage with tiny white wings encircled the crown.

The bride, familiarly known as Nurse Sullivan, will be much missed, being a professional nurse, a graduate of St. Boniface Hospital."

As she walked up the aisle on her father's arm, Maggie could see Thomas waiting for her by the two prie-dieux that had been placed in the middle of the aisle just in front of the altar. Both the bride's and groom's eyes reflected the happiness that they felt on their wedding day. As the newlyweds and their two witnesses signed the marriage register, in recognition of the groom's attachment to the country of his birth, Declan sang the new Irish ballad, "When Irish Eyes Are Smiling", which had become very popular since its introduction in 1912.

As the bride and groom walked down the aisle, Maggie smiled at her immediate family and relatives who were there to share in the joy of this special occasion. How lovely that the Flanagan family and Alexander MacTavish were in attendance as well! Declan's singing of "Danny Boy" brought tears to Thomas's eyes as he thought of his Irish family thousands of miles away in Galway who were undoubtedly wishing that they could be with him and his bride at this very minute. However, he took comfort in the thought that very soon Maggie and he would be taking the train to New Brunswick and from there a ferry to Prince Edward Island where he would be reunited with his brother Patrick whom he had not seen for five years.

Outside the church in the warm sunshine, guests threw confetti on the bride and groom, wishing them a long and happy life together. Mirroring the custom of the time, Maggie and Thomas's wedding ceremony was followed by a reception at the bride's home and the departure of the newlyweds by train on their honeymoon. For Thomas, it was an opportunity to spend two glorious weeks with his bride, as well as the occasion to reconnect with his older brother who had left Ireland a few years before him and to meet his new sister-in-law and niece. For Maggie, the honeymoon promised time with her new husband whom she had grown to love more and more, as well as the opportunity to travel for the first time outside of her province. Perhaps it was not as far as she had once hoped but she looked forward to seeing the sandy beaches, red soil and white lighthouses of the island that was the backdrop to the story of *Anne of Green Gables* and the adopted home of her new in-laws. Hugging each other, the newlyweds waved goodbye to well-wishers on the platform as the train's whistle blew and the cries of "Bon voyage!" grew fainter and fainter.

Thomas turned to Maggie, telling her that he was the luckiest man alive. "Good things have happened to me ever since I arrived in Winnipeg. Even my accident was a positive experience for it led me to you. I'll try my very best to make you happy throughout our marriage."

"And meeting you, Thomas, has been wonderful for me as well. You've brought much happiness into my life and I know that we will have a most successful marriage."

"Now, it's time for dinner, our first meal together as man and wife," declared Thomas as he escorted his new wife to the dining car.

A few days later, the newlyweds were exploring the beauty of Prince Edward Island with Thomas's brother Patrick, his wife Colleen and their young daughter, Brigid. Patrick pointed out the ferrous red earth which yielded huge potato crops and then led his guests to the waterfront area. Thomas was eager for Maggie to witness the spellbinding pull of the ocean that he knew so well, having lived close to the sea in Ireland. "Dear heart, have you ever seen the power of the ocean with its foaming waves rushing to meet the shore and crashing angrily against the rocks that stand in their way?"

"No, but I've seen the waves breaking against the shore at Lake Winnipeg," she replied.

"Ah, but you cannot compare a lake to an ocean!" he declared. "Once you have experienced the power of the wild ocean, the waves lapping against the lakeshore appear very peaceful indeed."

Thomas's words suddenly conjured suppressed images of a bright summer day at Winnipeg Beach with Eduardo, recollections of a first love that Maggie sought to dispel immediately. She took in a deep breath of the salty sea air and took her new husband's arm in hers, smiling as she said, "You're probably right, Thomas, but, for now, let's walk by the shore and enjoy the picturesque sight of the fishing boats and pleasure craft returning to the dock."

Chapter 18

Winnipeg, May 1976

My wedding day! Standing in my old bedroom at my parents' home, I took one last look in the mirror, smiling as I admired my floor-length gown of white delustred satin with its fitted bodice featuring a high neckline of lace appliqued with lace and pearls. The gown's skirt extended into a train bordered with lace that was overlaid by a striking cathedral veil. My matron of honour and very good friend, Lisa, handed me the cascade of red roses and white carnations that David had ordered for my wedding bouquet. Happiness filled my heart as I hugged my family before leaving for church and my new life with David as my husband.

As the first majestic notes of the church organ sounded, I took my father's arm, intent on enjoying every minute of the wedding ceremony that David and I had planned so meticulously. The nuptial mass began with the tenor singing Beethoven's "Ode to Joy" in English, French and Spanish as I walked solemnly up the aisle with my father, careful to avoid the heel-grasping air grates that gently lifted my long cathedral train. As I reached the two prie-dieux in front of the altar, I smiled at David who whispered, "How lovely you look!" Just after the priest pronounced us man and wife, at my request, my father read Shakespeare's memorable sonnet no. 116 that pays tribute to the timeless nature of true love:

Let me not to the marriage of true minds
Admit impediments.

As we walked down the aisle to the music of *The Bridal March*, David and I smiled at all our family and friends who were there to share the joy of our wedding day. Outside the church in the warm sunshine, guests threw confetti on us and wished us well before making their way to the reception and dinner which concluded with the familiar Irish blessing:

May the road rise up to meet you.
May the wind be always at your back.
May the sun shine warm upon your face;
The rains fall soft upon your fields and until we meet again,
May God hold you in the palm of His hand.

The next day, we flew to Spain where we began our month-long honeymoon in the land of my dreams.

Chapter 19

Madrid, November 1915

Querida Margarita,

I was so delighted to read about your lovely wedding, both in your letter and in the attached newspaper article describing your special day. How I would have enjoyed being there with you and sharing the joy of that wonderful moment in your life! I am truly happy that you have found a husband who is a warm and sensitive man with a striking sense of humour and a boundless love for you. Wouldn't it be wonderful if Felipe and I could visit you and Thomas in Winnipeg? I have already spoken to Felipe about my wish and he is in agreement, knowing the strong bond that exists between the two of us. How I pray that we will be able to see each other soon! Although the period that we spent together was brief, it seems to me that we immediately recognized that we were kindred spirits and experienced a friendship over a few months that few are fortunate enough to know in their lifetime. Moreover, you are attracted to my country and would so enjoy visiting all those places that I described to you while I was in Winnipeg. Of course, it would also be a very special pleasure for us to introduce you to your namesake who was born on May 21.

Our little Margarita is doing very well and brings so much joy to our life. She smiles at Felipe and me constantly and makes each day so bright.

Do you remember my telling you about the charms of Seville? Felipe has suggested that we travel there next spring to witness the beautiful religious floats for which the city is famous during Holy Week. My mother and mother-in-law are already vying for the honour of looking after Margarita.

Maggie, you had the opportunity to travel to Prince Edward Island for your honeymoon. I remember when I was teaching at St. Mary's Academy that many of my students were excited to read Anne of Green Gables *by Lucy Maud Montgomery, a resident of that island. How did you enjoy visiting the province? Thomas must have been so happy to be reunited with his brother and family while you were there!*

I was also happy to read that Mr. MacTavish and Grace are now courting. Isn't it interesting to observe how our little circle of friends has grown, leading to new connections such as your Thomas who is now working with Mr. Flanagan?

I must say goodbye to you for now but Felipe and I send you and Thomas all our love and best wishes for the future.

Un gran abrazo
Maria Cristina

Chapter 20

Spain, June 1976

Jan Morris's introduction to the charms of Andalusia, which she describes as "bewitching", set the tone for our honeymoon in the Spanish South, a land embellished with jasmine and bougainvillea, enlivened by the sound of castanets and guitars, fragrant with olive, orange and almond trees and made magical by its *pueblo blancos* and storied hilltop castles…

Our honeymoon began in Málaga, birthplace of Picasso and one of the oldest Mediterranean ports on the southern coast of Spain. David and I had reserved a few nights' accommodation at the lovely Parador de Gibralfaro, part of the network of atmospheric or historic hotels in scenic settings managed by the Spanish government. Perched on a hill overlooking the Mediterranean (and the city's iconic bullring!) with magenta-coloured bougainvillea running like thick floral braids across the arcaded balconies of the old stone mansion with its many wrought-iron grilles, the parador was a veritable delight. Pleasantly secluded but within close proximity to Málaga, it also offered a scenic walk to the ruins of a Moorish castle (the *Castillo de Gibralfaro*) with magnificent views from all sides.

This is how I described our lovely stay in Málaga in a quick postcard to my parents:

We arrived safely in Málaga and are enjoying the parador's comfortable, traditional décor. The key to our room is the size of the medieval ones used by knights to open castle doors! From our balcony, the view of the turquoise ocean framed by palm trees is breathtaking. It will be difficult to leave this paradise for our next destination, Marbella.

After drinks on our balcony, we headed to the parador's dining room where we ordered the specialty of the house: *entremeses variados* (a variety of hors-d'oeuvres), followed by a *fritura malagueña,* a platter of fried fish based on the local catch of the day. To our amazement, FOURTEEN different types of hors-d'oeuvres in separate dishes were placed before us! Of course, after this massive first course, we could barely eat any of the fish piled high on the huge silver platter that contained our second course.

While in Málaga, we visited the *Alcazaba*, a combination palace and fortress built by the Moors, and strolled down the narrow streets of the city's Old Quarter where horse-drawn carriages take tourists by the cathedral and episcopal palace.

Our next stop was charming Marbella, an upscale seaside town along the Costa del Sol which was well deserving of its name, "beautiful sea". We stayed at a pleasant hotel close to the *Plaza de los Naranjos* (Courtyard of the Orange Trees) where narrow cobblestone streets converge and attractive shops and restaurants line the square. The beautiful promenade along the ocean was perfect for an early evening stroll. The Spanish enjoy this pre-prandial walk, known as the *paseo,* which allows them to socialize with the members of their community.

After a few days in Marbella, we decided to visit one of the most striking towns along the route of Andalusia's beautiful whitewashed towns and took the bus to Ronda. My next postcard to my parents captured all of our fears, as well as our relief upon returning safely to Marbella:

Dear Mom and Dad,

This has been one of the most frightening days of our lives. David and I began to think that the vows we took under a week ago "to honour and love each other.... until death do us part" were going to prove to be prophetic – way too soon! We took a bus to Ronda and thought we would never return to Marbella alive. However, gracias a Dios, *we are safely back at our hotel, enjoying a well-deserved drink. We will describe our experience to you upon our return home: be prepared for a good story!*

We embarked on our bus for Ronda in the late morning and soon noticed that our driver appeared to be intoxicated. The smell emanating from his breath and his complete insouciance about the hairpin curves he faced along the narrow mountain road rapidly convinced us that something was wrong. The higher he drove up the winding road, the more determined the driver was to reach his destination quickly. As he rounded each bend in the serpentine road, he would merely honk his horn and then unconcernedly proceed despite the fact that the zigzag road hugging the mountain prevented him from seeing any vehicle travelling in the opposite direction. His driving became increasingly erratic and many passengers began to voice their concerns. Soon, concern turned to fear and fear to panic as the bus veered wildly from its inside lane by the mountain face into the outside lane overlooking the precipice. We somehow made it to our destination safe and sound and began exploring one of the most scenic of all the towns included on the *Ruta de los Pueblos Blancos*.

Ronda is truly a marvel, a city split by a gorge (El Tajo) into two sections: the old Moorish Quarter on one side and the newer section built after the Reconquista. The latter includes the New Bridge with its spectacular views of the gorge and the cliffside houses hanging precariously over the edge, as well as the oldest bullring in Spain. We also wandered through the Old Quarter with its winding streets, wrought-iron balconies covered with pots of geraniums (fancifully called *gitanillas* or little gypsies in Spanish) and magnificent old private residences boasting of bubbling fountains, classic-styled statues and tiled patios. Walking through these labyrinthine streets was truly like being transported to another world, almost as if we had travelled on a magic carpet to a forgotten land frozen in time like Sleeping Beauty's castle hidden in the deep overgrowth of a one-hundred-year-old forest. David and I sought the comfort of a church to express our thanks to God for having arrived safely in Ronda despite our inebriated driver, as well as to pray for an uneventful return to Marbella!

We could not help but reflect that, just a few days earlier, we had embraced the sacred vows of matrimony for our *entire* lives …

Of course, while we were enjoying lunch and admiring the beautiful city of Ronda, our bus driver had been enjoying more Bacchanalian pleasures before stumbling onto the bus for the late afternoon return trip to Marbella. We were not reassured by his slurred speech and unsteady gait but there appeared to be no other option that we could take for our return journey. Our anxiety mounted as women and children began screaming in terror. At one point, one of the bus's back wheels hit a stone abutment and knocked it down the precipice. Worse yet, the wheel stood over the precipice, poised in midair without any support. The driver exited the vehicle and checked the situation. Confident that he could safely maneuver the bus back onto the road, he returned to his seat and drove us back to Marbella. Miraculously, we all arrived safely after such an ordeal!

After our experience in Ronda, David and I were happy to spend some lazy hours on the beaches of Cadiz, our next stop. A seaport with a long and fascinating history, Cadiz welcomed the many Spanish galleons leaving for and returning from the New World. Today, its lovely seaside promenades and enchanting parks filled with exotic flora from the New World beckon to the weary traveler looking for relaxation.

I sent the following postcard from our next destination, Jerez de la Frontera, to my parents:

> *Today, David and I visited the charming town of Jerez de la Frontera where we were introduced to the subtleties of sherry. I always thought that sherry was a sweet fortified wine sipped in the afternoon by little old ladies. Was I wrong! No, sherry definitely has a multi-faceted personality which we will be happy to explore in the future!*

Yes, tasting *Tio Pepe* and *La Ina* was definitely a novel experience for us, particularly given the special ambiance of the bodegas in Jerez. Having only enough time to visit one attraction, we unfortunately had to skip the *Fundación Real Escuela Andaluza del Arte Ecuestre* where Andalusian horses are trained to "dance" with their human partners. Instead, we elected to visit the Domecq Bodega where we were given a complete tour of the facilities, as well as a tasting of various sherries ranging from the very dry to the cloyingly sweet. The bodega also produced a number of fine brandies which we also tasted.

Sherry was introduced to the English by British sailors and pirates. Reputedly, Sir Francis Drake stole many casks of sherry from Cadiz when he attacked the city in 1587, providing British sailors with a regular supply that they shipped back to their homeland, further popularizing the fortified wine.

We did not leave the Domecq Bodega empty-handed. When we told our guide that we were honeymooners, she gave us a handsome red-velvet box containing a small bottle of *La Ina* sherry and another of *Fundador* brandy, as well as several mini bottles. We decided then to drink the sherry on the occasion of our twenty-fifth wedding anniversary and the brandy for our fiftieth wedding anniversary. (We did savour the bottle of *La Ina* as planned to celebrate our silver anniversary and hope to enjoy the brandy on our golden anniversary.)

Ah, Sevilla! Who can resist her seductive charms? This enchantress with her many wiles can bewitch you unknowingly as she instantly appeals to all the senses: the amazing fragrance of orange trees perfuming a square; the vivid mauve, pink and orange hues of bougainvillea cascading down a whitewashed building; the clack-clack of castanets, the stamping of heels and the snapping of fingers as colourful gypsy skirts swish during a flamenco performance; the taste of almonds and sherry followed by garlicky spoonfuls of ice-cold gazpacho redolent with the flavours of a summer garden and the enticing kiss of a delicate fan's gentle breeze against one's hair – all of these encapsulate this enchanting Andalusian city of romance.

In a postcard to my parents, I tried to capture the magic of Seville:

> *What a perfect city to select for one's honeymoon! We feel that we have just stepped onto a movie set with all the necessary props to film the stereotypical images of Seville: the Royal Tobacco Factory which Bizet used as the background for his opera* Carmen; *the ibérico and serrano*

hams hanging from the ceilings of tapa bars; the countless shops with their flounced flamenco dresses, silk shawls, mantilla combs and lovely fans; the flowered courtyards spilling over with geraniums and the refreshing sound of water trickling from fountains. ¡Viva España!

Speaking of "¡Y Viva España!", this is the song that we shall forever associate with our honeymoon in Spain. In 1973, Manola Escobar popularized the song, originally a Belgian melody, with a Spanish version extolling his country's many attractions and it soon became an international hit. How many times David and I tapped our feet, hummed the tune or even danced to this popular ode to Spain during our honeymoon!

David` and I visited Seville's Cathedral, the third largest church in Europe, and marveled at all its glistening gold. We thought of the quantity of precious metals plundered from the New World for the construction of such magnificent buildings in Spain. All that remains of the original Moorish structure is the *Patio de los Naranjos* (Courtyard of the Orange Trees*)* where the faithful there once performed their ritual cleansing before praying under the shade of the orange trees and the Giralda, the former minaret, now transformed into a Christian bell tower and weathervane.

From the Cathedral, it is a short walk to the entrance of the Alcazar, a palace built for the governors of the local Moorish jurisdiction, and today a royal residence for the Spanish sovereigns. The gardens closer to the building are in the geometric style favoured by the Moors while the lusher gardens of palm trees, roses and myrtle shrubs located further back were built after the Reconquista. The many beautiful fountains enhance these charming gardens and remind visitors of the great importance that water had in the lives of the Moors who, as desert people, depended on it even more than most. The abundance of water in Spain amazed them and water features became an integral part of their lives.

We then strolled through the old Jewish quarter of Santa Cruz with its flower-draped balconies, wrought-iron latticework, small plazas boasting stone fountains, tiled-lined patios and benches, as well as streets so narrow that they are called "kissing lanes". We saw the house where Bartolomé Murillo, the famous Sevillian artist, once lived. Orange trees lend shade and ambiance to the lovely area of Santa Cruz; however, their fruit is not really edible, given that the oranges are extremely bitter and only used to make vitamins, perfumes and marmalade. Our appreciation of Santa Cruz was heightened by our stay at the Hotel Murillo, named after the beloved artist, and located in the centre of the quarter, only minutes away from the Cathedral. The hotel's rooftop terrace offers striking views of the Giralda and other Sevillian landmarks and the rooms with their wrought-iron grill work and flower-bedecked balconies testify to Andalusia's heritage.

To continue with our visit of Seville's beautiful residences, we made our way to the Casa de Pilatos where we toured the lovely sixteenth-century aristocratic home of a Spanish duke and walked through its resplendent bougainvillea-filled gardens. As we strolled down the perfumed pathways, David noticed that I was wearing my grandmother's amethyst pendant and asked me why I had taken it to Spain. "You will probably think that it was a rather romantic notion of mine," I admitted, "but somehow I feel that I am taking a small part of her to Spain, the country that I imagine she wished she could have visited so many years ago."

"And why do you think that Spain was so important to her?"

I reminded David of the Spanish fan, the message from Eduardo and the letters from Spain which had been carefully placed at the bottom of my grandmother's trunk in the attic.

"But you haven't even read the letters from Maria Cristina; they may not refer to Eduardo at all."

"You may be right, David, but I feel that, one day, this Spanish connection will reveal itself and that we will be part of it. I feel it very strongly here in Seville."

"As you say, Sophie, it is a very fanciful impression of yours but intuition sometimes provides a strong foreshadowing of the future. In the meantime, let's have lunch here in the present before continuing with our tour of Seville and visiting Maria Luisa Park."

How we enjoyed our visit to The *Parque Maria Luisa*, a large urban park that is popular with Sevillians and tourists alike! It is the perfect place for a stroll with its plethora of palm and orange trees, its multitude of flowers, its waterfalls and lily ponds and its beautiful statuary and fountains. As my old friend Iago was responsible for my familiarity with the works of Gustavo Bécquer who was born in Seville, I paused for a few minutes before the impressive monument to this Romantic writer. The marble group comprises a bust of the writer, as well as statues of three well-dressed women sitting on a bench who symbolize the three states of love that the poet describes in his *Rimas*: the first stirrings of passion, the culmination of love and its waning. Two bronze figures including a young cupid with his arrow poised for his next "victim" complete the tribute to Bécquer.

Plaza de España was the final visit of our tour; it was built in 1929 for the Ibero-American Exposition. Its crescent-shaped structure boasts of fifty alcoves representing all of Spain's provinces with each one featuring a tiled mural highlighting specific aspects of the particular province to which it is dedicated. Graceful bridges over canals span this impressive semi-circle of Spanish history and culture.

While in Seville, "*Una ración de almendras con una copa de jerez*" (A serving of almonds with a glass of sherry) was our most frequent request. As we became increasingly accustomed to Spain's late dining hours, we were amazed to discover one day that we actually arrived at a restaurant at 4:00 p.m. for lunch only to discover that the kitchen had closed until dinner time!

On our last night in Seville, David suggested a romantic moonlit carriage ride through the streets of the Old Quarter. Seeing all the lovely sights at night that we had admired during the day added a special charm to our tour and was a unique way of ending our stay in this unforgettable city. David and I noticed that one orange tree seemed to be so completely covered with white flowers that it almost appeared to be wearing a wedding dress. When we asked the carriage driver why the tree was so white, he told us that the many doves (*palomas*) sitting on the branches had led to the creation of our whimsical impression!

We left Seville with a lacy shawl that I had purchased, as well as a doll attired in the red and white striped dress of a Malagueña and another proudly wearing the gypsy garments, shawl and comb of an Andalusian native. We also bought a group of three paintings representing scenes from a typical Andalusian village as well as jackets of incredibly buttery leather.

Of course, our best souvenirs were those intangible memories of a honeymoon spent in a city known for its atmosphere and romance.

Dear Mom and Dad,

You will not believe what we just purchased in Toledo! David and I are now the proud possessors of three damascene swords… and a large shield to display them. How we will transport these souvenirs on the rest of our trip remains to be seen.

We will spend a few days in Madrid before boarding our train for San Sebastian and then France.

Sophie

Yes, after visiting the Cathedral and El Greco's house, our trip to Toledo did indeed focus on shopping. In this city of artisans, handicrafts have reigned supreme since the days of the Moors. Later, medieval artisans fashioned the swords used by knights in the Crusades and later still the swords used by matadors. Today, high-quality knives continue to be crafted by hand in Toledo and visitors can observe goldsmiths pounding gold threads into a steel base to create the resplendent art of inlaid plates, jewelry and artifacts known as damascene. As David had expressed a strong wish to learn more about the traditional damascene craft so characteristic of Toledo, we decided to devote an afternoon to visiting the many shops specializing in the technique of inlaying 24-karat-gold over steel. Thus, after many questions, we left Toledo with three swords (with blunted tips) whose hilts were decorated in damascene, as well as several letter openers, a pendant and a lovely plate with two small accompanying vases decorated with birds and flowers. Burdened as we were at the time with all these purchases, especially the cumbersome swords and escutcheon, we soon realized how difficult it was going to be to carry these items up and down the many non-automated staircases at train stations leading from one platform to another and then across the very narrow corridors of the trains of the day with their tight compartments. Furthermore, that didn't even take into account the heavy suitcases that we had to carry, along with all our souvenirs!

In Madrid, I showed David the sights that I knew so well. After visiting the Royal Palace, the Prado, Plaza Mayor, the Puerta del Sol, etc., we enjoyed a fine dinner at *La Bola Taverna*, a venerable Madrid institution whose specialty is *Cocido madrileño*, a hearty pork stew with potatoes, garbanzo beans and vegetables cooked in individual clay pots over a wood fire. The traditional décor and ambiance, as well as the food, made for a lovely evening.

For our final evening in Madrid, we had made reservations by mail from Canada (There were no e-mails in 1976 and international telephone calls were prohibitively expensive at the time!) to dine at the illustrious *Casa Botín*, reputedly the oldest restaurant in the world (since 1725) and the establishment described by Hemingway in *The Sun Also Rises* as "one of the best restaurants in the world". The specialty of the house is roast suckling pig, which we very much enjoyed, and we were particularly fortunate that the evening that we dined there, *la Tuna* made an appearance. A *tuna* refers to a group of university students in traditional dress who play the lute, tambourine and guitar to serenade their audience. While they originally performed as a way of earning money or food, today they are more focused on travelling and meeting people from around the world. Their cloaks testify to this as they are covered with the shields of the cities and countries that they have visited. The students also display ribbons on their cloaks which they receive from their loved ones or friends who wish to express their affection and good wishes.

As we savoured our last glass of wine at the *Casa Botín* and reflected on the wonderful experiences that we had enjoyed in Spain, my thoughts turned once again to Maria Cristina and Eduardo. "David, do you think that their children and grandchildren live here in Madrid today? How I would love to meet them and find out more about their ancestors!"

"Well, Sophie, you could try to contact them but you would need an old address to begin your research."

"When we get back to Canada, I will try once again to obtain those elusive letters from my cousin or aunt. Do you believe, David, that there is something they contain that the family doesn't want to share with me?"

"I think that you have read too many mystery novels. It is probably just normal human procrastination that has led to the delay in sending the letters to you."

The next morning, we boarded the train for San Sebastían with all our luggage and souvenirs. This lovely Belle Époque city by the sea resembles its French sister of Biarritz across the border with its seaside promenades, sandy beaches, impressive hotels and venerable mansions, as well as its atmospheric harbor with bobbing boats. We spent two relaxing days in the coastal city before taking the train to the fortified medieval city of Carcassonne and the beginning of the French portion of our honeymoon.

We did manage to return home with all our damascene pieces but it was not easy as we had many trains to catch before reaching Paris, our ultimate destination. Fortunately for us, my great-uncle in Tours wrapped the swords and escutcheon in special packaging and fashioned a handle for easier carrying. While this did not reduce their weight, it made them less of a burden to transport on our way home to Canada. When we finally left Paris with all our belongings, we were fortunate that the airline's weight restrictions were generous and that the security regulations in the seventies were so lax that we were even allowed to take our swords into the cabin of the Air France plane we took on our return journey to Canada!

Chapter 21

Winnipeg, May 1916

Maggie adjusted her nurse's cap, checked her uniform and smiled at Thomas before she kissed him goodbye as she left for the hospital. She was excited to resume her work as a nurse after a six-month hiatus at home. Although most married women did not work outside the home in her era, she wished to return to her profession not to mark her independence but, rather, simply because she enjoyed helping others and the additional income would help her and Thomas with the purchase of a house for their future family.

Upon arrival at the hospital, she noticed a flurry of activity as construction projects which had been launched a few years earlier were in the process of being completed. A new pathology department with a fully equipped laboratory had been constructed, allowing blood and urine samples to be analyzed on site rather than having to send them out to other hospitals in Winnipeg. New modern operating rooms were also being built, enabling the hospital to keep pace with ever evolving medical technologies. World War 1 had also increased hospital requirements for the care of sick and wounded soldiers and some 300 of them could now be accommodated if necessary. Those who were well enough could even spend a few minutes on the rooftop garden where they could enjoy a breath of fresh air and a view of the city. In 1916, the hospital switched from coal to electricity; adding to the benefits of the hospital's central heating system was the installation of thermostats in each room, a major innovation for its time. Maggie marvelled at the progress that had been made as she quickly checked in with the head nurse of the maternity ward where she would be working.

Upon returning home, Maggie was pleased to report on her first day back at the hospital, telling Thomas that she had made the right decision to return to work. She was so excited about her own news that she didn't notice her husband's elated mood until she finished talking. "Why, Thomas, forgive me for rattling on for so long. I think that you, too, have something to tell me."

"Yes, indeed, Maggie. Can you believe that Mr. Flanagan offered me a partnership in his store? Not only will this mean a significantly higher income for us but it will also allow me to go on business trips to Europe to choose the latest textiles for our store. Our store! Doesn't that sound wonderful, Maggie? Mr. Flanagan told me that I could even take a few extra days to visit my family in Galway on my first trip to Ireland. Of course, this won't be right away, he said, but soon after the war ends and conditions are safer overseas. What do you think, Maggie? Shall we celebrate this weekend by having dinner at a special restaurant? How about the Fort Garry Hotel? I have never been there. We could also see a moving picture show at either the Dominion or the Bijou Theatre."

'That sounds wonderful, Thomas," replied Maggie as the couple danced happily around their small apartment.

A week later, Maggie had tea with Grace who informed her that she and Alexander MacTavish would be married in August. Grace confided that her parents were somewhat concerned about the engagement, given the age difference between the two fiancés and the possibility that Mr. MacTavish might be marrying her on the rebound after being rejected by his first love. However, they balanced their arguments with the fact that they both liked their future son-in-law and felt that their daughter's and his interests were very compatible. Maggie offered Grace her sincerest wishes for the couple's future happiness, adding that life sometimes offers us a second chance at happiness when we least expect it.

Chapter 22

Seville, June 1916

Dearest Margarita,

I was delighted to read your good news about your return to work. How wonderful that you are enjoying your profession so much and that Thomas has secured a partnership with Mr. Flanagan!

Felipe and I also have good news: we are expecting our second child in November and are so very happy. Our little Margarita is so sweet and we know that she will welcome a new sibling. Thank you so much for the miniature nurse's uniform that you made for her; I am sure that she will enjoy wearing it in a few years. Who knows? It may inspire Margarita's future choice of career.

*Seville's beauty cannot be exaggerated: the architecture, the striking white buildings brightened with geraniums and bougainvillea of every colour, the majesty of the cathedral, the perfumed orange trees, etc. Our first trip there in April was absolutely incredible. You have to see the religious floats yourself to believe how truly outstanding they are, especially at night when they are illuminated by hundreds of wax candles and carried by robed penitents (*Nazarenos*). It is quite astonishing to see how reverent the crowds are. And the flowers! Their perfume* *is ubiquitous and their beauty is unsurpassed, mounds and mounds of blooms decorating the floats dedicated to Mary and Christ. I lit a candle for you, looking forward to the day that we will meet again.*

Eduardo is working very hard to promote the success of his new vineyard. Cava has become increasingly popular in Spain, especially with the Royal Family being supplied with sparkling wine by the Raventos family, producers of Codorníu. *Papá is offering Eduardo all the assistance that he can with his many connections in the world of oenophiles.*

Felipe works extremely long days at the hospital and has become an expert in highly infectious diseases. He often says that the next pandemic is only a threat away and wishes to be prepared as much as possible. Thus, he pursues his studies in epidemiology and is very familiar with all the viruses which are currently known. He often says, "If only I could predict what lies ahead!"

Your friend Maria Cristina who thinks of you often and sends you an abrazo.

Chapter 23

WINNIPEG, JULY—DECEMBER 1916

Moving day! Maggie and Thomas had a final look at their modest apartment before taking the last of their possessions down to the trailer that held all of the goods that they would be moving into their new, more spacious home. Fortunately, they would have a month to get settled before Thomas's brother and his family arrived from Prince Edward Island to holiday in the Manitoba capital. Thomas was very excited at the prospect of seeing Patrick, Colleen and their daughter Brigid once again and of showing them the flourishing city of Winnipeg. At the beginning of the 20th century, it was a rare privilege indeed to see one's relatives once they were separated by such large distances.

Maggie was pleased to tell Thomas that not only had they been invited to Grace's wedding to Alexander MacTavish the next month but that the Flanagans had kindly included Patrick and his family as well. It would be an opportunity for them not only to experience a Canadian wedding but, also, to see the legendary Royal Alexandra Hotel. Moreover, on the eve of the wedding, there would be a dinner and reception at the Flanagans in honour of Grace's wedding. Thomas happily added these invitations to the roster of activities that he and

Maggie had planned for Patrick's visit, including a stop at Maggie's parents' farm. They would also take the train to Grand Beach for a day. Although Thomas had wished to travel to Winnipeg Beach, Maggie, remembering her engagement day there with Eduardo, had steadfastly refused to go, saying that she had already visited Winnipeg Beach and would prefer to see something new. In truth, she could not bear to return to the scene that had played host to such wonderful memories. Thomas, seeing how determined she was about this, finally acquiesced and agreed that a trip to Grand Beach would be a suitable substitute indeed with its fine, powdery sand beaches and tall, grass-blanketed dunes.

"I have heard that, except for its fresh water, Grand Beach could easily be mistaken for an ocean beach. Brigid will be delighted to play on the beach, to make sandcastles with her uncle and aunt and to jump in the lake to meet the waves," he confirmed. His face radiated such warmth at the prospect of seeing his family members once again and of sharing time with them that Maggie was once again reminded of the depth of her love for her husband.

"You know, Maggie, I have never been as happy as I am now, with you by my side, my darling wife. I love you so much." Looking into his calm, honest eyes, Maggie replied, "And you, dearest husband, bring to mind all that is good and special in life. I love you with all my heart."

After all these happy events, Maggie received a much-anticipated letter from Maria Cristina who was also pleased to share her latest good news with her close friend:

Dear Margarita,

Well, I must give you the most important news first. Our little Miguel Felipe Eduardo was born on November 15 and has been warmly welcomed not only by his parents but also by his big sister, Margarita. She dotes over the baby, frequently dressing up in the little nurse's uniform that you made for her and placing her hand on Miguel's forehead in an attempt to gauge his temperature as she has seen her father do when she is ill. Who knows, dear friend? She may one day become a nurse like you.

Miguel's christening was held last week and Eduardo agreed to be his godfather and Felipe's sister Felicia his godmother. Should anything ever happen to us, I know that Miguel will be in good hands.

I was very happy to read that Grace's wedding to Mr. MacTavish was so lovely and that Eduardo's Cava reached the Flanagan home in time for the wedding eve reception. (With Prohibition in Manitoba now, Eduardo felt that the Flanagans and their guests would enjoy a little wine with their special meal.) I laughed when I read your account of Thomas's brother who especially enjoyed the opportunity to imbibe rather generously after experiencing a long, dry period in Prince Edward Island due to the strict liquor laws there... Please convey Eduardo's and my warmest wishes to the newlyweds whom we remember very well from our journey together on the Empress.

In early September, Felipe and I are visited the Region of Catalonia which produces many fine sparkling wines. We saw Eduardo's vineyard and were impressed with the passion he devotes to his craft. The vines planted by our uncle are strong and healthy and Eduardo is expecting a good yield as he prepares to produce his first bottles of Cava. (The case of Cava that he sent to the Flanagans was part of the inheritance that he received from our uncle.)

I know that, with each visit to various parts of Spain, I always tell you how much you would enjoy touring the region but, nevertheless, it is the truth. Visiting Catalonia and the beautiful island of Mallorca was a very special experience. Wouldn't it be wonderful if we could all meet together in Spain one day!

Mallorca is resplendent with almond, orange and olive trees and was a quiet oasis for Felipe and me as we enjoyed our time together with Margarita. Felipe is always so busy in Madrid, rushing from one patient to another that I truly appreciate these special moments with him. We spent time at the beach where Margarita laughed as the waves reached her knees. We also visited the cathedral and the Royal Palace in

Palma, the capital. Of course, we couldn't resist the opportunity to spend a little time in Valencia, the home of paella, before returning home.

I hope that you and Thomas have a wonderful Christmas.

Your friend,
Maria Cristina

Chapter 24

WINNIPEG, NOVEMBER 1918—JUNE 1919

"Thomas, I am completely worn out after my day on the wards."

"Is your new position as nursing supervisor more challenging than you expected, my dear?"

"No, it's not the position but, rather, the extra-long hours all the medical staff must work. As you know, we just finished handling a typhoid outbreak at the hospital and, no sooner was that over than we admitted the first patients suffering from the new, terrible influenza virus known as the Spanish Flu, a highly contagious disease that is spread very easily through contact with the droplets that we expel from our mouth and nose. Today, alone, I cared for 10 patients who contracted the disease and who are very ill and can barely breathe. It is very sad to see them struggle for each breath. We have so little with which to work and the doctors have few means of treating the disease other than isolating patients as best they can in crowded and often makeshift hospitals and offering them aspirin to alleviate their pain. As so many hospital employees are ill, the Grey Nuns have asked other religious orders for assistance. Jesuit priests, Oblate Sisters and the Sisters of the Holy Family have all responded to the call and have joined forces with us to help care for the sick. Nevertheless, the situation is dire."

"I read that, due to the shortage of nurses, St. John Ambulance is offering an intensive course in nursing to those who wish to tend to the sick, including teachers who are not working due to the ban on public gatherings, including schools," added Thomas.

"Yes, while this will help, I am concerned, Thomas, that not only has the current strain of influenza struck its usual vulnerable victims of the very young and the very old, but it has also killed many more in the prime of life. Please be very careful and try to maintain a distance from your clients. I'm also afraid that I may bring this virus home to you after being exposed to so many sick patients."

"What about you, Maggie? I'm worried that you will contract the virus, too. Just as you can't avoid being close to your patients, I can't avoid being close to my customers whose measurements must be taken and clothing adjusted."

"At least, I have a medical mask. Please ensure that the cloth masks which I made for you are boiled after each use. Remember that cloth masks can be virus carriers if their wearers are negligent about cleaning them."

"Don't worry, Maggie. I will boil my masks and keep my distance as much as possible. Fortunately for me, Mr. Flanagan is also very concerned about protecting employees and, as his partner, the two of us have liberated more storage space to enlarge our work area and better distance our employees."

"I'm glad to hear it, especially as this is in keeping with all the restrictions imposed on churches, schools, theatres and public gatherings. I know that the use of disinfectants and the adoption of quarantine procedures and more stringent personal hygiene as well as the wearing of masks are all playing an important role in limiting the spread of the Spanish Flu but we have very few weapons in our arsenal: no vaccines, no effective treatments or medications and no means of testing for the virus, only our collective will to conquer this disease. Whenever I see a new patient arrive who complains of fatigue and shortness of breath, a sore throat, a fever and a cough, I cringe, knowing that there is a strong probability that he or she will not leave the hospital alive.

Nevertheless, in the midst of all this serious talk, Thomas, I have good news to share with you. I am with child and will give birth to our baby in May. I am so excited! Now that I am about to become a mother, I plan to retire from nursing to protect our child from the influenza virus and other diseases."

"What wonderful news, Maggie! I am so pleased that we shall become parents soon. Should I begin to build a crib for our baby, my darling?"

"We still have a lot of time, Thomas," answered Maggie with a laugh. "Why don't we go for a walk in the park and begin thinking about the name we will give our little one?" she suggested.

A few weeks later, Maggie settled comfortably in her favourite chair to read Maria Cristina's latest letter, dated December 1, 1918.

Dear Margarita,

What wonderful news about your pregnancy you shared with me in your last letter! I am so pleased for you and Thomas.

How are you managing to protect yourself from the influenza virus as you treat patients? I am relieved that you are no longer working at the hospital. I worry so much about Felipe as he is constantly in close contact with the sick. The war has now ended but new casualties related to the Spanish Flu continue to arrive every day.

Felipe tells me that approximately one-third of the world's population may eventually be infected by the flu pandemic virus, resulting in a death toll that could reach over 50 million people. Overcrowded war camps and hospitals are ideal breeding grounds for the spread of the respiratory virus as are the increased travel by rail and ship of soldiers from one country to another and the huge, post-war celebratory crowds that have gathered in the streets over the past few weeks. Moreover, Felipe believes that the soldiers' immune systems, weakened by the effects of war such as malnutrition, poor hygiene and the stress of combat and chemical attacks, have increased their susceptibility to the influenza virus. He feels so helpless as he sees one patient after another succumb to the flu, their lungs filling with liquids as they gasp for air. Working from morning to night, he sometimes grabs a few hours of sleep at the hospital before rushing home to change and eat. He is afraid of bringing the virus to us and refrains from contact with Margarita who does not understand why her father no longer wishes to hold her and playfully throw her up in the air.

Christmas will be celebrated soon in a world that hopes for a brighter future. Felipe has promised me a trip to anywhere I wish to visit next summer when conditions are predicted to be much better. I told him that my dream is to return to Winnipeg to see you again and to meet Thomas and your baby. He has agreed and suggested that we follow a trip to your capital with a train ride to the Rockies where we would stay at the magnificent Château Lake Louise. Think of it, Maggie! In seven months, we may be together again, dearest friend!

Affectionately,
Maria Cristina

Maggie's heart was full of happiness as she reflected upon the prospect of Maria Cristina's and Felipe's visit to Winnipeg, as well as on the arrival of Thomas's and her child in the New Year.

Having retired from nursing for a second time, given her concerns about the influenza pandemic, Maggie began to prepare for the arrival of her baby, a daughter who was born in early May. Despite her busy schedule as a new mother, she, of course, took the time to inform Maria Cristina of baby Maureen's birth.

June 15, 1919

Dearest Margarita,

Felipe is currently making plans for our early September visit to Canada. He feels that waiting a few more months for our visit will make it safer. I can't wait to see you again! Also, it is important for Felipe to have a good rest after the past year and a half during which he has been working tirelessly. The fresh air of the Rockies and tranquility of the lakes, woods and mountains will do him so much good. We will take the children with us but please do not worry about accommodating us in Winnipeg as we have reserved rooms at the Fort Garry Hotel.

I can't believe that we will finally see each other again in just a few months!

Sending you all my love and un gran abrazo,

Tu amiga para siempre,
Maria Cristina

P.S. *I have just collected today's post and see that there is a letter from you. How delighted I am to learn of baby Maureen's birth! I will be sending you a child's china tea set from Spain that Maureen will be able to play with when she is a little older. I saw the lovely set in the store window last week and purchased it, having had the premonition that you were going to have a daughter. I know how happy you must be now as you cradle your infant in your arms.*

Chapter 25

Toronto, April 1977

I was just starting to wonder if I would ever see the long-awaited letters from Maria Cristina that I had found in my grandmother's attic when I received a call from my aunt Maeve who informed me that she would be in Toronto for a few days to attend a nurses' conference and that she hoped to see me during this period. She also mentioned that she would give me the old letters from Spain that I was so eager to read as she had just seen her daughter who had returned them to her, along with the ornate fan that I remembered. I tried to restrain the eagerness in my voice as I thanked her and invited her to join David and me for dinner. Would I finally be able to solve the mystery of Eduardo's presence in my grandmother's life or would it remain an elusive tale of passion fated to vanish like the gossamer of young lovers' dreams? The message that he had written to my grandmother so many years earlier still resonated with me: *A mi preciosa Margarita, un recuerdo de un verano que nunca olvidaré y una promesa de un futuro feliz a tu lado. Con todo mi amor, Eduardo. (To my precious Margarita, a souvenir of a summer that I will never forget and a promise of a happy future together by your side. With all my love, Eduardo.)* Of course, there were also the ticket stubs that I had found that led me to undertake some research on the Moonlight Train and on the existence of the old Walker Theatre. David was able to enlighten me about the once ornate theatre which had become the Odeon Cinema where I used to see movies during my university days and I had read a few articles about the titillating late-evening train ride from Winnipeg Beach to Winnipeg during the first half of the twentieth century. Had my usually prudent grandmother really gone on such a potentially risqué trip with Eduardo?

After my aunt left, I carefully undid the fancy ribbon that held the bundles of letters together, opened the lovely, hand-painted fan that Maria Cristina had given my grandmother so long ago and began reading the beautifully calligraphed letters that had lain dormant for some sixty years. How close the two friends had been despite their differences in culture and background! Through various references in Maria Cristina's letters, I gradually learned about how the two had first met, which places they had visited together, their career aspirations and hopes for the future. I also realized how strong a bond existed between Maria Cristina and her brother Eduardo. However, despite all the information that I gleaned about the friendship between the two women, there were very few details revealed about the nature of the relationship between Eduardo and my grandmother as Maria Cristina's comments were always carefully veiled in neutral language whenever she mentioned her brother. Nevertheless, I reminded myself that the short message that he had written to my grandmother spoke volumes.

As I was reading the last letter from Maria Cristina which referred to her planned trip to Winnipeg in September of 1919, I suddenly stopped. Where were the other letters that must have followed? Why did they end with that warm missive of 1919? And then I saw one more envelope, this one bordered in black, an envelope which I had obviously overlooked when I discovered the letters in my grandmother's attic. With a feeling of foreboding, I opened it and saw that it was signed by Felipe Gomez y Garcia, Maria Cristina's husband, and was dated July 1919. It was a short but very touching letter and I felt my throat constrict as I read it.

Dear Mrs. O'Toole,

It is with a broken heart that I write to you today to share the sad news of Maria Cristina's death last month from the influenza virus that is plaguing the world.

My dear wife was always so worried that I would contract the disease but, in the end, I fear that I gave her the Spanish Flu myself due to my constant contact with patients afflicted with it. The guilt and grief I feel are quite overwhelming as I look at my two, now motherless children: your namesake, little Margarita, who is only four years old and Miguel, just two. Miguel and Margarita will never feel their mother's gentle touch again or hear her sing another soothing lullaby. I am devastated as Maria Cristina was the love of my life, the beautiful constant star that never failed to guide me, and now she is gone forever...

In her final days when she realized that she would not get better, Maria Cristina asked me to write to you as she was too weak to hold a pen and could barely breathe. Her words to you were, "Thank you, my dearest Margarita, for your gift of friendship over the past six years. How you enriched my life with your kindness and joie de vivre! I bid you good-bye, regretting that I was not able to see you again as planned for this September. May we meet again in paradise!"

Felipe Gomez y Garcia

Choking back my tears for this person that I had never known, I felt the pain that my grandmother must have experienced when she read Felipe's sad letter. I was reminded of Alfred, Lord Tennyson's haunting words about a happier past, now forever vanished, as he contemplated the death of his good friend, Arthur Hallam:

But the tender grace of a day that is dead
Will never come back to me.

Observing the tears running freely down my cheeks, David asked me, of course, about the contents of the letters which I had been reading. "I am sorry that you did not discover more about Eduardo but, at least, now you know what ended the warm relationship between your grandmother and Maria Cristina.“

"You are right, David, but it is disappointing after waiting so long for those letters that I am no further ahead in my attempts to learn more about the mysterious Eduardo," I added.

"Just think that he and Maggie enjoyed a special but short-lived love story. Do you not like to quote Tennyson's reflection on lost love: 'Tis better to have loved and lost than never to have loved at all'?"

Three weeks later, I received another call from my aunt Maeve who informed me that, while finally sorting through a large box of old letters and cards that her sister Maureen had given her upon my grandmother's death, she had found another letter from Felipe, postmarked some five years after his first one to my grandmother, as well as a golden wedding anniversary greeting card from "Eduardo and Ariana". "I'm sorry that it took me so long to rummage through that box but I finally opened it and thought that you might wish to see these items, given your interest in this Maria Cristina and her brother from Spain." She promised to send the items to me that very day.

When I opened Felipe's second letter, I was happy to read that, five years after Maria Cristina's death, he had married a hospital colleague of his who was also an epidemiologist working at the same hospital as he was. Lucia had been very kind to him and, more importantly in his estimation, she was very good to his children who instantly warmed to this woman who so wanted to be a mother but whose advancing age made this highly unlikely. The new couple provided Margarita and Miguel with a happy home and constant love. Apparently, Eduardo was a frequent visitor to their residence as he was very attached to the children. Moreover, the family would spend summer holidays at his estate, *Villa Sol y Iris*, in Catalonia where they enjoyed the hilly countryside, fresh air and their excursions to the nearby seaside.

"David, at least, I have learned that Eduardo maintained close ties with Felipe and his children, but I notice that there is no mention of a wife or of his own children at that time. Surely, he would have married by then. Do you think that he actually waited until much later in life to marry Ariana?

And why did the couple send a note to my grandparents on the occasion of their fiftieth wedding anniversary? I doubt that there was any contact between the two couples prior to my grandparents' golden anniversary," I added as I held up the greeting card. "It reads, 'We send you our warmest wishes on the occasion of your golden wedding anniversary. May you have many more happy years together! We hope that you will enjoy this bottle of special Cava named in memory of my dear sister Maria Cristina as you celebrate your milestone anniversary and perhaps toast each other with our traditional Spanish wish: *¡Salud, dinero, amor, y tiempo para gozarlos!* (Health, money, love and time to enjoy them!). Eduardo and Adriana Martínez.' What do you make of that, David?"

"It's rather puzzling to be sure but who knows what motivates people to do certain things, Sophie?"

"The toast to which Eduardo and Ariana refer is the same drinking toast that I learned from Iago in Madrid during my student days there and brings back good memories. Incidentally, did you notice the beautiful name that Eduardo gave to his estate, *Villa Sol y Iris*? That means the House of Sun and Rainbows, a name which certainly hints at happiness. Perhaps Eduardo's marriage to Ariana was his second chance at happiness?"

"Sophie, I never cease to be amazed by your endless optimism!"

"Just think, if Eduardo sent good wishes to my grandparents on the occasion of their fiftieth wedding anniversary, that would have been in 1965, some twelve years ago. As a matter of fact, I remember attending the reception that was organized for them and helping to serve some of the refreshments to the guests who attended it. My grandfather died in 1969 and my grandmother in 1971, six years ago. It is possible that Eduardo is still alive today although he would probably be about ninety years old now. Wouldn't it be wonderful if we could meet him, David?"

"I'm sure that such an opportunity would please you very much but it's unlikely that he's still alive today," my husband replied.

"I suppose that you're right, but it would have been satisfying to discover the end to this love story which has fascinated me for so long," I concluded. "It's almost like the game of snakes and ladders, which I used to play as a little girl. In one move, you make a little progress in solving the mystery but, no sooner are you cheering your success, that you are sliding down once again into uncertainty."

Felipe had included his new address in Seville and added that, if ever Maggie and her husband were to travel to Spain, he and Lucia would be delighted to welcome them to their home. Of course, in her day, my grandmother must have thought that travelling to Seville was equivalent to travelling to the moon and set the letter aside. At that point in her life, she had five children and little extra money to spend on such luxuries as overseas travel. She was proud of her children and their accomplishments and was pleased that my aunt Maeve had followed in her footsteps by training as a nurse and that my father had become a physician. Although Maggie was unable to accompany her husband on his overseas trips, I'm sure that she must have rejoiced with Thomas whose new position not only enabled him to travel to Ireland from time to time on business, selecting new textiles for men's clothing, but also to visit his parents and siblings. How delighted they must have been to see him once again!

After reading Felipe's letter, I suddenly remembered that, when sorting the items in my grandmother's attic, I had decided to take her copy of Mark Twain's travel book, *The Innocents Abroad*, in order to read it later but never had. I located the book in one of the many boxes stacked in our basement and started reading it when I noticed that there was a bookmark placed at the beginning of the section which covered Spain. I examined it, noting that it was not a store-bought item but rather that it had been fashioned using everyday materials found at home. Behind a protective cover of plastic had been placed a dried, preserved red rose and a small card which read, "To the woman who once loved roses, may she also continue to appreciate the many other flowers in the garden of life!"

I knew that I had seen that distinctive handwriting before but where? It finally dawned upon me… Did it not match the handwriting on Eduardo's love note to my grandmother? Curious, I slit the side of the bookmark and discovered that fabric covered the name of the writer and the date of his note: "Eduardo, May 1950." While I was not surprised to learn that Eduardo had written the note, I was very surprised to note that it had been penned more than 35 years after the one that I had found in my grandmother's attic. The note left a great deal unsaid and yet it seemed to hint at the end of a strong, romantic relationship. Had Eduardo really seen Maggie again after so many years? I rushed to the study to inform David of my latest discovery and to ask him what he thought of this second, rather puzzling message that appeared to have been written in such a way as to only be fully understood by its intended recipient. Would I ever really discover what had happened between Eduardo and Maggie?

Chapter 26

Spain, May—June 1979

In May of 1979, David and I flew to Spain once again and enjoyed another very special trip to this fabled country. As I had done before, I continued to keep my parents abreast of our travels by sending them postcards from the various cities that we visited, hoping that they would enjoy reading them as much as I enjoyed writing them. I also prepared drafts of future travel articles which I hoped to have published as a collection entitled "Spain: Sketches of a Sunny, Storied and Seductive Land". Why did I continue to feel such a strong attraction to Spain? Why had my grandmother shared this same interest? There were no answers to my questions but it was always interesting to search for them.

May 28, 1979

Dear Mom and Dad,

We arrived in Cordoba late this afternoon and I thought that I had trespassed on a movie set where a film about a fiesta in Spain was being produced. Everywhere we looked on the way to our hotel, we saw women and girls attired in flamenco dresses, accompanied by men in traditional short suits. The streets were so festive and colourful that I instinctively wanted to clap my hands in unreserved joy!

I was ill the day that we boarded the train from the Algarve to Cordoba but even a high fever could not dampen my enthusiasm for this city of patios and courtyards. Moreover, unbeknown to David and me, we arrived in Cordoba at the time of its Spring Fair, known as "La Feria de Nuestra Señora de la Salud" (The Feast of Our Lady of Health). This fiesta, similar to Seville's famous fair, takes place at the end of May and sparkles with Andalusian flavour. Many of the city's streets are filled with horse-drawn carriages transporting women and girls proudly wearing their flamboyant, flamenco dresses with ruffled skirts and sleeves. Other women ride side-saddle with their handsome caballeros, many of whom doffed their hats as I rushed to take their photographs. Children dressed in miniature outfits resembling those of their parents were everywhere and happy to pose for a photo as well. What a unique experience! Moreover, the excitement of witnessing the feria appeared to have been just the right medicine for me: my fever disappeared and I was soon back to normal as my bemused husband noted.

The next day, David and I visited some of Cordoba's famous attractions including, of course, the Mesquita whose construction began in the eighth century. Its many alternating red and white striped columns have frequently led to its comparison to a vast desert tent. While the cathedral that was built later in the center of the mosque is perceived by some as a rather jarring addition, it is a reflection of the many religions that were practiced in harmony in southern Spain at that time. A millennium ago, Muslims, Christians and Jews lived together in Cordoba, creating a sophisticated city recognized throughout Europe as a leading centre of scholarship, poetry, music, medicine and science. Artisans made delicate jewelry and colourful tiles; scholars discussed astronomy and philosophy; architects built lovely private and public buildings; translators helped to disseminate the knowledge of the time and doctors were even operating on cataracts in the 10th century!

After visiting the Mesquita, we walked through the narrow, winding streets of the Judería (Jewish Quarter) where we purchased a small decorative table with Arabic inscriptions which was inlaid with ivory, onyx and several varieties of wood. To our surprise, upon lifting the ornate lid of the table, we heard the first bars of the song *Granada*, composed by the Mexican Agustín Lara and later popularized by many celebrated singers such as José Carreras and Plácido Domingo. We admired the wooden compartment inside which was divided into little sections for storing jewelry. Quite interestingly, the sections were grouped together to form a Star of David!

That evening, we dined at the *Caballo Rojo* (Red Horse) where the restaurant courtyard, fountains, abundance of flowers and tiled patios created the perfect ambiance for an Andalusian dinner. Walking back to our hotel, we passed by the Alcazar with its impressive illuminated gardens, enhanced by cypress and orange trees which, lovely by day, were truly magical by night. How enchanted we were to listen to the lovely *Noches en los jardines de España* by the Andalusian composer Manuel de Falla, the notes of which seemed to float harmoniously over the old stone walls!

From Cordoba, we travelled to Nerja renowned for its prehistoric stalactite and stalagmite caves stretching almost five kilometres. Dance performances are held regularly in one of the cave's chambers with its natural amphitheater and seating. We enjoyed a classical ballet on our evening there and, later, walked to the Balcón de Europa, a palm-shaded overlook in Nerja with a panoramic view of the Mediterranean.

June 5, 1979

Dear Mom and Dad,

We are now in the lovely city of Granada, which means pomegranate in English. Of course, this adds to its romantic appeal, summoning images of exotic Moorish dishes flavoured not only with this scarlet fruit but also with dates and apricots and pungent with cinnamon, cloves and orange zest. It is here in this magical city that we first heard the famous quote by Francisco de Icaza, a Mexican poet living in Spain who upon seeing a blind beggar, exhorted a passerby to "Give him alms, woman, because there is nothing sadder in life than being blind in Granada."

Water, so rare in the desert where the Moors had lived, is the most unifying element of the Alhambra, both its raison-d'être and its most common decorative feature. Barely rippling in ponds, cascading in waterfalls, trickling or gurgling in fountains, water is both the background and the main focus of all the rooms and gardens of this splendid retreat. It offers coolness in the heat of the summer and gives life to the flowers and vegetation in the surrounding area; it protects intimate conversations from eavesdropping ears; relaxes the spirits of the weary and pleases the eye and ear as it falls soothingly into the basins of tiled fountains. No wonder that the Moors glorified water in their last and greatest palace in Spain. The Alhambra, built mostly in the fourteenth century, provides a view of the refined, elegant civilization developed by the Moors during their close to eight centuries of dominion over Spain. Honeycombed stucco ceilings, ceramic tiles, molded-plaster walls and filigreed windows combine with open courtyards featuring beautiful fountains and lush vegetation to achieve a paradisiacal setting. The Courtyard of the Lions with its famous fountain supported by twelve marble lions spouting water into channels irrigating the gardens, the Grand Hall of the Ambassadors where the sultan received foreign emissaries, the Courtyard of the Myrtles with its reflecting pool lined by myrtle trees are all highlights of the palace. If one looks above while visiting the baths, one can see the balcony where blind musicians used to play as the sultan's naked wives danced before him. Finally, the culmination of the visit is strolling through and admiring the exquisite gardens of the *Generalife* with their lovely roses, fragrant herbs and countless water features.

It is not difficult to imagine the feelings of the last Moorish king Boabdil as he relinquished his palace to the forces of Ferdinand and Isabella on the last wave of the Reconquista tide which swept across the Iberian Peninsula in 1492, that fateful, glorious year for the country. As Boabdil fled the Alhambra, he wept for his loss and his unforgiving mother scornfully rebuked him by saying, "Do not weep like a woman for what you could not defend as a man." In that same year, the Spanish sovereigns received Christopher Columbus in the Alhambra where they offered to endorse his expedition to "India".

Given that Isabella and Ferdinand united the Kingdoms of Aragon and Castile with their marriage and played major roles in the Reconquest of Christian Spain, as well as in the discovery of the New World, David and I were interested in visiting the Royal Chapel where the royal sovereigns are buried. The Chapel, decorated in the lacy silver-filigree style favoured by the Moors, honours the couple with marble tombs bearing their likenesses.

In Granada, home of the great Spanish poet Frederico Garcia Lorca, we also enjoyed the flamenco tradition credited to the (Roma) Gypsies of Sacromonte. Their variation of flamenco is known as *zambra* and is performed by singing dancers. A half-dozen whitewashed caves cut into the rock and used as residences in the picturesque Sacromonte neighbourhood offer *zambra* in the evenings, a popular attraction in Granada. While touristy, it is atmospheric and fun but one must be careful, nevertheless, as quick-fingered thieves are always ready to take advantage of carefree visitors on holidays.

From Granada, David and I travelled to Toledo where we enjoyed lunch at the beautiful parador before taking the overnight train to Tours, France where we planned to visit some of the famous châteaux in that area. A rather amusing anecdote is associated with that trip. Historically, Spain has had a railway system that isolated it from the other countries of Europe, given that it used a broader gauge track than the rest of the continent. Until 2011, no Spanish train could connect with the rest of Europe without disembarking all of its passengers or unloading its freight. Consequently, in 1979 upon arriving at the Spanish-French border at Irun/Hendaye, it was necessary to change trains in order to proceed on one's journey to France. (Today, elaborate gauge-changing facilities allow both freight and passenger trains to travel freely across the Spanish-French border.) However, David, feeling particularly tired the morning of our arrival at the border and enjoying our private compartment on the train, kept insisting that he had enough time to rise, shave and dress before disembarking to catch the train to France waiting on the tracks for our Spanish train's passengers. Without a warning knock on the door by the porter, my pleas to David went unheeded… It was only when I told him that I had just heard an announcement in Spanish saying that our train would be leaving for Madrid in ten minutes that he jumped out of bed in the nick of time and ran, unshaved and in his previous day's clothing, to catch our waiting train for France!

Chapter 27

Villa Sol y Iris, Spain, December 1949

Still striking a dashing figure as he approached sixty, Eduardo Martínez looked out across the vast expanse of vineyards that were part of his estate and smiled in the pale December sunshine. This was the best year yet for the production of his premium sparkling wines. He was very proud of his Cavas which were made in accordance with the "méthode champenoise" which meant that the traditional method of secondary fermentation took place in the bottle as opposed to a large tank ("Charmat" fermentation). The "méthode champenoise" ensured a higher quality wine rich in plentiful, smaller bubbles, resembling its classic French cousin, Champagne, more than its effervescent Italian relative whose secondary fermentation occurred in a tank.

Yes, indeed, *Las Cavas Martínez* had found their own profitable niche and Eduardo was confident that, in Miguel's capable hands, the vineyard would continue to flourish for many years to come. Moreover, with the recent arrival of Miguel's son, the future of the winery appeared promising. Eduardo thanked God for the warm presence of his nephew and wife Teresa and now their infant son Diego who had created a family for him at Villa Sol y Iris.

As he walked among the rows of his vineyard, Eduardo also reflected on another issue which had to be settled soon. Cancer had claimed the life of his wife Victoria nine years earlier, thus ending an unhappy marriage that had stretched across a very long twenty-six years. Since then, he had been actively pursued by many of the eligible women of the area, some of whom were widows and others young, single women looking for a comfortable, prosperous "catch" to sweeten their life. While he had no desire to embark on a second disastrous marriage, for the past two years he had been dating an intelligent, attractive widow who was younger but not too much younger than he was. They were very compatible, sharing many interests and very comfortable with each other. The problem was that Ariana wished to marry and he knew that, if he did not propose soon, he would lose her. She was too diplomatic to issue an ultimatum but the writing was on the wall and he had to take action in the very near future. Ariana had brightened his life after so many dreary years and he was sorely tempted to reach for this second chance at happiness. But why did Maggie's image constantly appear, preventing him from making a definitive decision to marry Ariana whom he loved? After all, Maggie was happily married and he hadn't seen her for over thirty-five years.

There were three letters in Eduardo's hands, all inviting him to travel to Winnipeg next May. The first one was from a hotel association requesting that he present his premium Cavas to their members while the second was from an influential group of business men who were planning a number of prestigious events for the city's elite and had indicated their desire to purchase dozens of cases of his wines for upscale receptions. Both invitations appealed to him and yet... So many years later, why did he hesitate to visit the city that had introduced him to Maggie?

Eduardo's old friend, Pierre, still the Royal Alexandra's trusty concierge, had also written to him with two personal invitations.

Dear Eduardo,

My Christmas letter to you this year will be a little different from the many previous ones I have sent you over the years. I will be retiring next May from my position as concierge and, as I am the Royal

Alexandra's longest-serving employee, hotel management has decided to mark this event in grand style. A dinner and dance will be held in May the weekend after my retirement and I would be so very pleased if you could attend. Also, next May, Françoise and I will be celebrating our forty-fifth wedding anniversary and our children will be holding a special party for family and friends on this occasion. How special it would be for me if you could finally meet my wife and children!

You may be interested to know that Mr. and Mrs. O'Toole have reserved a table in our dining room at the end of this month on the occasion of their son Michael's marriage. After the church ceremony and reception, the bride and groom, as well as their parents and the maid of honour and best man will have dinner here in our venerable hotel.

My warmest holiday wishes to you, Eduardo, and your adopted family at this special time of the year. I look forward with great anticipation to hearing from you soon.

By the time that he reached his residence, Eduardo had made a number of decisions. He would travel to Winnipeg next May and meet with the hotel association members as well as the business leaders. He would also attend Pierre's retirement party at the Royal Alexandra and the private family celebration on the occasion of his and Françoise's forty-fifth wedding anniversary. Finally, and this would be difficult but necessary to seal his decision, he would also attempt to see Maggie and explain to her in person what had happened thirty-five years earlier to change the course of both their lives. Then, barring any new developments, upon his return to Spain, he would propose to Ariana.

Upon entering Villa Sol y Iris, Eduardo felt the warmth of his home envelop him as he stooped to pick up little Diego who ran excitedly into his arms, saw Teresa and Miguel decorating the Christmas tree and breathed in the fragrant aromas emanating from the kitchen. Life was good and he was fortunate to be surrounded by a loving family, as well as by Ariana who would be joining him soon for the holidays. Christmas, his favourite time of the year, was fast approaching and his niece Margarita and her husband Carlos would be arriving in a few more days. What a lovely holiday they would all enjoy together!

Chapter 28

Winnipeg, May 1950

On a warm May evening, Maggie was seated in a comfortable chair on her veranda, engrossed in a book, when she suddenly heard a familiar voice from the past greet her with the words, "Hola Margarita". That voice, accompanied by its lovely Spanish accent, could only belong to one man, a man whom she had not seen for almost four decades. She looked up from her book into the eyes of the man to whom she had given her heart so many years earlier and saw the same kindness and sparkle reflected in them. The years had been extraordinarily kind to him with only his silver hair and a few wrinkles testifying to the passage of time. Why was he standing at her veranda door? "Well, Maggie, aren't you going to invite me in?" he asked teasingly.

Maggie rose from her chair to open the screen door for him, her fingers trembling on the latch. "Why Eduardo, of course, you are welcome to come in. I am just so surprised to see you after such a long time," she said as she fussed with a few wayward strands of hair and pinched her hands to assure herself that she wasn't waking from a very pleasant dream.

"How lovely to see you again! It is so quiet here that I was afraid that I might frighten you upon speaking," Eduardo declared as he reached for Maggie's hand and kissed it gently in the Latin fashion.

"Yes, indeed. Thomas is away on a business trip to the United Kingdom for two weeks; my daughters are currently visiting relatives in Prince Edward Island and my sons are married now and have left home. It is too bad that you have missed them," she added uncertainly, feeling rather confused about the situation.

"While I would have enjoyed meeting them, I had honestly hoped to catch you alone in order to talk to you, Maggie, and to explain in person what happened so many decades ago. Would you be free to join me for dinner tomorrow at the Fort Garry?"

It was an invitation that Maggie could not refuse despite the warning bells that she tried to silence. "Why yes, of course. That would be wonderful."

The next day, Maggie rather guiltily spent many hours primping before her dinner with Eduardo in the magnificent setting of the Provencher Room at the Fort Garry Hotel. While she was excited to see him again, she wondered what Thomas would say if he knew that she was dining out with the handsome man who had been her first love. She quashed that thought, telling herself that it was only a meal with an old friend. Only, of course, Eduardo was an old friend who was going to explain why he hadn't come back to Winnipeg in 1914 to marry her as promised.

They began their meal with the usual questions about family and work and then, after a few glasses of wine, Eduardo proceeded to talk about Victoria. "As I told you in my letter, when I returned to Madrid in 1913 and explained to my parents that I intended to marry you, the daughter of a farmer, they were apoplectic. They were mostly upset that I refused to marry Victoria whose parents had been their closest friends for decades and who had planned the match between the two of us since our birth. Moreover, Victoria insisted that I had proposed to her before leaving for Canada, which was entirely untrue. While she was intelligent and attractive, I felt no special connection with her. Nevertheless, my parents stressed the many links that bound us together, many more than those, apparently, that would ensure a successful marriage with you. Finally, my parents whom I loved very much despite the obstacles that they placed in my path to marital happiness, stated that they would disown me if I did not marry someone of whom they approved. I could live with the financial limitations but I was unable to accept that the ties with my family would be severed permanently. I know it was cowardly but I felt so overwhelmed with only Maria Cristina to support me at her peril that I finally yielded to my parents' wishes. My punishment was a miserable marriage without the children that I so desired and the constant memory that haunted me of the wonderful woman I cast aside. I hope that you can find it in your heart to forgive me. Please remember how much I always loved you."

"Yes, Eduardo, I understand why you acted as you did and I forgive you. Besides, I was given a second chance at happiness with my Thomas who has been such a great husband and father to our children. What about you? What happened to Victoria?"

"She died of cancer in 1940. However, I found my happiness in Maria Cristina's and Felipe's children, Margarita and Miguel, who frequently visited me at the Villa and were the reason behind the name I gave it, *Villa Sol y Iris,* with its happy connotations of sunshine and rainbows. As Victoria did not much care for children, she would frequently travel when they came to visit and I did not object."

"I feel so sorry for you, Eduardo. However, surely you must have met some eligible women after Victoria's death?"

"You are so kind, dearest Margarita, especially after the pain that I caused you. Yes, I have met a number of women and actually am thinking of proposing to a special person when I return to Spain."

Eduardo then told Maggie about Ariana and what a suitable match she was and how much she meant to him.

"You know, Eduardo, what you are saying reminds me of something that my mother told me when I met Thomas after you left. She referred to choices in the garden of life and how I had been attracted to the short-lived but beautiful rose when I was surrounded by many other less flamboyant but hardier flowers. 'Perhaps it is time to appreciate the other blooms in the garden,' she told me. Take a second chance at happiness as I did, Eduardo, and you will not regret it."

As he saw Maggie to her door, Eduardo thanked her for a most enjoyable evening, but especially for her understanding. "How about a picnic tomorrow at Assiniboine Park? I am sure that the hotel will arrange for a basket of delicious food for the two of us."

Maggie accepted the invitation, knowing that it was probably not a wise thing to do and Eduardo gave her a chaste kiss on the cheek before leaving.

The next day, Maggie and Eduardo were enjoying a picnic lunch at Assiniboine Park as they reminisced over their earlier visits there. They then strolled through the lovely gardens and sat on a bench, recalling their time together in Winnipeg, as well as Maria Cristina's tragic death as a result of the Spanish Flu. As she remembered her dear friend, a tear flowed down Maggie's cheek and Eduardo wiped it away with his finger. He then held her tight to console her and when Maggie looked up at him, he pressed his lips against hers in a loving but lingering kiss to which she responded tenderly. She could feel his moist lips kissing the curve of her neck, his warm breath against her cheek and his gentle whispers in her ear. Reveling in the feel of his body against hers and in the smell of his skin, she nevertheless reached a difficult decision. Tearing herself away from Eduardo's arms, she told him, "We cannot do this, Eduardo. You are treading on dangerous territory for I am a happily married woman. Nevertheless, you were my first love and it is so tempting at this very moment to rekindle that fire while you are sitting here, ever so close to me and as handsome as ever. Tempting but wrong."

"You are right, Margarita. The love that we felt for each other was very strong but it is now part of the past despite current temptations. However, please promise me that you will see me once more before I leave. You remember Pierre, the concierge at the Royal Alexandra? Well, on Friday night, the hotel will be hosting a retirement party for him, its longest serving employee, and he has asked me to attend. Would you accompany me one last time to this dinner and dance before I leave for Madrid?"

"I will, Eduardo as I cannot refuse the opportunity to see you one more time, God forgive me. 'The spirit is strong but the flesh is weak.'"

"Thank you, Margarita. Tomorrow, I will attend the reception for Pierre and his wife that their children are hosting for them but Friday will be our special farewell evening to remember," added Eduardo as he kissed Maggie's hand ever so gently.

Maggie and Eduardo were so engrossed in each other that they did not notice another middle-aged couple out for a stroll who remained discreetly out of their sight. "Is that not Maggie with Eduardo?", asked a bewildered Alexander MacTavish.

"Yes, I think that you are right," answered Grace. "After all these years, he still stands out in a crowd," she observed wistfully, remembering a few magic hours on the *Empress of Ireland.* Let's not disturb them or share any premature conclusions about their intentions with anyone."

"No, such talk can only lead to trouble for Maggie and Thomas. We shall keep this to ourselves," he agreed.

On Friday, Maggie, attired in her best dress and wearing the amethyst pendant that Eduardo had given her just before leaving for Spain, entered the ballroom in the Royal Alexandra Hotel on his arm. She was soon talking to Pierre, his wife and children, all of whom had enjoyed a very pleasant forty-fifth wedding anniversary reception the evening before. Pierre enthused, "We were so very happy to have Eduardo with us yesterday. He and I have exchanged news for so many years after the summer of 1913 when he first requested my services to secure theatre tickets, picnic baskets and even cars. How many premium bottles of Cava Françoise and I have drunk, thanks to him!" he laughed.

After cocktails, a special meal was served and then the departing concierge was presented with a gold watch in recognition of his forty years of service at the hotel, as well as a voucher for a weekend's free accommodation for two in one of the hotel's suites with complimentary meals in the hotel's dining venues. Four long-time guests at the hotel over the decades, including Eduardo, all spoke of the excellent service that Pierre had provided over the years. Then the orchestra began to play selections from the past few decades as the lights dimmed and guests proceeded to the dance floor. "Will you dance with me, Margarita?" asked Eduardo and soon the couple was wrapped in each other's arms as they glided across the ballroom. Towards the end of the evening, the orchestra played "Bésame Mucho", an iconic Mexican love song from the 1940s written by Consuelo Velázquez. "Would you like me to translate the words for you as we dance?" asked Eduardo.

"Yes, of course, Eduardo. I would like that," answered his dancing partner.

The deep longing expressed in the song echoed the feelings of the couple as they danced around the ballroom, remembering the magic of their past love and the pain of its loss so many years earlier. At the same time, as they held each other in a tight embrace, Maggie and Eduardo were enveloped in the heat of the moment, responding to the crescendo of emotion unwittingly unleashed by their recent time together. Nevertheless, they were both acutely aware that the final curtain call on their love story was about to drop and that they would soon be separated from each other for the last time.

"Oh, Eduardo, the words are so appropriate but so sad!" whispered Maggie. With Eduardo's warm breath against her cheek, he replied, "They express what I feel. How I want to kiss you and feel you close to me tonight! I want you so much that, if you were to give me the signal, I would carry you away and ravish you as the pirates did to the beautiful young maidens in the tales that I used to read as an adolescent."

"You never change, Eduardo, always the romantic. However, you know that I wouldn't be the screaming, kicking maiden railing against her fate but rather a most willing participant. I want you so much, too, dear Eduardo, but unfortunately it was never meant to be."

After thanking their hosts for the lovely evening, they left the ballroom, walking outside towards Eduardo's rental car, which was parked in a secluded area.

"Please let me kiss you properly, Margarita, before I leave tomorrow." She raised her lips to his and Maggie could feel the heat of his desire as much as her own as he held her close to his chest, pressing down against her lips with increasing passion. Then timidly at first and gradually more boldly, he traced the contours of her body with his exploring hands, further igniting her ardour. Battling between the dictates of her conscience and the increasing demands of her body, Maggie prayed for the strength to resist and suddenly broke away from their embrace. Looking deep into her eyes, Eduardo asked her, "Do you remember that ride on the Moonlight Train from Winnipeg Beach to Winnipeg so many years ago?"

"How could I forget it?"

"Then, come to my room and let's pursue the journey tonight before the train leaves the station one last time."

"While I am sorely tempted, I remember not only my ride with you on the Moonlight Train but also the day I promised to be faithful to my husband for the rest of my life. I fear that I have already broken the spirit of my vows but, at least, I can stop now before going any further. Please, Eduardo, never contact me again if ever you come back to Winnipeg. I love my husband but the temptation with you is too great. Marry Ariana upon your return to Spain and be as happy with her as I am with Thomas! It is what I wish for you with all my heart."

"Alas for me, you are a wonderful and principled woman, Margarita querida. I was a fool not to have come back for you in 1914 as planned. Thank you for the special moments you have given me this past week but it is time now to take you home and say farewell, my dearest one."

The next day, Pierre picked up Eduardo as planned to drive him to the airport. "It was you, Pierre, who suggested that the orchestra play "Bésame Mucho" yesterday, wasn't it?"

"Yes, it was, I must admit. Did the song lead to a resolution of your feelings for Margarita?"

"A gentleman never tells, Pierre, but in a way it did. While Maggie and I enjoyed a very special evening together, we also finally had the opportunity to say our goodbyes in person without betraying anyone. Moreover, upon further reflection, I have decided to propose to Ariana when I return to Spain."

"I am pleased to hear it. Speaking as a happily married man, Eduardo, I am delighted that a good marriage will not be jeopardized and that you will finally find the happiness that you deserve."

Later, that day, a week before Thomas's return from Europe, Maggie received a magnificent bouquet of nine red roses encircling three white ones placed in the centre. Was this a symbolic reminder of purity battling against the forces of passion? The short message accompanying the bouquet read, "To the woman who once loved roses, may she also continue to appreciate the many other lovely flowers in the garden of life. Eduardo. May 1950."

Chapter 29

WINNIPEG, JUNE-AUGUST 1965

Maggie and Thomas were enjoying a cup of tea on their veranda on a warm Manitoba summer evening which refused to yield its fading light to the stars until almost the final hour of the day. The carefully tended purple irises, pink peonies and bright yellow marigolds fronting the veranda were the envy of the neighbourhood and the couple was relaxing after a long day's work in their large vegetable garden. They were talking animatedly about the upcoming reception which their children were planning for them on the occasion of their fiftieth wedding anniversary. "How lovely it will be to see all of our children together again for this happy celebration! Deirdre and Christopher will be flying down from Charlottetown to join Maureen, Michael and Maeve who are working so hard to make this a very special event for us. Moreover, my siblings and cousins, as well as many of our friends will also be attending the reception. Would you mind, Thomas, if I invited Grace and Alexander MacTavish to join us?"

"Of course not, my dear. Even my brother Patrick and Colleen have indicated that they will be attending, as well as my old friends Declan and Timothy and Emily Flanagan. It will be a most memorable occasion. However, after our celebration, I am planning something else that you will enjoy very much, Maggie. Ever since we met, I have noticed the special place that Spain holds in your heart and how your eyes sparkle whenever you hear about the country on the radio or read a travel article about it or even a recipe book extolling its dishes. Consequently, I am planning to take you to Spain so that you can finally realize your wish to visit the land that seems to fascinate you so much."

Maggie looked at her dear husband so earnest in his wish to please her and was crestfallen as she listened to him speak. She had no idea that she had been so transparent about her interest in Spain and its culture and Thomas's generous offer to travel to that country on their limited savings instead of to his beloved Ireland touched her deeply. She knew how he wished to return to the country of his birth which he had not seen since his retirement ten years earlier. As her husband's confusion about her reaction to his generous plans became evident, Maggie spoke confidently, "Actually, Thomas, while it is true that I was once fascinated by Spain, over the past decade I have started dreaming of visiting Ireland and all the places there that you have described to me over the years. I have Irish blood too and feel the country beckoning to me. Why not travel to Ireland now before it's too late? We could walk together by the Cliffs of Moher and through the streets of Galway where you were born and I could finally meet all of your family."

"How I would love to return to Ireland with you and introduce you to my two sisters and three brothers who are still living there with their spouses! Perhaps I could even persuade Patrick and Colleen to join us there rather than in Winnipeg for a real family reunion… Oh, the prospect brings tears to my eyes," admitted Thomas. "Are you sure that you really want this, Maggie?"

"I have never been surer of anything in my life, sweetheart."

"Then, I will be off to the travel agent tomorrow to begin planning our trip."

"And let's make it an extended one: at least four to six weeks to see everyone properly as well as to have time for our own wanderings by the sea and across the lush, green countryside," added Maggie.

As Maggie and Thomas were talking, a car rolled up before their house and a couple that was about their age started walking towards their veranda. "Who could that be?" wondered Thomas, aloud.

"Of course, he is a lot older now but he looks like the former concierge at the Royal Alexandra Hotel. Why is he here?" asked a puzzled Maggie.

"Remember me, Mrs. O'Toole? I am Pierre Lajeunesse and this is my wife Françoise. I met you many years ago at the Royal Alexandra Hotel when you were close friends with Miss Martínez and her brother and, years later, at your son's wedding supper. We are here to drop off a gift if we may." Maggie's eyes pleaded with him not to mention the last time she had seen him, which was at his retirement party, a very memorable event which she had attended with Eduardo during Thomas's trip to Europe.

"I am pleased to see you again. Would you like to come in? Do you remember my husband, Thomas O'Toole?"

When they were comfortably seated in the veranda, Maggie offered them tea and a slice of her famous "wacky" cake, which they accepted.

"I am sure that you are wondering why we are here," Pierre stated as he began to describe how he had continued to correspond with Eduardo Martínez once he left Winnipeg after escorting his sister there. "As a matter of fact, Eduardo invited my wife and me to spend a week with him and his wife Ariana just recently as part of our travels this year to mark our diamond wedding anniversary. We had a lovely time with them before leaving for France where we spent a month with our relatives."

While Pierre and Françoise proceeded to describe their trip to France, Maggie was thinking about the reference to Ariana as Eduardo's wife. So, he had finally decided to marry her! She was pleased to learn about this development and hoped that his marriage was as happy as her own.

Maggie's attention focused sharply on Pierre's account of his and his wife's travels when he mentioned *Villa Sol y Iris* where Eduardo and Ariana lived, along with his nephew Miguel, his wife Teresa and their son Diego. Pierre smiled at Maggie and continued his story, "Eduardo and Ariana married 15 years ago and theirs is a joyous union with a strong emphasis on family life. Moreover, the company that he founded many years ago, *Las Cavas Martínez*, has been incredibly successful both domestically and internationally. Now, I'll finally get to the point! Two years ago, Eduardo produced a premium Cava called *Maria Cristina* on the occasion of what would have been his beloved sister's 70th birthday and he asked me to give you a bottle of it and this card to mark your golden wedding anniversary. He thought, Maggie, that you might wish to drink it in remembrance of your good friend Maria Cristina, as well as in celebration of your milestone anniversary."

After their guests had left, Thomas picked up the card addressed to him and Maggie and handed it to her. Maggie read the card to her husband, carefully trying to keep any strong emotion from her voice:

> "*We send you our warmest wishes on the occasion of your golden wedding anniversary. May you have many more happy years together! We hope that you will enjoy this bottle of special Cava named in memory of my dear sister Maria Cristina as you celebrate your anniversary and perhaps toast each other with this traditional Spanish wish*: ¡Salud, dinero, amor y tiempo para gozarlos! *Eduardo and Adriana Martínez.*"

"What a lovely message, Maggie, from Mr. Martínez! And how thoughtful of him and his wife to send us a bottle of his premium Cava on the occasion of our anniversary. Mr. Martínez must have a very good memory to recall the date of our golden wedding anniversary, which he would only have known through his sister way back in 1915."

"Yes, indeed, Thomas, but for now I wish to concentrate on the special man who will accompany me to Ireland," declared Maggie as she and Thomas went for a long, moonlit walk, hand in hand, before retiring.

In early August, Maggie and Thomas were busy greeting their guests at the reception planned by their children. How happy they were to be surrounded by all their family and friends amid the excited cries of their younger grandchildren who were running through the house and yard in an explosion of youthful energy! Maggie spotted Grace MacTavish among the guests and made her way to speak to her. It had been years since they had seen each other. After chatting animatedly about their travel plans and grandchildren, Grace's demeanor became more serious as she told Maggie about the time some fifteen years earlier when she and her husband had seen her at Assiniboine Park with Eduardo. "Obviously, we didn't mention this to anyone but we were worried that this signaled trouble for you and Thomas. Please assure me that all is well between the two of you."

"Set aside your concerns, Grace. Thomas and I are very happy together as are Eduardo and his wife Ariana. The time that you saw him and me together at Assiniboine Park occurred during his last business trip to Winnipeg in 1950. We were speaking of old times and, when he spoke of Maria Cristina, the remembrance of our good friendship brought tears to my eyes. You may have seen Eduardo consoling me at that moment but that was all."

"Thank you for confiding in me, Maggie. I am so relieved to know that all is well. Ah, here is Alexander who wishes to offer you his congratulations. After your trip to Ireland, we will invite you and Thomas over for dinner and catch up on our news."

After speaking to Alexander MacTavish, Maggie turned to her teenaged grand-daughter who was taking a short break from her hosting duties at the reception. "Sophie, how do you find your courses? Any travel scheduled for this summer? What are your plans for the future?"

Sophie began to tell her grandmother about her high school experiences, her history and literature courses and a possible school trip to Prince Edward Island during the summer. She added, "One day, I hope to travel to Spain, a country that has attracted me for so long. In the meantime, I'm glad that you and Grandpa will soon be travelling to Ireland, which I also hope to visit eventually. Perhaps I will be a travel writer or a doctor? I'm torn between a career in medicine and one involving writing, changing my plans from month to month. Did you always know that you wanted to be a nurse, Grandma?"

"Yes, it was the only career to which I ever aspired although I, too, hoped to travel around the world and become familiar with different cultures. Not all our dreams can be realized but many of them can if we are really motivated to realize them. I wish you much success in life, Sophie. When your grandfather and I return from Ireland, I'll plan a little outing just for the two of us and I will tell you all about our trip."

"I look forward to that," confirmed Sophie as she returned to her duties at the reception.

A week later, on the eve of their departure for Ireland, Maggie and Thomas were savouring their premium Cava from Spain as they toasted Maria Cristina, the success of their trip and their continued happiness as a couple. "Marrying you, Maggie, was the best decision that I ever made," declared her contented husband.

"Thank you, Thomas, for fifty beautiful and happy years. Marrying you was also the best decision that I ever made."

"I am so looking forward to seeing my family again and to introducing you to them all. Even Patrick and Colleen will fly to Ireland to join the family reunion. I am definitely the lucky Irishman who found a pot of gold at the end of the rainbow when I first set eyes upon you five decades ago," Thomas added before kissing Maggie and tasting the last drop of Cava on her lips.

Two months later, as promised, Maggie invited Sophie to join her for lunch at The Bay's iconic Paddlewheel Restaurant. Opened in 1954, the restaurant sported a riverboat décor that was a reminder of the role the Hudson's Bay Company played in the river trade of the 1870s. The sign heralding the "Red River Steamship Company" encouraged patrons not only to enjoy the restaurant but also the fanciful illusion of strolling on a Mississippi paddlewheel deck with painted steam clouds floating on the ceiling. The vast cafeteria was surrounded by faux facades of southern buildings and boasted an enormous mural depicting a wide, meandering river. Sophie remembered earlier visits there with her parents when she threw coins into the water surrounding the paddlewheel and made a wish, one of which was to travel to Spain. However, today, she was listening to her grandmother's moving account of her trip to Ireland.

"Grandma, what a lovely ring!" exclaimed Sophie who was most impressed with her grandmother's new acquisition, which featured an emerald heart clasped by two hands, above which sat a crown.

"Your grandfather bought this ring for me in Ireland as a gift to mark our fiftieth wedding anniversary. It is known as a Claddagh Ring and the heart represents love, the hands friendship and the crown loyalty. The design of the ring actually originated in the Irish fishing village of the same name in County Galway close to where your grandfather was born. While Claddagh Rings are traditionally given for engagements and weddings, my sweetheart told me that mine highlights the fifty years of happiness that he has shared with me since our wedding."

"How very romantic, Grandma! And what did you visit while you were in Ireland?"

"It was a very special trip that allowed us to see the staggering majesty of the Cliffs of Moher, the wild beauty of the Aran Islands, the very green and tranquil Killarney Region where we explored lovely lakes by jaunting car and, of course, the seaport of Galway with its traditional Irish music and dances. I met your grandfather's siblings and cousins and had the opportunity to enjoy many harp concerts. Let me show you some photos of our trip."

As Sophie looked at the photos with her grandmother, she was struck by the happiness that she radiated. "You seem so content, Grandma."

"I am, indeed, Sophie," was her simple reply.

Chapter 30

Villa Sol y Iris, Spain, fall 1965

Eduardo and Ariana were sipping a cup of coffee in the courtyard of their villa, reviewing the wonderful year that they had just enjoyed together. It had begun in February with an extended cruise through South America after spending a week in Rio de Janeiro where they were immersed in the steamy atmosphere of Copacabana Beach and the lavish spectacle of the Rio Carnival. Even now, they found it difficult to believe that they had witnessed the world's longest parade, consisting of thousands of artists attired in the most extravagant of costumes, dancing on magical floats that challenged the imagination. "Ariana, do you remember how enchanted you were at the sight of dozens of women parading as birthday cakes in their frothy white gowns stretched over wide layers of crinolines and wearing a crown of candles on their head?"

"Not as much as you, darling Eduardo, admiring the floats featuring huge mechanical whales disgorging twenty or so scantily clad attractive women covered in feathers!" laughed Ariana. She added, "Cruising down the legendary Amazon, home to parrots, toucans and crocodiles was also interesting but not as wonderful as attending *La Traviata* in Manaus's famous pink *Teatro Amazonas.* It is amazing that such a structure could have been constructed some seventy years ago in the heart of the Amazon jungle, the product of the era of rubber barons who dreamt of building a vibrant European city in the middle of the rainforest."

After Brazil, Eduardo and Ariana had enjoyed the sights of Buenos Aires including its emblematic *Casa Rosada* and magnificent *Teatro Colón.* Hand in hand, they had strolled through *La Boca* District with its brightly painted houses and tango street dancers and then savoured a romantic dinner at the legendary Café Tortoni, still cloaked in its iconic *fin de siècle* décor. "Wasn't that a special evening!", reminisced Ariana, to which her husband gallantly replied, "Every evening with you is special, my dear."

After visiting Ushuaia, the world's southernmost city, Eduardo and Ariana attempted to count the many penguins they spotted among the fjords and glaciers surrounding Cape Horn before concluding their cruise in Valparaiso with its colourful, cliff-hugging houses and narrow, winding streets. They then made their way to Santiago with its striking Spanish colonial buildings and, of course, to the many vineyards near the Chilean capital where they tasted the wines and compared them to their own.

Upon their return to Spain in April, Eduardo and Ariana had been pleased to welcome Eduardo's old friend Pierre, the former concierge at the Royal Alexandra Hotel, and his wife Françoise who had finally accepted their invitation to visit Villa Sol y Iris on the occasion of their sixtieth wedding anniversary. What a delightful week they had spent with them, explaining the intricacies of their Cava operation, as well as touring a number of local areas together! Pierre was delighted to meet Ariana and told Eduardo that he was very happy to note how well things had worked out for him.

The summer brought its usual family visitors including Felipe and Lucia who were always happy to spend time with Miguel and Margarita and their children at Villa Sol y Iris. "Isn't it special, Ariana, to spend the summer months with all the family, watching them getting to know each other as they frolic in the pool, run around the vineyard playing hide and seek and enjoy day excursions to the ocean?" asked Eduardo. "I always look forward to July and August and to spending time with your grandchildren who get along so well with my own great nephews and nieces."

"It's wonderful the way that you play with them, hoisting them on your shoulders, swimming with them, telling them stories and listening to the older ones describe their hopes and worries," observed Ariana. "I have been very fortunate to inherit your family members who have accepted me so whole-heartedly."

"And the same applies to me," confirmed Eduardo who was always eager to enjoy the rituals of summer when he could spend special moments with his niece Margarita as she and her husband Carlos helped Miguel and his wife Teresa with the various operations of the vineyard. Eduardo also took pride in noting how Diego, Miguel and Teresa's young son, constantly questioned his father and him about the vineyard and how to improve yields and spot potential problems. Diego had even mentioned his interest in taking a course in viticulture to acquire additional knowledge of the family business.

Now, autumn was bidding a proud farewell to the dying summer by offering its spectators a cornucopia of mellow delights: the abundance of the vines with their plump grapes basking in the still warm rays of the maturing sun, the aromas of ripe fruit and fragrant flowers, the crimson and gold sunsets setting the horizon on fire. The last of their visitors had just departed after a long weekend of celebrations marking Eduardo and Ariana's fifteenth wedding anniversary. They had been so grateful to welcome the friends and family who had gathered at the Villa once again to wish them well. Although advancing in years, Felipe and Lucia were also there, another couple that had been given a second chance at happiness and who were very proud of their children Margarita and Miguel. Eduardo nursed a soft spot for Miguel who shared his passion for viticulture and who had accepted his uncle's offer to become a business partner and to live at the Villa with his family.

After one of the most successful years yet for *Las Cavas Martínez*, Eduardo had been delighted to present a vintage sparkling wine to Ariana at the family celebration held at Villa Sol y Iris. He proudly raised a bottle of the Cava, describing its specific traits to those who had gathered with them. "*Ariana* is characterized by its crisp apple notes with a lingering trace of zesty lemon; its fine bubbles and lively acidity are suggestive of an aristocratic wine. I have named it in honour of my wife, Ariana, who has brought such happiness into my life. Thank you for fifteen wonderful years together." Eduardo then opened the first bottle of the vintage and poured a glass for his wife and himself. Raising their glasses to each other, they took a sip of the sparkling wine and then indulged in a long kiss, much to the delight of their audience.

In another two months, they would begin preparations for Christmas, another welcome holiday in the cycle of the year and an integral part of the rhythm of their lives. Already, Eduardo could anticipate the delights of Christmas: the glitter and lights of the trees, the sound of carols and joyous music, the aromas from the kitchen which would tease his palate, the taste of special treats reserved especially for that time of the year and the warm embraces of friends and relatives gathering together. What a fortunate man he was! He raised his eyes to the heavens and thanked God for the special graces He had bestowed upon him in the autumn of his life. He smiled to himself as he reflected that, on such golden days, he truly felt that he was reliving the summer of his life, rather than approaching its winter.

Chapter 31

Toronto, November 1979—January 1980

David is now into his fifth year of university teaching and is enjoying his work very much. He is currently developing a new history course dealing with the challenges of the first half of the twentieth century in Canada such as the Winnipeg General Strike in 1919, typhoid and polio epidemics as well as the Spanish Flu, the Prohibition, the Dust Bowl on the Prairies, the Great Depression, etc.

"Sophie, did you see the envelope that was delivered here earlier today and addressed to you? It might be that contract that you were hoping to receive." I rushed to open the envelope and was elated to find a contract for several articles that I had proposed to write for a prestigious travel magazine. That would certainly keep me busy, especially with my weekly book critiques for the local paper and a magazine article that I was preparing on the history of the Spanish Flu for a medical journal. One day, when I had the time, I promised myself I would write the novel that had gradually taken root in my mind ever since my university days.

"David, do you know why the 1918 influenza pandemic was called the Spanish Flu?" He replied, "It seems that King Alfonso XIII was one of the first Spaniards to contract the illness and he passed it on to the country's

Prime Minister and several members of the government. This created a false impression that Spain was especially hard hit by the flu, giving rise to the name by which the pandemic is commonly known, the Spanish Flu. Also, during World War I, Spain was a neutral country and its newspapers had more freedom to write about the flu as it started to move across Europe. Most of the other countries at war did not allow their newspapers to report on the influenza outbreak, fearing it might lower morale among the troops."

"Excellent reply," I answered laughingly, having just completed some research on the topic.

"David, to change the subject to something more optimistic, I have been rereading Felipe's last letter lately and was wondering if you thought that Maria Cristina's daughter, Margarita, would find it odd if I wrote to her? I don't know if she still lives at Felipe's old address but I'm willing to give it a try. Perhaps she inherited the house in Seville from her father?"

"Why not? You've been fascinated by this Martínez family for so long that it's worth a try if it really means that much to you."

Accordingly, I wrote a long letter to Margarita in Spanish explaining who I was and why I was writing. I checked the address once more and mailed my letter, hoping that she would write back to me if she were still alive and living in Seville.

Like a young child waiting for a birthday package or a lovelorn teenager hoping to receive a letter from her sweetheart, I faithfully checked the mailbox daily for a reply to my letter to Margarita. At last, on a frigid January day, a letter from Seville arrived and I eagerly rushed home to read it.

It appeared that Margarita had indeed received my letter at her father's old address in Seville where she and her family were currently living. After telling me what a surprise and delight it was to hear from me, she provided a summary of her family's activities. As her mother, Maria Cristina, had predicted, Margarita had become a nurse and had only recently retired. Her two children, Carolina and Rafael, were also living in Seville and Margarita and her husband Carlos saw them regularly. Carolina was married and was expecting her first child while her younger brother was still living at the family home.

Margarita's father, Felipe, had died several years earlier after a happy second marriage to his colleague Lucia with whom he had shared many interests. Margarita's brother Miguel, who shared his uncle's passion for winemaking, was managing *Las Cavas Martínez,* given that Eduardo and his first wife Victoria had never had any children to inherit the family business. Miguel and his wife, along with their son Diego, lived with Eduardo on the family estate. Eduardo was alive and in good health at 89 years young!

Margarita wrote that she had called her uncle to tell him about my letter and she had been surprised to note the intensity of his reaction to hearing about his and Maria Cristina's Canadian friend's granddaughter. He asked many questions and told his niece that he wished that an invitation be extended to my husband and me to attend his ninetieth birthday celebration in May.

"David, can you believe that Eduardo is still alive and has invited us to attend his 90th birthday celebration in Spain!" I cried out as I raced to my husband's study.

"That's wonderful, Sophie. Haven't you purchased our plane tickets yet?" he teased me as I stood excitedly before his desk.

"Do you really want to attend this event?" I asked.

"Sophie, how can I deny you the pleasure of finally meeting this Eduardo and his family who have captured your imagination for so long? Moreover, his birthday will coincide with our fourth wedding anniversary and what better place to celebrate it than in the land of Cava!"

"How I love you, David! I'll call the travel agency immediately to check on tickets to Barcelona."

Chapter 32

VILLA SOL Y IRIS, DECEMBER 1970

This would be his fourth Christmas without Ariana since a tragic car accident had claimed her life. Throughout his deepest moments of grief, Eduardo had always been comforted by his extended family and, as this Christmas approached, he began to smile as he reflected on all the special holiday celebrations that were coming to life once again. From his study, he could smell the wonderful fragrances emanating from the kitchen where Teresa and her daughter-in-law Alicia were preparing their usual Christmas treats. Diego, Miguel and Alicia's son, was just back from university where he was studying viticulture and had spent the afternoon touring the vineyards with his father. When the door to the residence opened with a clatter, Alicia called out to Diego, asking him to bring the large crèche and heavy figurines down from the attic to the living room for their annual appearance. Soon, in accordance with the established Christmas tradition at Villa Sol y Iris, it would be Eduardo's turn to place the Holy Family, the Three Wise Men, the angels and the shepherds in their appropriate places by the hearth as the family listened to Christmas carols.

Eduardo picked up his Christmas mail from his desk and decided that he had just enough time to reread the good wishes from family and friends whose letters and cards from far away had reached him that day. He reserved the letter from his old friend Pierre for last.

December 1, 1970

My dear friend Eduardo,

I do hope that his letter finds you happy and in good health. I am always amazed to read about the activities of your family and the strong links that bind you together so comfortably. I know how proud you are of your great-nephew Diego and I can understand why: not only does he share your interest in winemaking but you appear to be kindred spirits.

While on the topic of wine, I thought that you would be interested to learn that, in my old age, I am taking sommelier courses. (Your many bottles of Cava over the years may be partially responsible for this decision.) I was pleased to read that you, too, are taking courses but I wonder what motivated you to study Irish culture and literature… Could an old Irish flame in Winnipeg have inspired you?

You may not know that Mr. Thomas O'Toole died in January of this year after a lengthy illness. I read his obituary in the paper and have enclosed it should you wish to read it.

The iconic Royal Alex Hotel will be razed in 1971 after years of neglect. While it did reopen briefly this year after closing in 1967 and there was talk of converting it into a residence for the elderly, a final decision has now been made to demolish it. The hotel could not survive due to its poor location in Winnipeg. How sad for those of us who loved her and knew her so well! However, should you ever wish to travel to Winnipeg, Françoise and I would be more than pleased to welcome you to our home. You supply the Cava; I will provide the critique (Just kidding, of course.)!

Once again, Françoise and I take this opportunity to wish you health, happiness and continued success with Las Cavas Martínez. *May the dark skies which loomed over you during the past few years be replaced by ever increasing sunshine!*

With great affection,
Pierre

An idea began to take root in Eduardo's mind by the time that he had finished rereading Pierre's letter but he could hear Teresa calling out to him and reminding him that it was time to take care of the Christmas crèche. He would have to wait until the holidays were over and all their many visitors had left before taking any action …

Chapter 33

SPAIN, MAY-JUNE 1980

How wonderful it is to be back in Spain! I have to pinch myself to believe that I am actually here once again with David and that we will have two weeks to ourselves here in Catalonia, including one very special trip to the Martínez Winery where we will meet Eduardo, Margarita and other members of the family. Eduardo has actually invited us to spend the weekend on his estate after the birthday celebrations on Friday as he apparently wishes to have the opportunity to talk to us at greater length.

We boarded the plane to Madrid and then flew to Palma de Mallorca. Once there, I took the time to bask in the bright sunshine as I penned a letter to my parents about the island's many attractions. At the same time, I also made notes for the travel article that I was contracted to submit a few days after our return to Ottawa.

May 22, 1980

Dear Mom and Dad,

How delightful it is to be spending a few days on the lovely island of Mallorca! Yesterday, we strolled by the Cathedral with its altar canopy by Gaudí and admired the building's enviable location by the sea, as well as the adjoining Palace of Almudaina where members of the Spanish Royal Family spend their holidays.

David and I did take the time to relax on the golden sand beaches of El Arenal. We also climbed the hill to Castell de Bellver, *a round hilltop castle which was the summer palace for royalty during the brief period that Mallorca had its own sovereigns. What a spectacular panorama we enjoyed from this location!*

After walking down the old cobblestone streets of Palma, we decided to travel to some of the other towns and villages on the island. Our first stop was the Pearl Factory in Manacor where we admired the Majorica pearls fashioned into a variety of jewelry items. While not a true "natural" pearl, the Majorica pearl does nevertheless display the iridescence of its purebred cousins, thanks to the processing of an extract obtained from natural organic elements found in the Mediterranean Sea.

Leaving the Pearl Factory, we headed for the Cuevas del Drach *(Caves of the Dragon) in the town of Porto Cristo. These caves are most impressive, given that they are covered with stalactites and stalagmites and their walls are coloured by the minerals leaching through them. The most unique feature of the caves, however, is the presence of lakes. Concerts are given on Lake Martel, reputed to be the largest underground lake in the world. When we were there, four musicians performed as their boat travelled across the lake.*

Before flying to Barcelona for a few days, I stopped at a local market to admire a display of dolls wearing the traditional costume of a Majorcan woman, a warm outfit with a richly adorned velvet skirt and cape and a black bodice trimmed with embroidery. When I asked the elderly woman who was selling the dolls why the outfits worn on the island were so heavy, given the mild temperature on Mallorca, she replied that they represented the fancy folk costume worn during the winter for special events or at church. She commented on the irony of selling, in her old age, the very same costume that she had disliked so much as a child. When, after purchasing one of her dolls, I wished her well, she smiled and used the grand yet simple traditional Spanish farewell, "¡Y vaya con Dios!*" (May God be with you!).*

After our stay in Palma, we will fly to Barcelona and travel to the Martínez Winery where we will finally meet Eduardo, his niece Margarita and nephew Miguel at Eduardo's ninetieth birthday celebration. What a special weekend this will be!

May 29, 1980

David and I are enjoying our short stay in Barcelona: with its broad avenues and Art Deco architecture, it is reminiscent of Paris but with palm trees! On our first night here, we celebrated our fourth wedding anniversary in a lovely restaurant where the food was delicious and the service most attentive: they even placed a cushion under my feet so that they would reach the floor!

We began our visit of Barcelona with a long stroll along las Ramblas, the extensive pedestrian promenade that is such a delight for tourists and residents alike. It begins at the sea with the statue of Christopher Columbus and ends at Plaza de Catalonia with its lovely fountains. Along the way, there is a plethora of goods for sale from magazines at newsstands, to a variety of flowers and local paintings, to chirping birds imprisoned in cages. The St. Joseph *La Boqueria* is one of the most striking markets in the world. This temple to Ceres features a rich and vast array of foodstuffs from fish of all description; meat including, of course, a striking number of *ibérico* and *serrano* hams suspended from the ceiling; exotic fruits ranging from pomegranates and persimmons to quince; vegetables such as artichokes, assorted mushrooms and multicoloured peppers and a multitude of spices such as golden-red saffron threads, orange turmeric and fragrant cinnamon and, of course, the ubiquitous black and green olives associated with Mediterranean countries.

After satisfying our epicurean interests, David and I decided to contemplate the wonders of the soul and spirit by visiting the old, narrow Gothic Quarter of the city, the birthplace of the community first settled by the Romans and then further developed by Christians and Jews who designed medieval streets with hidden courtyards. We stopped for a few moments of reflection at the magnificent Cathedral of Barcelona, an example of Catalan Gothic architecture. Gargoyles and spires and a cloister embellished with magnolia and palm trees all add to the Cathedral's interest and, if one is fortunate enough to be there on a weekend, folk dancers may suddenly appear on the cathedral steps to dance the traditional Catalan *sardana*.

We toured the "Poble Espanyol", a Spanish theme park which features the architecture of the various regions of Spain. The many buildings which the park contains were originally built for Spain's 1929 International Exhibition but, like the Eiffel Tower in Paris constructed for the 1889 World Fair, proved to be so popular that they have been maintained for the pleasure of Barcelona's citizens and many visitors. Today, one can visit Seville in miniature, buy a fan in Cordoba and enjoy a churro in Madrid, all within this theme park which features a little of each major region in Spain.

David and I decided to visit the mountainside monastery of Montserrat on our way to the Martínez estate. It would prove to be a memorable trip in more ways than one as I describe in another letter to my parents...

June 1, 1980

Dear Mom and Dad,

Another frightening ride through the mountains of Spain! Shadows of our trip to Ronda four years ago haunted us as we rode by taxi to visit Montserrat in its beautiful mountain setting. Our driver, while sober and friendly, had the disconcerting habit of turning his head away from the busy highway to engage in long conversations with me in Spanish!

It is difficult to describe the striking beauty of Montserrat with its rich jewel hues of emerald, amethyst and topaz dusting the mountains against the cerulean blue of the sky which forms a magnificent backdrop to the monastery. The enameled altar contains the small wooden statue of the Black Virgin of Montserrat who is the patroness of Catalonia. As many miracles are attributed to the statue, the curious and the faithful come to the Benedictine Monastery to walk past the Virgin and kiss her outstretched hand. We were fortunate enough to hear the Escolania Choir, *a renowned boys' choir dating back to the fourteenth century as it interpreted religious choral music.*

After visiting Montserrat, we took a taxi to the Martínez Estate where we were warmly welcomed by Margarita, Maria Cristina's daughter, who showed us to our suite decorated in traditional Spanish style. It would take too long to describe our memorable weekend there on paper but I will give you a call upon our return to Toronto and tell you all about it.

Much love from Sophie

The heavy wooden doors studded with tiny medallions of steel bearing images of wine bottles opened slowly on their silent hinges in response to our intercom message, allowing our driver to take the long, palm-shaded drive to the residence. A canopy of trees near the entrance to the main office building provided welcome shade on the hot day. As far as the eye could see, tidy rows of vines grew on flat ground while other vines further away sloped down the hills, reminding us that we were on a prosperous wine estate. As we approached the residence, we admired the magnificent floral arch of purple bougainvillea framing the entrance and enjoyed the cooling sound of water as it cascaded from the large fountain dedicated to Bacchus. At the door stood a tall woman in her late sixties, coiffed and dressed impeccably. As we alighted from the car, she walked towards us and held out her arms to embrace us. "Sofía and David, how wonderful to finally meet you! I'll take you to your suite where you can relax for an hour before the celebration begins in the courtyard behind us. If you need anything, just call for it from your room. Jósé will take your bags up for you. I look forward to talking to you at greater length later today."

Our suite was spectacular as was the view of the vineyards from our bedroom window. After showering and changing, we made our way to the courtyard where a large group of people had assembled. We were shown to our places in the second row and waited for the activities to start.

Miguel Gomez y Martínez, Felipe and Maria Cristina's son, and Margarita, their daughter, were the first ones to address the group and enthusiastically welcome all those who had gathered to pay tribute to Eduardo on the occasion of his ninetieth birthday. Next on the podium was Diego, Miguel's son, who like his father and great-uncle, was instrumental to the success of *Las Cavas Martínez.* Diego then introduced Eduardo and asked him to speak. I expected to see a small wizened man holding on to a cane but was surprised to watch a tall, lithe gentleman with a silver mane of hair climb the few steps to the podium. Dressed in a cream-coloured summer suit with a light blue shirt and a tie that reflected the vineyard's trademark colours of azure and gold, the confident and proud owner of *Las Cavas Martínez* made his way to the microphone without assistance. In a strong voice belying his age, he addressed his relatives, friends, acquaintances and competitors.

"Well, I've made it to ninety and am proud of my age and of the longevity of this vineyard which I inherited close to sixty-five years ago from my uncle José Luis Martínez," he asserted boldly. My father's older brother had hoped to keep the vineyard in the family but neither his own children nor his siblings expressed any interest in it. He travelled to Madrid in one last bid to save it and asked me if I would like to take over the vineyard. I don't think that he believed me when I first agreed but I jumped at the opportunity and the vineyard became Victoria's and my wedding present from my parents who purchased it from José. My experience as a wine merchant would serve me well but my passion for the work was one my uncle recognized as I had spent many summers on this estate helping him, returning in the fall for the grape harvest. My wife Victoria was less enthusiastic about leaving life in Madrid but I eventually convinced her that she would find the vineyard rewarding. While she never loved it the way I did, she did work hard along with me and the vineyard became a success.

"My biggest regret was that Victoria and I were unable to have children. When my beloved sister died, leaving behind her two young children, I told my brother-in-law Felipe that I would love them as my own and I have. Margarita and Miguel, you have been the joy of my life and the summers which you spent here at Villa Sol y Iris, along with your father Felipe and, later, his wife Lucia, were among the happiest that I can recall. I remember how Miguel would stop every so often as we walked through the vineyards to ask me if a certain vine required special care as its leaves looked wilted or yellow or he felt the grapes were too small and bitter. I taught him everything I knew about winemaking and then, Miguel and his wife Teresa welcomed Diego into their lives and mine and I started the same process with him. The cycle continues as, last month, Diego's wife Alicia gave birth to a boy who was christened just yesterday as Eduardo Miguel Diego after me, his grand-father and his father." At that point, Diego placed the young Eduardo in his great great-uncle's arms and the guests cheered, chanting "*¡Vivan los dos Eduardos*! (Long live the two Eduardos!)."

Diego embraced his great-uncle and declared, "Today, Eduardo will be introducing a new premium Cava that we have been perfecting for some time."

Eduardo then rose once again with a bottle of the special wine in his hands. "This Cava will be known as *Margarita*, my niece's name, but also the name of someone who was very dear to my heart many decades ago. Most of you here do not know that, in my youth, I travelled to Canada and met Maggie, a wonderful woman with whom I fell in love and planned to marry. Things didn't work out for us but I never forgot her and this sparkling wine was developed in her honour. *Margarita* boasts an impressive bouquet of lemon and grapefruit notes with a bouquet of freshly-baked bread and a fleeting soupçon of roses. It also has an abundant mousse of fine-textured bubbles. May I ask Maggie's granddaughter, Sophie, who is here today with us to come to the podium and join me as we drink a glass of *Margarita* in her memory."

Overcome with emotion, I walked to the podium and hugged Eduardo, kissing his cheeks. "How lovely you are, *querida*, and how I appreciate your presence here today," he commented, his voice charged with emotion. Then, to lighten the mood, he added, "If only I were a few years younger, I would take you for a long walk in the vineyards and show you off to all the workers!"

"I see that you have not lost your Latin charm, but, if you like, tomorrow will not be too late for that walk," I offered while secretly blessing my husband at that moment for having supported our trip to Spain to meet Eduardo and his family.

"The wine that you have made to honour your niece and my grandmother is truly excellent," I commented. "May I toast the winemaker, as well?"

"Thank you so much for your kind words. I look forward to speaking to you and your husband later but, for now, I must mingle with the many guests who have come here today to offer me their congratulations on my ninetieth birthday. We will see each other at the family dinner tonight and, tomorrow, I would like to show you my garden and, if you and your husband are interested, the wine cellars at *Las Cavas Martínez*. We could even go for that walk in the vineyards. Would you like that?"

"It sounds delightful, Señor Martínez."

"Please call me Eduardo. And may I call you Sofía?"

As we enjoyed a glass of Cava and some accompanying tapas during the reception that followed the speeches, David and I discussed the ceremony we had just witnessed. "How touching it must be for Eduardo to reflect over his long life and to see four generations of his family gathered here today!" I reflected.

"It is indeed a privileged moment for him," agreed David.

"Doesn't this remind you of the reception in the Niagara Region vineyards that we enjoyed the day that we met? At that time, we were also drinking sparkling wine in a vineyard."

"Yes, I do remember those 'beaded bubbles winking at the brim', a quote from Keats that certainly caught your attention. Already four wonderful years of being married to you!" David declared as he kissed me just as Eduardo arrived.

"I wished to stop to say 'Hello' as I haven't met you yet, David. May I address you this way?" Eduardo asked.

"Of course, Señor Martínez. And, may I add, what a lovely celebration in your honour this is!"

"Thank you but please call me Eduardo. It makes me feel younger! Also, as I am leaving now, you may wish to return to your previous activity," he added with a mischievous look at David and me.

David replied, "I shall do both with pleasure, Eduardo. May I add that you are wearing a very striking black pearl tie pin."

"It's old but very lovely, a gift from the Canadian girl whom I left behind," replied Eduardo before taking his leave to meet more guests.

The family dinner that evening was held al fresco in the gardens with the perfume of orange blossoms enveloping the guests gathered under the star-lit sky, the sound of water softly gurgling in several fountains and the huge braids of pink, purple and fuchsia bougainvillea running across the trellises. Modernista-styled light standards illuminated the area while the stirring music of the *Concierto de Aranjuez* played in the background. A traditional Spanish dinner was served beginning with platters of tapas offered to the guests as they mingled before dinner: olive-stuffed cheese pastries, marinated mushrooms, chorizo and red pepper canapés, *jamón ibérico* and grilled garlic shrimp. Once seated, a cooling gazpacho soup blending cucumbers, peppers, onions, garlic and tomatoes was served on a bed of ice. A gargantuan *paella a la Valenciana* topped with chicken, mussels, shrimp, squid and lobster and enhanced with the distinctive taste of saffron, was set before the diners. Finally, almond and lemon pastries concluded the meal with marzipan delicacies elaborately shaped in a variety of fruit as well as wine bottles. Of course, Miguel had ensured that the appropriate wines had accompanied each course, ending with some Icewine from the Niagara Region in honour of his Canadian guests.

During the course of the meal, David and I spoke to Margarita and her husband Carlos and met their daughter Carolina and son-in-law Juan as well as their son Rafael and his wife Eva. Carolina and I were surprised to note how effortlessly we found topics of interest and vowed to keep in touch in the future. I was also pleased to observe that David was talking enthusiastically to Miguel and his family, learning more about wines.

The next morning, David and I enjoyed breakfast outside on the patio and were happy to share a table with Margarita and Miguel who were eager to learn more about the mother whom they had barely known. I provided them with copies of the letters that Maria Cristina had sent to my grandmother so that they could have a snapshot view of her Manitoba experience, as well as an insight into her life as a young wife and mother. Margarita told us that she knew little of their mother's last years and even, as a very young child, she had sensed her father's deep grief and had not wished to intensify it by her questions. Both siblings were very grateful to me for having given them the opportunity to glean a few more details about their mother. Miguel added, "I would not wish you, however, to think that we had a sad life as children. Nothing could be further from the truth. Our father spent every free moment that he had with us and we loved him dearly. When he remarried, he chose a woman who clearly loved us and who was besotted with him. We were very fortunate, indeed."

As the four of us were finishing our coffee, Eduardo arrived and offered to show David and me his garden and then the wine cellars. "If you don't mind, Eduardo, I will join Margarita and Miguel for a tour of the vineyard while you show Sophie your garden. I think that the two of you would appreciate some time together," concluded David. "I will accompany you later for the tour of the wine cellars, if you agree." Eduardo thanked him for his consideration and left with me on his arm while the other three headed towards the vines growing tall under the warm sun.

I could tell that Eduardo was very proud of his garden which boasted a lovely collection of roses and bougainvillea, as well as a vast number of potted geraniums hanging against a stone wall. He pointed to a section of daisies that he had planted in Maggie's memory decades earlier and directed me to a colourful *azuelo* bench forming a ring around a flowering lemon tree. "Here, my dear, we will have some shade from the strong sun. Ah, I see that you're holding Maria Cristina's old fan made of ivory with hand-painted pink roses, undoubtedly a souvenir she gave to your grandmother. Let me show you how to use it properly."

"Actually, Eduardo, I am somewhat knowledgeable in using fans but obviously I could perfect my technique. When I was a student in Madrid in 1972, a young Spaniard called Iago gave me some lessons in the art that you call 'the silent language of love'. I would hazard a guess that you also taught my grandmother how to use a Spanish fan."

"Yes, you're correct. It was 67 years ago that I showed Margarita how to use that very fan that you are holding now, which I borrowed from my sister."

"Eduardo, I can't believe that I'm actually here with you and your family as you have been an enigmatic part of a puzzle that I have been trying to solve ever since I found that fan, as well as letters from Maria Cristina in my grandmother's attic after she died."

"And I can't tell you how happy I was when Margarita told me that you had written to her. To think that you and your husband actually came this far to meet the family. *Maravilloso*! I am moved beyond words. You know, Sofía, that it was my fault that Maggie and I did not marry."

Eduardo then explained what had happened so many years earlier when he returned to Madrid and how circumstances had conspired against his marrying my grandmother. "I'm not proud of my decision but perhaps, having lived in Spain for a period, you have some idea of our conventions and of how difficult it was for me to break away from them and from my beloved parents' wishes."

A few tears rolled down my cheeks as I heard Eduardo tell me about his love for my grandmother, tears which he gently wiped away with his monogramed handkerchief.

"Eduardo, I thought that it was only in the movies that men kept handkerchiefs on hand just for such occasions!"

"It appears that they do come in handy from time to time. I'm not sure if I am seeing things but, Sofía, are you not wearing the amethyst pendant that I gave your grandmother the day that we were engaged?"

"Yes, she left it to me in her will. For some reason, I was always curious about this pendant and imagined various stories about its origin. She told me that it was from a distant relative but I always suspected that it held great significance for her. My suspicions were proven to be true when, nine years ago, I found the note which accompanied the pendant while I was clearing out my grandmother's attic after her death. I still remember the words from that note: '*A mi preciosa Margarita, un recuerdo de un verano que nunca olvidaré y una promesa de un futuro feliz a tu lado. Con todo mi amor, Eduardo.*'"

"*Muy bien dicho, Sofía.* Your Spanish is very good. I do remember that amethyst pendant," he confirmed as, with glistening eyes, he turned it over and traced his finger over the initials E and M that had been inscribed on the locket's back almost seven decades earlier."

"It was the note that accompanied it that started my quest for more information about you and eventually led to my husband's and my visit here. However, along the way to obtaining more details about your romance with my grandmother, I found a few clues which intrigued me. May I ask you about them?"

"Of course, Sofía."

"Did you attend the opera *Carmen* with Maggie?"

"Yes, and it was on that occasion that I borrowed Maria Cristina's fan and showed your grandmother how to use it.... with some success, I must admit."

"I also found a ticket stub in her attic for a ride on the Moonlight Train. I was always intrigued by that name."

"That was a special experience that I shall always remember, a romantic ride in a dark train car on the way back to Winnipeg after our engagement at Winnipeg Beach. Remember, Sofía, we were young and in love."

"May I ask you another question? One day when I was reading an old book of my grandmother's, I found a bookmark containing a pressed rose. When I slit the side of the bookmark open, I discovered a message referring to 'the garden of life' dated 1950 and signed Eduardo. I always wondered about that: did you ever see Maggie again after you left Winnipeg in 1913?"

"Yes, in 1950 I had the opportunity to travel to Winnipeg on business and to attend an event celebrating my old friend Pierre's retirement as a concierge at the Royal Alexandra Hotel. I couldn't resist seeing Maggie again to explain in person why I had not come back for her. As luck would have it, her husband and children were all away that week and one meeting led to another and finally to a very romantic last evening at the Royal Alexandra Hotel."

Noting my perplexed look, Eduardo quickly added, "I see that you are surprised. Although it pains me to jeopardize my well-established reputation in Spain as a Don Juan," he joked, "I actually am proud to say that, while we came close to straying, we resisted, thanks mostly to Maggie's strong willpower and conscience. After all, it would have been wrong on several counts. Your grandmother was married and she loved her husband. I wasn't yet engaged to Ariana whom I loved in a different way, but I was contemplating proposing to her upon my return to Spain."

"Robert Browning once wrote of a love experience, 'How sad and bad and mad it was—but then, how it was sweet!' The poet's words seem to describe your situation so well, Eduardo. Did you send my grandmother a bouquet of roses after that evening? That would explain the pressed rose and accompanying message in the bookmark which I found."

"Did your grandmother really keep a rose from that bouquet, along with my accompanying message, in a bookmark for all those years?" Eduardo's eyes were misting as he continued, "Indeed, Browning's words would have been most appropriate for the circumstances, but they would have revealed too much had the message fallen into other hands. Yes, I sent Maggie a bouquet of roses to thank her for a wonderful evening and to remind her of her mother's words in describing the different types of love that one can experience in life and how each variety, like the flowers in a garden, has its own special qualities. I only wished for her happiness and she prayed for mine."

"Thank you, Eduardo, for being so frank with me. May I add that I am so very happy to have met you after all these years."

"As I am, too. And now it is time for me to show you off to the workers! Let's make our way to the vineyards and join the others for our tour of the wine cellars."

As Eduardo and I walked to the vineyards, I noted with some amusement that he took every opportunity to introduce me to his workers as he proudly informed them that I was the relative of an old friend of his from Canada…

After joining David, Margarita and Miguel, Eduardo began the tour of the wine cellars by giving us some background information about the production of Cava. He described how the introduction of an automated process to turn the bottles of sparkling wine ever so slightly every day, thus replacing the laborious manual tilting still used by *remueurs* in the production of some prestige French Champagnes, had provided Cava producers with a strong price advantage. This helped to ensure the popularity of Cava with aficionados worldwide," Eduardo added.

"Are there different types of Cava and how long are they aged?" asked David.

"Yes," replied Eduardo. "There are six types distinguished by their sweetness, a process that is controlled by the vintner's addition of sugar and wine once the yeast sediment is removed. These types range from *Extra Brut* with under six grams of sugar per litre to *Dulce* with more than fifty grams of sugar per liter. Here at *Las Cavas Martínez*, our regular sparkling wine is aged for nine months but our *Cava Reserva* spends at least fifteen months in our cellars and our *Cava Gran Reserva* matures for a minimum thirty months.

"While we are not as well known as *Codorníu* and *Freixenet*, *Martínez* is a well-respected vintner on both the national and international scene," declared Eduardo proudly. "With Diego learning the vigneron trade under Miguel's careful tutelage, Martínez's future is assured. Come now, let's walk through the cellar and see our various vintages."

Eduardo and his guests walked through the cool, damp cellar as the winemaker pointed out bottles from his *Gran Reserva Cava Maria Cristina* and finally, his last two *Gran Reserva Cava Ariana* and *Gran Reserva Cava*

Margarita. "Let's take a bottle of each of these three vintages with us to the house for tonight's dinner," suggested Eduardo.

When a glass of the *Gran Reserva Cava Margarita* had been poured for every guest, David rose and asked if he could propose a toast. With Eduardo's assent, he began, "Sophie and I have so thoroughly enjoyed our stay here, meeting your family, touring the vineyards and cellars, savouring authentic Spanish food and tasting your wines in such special surroundings that we would be remiss if we did not express our appreciation to Eduardo, the author of this wonderful experience, as well as to Miguel, Teresa, Diego and Alicia for having hosted us during our visit. Please raise your glass with me as we wish Eduardo continued success! *Salud, dinero, amor y tiempo para gozarles.* That's a toast that my wife taught me from her experiences in Spain as a student."

During the meal which followed, Carolina and I began to exchange more information about our families, careers and aspirations. I learned that she was a high fashion designer who had recently opened her own boutique specializing in flamenco, wedding and other specialty wear whereas my interests were deeply rooted in writing, travel and gastronomy. How fascinating to realize that, despite different professional directions and cultures, we shared so many similar thoughts and values! After an engaging conversation with Carolina and her husband Juan, I turned to Diego and his wife Alicia who was holding her baby son in her arms. She shared her first joys and worries of motherhood with me while Diego talked about his childhood on the estate and his hopes for the future and for his new son.

All too soon, the evening ended as David and I planned the next day at the beach with our new friends, Carolina, Juan, Diego and Alicia. They planned to drop us off at our hotel in Barcelona, wait for us to change into our bathing suits and then take us to a lovely beach that they knew. It sounded like the perfect ending to a busy but short holiday in Spain. Alas, it also meant saying good-bye to Eduardo and, at his venerable age, probably a last farewell. I kissed his cheek and thanked him for all his kindness.

"Thank you so much for taking the time to come to Spain for my special birthday; I shall treasure these moments for the rest of my days," he concluded as we hugged for what I thought would be the last time.

"*¡Y vaya con Dios!*" I responded as David and I left Villa Sol y Iris.

Chapter 34

SPAIN, MAY—JUNE 1990

Ten years after our momentous visit to Spain, David and I were extremely busy with our jobs and young family. We first welcomed into this world twins Nicholas and Charles, followed by our daughter Alexandra and, finally, our son Maximo. With the birth of each child, I experienced the incredible sensation that a mother feels as she holds such a fragile human being in her arms. How can one resist that appealing little face that lights up when it sees yours?

David had secured tenure at the university and was enthusiastic about developing history courses that would be of special interest to his students. Despite the time constraints imposed by looking after four young children, I continued to enjoy writing although I missed the opportunity to travel overseas. Nevertheless, travel with the children to closer destinations led to the joy of holidaying together and sharing memorable family experiences.

Over the years, Carolina and I had become faithful correspondents and, consequently, we shared many of life's joys and challenges vicariously. Dear Eduardo had sent David and me a dozen bottles of his prized vintage *Gran Reserva Cava Margarita* to celebrate our tenth wedding anniversary in 1986. In my letter of thanks to Eduardo, I included a photo of David and me enjoying a glass of his Cava, happily surrounded by our children. According to his nephew Miguel, the photo had given Eduardo no end of pleasure and he kept it by his bedside.

I was sitting at my desk writing to Carolina when David informed me that he had been invited to attend a conference for university history professors in Barcelona at the end of May. Was there any chance that we could find a sitter and that I could accompany him? If so, David suggested that I join him after the conference and that we travel to Andalusia for ten days or so. If everything worked out, we might even be able to visit Carolina and Juan during that period. A few days later, it seemed serendipitous that we should receive a joint invitation from Margarita and Miguel to attend Eduardo's one hundredth birthday celebration at Villa Sol y Iris. What a lovely and unexpected opportunity, after a ten-year hiatus, to explore more of the country that had enchanted me for so long, to accumulate updated information for another travel article about southern Spain and to see Margarita and Carlos, Miguel and Teresa and Carolina and Juan once again, as well as Eduardo!

From Barcelona we flew to Marbella where we had enjoyed two days by the sea during our honeymoon. While visiting a church in the city, I noted once again how many of the statues in Spanish churches are clothed in ornate garments which are changed regularly, a practice not observed in North American. This tradition of attiring statues in Spain started in the Middle Ages when moveable arms were affixed to simple wooden statues of the Virgin with the Christ Child to allow both statues to be dressed. By the 17th century, artists in Spain and Portugal, as well as their colonies, were fashioning statues with articulated limbs to allow for easier clothing changes. Some statues even boast real hair and wear rich gowns of brocade, satin or velvet, as well as jewelry and diadems. Famous statues such as *Nuestra Señora de los Dolores* (Our Lady of Sorrows) in Guadalajara, Mexico and *La Macarena (*The Weeping Virgin*)* in Seville have become very popular objects of devotion. *La Macarena,* for example, holds a position of honour among the two most important floats of the Holy Week Processions.

We took the bus from Marbella to Arcos de la Frontera, a whitewashed city with a spectacular location in the mountains. Once there, I sent a quick postcard to my parents after which we called our children and spoke to David's parents, who were looking after them, to ascertain that all was well. How fortunate we were to be once again in Spain, reminiscing over the past, enjoying the present and looking forward to the future!

Dear Mom and Dad,

We are now in the delightful town of Arcos de la Frontera which traces its origins to the great Reconquista of Spain from the Moors. This is a city to be visited just for the sheer pleasure of experiencing an ancient town with labyrinthine streets inching their way up or down the cliff: unlike Ronda or Jerez, there are no major sites to tour but, rather, the opportunity to stroll through an old Andalusian village where children play soccer on the church square under the watchful eyes of dozens of cats and where pedestrians walk under arches that support earthquake-damaged structures from long ago. Also of note is the warm, dust-laden sirocco wind originating from the Sahara, which is often blamed for the fatigue and headaches experienced by the locals.

We are eagerly waiting for Carolina and Juan to join us at our lovely parador here in Arcos.

How delighted we were with our accommodations! The *Parador de Arcos de la Frontera* is perched on the top of a hill on the site of an old mansion in the centre of Arcos. The hotel's elegant courtyard with its fountain and stone well, its iron grills, pink arches and tiled floor reminds one of a gracious old Spanish home. Our bedroom terrace allowed us to enjoy the same magnificent view seen from the dining room with its wall of windows overlooking the orange trees to one side and the terraced silver-green olive groves leading down to the river on the other.

Carolina and Juan arrived in mid-afternoon and we soon found ourselves in the courtyard sipping a glass of sherry, accompanied by tapa plates of almonds and olives. Margarita and Carlos were taking care of Carolina and Juan's two sons and young daughter during their brief trip with us to Arcos and Cadiz. We strolled leisurely through the lovely old town before enjoying a late-night dinner with our Spanish friends on the hotel terrace. Predictably, we talked late into the night, catching up on our news until we were almost ushered out of the restaurant by the tired waiters!

When we returned to our room, David presented me with a box of jewelry which contained a striking necklace in damascene bearing several miniature gold fans. "Sophie, when I saw this necklace, I had to buy it for you as a special souvenir of this year's trip to Spain, knowing how much it would delight you. I hope that the fans which decorate it will also remind you of love's secret language and how much you mean to me."

"Ah, David, what a romantic thought and how beautifully expressed in this elegant necklace!" I said as he silenced me with a passionate kiss.

From Arcos de la Frontera, we travelled to the port of Cadiz which is considered to be the oldest city in Western Europe. With its many baroque palaces and stately pastel homes lining the seaside promenades, Cadiz offers a reminder of the wealth accumulated by conquistadores who made their fortunes in the New World. The four of us were happy to stroll along the ocean, imagining the turbulent history of the Spanish galleons returning to the city, their holds bursting with gold and silver from South America. We were pleased to stay at the *Hotel Atlántico, Parador de Cadiz*, whose glass walls offered a magnificent view of the ocean and whose rooftop infinity pool was not only striking but refreshing. After two days of exploring Cadiz's impressive parks, strolling on its beaches and enjoying our hotel's pool, we bade a fond farewell to our friends, reminding them that we would soon be together again at Villa Sol y Iris for Eduardo's centenary celebrations.

After the lazy charms of Cadiz, David and I travelled to Gibraltar where we enjoyed the historic attributes of "The Rock". I took a few minutes to squeeze as many words as I could onto a postcard to my parents who always followed our travels with great interest and who were busy planning their own trip to Ireland where they hoped to learn more about my father's Irish heritage.

May 18, 1990

Dear Mom and Dad,

Today, David and I explored "The Rock" which, as you know, is a narrow extension off the southern coast of Spain that, much to the frustration of the Spanish, has been under British control since 1704.

What an unusual border between the two countries! Upon entering, one actually crosses an air-strip which has a traffic light for pedestrians and motorists. There can be planes flying overhead – watch out!

We took a taxi to a point near the top of the Rock where apparently a Muslim chieftain crossed over from Africa in 711, beginning the Moorish conquest of Spain. The views of the African continent from Gibraltar are most impressive.

After admiring the panorama from the height of the Rock, we visited the Apes' Den, home to a couple of hundred apes (Barbary macaques). Legend has it that as long as the monkeys remain there, so will the British. One has to be careful of these monkeys, nevertheless: while they appear to be friendly and playful, they are actually great thieves and will skillfully steal your glasses, your purse or your ice-cream cone before you can stop them!

Love,
Sophie

After visiting Gibraltar, David and I flew to Barcelona and were soon on our way to Villa Sol y Iris. After ringing the bell at the front entrance, we were surprised to see Eduardo himself opening the door and welcoming us with great enthusiasm. "Ah, dearest Sofía and David, I can't tell you how pleased I am to see you again. Welcome to Villa Sol y Iris, *amigos queridos* (beloved friends)! Margarita and Carlos, as well as Carolina and Juan and Rafael and Eva with their children have already arrived from Seville. Please join us for a sherry and tapas in the courtyard in an hour."

After drinks, all the guests eagerly met for dinner in a cacophonous celebration of life and family. We saw young Eduardo, now ten years old, and his two sisters Maria and Allegra happily playing with their cousins from Seville and thought once again of our beloved children back home. Eduardo, Miguel and Teresa, as well as Diego and Alicia, were eager to catch up on family news from Margarita and Carlos, as well as on our own family before retiring for the night. David and I felt that we were with our second family as questions were asked and answers given in rapid succession. We would barely have time to speak to Carolina and Juan before the ceremony the next day when the rest of the extended family, including Ariana's daughters and their children and a few old friends of Eduardo's arrived for his milestone birthday celebration.

While Alicia and Diego attended to the last-minute details, David and I greeted the guests who were excited about extending their best wishes to the centenarian. The short ceremony began with Miguel teasing his uncle about having the challenge now of outliving him and then Diego spoke of Eduardo's many contributions on both a personal and professional level and how his own son, young Eduardo, was a devoted fan of his great-great-uncle, seeking his advice on many questions. "Whenever we look for him, he can usually be found in the vineyard with his wise counsellor or so he thinks!" Diego joked. Eduardo was last to speak and he proudly reached the podium without help, dapper in a new suit with an abundance of silver hair crowning his head. He looked at the people who were gathered for his special birthday and his thoughts focused on the past, to the days when he would race past Maria Cristina as they walked to school in Madrid, teasing her by pulling her braids and later hiding her many fans. She was always so good-natured that it wasn't much fun to tease her, he recalled as he smiled at the thought of the dear sister whom he had lost so long ago.

Later, he remembered playing hide and seek with Margarita and Miguel when Felipe would bring them to the villa for the summer holidays. He would regale the children with stories about monsters hidden in the vineyards but Margarita would beg him for more traditional tales about princesses living in castles. He always had special treats for the children despite their father's warning that they would spoil their meals.

By the time that Margarita and Miguel had grown up and had their own children, he had a pool built on the villa grounds and used to swim with Carolina, Rafael and Diego and then Ariana's grandchildren. How many times had he raced against them all and won! And how could he forget the exciting treasure hunts that he and Ariana had organized for the children, teasing them by offering the winner a tour of the wine cellars or of the vineyards until the real prize was revealed. Now, they were all grown up and it was his great-great-nieces and nephews who played in the pool with the still avid swimmer although he rarely won the races now... Still, they all loved his many stories perfected through the years and told with great enthusiasm.

It was time to speak as the guests were beginning to fidget in their chairs, waiting for Eduardo to address them while his thoughts dwelled on past good times. He cleared his throat and spoke with confidence, telling his audience what a fortunate man he was and how happy he felt to be among those he loved. He concluded with the wish that his namesake continue with the family tradition of viticulture and, from the back of the courtyard, he heard a young voice declaring confidently, "Of course, great-great-uncle Eduardo, that is my plan!"

After the lovely reception during which the senior Eduardo was much fêted, I could see him looking for me and I walked quickly towards him. "What a wonderful day this is!" I commented. "I am so happy that David and I were able to accept your kind invitation to join you for your milestone birthday celebration."

"Surely not as happy as I was when I heard that you and David would be attending it! Come, let's walk to my garden and have a little chat. We sat on the same tiled bench where we had talked a decade earlier and then Eduardo removed an elaborate box from his breast pocket and gave it to me. "This is the ring that I planned to give your grandmother; it has turquoise sapphires to reflect the bright blue of her eyes, pink sapphires to remind me of her innocence and a large white diamond representing our love. I would like you to have this ring. It has been in my will for years as I could never bring myself to give it to Victoria and, after her death, I planned to make the ring a family heirloom, perhaps an engagement ring for young Eduardo to give to his future bride. However, I have now changed my mind, Sofía, and wish to give you this ring as it truly belongs more to your family than to mine."

"It is truly a magnificent ring but how can I accept something so valuable?"

"It would make an old man very happy if you were to accept it, bis*nieta querida*."

Truly moved by Eduardo's reference to me as his "beloved great-granddaughter", I smiled, saying, "Well then, bis*abuelo querido* (beloved great-grand-father), how can I refuse?"

That evening as the family gathered for another meal al fresco, I admired the striking ring on my right hand that Eduardo had given me and that I had worn at my husband's suggestion. "This will probably be the only time that he will ever see the ring that he wished to give to your grandmother worn by someone from her family who so clearly cares for him. Besides, the turquoise sapphires match your blue eyes!" added David.

"I am so happy to see you wearing the ring that has lain dormant for all these years. May it bring you and perhaps eventually your daughter the same pleasure that I had in dreaming of giving it to your grandmother!" said Eduardo, much moved as he noticed the family heirloom on my finger.

The next day, as we prepared to return to Toronto, we said good-bye to Eduardo in a moment charged with deep emotion. I hugged him for a long time and, just before leaving *Villa Sol y Iris,* I reflected upon the lovely words of the old Spanish farewell and said with conviction, "*¡Y vaya con Dios, bisabuelo querido!*"

"*¡Y vaya con Dios, bisnieta querida!*" replied Eduardo as he hugged me for the last time.

When I returned home, I placed Eduardo's ring in its ornate box and stored it in our safety deposit box at the bank as I felt that it now belonged to another generation. That, however, would not prevent me from "borrowing" the magnificent ring from time to time in the interval…

Chapter 35

Toronto, December 31, 1999

Dear Carolina,

On this last day of the decade, century and millennium, I have gathered the letters which you have sent me for almost 20 years now and reread them, causing me to reflect on the many changes in our lives since we first met in Spain to celebrate Eduardo's ninetieth birthday. His death in 1992 affected me more than I would have thought. It is strange how some relationships develop so fully in a short period of time while other long-established ones sometimes do not withstand the test of time and wither into oblivion.

In contemplating the various friendships I have made over the years, I consider the traits that have made some of them so lasting while others prove to be as ephemeral as the strike of a match resulting in a bright but small flame that flickers and dies almost as soon as it is born. I remember some friendships destined, I thought, to last forever but, after a very short period of time, were consigned to the forgotten, dusty cobwebs of our minds and hearts while others, often unexpected, remain strong and vivid even when circumstances do not favour their development. They remind me of old candles which, even after months and years of storage, can be lit once again to shed their warm glow of light in the darkness.

Isn't it wonderful that, despite the geographical and cultural barriers that could potentially separate us, we maintain a friendship that is as meaningful as when we first met, much like the friendship which united our grandmothers so many years ago? Well, enough of this philosophical talk of friendship as David and I will soon be raising a glass of Eduardo's vintage Gran Reserva Cava Margarita to toast the arrival of the new millennium with the last bottle from the case of twelve that he sent us to mark our tenth wedding anniversary thirteen years ago. He will certainly be on our minds as we savour that special bottle…

Our children are all well and happy and what more could parents wish for them? Our two eldest, twins Nicholas and Charles, have decided to pursue their studies in tourism and education while Maximo is seriously contemplating a career in medicine. Our daughter Alexandra is very talented in the field of illustration, being able to capture in a drawing the essence of a person's mood or of a significant moment in life but is still wondering where to cast her net.

What about your children? Have they revealed their career choices to you yet?

I continue to review books and write travel articles although, one day, I hope to write a novel. Next year, I will register for an advanced Spanish course and, believe it or not, act in a play presented by a local theatre group.

David has been busy adding to his latest Canadian history course by including a chapter on the major contributions of Canadian physicians to society. He will discuss the work of Dr. Norman Bethune, a Canadian doctor who served as a frontline surgeon during the Spanish Civil War and who promoted the use of mobile blood transfusion services, thus saving more lives on the battlefield than was common at that time when blood loss frequently led to death. When he returned to Canada in 1937, Dr. Bethune devoted his efforts to raising funds and recruiting volunteers for the anti-fascist struggle in Spain.

David joins me in sending you, Juan and your family our warmest wishes for the New Year and the New Millennium.

Un gran abrazo de Sofía.

Ten days later, I received a reply from Carolina.

Dear Sofía,

How pleased I was to receive your last letter! I share your musings about friendship and the different forms it can take in our lives.

In answer to your question, Alonzo is currently debating the various merits of a career as a famous actor or singer! I think that he has seen too many films featuring Antonio Banderas and listened to too many videos with Enrique Iglesias performing before adoring fans... Francisco is considering a career as a soccer player or bullfighter! I venture to say that their plans will change very quickly … Esmeralda, on the other hand, is a very serious student but it is still too soon to tell which path she will follow in life. She often helps me in the store but I'm not sure that fashion holds the same appeal for her as for me. She appears to be very attracted to music and dance and will sit transfixed for hours listening to Placido Domingo's recordings or to watching performances by flamenco artists. Esmeralda also sings in the school choir and at church. She has started to take voice and dance lessons after school and occasionally performs in local musicals.

Diego and Alicia are busy with their increasing workload at Las Cavas Martínez, *as well as with following the lively schedules of their children, Eduardo, María and Allegra. We continue to see each other regularly during the Christmas, Easter and summer holidays.*

While on the topic of fashion, I am currently selecting the latest flamenco dresses to carry in my boutique for Seville's all-important Spring Fair. I think that you would be very impressed with my current collection of flamenco dresses, mantillas and shawls and, of course, beautiful, ornate fans. I do hope that you and David will be able to travel to Seville for this special occasion one day.

Juan continues to enjoy promoting and selling wines in our long family tradition.

Sadly, both my mother and father passed away this year, as well as Miguel's wife Teresa just after Christmas. Miguel continues to supervise some of the operations at Las Cavas Martínez *but Diego has assumed most of the day-to-day work of the estate. His son Eduardo is also playing an important role and has exhibited great interest in and knowledge of the operations. He is encouraging Diego to begin offering tours and wine tastings, which would certainly enhance recognition of* Las Cavas Martínez.

I look forward to hearing from you soon, amiga querida, and may the New Year smile upon you, David and your family!

Carolina

Chapter 36

Toronto and Seville, December 2009—April 2010

Dear Carolina,

It is difficult to believe that yet another decade has slipped by so quickly, a decade that has witnessed the sad death of my mother, the marriage of our son Nicholas to a delightful woman and the birth of our first grandchild. Nicholas's work in promoting Canadian tourism abroad took him and his wife to New York City for two years but they returned to Toronto just before the birth of their daughter.

Charles is now teaching in Newfoundland where he is enjoying maritime life and the seafaring traditions of that island. We believe that the Irish-Canadian girl whom he met there is also part of the island's attractions!

We had hoped that we would have the opportunity to return to Spain during the past decade and enjoy a visit with you and Juan. While this didn't occur, I believe that the near future holds an opportunity for us to see you again.

You may recall that, some ten years ago, I mentioned that David was working on a university course that would include a section on

Dr. Norman Bethune. Well, since then, the city of Malaga has opened the Canadians' Promenade in tribute to the doctor's humanitarian work. This route, which hugs the scenic coastline to Almeria Beach, is a way of honouring Dr. Bethune and his colleagues who rescued citizens at risk in their exodus from Malaga during the Spanish Civil War. During the ceremony, a commemorative plaque was unveiled with the inscription: "Walk of Canadians – In memory of aid from the people of Canada at the hands of Norman Bethune, provided to the refugees of Málaga in February 1937". An olive tree and a maple tree were planted as tangible symbols of this international cooperation.

We have already visited Dr. Bethune's home in Gravenhurst, Ontario where a museum has been erected in his memory. However, David is also very interested in walking down the Canadians' Promenade in Malaga and I, of course, would like to accompany him there. We are thinking of taking the train from Malaga to Seville where hopefully we could visit you and Juan, as well as check on our son Maximo who will soon begin a new chapter in his life in your *charming city. He has received a scholarship to study infectious diseases at a hospital in Seville that specializes in this area. What a splendid opportunity for him! Fortunately, he has also acquired a working knowledge of Spanish in his travels across South America and the Caribbean and, with a little extra studying, should be able to cope with his courses. Of course, we are sure that he will also rely on the city's pretty señoritas to help him with the language…*

Maximo will be starting his studies in Seville as soon as he completes his residency in internal medicine, which should be sometime early this spring. As this will coincide with the legendary revelries of the Spring Fair in Seville, it would be a most opportune occasion for us to visit you and Juan if convenient for you. Moreover, as my publisher has asked me to prepare several more articles on Andalusia, what could be better timing for me than a visit to Seville during the Spring Fair!

It may be that we are too late to secure reservations but we will try our best as I have longed wished to witness the visual extravaganza that is the Spring Fair. It will also be a good time to visit your boutique with all its special flamenco clothing.

Alexandra has started a course as a graphic designer this year and is looking forward to a career in this field. However, in the interim, she would like to travel to Spain with us, given that she has heard so much from her mother about its great attractions and wishes to witness them for herself.

I can't wait to see you, dear Carolina.

Sophie

Seville, January 10, 2010

Dearest Sofía,

What wonderful news you conveyed in your last letter!

First of all, Juan and I do hope that you and David (and Alexandra) will accept our invitation to stay at our home during the Spring Fair, which will be held in mid-April. We shall be happy to be your guides and to introduce you to this traditional celebration. Besides, as reservations must be made at least a year in advance, you won't find any suitable accommodation at this late date.

Of course, we understand that your primary reason for travelling to Seville is to be with your son whom we very sincerely congratulate on his scholarship. While he is studying in Seville, he is most welcome to join us whenever he wishes for our traditional family dinners on Sunday should he like some company and a hot meal. You can count on us to provide whatever assistance Maximo requires.

It is interesting for you to have children involved in such different professions. I look forward to meeting them all one day.

We are also happy that our children are working in fields that interest them. Francisco has completed his studies in medicine and is employed in the emergency ward of one of our largest hospitals here in

Sevilla; he also works occasionally at the Plaza de Toros when there are bullfights that could result in injuries. Alonzo is now working as a wine merchant with his father while Esmeralda has realized her dream of becoming a successful flamenco dancer.

Looking forward to hearing from you very soon!

Carolina

P.S. Don't worry about the flamenco attire. Both Juan and I have extra outfits that we can lend to you for the Spring Fair and our Esmeralda will be able to take care of your daughter's attire. Also, we are fortunate enough to have our own little caseta for the duration of the event where we can all relax, enjoy a drink and savour a few tapas.

SEVILLE, APRIL 2010

During our brief stop in Malaga, David and I walked down the new Canadians' Promenade. We noticed all the major work being undertaken in the city's waterfront area and look forward to exploring the renovated port area on our next trip to Spain.

David, Alexandra and I took the train to Seville where we were met by Maximo who loves the city as much as I do although he has only been here three weeks. While savouring tapas and sherry in an atmospheric café, we learned about his new life in Seville and how he was adjusting. "The weather here is lovely, the atmosphere enchanting, the lifestyle captivating, the food delicious – in short, everything you claimed it would be, Mom," said our enthusiastic son.

"And what about your studies at the hospital?" asked David. "Are you finding them worthwhile?"

"No doubt about it. The work undertaken here has been eye-opening. We will be studying epidemics and pandemics from the Plague of Justinian that spread throughout the Mediterranean Region in the sixth century to the Bubonic Plague or Black Death which ravaged Europe during the Medieval Ages, reducing the continent's population by one-third. We will also consider the deadly invasion of smallpox beginning in Mexico in 1519 that accompanied the arrival of the Spanish conquistadores and ultimately led to the demise of the Aztec population. Almost a century ago, there was the deadly Spanish Flu pandemic that killed approximately 50 million. Can you believe that, even as late as the 1950s, smallpox was still responsible for the deaths of some two million people every year until its eradication was confirmed in 1980? We will also focus on more recent pandemics such as HIV/AIDS and the SARS outbreak."

"It sounds like a very challenging program, but we are happy that you are enjoying it. Have you discussed the possibility of another pandemic?"

Maximo answered very seriously, "Given the ease and frequency of travel today with people readily moving from one continent to another, it is likely that a pandemic will strike sooner rather than later."

"Sad but so true." David looked at his watch and said, "Well, I believe that it is about time for us to leave as Carolina and Juan are expecting all of us for drinks at 9:00 p.m. to be followed by dinner."

Maximo drove us through the narrow cobblestone streets of the old city and parked his car at an angle with the wheels on the right side resting on part of the curb. "I see that you have adjusted to the practices here, "observed his father as we alighted from the car and walked through a beautiful and very fragrant patio garden that led to a stone building covered by striking purple bougainvillea zigzagging across century-old white walls. Pots of red, orange and white geraniums lined the entire exterior of the house and two tall palm trees overlooked a tiled table with matching chairs set in the centre of the patio. The soothing sound of water filled the area and the whole patio was a picture postcard of Andalusia. Alexandra was soon echoing her mother's enthusiastic comments, referring to an Andalusian dream, a Spanish fantasy, etc.

"*Bienvenidos a nuestra casa*!" said Carolina and Juan as they greeted us with hugs and kisses. "How wonderful it is to see you again, Sofía and David, and to meet Alejandra and Maximo!"

"*Mucho gusto, señora, señor*," replied our son who had benefitted from his few weeks in Spain to learn more of the language.

"*Es un placer conocerlos.* You are all most welcome to our home. May we offer you a little sangria or sherry in the courtyard or would you prefer the coolness of the house?"

"And leave this magical paradise?" I asked in feigned disbelief. "May I ask if this beautiful home originally belonged to your grandfather Felipe and Lucia?"

"Yes," said Caroline. "My mother Margarita inherited it from him and it was passed on to me. If you like, we can catch up on our news here in the courtyard."

Carolina disappeared for a few minutes, reappearing with a large tray containing an earthenware jug of sangria, a bottle of Fino sherry, glasses and bowls of almonds and olives. She was accompanied by her handsome sons Francisco and Alonzo and by a beautiful young woman whom I assumed was Esmeralda.

"Meet our sons Francisco and Alonzo and our daughter Esmeralda."

Soon, the two families were busy discussing epidemiology, music, wine, fashion, history and literature, all of which appealed to one group or another. I observed that Maximo and Esmeralda were having a particularly animated conversation and I wondered if our son might not be a frequent visitor at her parents' home during his year in Seville... Francisco and Alonzo were busy entertaining Alexandra and talking about the upcoming activities in Seville.

"May I ask, Maximo, why you were given such a Spanish-sounding name?" queried Juan.

"Just ask my mother! You know of her interest in anything Spanish," replied our son.

David smiled, adding that he had already vetoed my earlier Hispanic name choices and had decided that it was time for a compromise.

At one point, Maximo was talking about viruses with Francisco who was describing his current work as an emergency physician. Before I could ask a question about the type of trauma cases that he treated, the conversation had already jumped to the various properties of different types of sherries. Alonzo and Juan provided David and me with some information on the subject while Maximo and Alexandra learned about the basic movements of flamenco from Esmeralda. She turned to us and in her soft voice explained some of the history behind the dance. "You may not know that flamenco was born here in Andalusia. As was the case with tango in Argentina, those on the fringes of Spanish society such as the remaining Moors after the Reconquista and the frequently scorned *gitanos* expressed their deep passions and strong sense of melancholy through this art form. Over the years, of course, flamenco, like tango, has acquired respectability and popularity but it remains mysterious, reminding us of the jealousy and pain associated with those in unhappy love situations." She added, "I am pleased to invite you all to experience true flamenco here in Sevilla later this week when I will dance at a tablao."

At 2:00 a.m., Carolina mentioned that we might wish to retire "early", given our busy program for the next day, which would include a visit to the Fair. Maximo declined to join as he would be attending classes but Esmeralda shyly suggested that she would be willing to accompany him to the Fair later that evening should he be interested. "Why, that would be fantastic, Esmeralda. May I pick you up at 7:00 then?" With that offer began the first stirrings of a romance between members of our two beloved families…

The next morning, Carolina and Juan greeted us at the breakfast table with oranges, coffee, churros and a cup of chocolate for dipping. After we had finished our tasty breakfast, Carolina excused herself for a few minutes, returning with a flamenco dress and a *traje corto* for David to wear at the Fair.

"Sofía, the *traje de flamenco* or *traje de gitana* (gypsy dress) is the outfit traditionally worn by women during the Spring Fair, which takes place about two weeks after Easter. Multiple layers of ruffles trim the skirt and sleeves of the dress which is frequently enlivened by polka dots. To complete the outfit, a shawl is often worn over the shoulders and a long mantilla flows from a decorative comb (*peineta*) placed in the woman's hair. Long earrings are a common accessory as is a lovely fan!"

"But Carolina, what prompted the women to dress in such striking but rather impractical splendour?"

"Well, actually, the flamenco dress originated in the late nineteenth century when women vendors wearing modest gowns trimmed with ruffles to disguise their humble origins accompanied livestock traders travelling to the fair. Eventually, more prosperous women began to copy these outfits and by the time that the Seville Exposition of 1929 was held, the *traje de flamenco* had earned its status as the official attire of the Spring Fair."

"What do you think of this dress, Sofía?" asked Carolina as she held up the magnificent white flamenco dress for my inspection.

"Is it really for me? I can't believe that I will actually be wearing this beautiful fantasy to the Fair. I feel like Cinderella being transformed by her fairy godmother with the stroke of a wand and wearing a ballgown to the dance held by the prince. How exciting! Thank you so much for lending me this beautiful creation," I concluded as I held the white dress with its fiery red polka dots and lacy, feminine ruffles against me.

"And you, David, what do you think of your *traje corto*? I don't detect the same enthusiasm expressed by your wife," teased Juan.

"Well, let's say that I will try it and see. I will admit, however, that we are very fortunate indeed to be here for the Spring Fair and to have the pleasure of your company and of your lovely accommodations."

At that point, Alexandra entered the breakfast room with Esmeralda, eager to show us the fine attire that she would be wearing to the Fair. "Isn't this outfit the ultimate, Mom, Dad? Esmeralda has been kind enough to lend me this black and white dress with its striking row of ruffles at the bottom and a bright scarlet shawl to wear over it. What do you think?"

"I think that you will look amazing and attract a number of *caballeros* in that dress," replied her father with conviction.

A few hours later, dressed in my flamenco finery with tiers of ruffles descending from the knee and wearing a red shawl and a crimson rose in my hair, I proudly walked up to my appropriately dressed husband who was wearing the short jacket and tight trousers with the flat hat called a *cordobes* associated with male attire at the Spring Fair. Twirling the ruffles of my dress, I asked a wife's typical question, "How do I look?"

David smiled and declared, "You will undoubtedly be the star of the Fair!"

I shot back, "And you will be just the man to accompany me in that *típico* outfit!"

We made our way to the *Feria de Abril*, the most colourful of all festivals in Spain, a mesmerizing, sensory experience. The pervasive perfume of orange blossoms mingles with the salty, pungent odour of thousands of sardines on the grill; the stamping of feet and clapping of hands accompany the rhythm of castanets and the strumming of guitars; handsome *cabelleros* sit imperiously on their horses with their lovely *señoritas* riding sidesaddle through the streets, their long, colourful dresses hanging to full advantage over the animal's quarters. Over 1000 *casetas* stood ready to welcome their guests, each one an individually decorated marquee tent with tables and chairs, lights and music, food and drink. The trick is to be invited to enter a *caseta* as the tents are private, belonging to a family, club or organization. Juan and Carolina directed us to their tent where we were immediately offered a glass of sherry and some almond-stuffed olives. Everyone in the tent was dressed impressively for the occasion and some were dancing the local sevillana, a folk dance reminiscent of flamenco but less difficult to perform.

We noticed Maximo and Esmeralda walking into the tent, hand in hand. We greeted them, shared a popular sherry spritzer with them and then left the fairgrounds with their carnival atmosphere. Alexandra barely noticed our departure as she was busy learning how to dance the sevillana with her tutors, Francisco and Alonzo.

Back at Carolina and Juan's residence, we returned to our room to freshen up when David suddenly asked me, "Have you noticed the strange quilt on our bed? It doesn't seem Spanish at all. Look at the squares: don't the embroidered images remind you of Winnipeg landmarks? Very bizarre indeed!"

When I asked Carolina about the quilt, she replied, "I'm glad that you noticed it. My mother Margarita inherited it from her mother, Maria Cristina, who received it from your grandmother as a farewell gift upon her departure from Winnipeg for Spain. Apparently, the images on the quilt are the places that the two friends visited so very long ago. I inherited the century-old quilt from my mother and thought that you might wish to enjoy it during your stay here."

Once more, the past made its presence felt.

The next day, Juan and Alonzo escorted David, Alexandra and me to their wine shop which was filled with the fragrant smells of sherry. "While we also sell brandy from Jerez, we specialize in the sale of all sherries from that area. Like Champagne, the only wines that can be sold as sherry must come from a designated area, in this case, the region comprised of Jerez de la Frontera, Sanlúcar de Barrameda and El Puerto de Santa María," stated Alonzo. 'There are many varieties of sherry, ranging from the very pale and dry wine know as *Fino* to darker and heavier versions such as *Amontillado* and *Oloroso* with its nutty flavour.

We asked Juan about *Manzanilla* which we had enjoyed on several occasions and he explained that it was a type of *Fino* produced in Sanlúcar de Barrameda that retained a slightly salty taste due to its proximity to the ocean.

"Of course, there are also sweet varieties made by adding Moscatel grapes to the white Palomino grapes from which sherry is produced. Come and try a few different sherries and see for yourself what you prefer," offered Juan.

We left the wine shop with a bottle of *Manzanillo* and headed for Carolina's boutique where we were shown the extravagant flamenco dresses that she sold, as well as shawls, mantillas and fans, the necessary accompaniments for the well-dressed woman in Spain. Carolina insisted that Alexandra and I choose a fan from the many lovely ones on display and we finally settled on ones which would match the lovely dresses that she and Esmeralda had lent us and that we would be wearing again on Sunday for the carriage ride through the city. I also looked at the long, lacy mantillas and wondered if there was a reason to choose white over black. "Yes, white mantillas are always worn during the Seville Fair," Carolina told me. "I will lend you one for Sunday as we will ride in the parade of carriages (*paseo de caballos*)."

On Sunday, dressed in our finery, we climbed aboard a horse-drawn carriage with Carolina and Juan. Alexandra and I truly felt like Cinderella!

Everywhere, people were partying in the street and enjoying the festive atmosphere. “Don’t worry: you won’t have to witness the bullfights as I know that you would prefer not to attend. We thought, however, that you might enjoy visiting a few of the attractions here before you leave. Juan, David and the boys will stay for the corrida. Francisco is on call today in case there are any injuries once the activities begin and will be our guide. Esmeralda is here as well with Maximo who will probably also wish to see the facilities,” mentioned Carolina. “The Plaza de Toros of the *Real Maestranza de Sevilla* hosts many of the more spectacular bullfights in Spain during the city’s Spring Fair. The *fiesta brava*, as it is called in Spain, allows matadors to earn their fame as they face the prospect of death courageously in the ring. Carolina turned to Alexandra, saying, “You may be surprised to learn that many young girls from here consider the matadors to be in the same category as popular Hollywood actors and paste their pictures all over their bedrooms.”

At that moment, Francisco arrived and greeted his parents and friends. “Hello everyone, I will take you to the little chapel here where the matadors pray before each corrida. Did you know, my Canadian friends, that the Virgin of Macarena is the patron of matadors and she is much revered by them?” asked Francisco.

After viewing the chapel, we made our way to the small trauma room where doctors would offer primary care to injured matadors before they were taken to the hospital.

“Are you kept busy here when you are on call?” asked Alexandra.

“No, not usually as serious injuries are not all that frequent but, occasionally, they can be life-threatening. The last death here was many years ago. Sevillians can be very passionate about bullfighting. When the popular matador Manolete was gored by a bull, even the mother of the animal that killed him was destroyed! Would you like to see the museum here? A guide will explain the attractions to you while I prepare the room here for any emergency. See you at the flamenco tablao and at dinner later tonight.”

As it was our last evening in Seville, Esmeralda had invited her family and ours to attend a flamenco show where she would be the principal dancer. Those attending were anticipating the lively music, passionate singing, flamboyant costumes and intense sensations to come. The first guitar notes were heard with their promise of frenetic music. Rhythmic hand clapping and the staccato of the musicians' and the singer's feet against the floor let us know that the dancers were about to arrive. A man, dressed in black pants with a polka-dotted scarf, accompanied Esmeralda who was wearing a striking red dress covered in a cascade of black ruffles. Her dark hair accentuated by a red rose, she paused for several seconds, looking intently at the audience. Then, her face half-hidden by her delicate embroidered fan, she turned towards the musicians and started to dance as the enthusiastic crowd cried "¡Olé!" It was another unforgettable experience in my favourite of all Spanish cities!

David and I enjoyed the show but were also watching our son as he admired Esmeralda's dance steps. "It appears that Maximo is quite captivated by Esmeralda's dancing," I remarked.

"I think that you can safely say that he is quite captivated by Esmeralda, period," my husband replied.

"Have you noticed the way she moves her fan quickly towards her heart whenever she looks at Maximo?"

"Perhaps you are being a little too fanciful, my love," commented my husband.

"Well, we are in Seville where the language of love can be expressed through the adept movement of fans!" I retorted.

Of course, our son busy with his medical studies for so many years, had had little time to pursue amorous activities before then. Now, in Spain, with a medical degree in hand and a very attractive and gentle woman by his side in a city imbued with charm, was he not also falling victim to Cupid's arrow?

Alexandra was enjoying all the attentions that were bestowed upon her by Francisco and Alonzo and basking in the seductive atmosphere of Seville. Given her interest in dance and fashion, she had much to share with Esmeralda and Carolina as well.

After another fine dinner with our hosts, we thanked them for their warm hospitality, as well as their children who had enabled us to better appreciate Seville and its many attractions. "You have all helped us to understand Sevilla as seen through the eyes of those who live here and love her. Carolina, by lending me a lovely flamenco dress, shawl, and mantilla, and by giving me a matching fan, you made my Cinderella experience here complete. Thank you so much for that and for sharing your family and home with us," I concluded.

"Today, Esmeralda, we learned more about flamenco and the beauty of the human form in movement through your dancing than we would ever have had just by reading about it. Also, Francisco and Alonzo, I really appreciated your help with the sevillana dance even if I did step on your toes a few times," Alexandra added.

David also expressed his gratitude by saying, "Thank you, as well, Alonzo and Juan, for helping us better appreciate the various nuances of sherry. And Francisco, despite the fact that we are not aficionados of the *fiesta brava*, we all enjoyed the tour of the Plaza de Torros and learning about its history and traditions. We thank you so much for everything and for welcoming Maximo to your family."

We turned to wish our son well in his studies but, as he was so engrossed in deep conversation with Esmeralda, we had to tap his shoulder before he realized that we were saying goodbye until his Christmas visit home.

"David, how perfect this trip to Seville has been! I've enjoyed myself so much and, as a bonus, what terrific material I've gathered for my next travel article on Spain! I'm sure that my publisher will be pleased."

"I have to agree, my sweet. I could almost dance once again to the tune of 'Viva España' as we did so often on our honeymoon. I can see how you are itching to write that article on Seville each time that you cast hungry eyes on your laptop."

"And Mom, I have to say, Spain was everything you described to me over the years. It was an incredible experience to be in Seville for the Fair and to dress up like a *Sevillana*. Thanks so much to both of you for allowing me to accompany you on this memorable trip," added Alexandra. "It was truly a dream come true!"

Chapter 37

Toronto and Spain, March—June 2012

"Sophie, how would you like to accompany me to Greece in May? There will be a very interesting conference for university professors taking place in Athens and, as I plan to retire within the next few years, why not attend it as I close my career?" asked David on a dreary, grey winter day.

"To quote Oscar Wilde, 'I can resist everything except temptation.' I've wanted to visit Greece for so long and it could be the springboard for a cruise through the Mediterranean. My publisher has offered me a contract for travel articles on this region of Europe and I could easily combine this with your plans. Of course, we could always add a stop in Spain and visit our friends there. What a wonderful prospect!"

As we were busy making plans, Alexandra called out excitedly, "Mom, Dad, can you believe that I have just received an exciting offer from your friends Miguel and Diego to work at their winery! It seems that, every year, they offer a work contract to a foreign student who is interested in some aspect of their Cava operations. In this case, my training as a graphic designer coincides with *Las Cavas Martínez's* interest in developing a new ad campaign, complete with a set of attractive posters that will help market their Cava products. Miguel and Diego hope that the production of these high-quality posters whose images could eventually be transferred to such items as premium stationery, towels and wine buckets will foster greater knowledge of and interest in their products in both the domestic and international markets."

"What marvelous news, Alexandra, but how did all this happen? I wasn't even aware that you had applied for a position at *Las Cavas Martínez*," I mentioned.

"It came as a surprise to me although I did have a long conversation with Carolina when we were in Seville about my interest in working for a winery. Apparently, she approached Miguel and Diego about hiring me as an international foreign student. I still can't believe it!"

"It's a wonderful opportunity but, of course, this means that you would move to Spain for a certain period. How long is your contract?"

"It is initially for one year but can be extended to two. Oh, I can't believe my good fortune! I must email Miguel and Diego immediately to accept their offer before they change their minds!" added Alexandra before rushing upstairs to her room.

A few months later, David and I set out on a special cruise of Mediterranean Europe, sailing to ports in Greece, France and Italy, following the conclusion of David's conference in Athens. Our cruise ended in Barcelona where Alexandra and Maximo would join us for a few days of touring before we all made our way to *Villa Sol y Iris*. It would be an opportunity for us to see Maximo once again, to help settle Alexandra in her new position with *Las Cavas Martínez* and, of course, to visit Miguel, Diego, Alicia and their family once more. Unfortunately, due to the close timing of Alonzo's wedding with our cruise, we wouldn't be able to see Carolina and Juan this time but we looked forward to their promised trip to Canada within a few years.

We landed in Athens and were excited to explore this city so steeped in history. Unlike previous holidays when we were away from home for a few weeks, we no longer worried about how our children, now all adults, were managing without us but instead thought of what the future held in store for them. How would Alexandra enjoy her experience in Spain? Would Maximo find a position at a hospital in Seville? Would Charles marry his

Irish sweetheart from Newfoundland? Would Nicholas and Paula's soon-to-be born second child be healthy? Our children grow into adulthood but, once a parent, always a parent, I told myself.

During our fascinating stay in Athens, on our cruise and finally upon our arrival in Spain, I continued to email my father about our experiences as, despite his advancing age, he always expressed great interest in all the travel adventures that David and I were enjoying.

June 15, 2012

Dear Dad,

What a happy reunion David and I had with Alexandra and Maximo whom we met at Barcelona Airport! After a brief rest, we elected to visit the old Roman foundations of Barcelona which are well preserved and easily accessible by taking the underground walkways extending over the excavations. Unlike the ruins of Pompeii which are open to the sky, Barcelona's early Roman history is viewed from raised platforms above the crumbling walls, stone columns and mosaic tiling preserved in the vast underground below the city's medieval courtyard known as the Plaça del Rei. *Among the ruins of particular interest to us were the factory where fish were chopped and salted, the dyeing and laundering facilities, the hot and cold baths and, especially, a wine-making facility where grapes were pressed and wine fermented in open vats. Unfortunately, the facility is no longer operating!*

We hope that you are well and look forward to seeing you soon in Toronto.

Your loving daughter, Sophie

Moving from the gloom of the subterranean ruins, we strolled down las Ramblas, stopping at the *Boqueria* to buy a delicious serrano ham sandwich and some saffron for future paellas at home before visiting the *Gran Teatro del Liceu*, an opulent Belle Époque opera house that, appropriately enough, had attractive posters of a seductive Carmen encouraging potential patrons to attend Bizet's captivating masterpiece. We also took the time to appreciate its café's theatrical décor that included a large number of upturned red velvet chairs secured onto the ceiling.

A highlight of our visit to Barcelona was a tour of the striking *Palau de la Musica Catalana*, a unique creation of stained glass, ceramics, statuary, ornate wrought iron and carved stone in the *Modernista* style developed by Catalan's late 19th century artists such as Gaudi and Montaner; the latter was the artist who designed this very special concert hall. Although the *Modernista Movement* shared many characteristics with *Art Nouveau* in France, in Catalonia it also became associated with the revival of Catalan culture in the context of urban and industrial development including intricately twisting iron balconies, decorative street lamps and the fanciful facades of buildings built in curving concrete enhanced with brightly-coloured glass and tiles. Barcelona was the focus of the *Modernista* Movement, which was particularly predominant in its architectural expression but which also influenced sculpture, poetry, theatre and painting. Just look at the lovely umbrellas fashioned in stone, superimposed on the walls of a corner building along the Ramblas or the broken glass chimneys on Gaudi's structures to have a better idea of the principles of the *Modernista* Movement!

As I wrote to my father, "*In the* Palau de la Musica Catalana, *rounded galleries, a kaleidoscopic skylight, ceramic mosaics and statues of the world's great musicians all pay tribute to the Modernista style. The Palau's excellent tour provided us with detailed explanations, as well as with lovely views of the building's interior, including its magnificent main hall.*

Our next stop was the Codorníu Winery which Alexandra asked us to tour prior to our visit of *Las Cavas Martínez* as she wished to see the many posters that *Codorníu* had produced over the years to familiarize the general public with its products. This would allow her to better understand the appeal of its advertisements to various audiences. Given that my father and I shared a strong predilection for Champagne and sparkling wine, I sent him an email describing our visit to the "Cathedral of Cava" whose cellars, completed in 1915, were recognized as a "National Artistic Historical Monument" and a masterpiece of Catalan *Modernismo* by King Juan Carlos.

June 16, 2012

Dear Dad,

What a wonderful visit we had today of the Codorníu Winery in Sant Sadurni, a town south of Barcelona in the Penandés Region famous for its sparkling wines!

After a detailed presentation on the history of Cava in Spain, we boarded a train that took us through a section of the almost 30 kilometres of cellars beneath the winery's buildings. What a splendid feeling for a sparkling wine enthusiast to be surrounded by thousands of bottles of Cava, smelling the yeasty fragrance and, best of all, drinking several samples of the golden elixir! We were shouting "¡Viva España! ¡Viva Cava!" by the end of the tour and thinking of how much you would have enjoyed the experience. Of course, we drank a toast to you as well and hope that you will soon be enjoying some bubbles with us on your upcoming visit to Toronto."

We did learn a great deal about the Codorníu operation before heading off to Villa Sol y Iris where we were warmly greeted by Miguel, Diego and Alicia, as well as the couple's son Eduardo who was just completing a viniculture program in Barcelona. Turning towards Alexandra, he congratulated her on her recent graduation from the graphic arts program that she had taken and expressed his hope that she would enjoy her new position with *Las Cavas Martínez*. "Would you and your brother like to have a quick visit of our vineyard and cellars now while your parents catch up on their latest news with my parents and grandfather?" Alexandra smiled warmly at the handsome Spaniard as she quickly accepted his offer and Maximo added that he would be happy to join the tour as well.

"Alicia, how are your daughters, Maria and Allegra?" I asked, not having seen them since their teenage years when David and I attended the senior Eduardo's 100th birthday celebration.

"They are doing very well, thank you. Allegra is now working as head nurse in the Intensive Care Unit of a large Madrid hospital, a position which she enjoys very much despite its many challenges. As you may know, she married a few years ago and she and her husband have two children and are expecting a third shortly. We wish that we could see them more often than we do but we are looking forward to their visit later this summer. Allegra will have more time to spend with us as she will be on maternity leave."

Diego continued, describing his other daughter's latest activities. "Maria is a language teacher who has travelled widely throughout Europe. A few years ago, she accepted a position in Galicia, a lush region in north-west Spain, where she taught English. She was so fascinated by the Celtic culture in that region that she decided to travel to Ireland where she is currently teaching Spanish. Who knows when she will return as she has recently met an Irishman who appears to be to her liking…

"Sofía and David, how I remember your first visit here when we were celebrating my uncle Eduardo's ninetieth birthday and then, of course, on the occasion of his one hundredth birthday! I am so pleased to see you once again, now with your daughter and one of your three sons." Miguel then added with a twinkle in his eyes, "And I can see that Alejandra and young Eduardo seem to be enjoying each other's company."

"Papá, they have just met," admonished Diego while Alicia smiled, remembering the instant rapport that she and her future husband had experienced when they were first introduced to each other.

"Welcome to our home, all of you. You may wish to refresh yourselves before we assemble prior to dinner with an aperitif and some tapas on the patio. Come, we will show you to your rooms," Alicia said as Eduardo returned with Alexandra and Maximo after their tour of the cellars and vineyard on the Martínez estate.

An hour later, with a glass of sherry in hand and some grilled garlic shrimp on which to nibble, the four Canadians were busy sharing their latest experiences with their Spanish hosts. "Tell me what you have visited in Spain, this time," urged Miguel. I know that you are great lovers of our country," he stated as he looked at David and me. After giving Miguel a brief description of what we had seen in Barcelona, Alexandra added," *Señor* Miguel, you don't know how happy I was when I received your offer of employment at this prestigious winery. It is truly a dream come true and

I have already started thinking of what might be considered for your new ad campaign."

"We are pleased to note your enthusiasm but, tonight, you must relax. We will serve you some special Cava with dinner from our *Maria Cristina* vintage, the vintage honouring my mother who died so young many years ago."

"Tomorrow," added Diego, "we have planned a very comprehensive tour of the facilities for all of you, followed by a tasting of several of our latest Cavas. I hope that this appeals to all of you. I will start the tour and then Eduardo will lead you into the tastings."

As the group enjoyed dinner, Alicia asked Maximo about the infectious diseases study program that he was taking in Seville.

"I learned a great deal about pandemics and infectious diseases over the past two years and have decided to accept an offer to work at one of the most respected hospitals in Seville. Now that I have acquired the knowledge, I wish to put it into practice and this will be a good opportunity for me. While on the topic of infectious diseases, I have an interesting story to share with you about your Spanish King Carlos IV and smallpox in the New World.

"As you know, the conquistadores and colonizers from Europe not only brought their religion, culture, books, animals and plants to the Americas but, unfortunately, they also helped to spread diseases from the Old World to the New World. It appears that half of the Aztec population died in the first century after the Europeans' arrival. The situation was worsened by the death of the Inca emperor and many more casualties caused as a result of the diseases carried by the slaves brought from Africa to Latin America to replace the decimated Indigenous population. Did you know that the major culprit among transported diseases was smallpox? Its deadly path was partially arrested after Edward Jenner developed a vaccination against the disease in 1796. Carlos IV wished to extend the vaccine's beneficial effect to the Americas by ordering a massive maritime vaccination program throughout the Spanish Empire.

"*The Royal Philanthropic Vaccine Expedition* became the first known global public health initiative whose mission was to eradicate disease, in this case smallpox, by developing a supply of vaccine and training personnel to administer it free of charge. The expedition left Spain for the New World in 1803. I was surprised to learn that its supply of live vaccine was assured by 22 young orphan boys travelling on a ship across the Atlantic. The first two boys were vaccinated with cowpox and, as pustules formed, doctors used material from them to inject two more in succession until all the boys were vaccinated during the long voyage to the New World."

"That's incredible!" exclaimed David who, like the rest of us, had never heard of this early and quite unusual humanitarian mission. "While I didn't know about this undertaking, I did read that John Clinch, an English clergyman and physician who studied medicine with Edward Jenner and who settled in Newfoundland was credited with administering the first smallpox vaccinations in the New World just ahead of the Spanish expedition. Dr. Clinch claimed to have inoculated some 700 people beginning with his wife's nephew in 1798. My father, who was a historian in St. John's, shared this interesting piece of information with me many years ago.

"And you, Alejandra (if I may use the Spanish version of your name?), what are your impressions of Spain so far?" asked Eduardo.

"Yes, please call me Alejandra. To answer your question, I am thoroughly enchanted by your country, Eduardo, and I am so happy that I will have the opportunity to learn more about it as I complete my internship here at the winery."

"If you need a guide, I will be pleased to be of assistance," offered the tall, attractive, olive-skinned Spaniard with deep brown eyes and an easy smile.

"Then, I shall be pleased to ask you for your help, Eduardo," replied Alexandra.

In the late morning of the next day, we began our tour with Miguel, Diego and Eduardo. Alexandra, in particular, had many questions to ask not only about the process involved in the production of Cava but, also, about the role that advertising played in the winemakers' world.

"Eduardo, I have been thinking of various new and startling images that we could associate with *Las Cavas Martínez* and its sparkling wines to highlight their appeal and versatility. For example, we could have an image of an opera singer in costume sitting at a table in one of your cellars, enjoying a flute of Cava or of a flamenco dancer performing in a *tablao* as she eyes a waiter pouring some Cava for patrons from a Martínez bottle. Perhaps an image of a web designer drinking Cava for inspiration as he creates a new site? As these images would be a departure from the more usual ones of couples sharing a glass of wine or of family gathered together for a special event, they could very well attract attention from a wider public. What do you think?

Without giving Eduardo time to reply, Alexandra continued, "Of course, we would also wish to reinforce the idea of Cava being the perfect libation for celebrations, large and small. The message is that Cava should not be reserved for weddings, birthdays and retirements but, like still wines, it should be part of the rituals of everyday life such as a companiable moment with a friend, a dinner with one's family, a happy interlude at a café after work, etc. Are you aware, Eduardo, of what Oscar Wilde said about the various reasons for drinking Champagne, which would apply to Cava, as well?"

"Why yes, Alejandra, my great-great-uncle Eduardo studied the Irish writer's works in later life and used to quote his words, 'Only the unimaginative can fail to find a reason for drinking Champagne.' I am intrigued by your ideas and look forward to spending more time with you in discussing how to develop them," commented Eduardo with another of his charming smiles.

"Eduardo, I just had another idea. Does Martínez produce Cava rosés? I can just picture the right advertisement for a salmon-coloured sparkling Cava."

"No, not yet, but I could discuss this possibility with my father and grandfather. I'm certain that it would be a good product to add to our stable of wines."

"Yes, they are so festive looking and their fruity notes would be a splendid accompaniment to Spain's iconic tapas, including its charcuterie."

"Sí sí, Alejandra, we shall bear that in mind but now it's time for lunch!"

After a light lunch, Diego continued our comprehensive tour of the facilities explaining, along with Miguel, the history of the winery while Eduardo educated the group about the subtle distinctions among the various types of wine produced by *Las Cavas Martínez.* As Eduardo poured each sample of wine for the participants, his eyes sought Alexandra's and when he presented her with the last flute in a flight of Cavas, I noticed how his fingers lingered ever so lightly over hers. Could there be another Spanish-Canadian romance developing in our family?

At dinner that evening, Miguel thanked us for our return visit to Villa Sol y Iris, saying, "Although I have only seen you a few times, I sense a strong connection between our families and am very pleased to have Alejandra working with us now."

"You are very kind, Miguel," I told him and, overcome with emotion, I hugged the elderly man who was the last close link to the love story that I had followed for so long. Would a new generation provide another similar connection?

Chapter 38

Spain, July 2012—May 2013

Alexandra was enjoying her position at the winery so much that she didn't even consider it to be work. Every day as she and Eduardo walked through the vineyards in the coolness of the early morning, she learned more and more about the vines that gave life to the three types of grapes, parellada, macabeo and xarello, used in the production of Cava. Eduardo would point out various vines, telling her which ones were in good health and which ones required special treatment to reach optimal growth and produce the best grapes. Later in the afternoon, she would work on the illustrations that she hoped would eventually be used in the company's promotional campaigns, keeping in mind the traditions and culture of the region. Often, at the end of her work day, Eduardo would stop by and ask her if she wished to go to a café for a pre-prandial aperitif. Diego and Alicia were generous with their dinner invitations and old Miguel never hesitated to draw her into a spirited conversation on a variety of subjects. It was a sunny, happy life and Alexandra had to admit that she was quickly falling in love with the kind man who was her tutor, friend and confidant.

In late July, Eduardo informed Alexandra that his parents were organizing a private reception at the end of August for the top executives of a number of foreign and domestic companies who regularly purchased wine from *Las Cavas Martínez*. He asked her if she would design place cards for each of the guests, reflecting their particular interests. It would be a challenging task but one that appealed to her. For the next few weeks, Alexandra spent extra hours at her desk daily, learning about the various companies that would be represented at the event featuring Cava tastings, a tour of the vineyards and cellars as well as a dance performance by Carolina's daughter, Esmeralda. The details which she gathered helped her to create unique place cards which would hopefully appeal to the guests who would be attending.

When the tables were set in the courtyard and all the cards accompanying each setting had been placed in a special holder featuring a collage of miniature bottles of Cava, Alexandra checked each table one last time, along with Eduardo. "It's perfect, querida," he whispered to her before taking her hand and kissing it gently. Surprised and a little embarrassed, she quickly told him that she had to leave in order to change for the reception.

When she returned in a lovely, form-fitting black cocktail dress highlighted by Mallorcan pearls and wearing stiletto heels, the appreciative look that she saw in Eduardo's eyes gave her the courage to walk up to him and ask if she should handle any last-minute details. "Just mingle with the guests and all will be well."

After the tours and wine tastings, the guests sat down under the stars for the flamenco performance by Esmeralda. Alexandra sat in the back row and was surprised to hear Eduardo ask her, "Is this seat taken?" During the performance, he held her hand and then asked her to wait for him after the guests had left.

Miguel, Diego and Alicia all came to see her and compliment her on her work, which had been well appreciated by the guests. "We are so glad that you are here," stated Miguel and then added, "You know, sometimes I like to pretend that you are the daughter that I never had. I hope that you don't mind."

"I am delighted, Miguel, and I can truthfully say that you are like my favourite uncle."

Later that evening, after a cup of coffee with Esmeralda whose flamenco dancing had impressed all the guests, Eduardo offered to escort Alexandra to her apartment on the estate. As they walked under a sky laden with stars, he complimented her on all her hard work and asked how she was enjoying her internship at *Las Cavas Martínez*.

"It is such a wonderful experience, Eduardo, and one that is beyond my wildest dreams," replied Alexandra who, by now, was thoroughly intoxicated by the magical evening, the glasses of Cava she had been offered and Eduardo's proximity. Eduardo drew her more closely to him and finally pressed his lips against hers. She responded to his long and passionate kiss with all the fervour that had been building in her for the past weeks since her arrival.

"Having you here has also been very special for me. I never imagined that I would be so attracted to you," admitted Eduardo. "What began as a simple flirtation for me has blossomed into something very special," he added with a lump in his throat.

"While I have enjoyed my career experience here, I must admit that working with you has been even better," replied Alexandra, her eyes reflecting the starlight overhead. "Every day, I look forward to spending time with you, as well as to discussing and realizing our joint projects for the winery."

"Do you think that my family suspects anything?", asked Eduardo.

"Miguel is certainly conscious of the attraction," confirmed Alexandra who was subject to his light teasing on a regular basis.

"What do you say to another kiss then as I can see him at his window, watching us?"

"Why not? It will make him happy and me even happier."

As Alexandra prepared to retire, she reflected on the day, wondering what the future held for her. She fell asleep dreaming of the special Spaniard who had won her heart so completely…

Toronto, December 2012

Dear Carolina,

How have you been? David and I were so sorry that we couldn't see you this year while we were in Spain but I know how busy you must have been preparing for Alonzo's wedding, given that we were doing the same thing a few months later for our son Charles.

We were delighted to read about all the celebrations which accompanied Alonzo's wedding. It seems as if every event in Spain is celebrated with unbridled enthusiasm!

Following the excitement of Charles's wedding to Shannon this past August, it was somewhat of a letdown to return to a quiet house after their departure on an extended honeymoon and work experience trip to South America. We will not see them again until next summer as they will be teaching French and English classes in Buenos Aires. What a wonderful experience for them!

It will be a strange Christmas for us this year as Nicholas and Alexandra will be the only two children celebrating with us. How wonderful that he and his family are living in Toronto and will be able to spend the holidays with us! We are very happy as well that Alexandra will be arriving from Barcelona tomorrow and will spend two weeks with the family. She seems so excited about her position at the winery and especially about a certain person working there….

Maximo is also enjoying his work in Spain and David and I are so grateful that you and Juan have welcomed him to your home on so many occasions. We know that he is very much looking forward to experiencing Spanish Christmas traditions with you and your family.

Both David and I continue to work part-time and with our employment, courses, the family and entertaining our friends, we maintain a full schedule. How about you? Have you decided to retire yet?

All the best to you both at Christmas and in the New Year! Give Maximo a big hug for us both!

Sophie

Alexandra was very excited to be home with her parents for Christmas and to spend time as well with her brother Nicholas, sister-in-law Paula and their children. "How is your new promotional campaign for *Martínez Cavas* working out?" Nicholas asked during the Christmas dinner hosted by their parents. "Are you pleased with the results?"

"To be honest, I think that it is quite a success," Alexandra replied proudly. Our slogan is 'We started small but have never stopped growing' and we are currently focusing on our younger customers who are gradually switching from beer to wine to Cava. Sales are increasing every month with this group. Soon, we will start another campaign, this one to reinforce the choice of Cava made by our older, more traditional buyers who associate our wines with the celebration of various milestones in their lives. We plan to convince them that Cava isn't just for special celebrations like Christmas and weddings but also for smaller, more intimate moments in life. How fortunate I am to have such a dream job!" she concluded.

"And how is the family with whom you work?" asked Nicholas very innocently.

Alexandra's enthusiastic reply, "They are just wonderful!", accompanied by the look of deep longing that her eyes revealed, convinced her brother and his wife that it was undoubtedly a specific member of that Spanish family who was responsible for her happiness.

"How about a glass of Cava to toast Christmas and the Martínez family?" suggested David.

"A great idea, Dad," replied Alexandra who vowed at that very moment that, despite the warm closeness that she felt in the embrace of her family, she would never again spend another Christmas without the man she loved at her side.

Mallorca, May 2013

"Alejandra, as I know how fascinated you are by the ocean, I wish to offer you the opportunity of visiting a beautiful region on the northern tip of the island of Mallorca called Cap de Formentor, which is located on a peninsula boasting a windswept lighthouse. Would you like to accompany me to this region for a weekend? We could explore its long, sandy beaches and visit its traditional markets. We have worked so hard lately on our new promotional campaigns that I feel we deserve a little relaxation."

"How wonderful that sounds, Eduardo! Yes, I would love to visit the area that you describe. When would we go?"

Two weeks later, Eduardo and Alexandra took the ferry from Barcelona to Palma and then drove a rental car through the vertiginous mountain road that snaked its way to the Formentor Peninsula where they found an isolated strip of sandy beach. There, they spread a comfortable blanket on the sand and opened the picnic lunch that they had purchased in Palma: smoked salmon sandwiches, an avocado and orange salad and *petits fours.* As the couple enjoyed the dramatic view of the sea before them, the thunderous cerulean waters creating a frothy wake before crashing against the shore in their endless quest to meet land, Eduardo took Alexandra's hand and kissed it. "*Mi amor*, I fell in love with you almost from the very first moment that I saw you and decided that you were the woman with whom I wished to spend the rest of my life. I hope that you feel the same way, dearest heart."

"Yes, I too was immediately attracted to you but dared not hope that the feeling was mutual. I love you so much, Eduardo."

On bended knee, Eduardo then asked Alexandra, "Will you marry me and make me the happiest man alive?"

"Yes, darling Eduardo, I will marry you and love you for the rest of my life."

The proposal was then sealed with a kiss before the couple returned to their car and made their way to the elegant hotel facing the ocean where they had made reservations for a special dinner. Eduardo and Alexandra walked through the beautiful gardens of the hotel property, enjoying the magnificent views of the ocean, the refreshing sea breezes and the idyllic charm of the area. While dining later that evening, Eduardo asked, "Would you like to get married next summer? Are you prepared to leave your home in Canada and move to Spain to be with me? The vineyard is my life and I hope that you wish to make it yours, too."

"While it will be difficult to leave my family, friends and country, I am willing to do so because I love you so much. However, I do hope to have our wedding in Toronto."

"Of course."

"I would also like to have the opportunity of returning home regularly to visit my family or have them visit us."

"Nothing would please me more. I would also like to spend time with them. Perhaps after our marriage in Toronto, we could have a big reception at Villa Sol y Iris for all my family and friends, as well as any of yours who would like to attend. That way, Miguel who is now ninety-seven and my sister María who is teaching in Ireland, as well as Allegra who has three very young children, would at least be able to attend our wedding reception in Spain, given that it is probable that they would not be able to fly to Canada for the actual ceremony."

"That sounds lovely. A wedding and two receptions!' "When shall we tell everyone about our engagement?" asked Alexandra.

"I can't wait. Let's tell them as soon as we return to the villa!"

"Alejandra, how was your weekend on Mallorca?" asked Miguel. "However, I think that it is a superfluous question as your smiles and sparkling eyes reveal your happiness. What did happen this weekend if I may ask?"

"We are engaged!" exclaimed Alexandra in unison with Eduardo.

A chorus of "What wonderful news!" followed. Alexandra explained how Eduardo proposed to her in the most romantic of settings as they faced the dramatic views of a wild ocean, its waves foaming against the shore.

Once the reality of the news sank in, Alicia asked somewhat timidly, "And what will your parents think of your living here so far from your home, Alejandra?"

"Are you prepared to spend your life here working for *Las Cavas Martínez*?" questioned Diego.

"Alejandra, do you love Eduardo enough to sacrifice seeing your family and friends on a regular basis and to adopt a new culture here?" wondered Miguel.

Alexandra thought for a minute and then replied, "To answer all your questions, I am certain that my parents, while sad to see me leave Canada for another country, will only wish for me to be happy. Moreover, Eduardo and I agree that I will travel to Canada or my family will travel here regularly. As to the vineyard, I never thought that I would be so interested in carrying out this work, but I am and I know that I can count on your guidance. Miguel, I love Eduardo enough to be very happy here with him and, besides, with all the modern means of communication at our disposal today, I will never be far away from family and friends. Also, with my marriage to Eduardo, I will inherit another family whom I already love," she stated as she smiled at Diego, Alicia and Miguel.

Miguel remained thoughtful and then said, "You know, I remember my uncle Eduardo telling me in his later years, 'If only I had placed love ahead of other considerations, I would have been a happier man in my earlier years! Never reject a love that you know is right for you.' I followed his advice and I am pleased that you are doing the same."

David and I received the enthusiastic call from the newly engaged couple just a few minutes later. We were, of course, very happy for them but sad that our only daughter would be moving so far away to begin a new life with Eduardo. However, as I reflected upon the situation, it felt right. My grandmother's loss of Eduardo had come full circle with Alexandra's marriage to his namesake.

I made a mental note to collect the magnificent ring that I had placed in a safety deposit box at the bank many years before, the ring that Eduardo had given me so long ago and that had been destined for my grandmother. As both David and I felt that it should be returned to the Martínez family, we offered it to the younger Eduardo during a private telephone conversation with him a few days later. He gladly accepted the gift, which not only would prove to be a striking engagement ring for our daughter, but also a reminder of the strong links between the two families. Had the senior Eduardo not told me when we first met that he had hoped that his namesake would one day give this very ring to his future bride? How right this felt!

Eduardo promised David and me that he would accompany Alexandra to Toronto in December and present her with this very special engagement ring at Christmas. I could barely wait to observe her reaction…

Chapter 39

TORONTO, DECEMBER 2013 TO JULY 2014

Toronto, December 2013

Dear Carolina,

What a Christmas celebration we will have this year! All of our children will finally be home: Nicholas and his family, Charles and Shannon who have returned to Toronto from Buenos Aires, Alexandra and Eduardo who will be flying here from Barcelona and Maximo who will be leaving Seville for Canada next week before starting a six-month contract with Médecins sans frontières *in Africa. David and I can barely believe our good fortune.*

We are very pleased with Alexandra's engagement to Eduardo and look forward to their wedding next July. While David and I will be sad to see our daughter leave Toronto permanently, we are so happy that she has found the right person with whom to spend the rest of her life. Moreover, we feel that we have our own Spanish family already with you and Juan and Diego and Alicia, as well as Miguel. How kind of Alonzo to offer to help Diego and Alicia with the vineyard while they are here! I'm sure that it must mean a great deal to them.

Is Esmeralda still enjoying her career as a professional flamenco dancer? How is Francisco? Maximo and he are such good friends and have many interests in common, in addition to their medical careers. David and I wish to thank you most sincerely for having made our son feel so comfortable while in Seville and for having given him a second place to call home while he was there.

Well, as I have a great deal of baking and shopping to do in preparation for Christmas, I will wish you "Feliz Navidad" and a Happy New Year. Now that David and I are both retired, we will have plenty of time to prepare for the July wedding!

Abrazos from Sofía

P.S. I can't wait to give Eduardo the magnificent heirloom engagement ring that his great-great-uncle had modified for my grandmother a century ago and to see Alexandra's reaction upon receiving this special gift. Remember: it's a secret until Christmas!

Toronto, March 2014

Dear Alicia,

It seems as if every year has more activities crammed into it than the preceding one! David and I are very much looking forward to Alexandra's return to Toronto for the three months preceding her wedding. Not only will this provide her with the opportunity to finalize all details in a more leisurely fashion, she will also be able to visit her friends and family here before her big day and her permanent move to Spain. Of course, as parents we are sorry that she will be living so far away but with today's modern communications, it is so much easier to keep in touch than it was before. We skype once a week and text each other almost daily. Since I couldn't be there for the all-important trip to a wedding boutique, I am grateful that you and Carolina stepped in to help guide Alexandra in her choice of a wedding gown; she tells me that it has a distinctive Spanish style that I will love!

Charles and Shannon continue to maintain contacts with their friends in Buenos Aires where they enjoyed the city's lifestyle and visited many interesting sites.

Nicholas and Paula are busy with their two young sons and, of course, with their baby daughter, the newest addition to their family. We are so happy that they live close to us, as do Charles and Shannon.

Maximo is truly enjoying his work with Médecins sans frontières *in Africa despite its many challenges. He will, however, take the time to fly down to Toronto for the wedding.*

You mentioned that you and Diego and Carolina and Juan would like to visit an area close to Toronto after the wedding for a short trip and asked for our suggestions. As you indicated that you were interested in seeing Niagara Falls, would you like to add a visit to the beautiful town of Niagara-on-the-Lake, famous for its annual Shaw Theatre Festival? You could then tour a few of the vineyards in the Niagara Region and try their wines which, as oenophiles, you might like to compare with your own. One activity that you must take in while you are in the National Capital is a trip to the Canadian Museum of History. It will be featuring a special exhibit on the one hundredth anniversary of the sinking of The Empress of Ireland, *the ship on which Eduardo and Maria Cristina sailed in 1913. I have taken the liberty of buying tickets for you all and, as requested, I have reserved rooms for you at the historic Château Laurier, one of our country's original railway hotels.*

Alexandra tells me that Miguel is doing well despite his advancing age and that he very much regrets that he will be unable to attend her wedding to Eduardo. However, he has begged her to ensure that a video of the wedding be made for him. We are looking forward to seeing Miguel again at the wedding reception to be held at Villa Sol y Iris *in late August.*

And how are your daughters? It is too bad that they will be unable to attend the wedding in Toronto but we are also looking forward to seeing them at the reception that you will be hosting afterwards.

David and I are eagerly awaiting your arrival in Toronto this summer.

Love from Sofía

Seville, May 2014

Dear Sofía,

Diego, Alicia, Juan and I are all very excited about the prospect of seeing you, David and your family very soon and especially at the wedding of your daughter to Eduardo. How enjoyable it will be to experience a Canadian wedding, as well as to see your country for the first time! For Spaniards, it is difficult to believe that the thermometer can reach thirty degrees C and higher during the summer as most of our stereotypical images of Canada are those of a winter wonderland!

Alonzo and Rocio have welcomed a son into this world and are quite besotted with him! Little Carlos is our first grandchild and we are thrilled to have him so close to us. After Rocio has completed her maternity leave, she will gradually assume much of the work at my boutique although I plan to continue helping her for another little while. The same applies to Juan's wine shop that Alonzo is now managing under his father's careful eye. We are pleased that we can enjoy more free time now but not be completely divorced from our interests.

Francisco will be completing his residency in emergency medicine in late May and hopes (if you don't mind) to accompany us to the wedding. It will be good for him as he needs a break after his long period of studies and he will be very happy to see his good friend Maximo again. Esmeralda continues to perform throughout Spain and frequently in South America, as well. Next year, she is scheduled to go on a world tour. She enjoys her life but I would find it too lonely without a family. However, as Juan constantly reminds me, we have to accept our children's choices.

Thank you for your suggestions for the trip that we shall take after the wedding. Diego and Alicia agree with us that a trip to Niagara Falls, Niagara-on-the-Lake and the wine region would be wonderful and, of course, we are thrilled that you have secured tickets for the Empress *exhibit at the Canadian Museum of History.*

Un gran abrazo!
Carolina

Toronto, June 2014

After emailing my reply to Carolina confirming that Francisco would be most welcome to attend Alexandra and Eduardo's wedding, I shared my concerns about Maximo with David. While we admired his humanitarian mission with *Médecins sans frontières*, we were naturally worried about the difficult and even perilous conditions under which he was living and working in Africa. We were also concerned about the future of his relationship with Esmeralda. We noticed that during our last phone calls with him, he had resisted all attempts to provide us with information about her and we feared that the romance was now on shaky ground.

Maximo made it back to Toronto two weeks before his sister's wedding after his six-month term in Africa had ended. During this period, he had inoculated hundreds of children, delivered countless babies and explained basic health care and hygiene to the many patients who sought the assistance of the MSF doctors.

The first week after his arrival, Maximo slept constantly, ate all of his favourite foods with gusto, enjoyed all the amenities of home and then, finally, began to speak of his experiences in Africa. While he had helped to save many lives, there were so many patients for whom he could do little but offer a comforting word and a gloved hand of sympathy. Gradually, as he resumed a more normal life in Canada after the spartan conditions he had known for six months, he opened up and told us more and more about life in Africa, including some of the happier moments he had spent there. Apparently, Francisco had been a great source of comfort to him by sending him several weekly emails offering support and encouragement. Actually, Francisco became so interested in Maximo's work that he decided to abandon sports medicine to study infectious diseases and enrolled in the same program that our son took in Seville.

"Maximo, you haven't spoken of Esmeralda for some time and it appears that you parted on somewhat acrimonious terms before flying to Toronto. Your father and I don't wish to intrude upon your privacy but we would like to know if it is all over between the two of you? I never know what to say when I write to Carolina and I have noticed that she, too, hesitates to mention anything about your relationship with Esmeralda."

"Mom, Dad, I guess that you deserve an honest answer after all the worries that I put you through while I was in Africa. As you know, Esmeralda and I were very much attracted to each other and we fell in love. I knew that dancing was her passion but I didn't realize that eventually it would come between us. You know, one usually expects a doctor's schedule to interfere with his private life but, of course, a dancer's schedule is in some ways worse due to constant travel and short stays in numerous cities. I proposed to her when I was preparing to leave Seville but she refused, saying that she would only marry me if I continued to live in Spain, given that her flamenco art received its inspiration and life from her own country. As I wasn't prepared to give up Canada and my own professional aspirations and she refused to leave Spain, that spelled the end of our relationship. It's sad but, ultimately, the right decision for both of us.

David echoed my thoughts when he placed his hand on Maximo's shoulder and said, "We are proud of you and only wish you the very best. I know that it is small comfort to hear but it is true: somewhere in this world, there is a girl who is waiting to meet you. You just have to find her as I found your mother in a vineyard!"

"Really David!"

"And what are your future plans now that you are back in Toronto?" David asked.

"I have found a few contracts filling in for various doctors' locums during the next few months and will enjoy being a regular family doctor, treating coughs, ear aches and fractures. I am also currently looking into a position with Canada's National Microbiology Lab in Winnipeg where I can put my knowledge of infectious diseases into practice."

"That sounds like an excellent position for you but, in the meantime, it is so wonderful to have you home once again," I said with a happy smile.

Toronto, early July 2014

How special these past few months at home with the family have been thought Alexandra as she admired her striking engagement ring whose pink and blue sapphires encircling a large diamond sparkled in the brilliant July sunshine! She was on her way to a local restaurant for a bridal luncheon that would gather many of her cherished friends and relatives. While she missed Eduardo and thought of him every day, she was also very happy to have the opportunity of seeing old friends once again and of dealing in person with the last details of their wedding and subsequent honeymoon in the wine country of British Columbia and California. She and Eduardo would be staying at two of the grand Canadian railway hotels: the Château Lake Louise near Banff and the Empress Hotel in Victoria before making their way to the Okanagan Valley and finally to the Napa Valley. She glanced at the program for the wine tour that they would be taking aboard an elegant, early twentieth century vintage train offering gourmet cuisine and stopping at some of the most celebrated terroirs in the Napa Valley including the Domaine Chandon, a pioneer of California sparkling wine founded by the French Champagne house of Moët & Chandon. It would be interesting, she mused, to view more of its advertisements and to compare its sparkling wine with that produced by Martínez.

Eduardo would be arriving tonight with his parents, as well as Carolina, Juan and Francisco and their hosts had planned a big barbecue for them all to introduce them to a typical Canadian experience. Alexandra felt like a child, counting the hours before Christmas and unable to wait any longer. After all, it had been three months since her tearful good-bye to Eduardo despite her good intentions not to shed any tears at all.

When Alexandra saw Eduardo descending the escalator at the airport, she rushed into his arms and raised her lips to his. Their kiss was so prolonged that when they turned around to greet the others, they were somewhat embarrassed to be treated to a long round of applause by other arrivals…

During the interval, David and I welcomed Diego, Alicia, Carolina and Juan while Maximo greeted his good friend Francisco enthusiastically.

"We are so happy to be here with you, dear friends and to have the opportunity to spend a little time in your country," commented Carolina.

"And how much warmer it is than we imagined!" observed Diego.

"Yes, indeed, Canada enjoys or endures great temperature extremes between summer and winter with a range of some 60 degrees Celsius or more," stated David.

"We have invited Nicholas and his wife Paula, as well as Charles and his wife Shannon, to join us tonight so that you will have the opportunity of meeting all of our family before the wedding," I informed our guests.

Two hours later with drinks in their hands and steaks on the barbecue, a very animated conversation was taking place among the Spaniards and Canadians forming the large group. In response to a question about his work, Nicholas explained how he planned and promoted themed tours of Canada for tourists. "For example, some visitors are attracted to our wine regions in Quebec, Ontario and British Columbia whereas others seek the tranquility of our lakes and mountains in Alberta and the North. We also familiarize tourists with our lighthouse accommodation in the Atlantic Region and with our famous museums. Others enjoy walking tours of Winnipeg's Exchange District and The Forks or theatrical tours such as the those taking place in the tunnels of Moose Jaw, Saskatchewan where tourists can relive Al Capone's bootlegging days or experience the hardships of Chinese immigrants. History buffs enjoy staying for a night or two in one of our grand hotels built by railway barons from coast to coast. Some of these hotels such as Winnipeg's Fort Garry even boast their own ghosts!"

"How interesting to learn all of these details! "stated Carolina. "And what about your year in Argentina; how did you enjoy the experience?" she asked Charles and Shannon.

"Ah, it was amazing. There was so much to see and do all the time that we were there," enthused Charles. "Actually, our barbecue tonight reminds me a little of the many *parrilladas* that we enjoyed in Argentina. Racks and racks of grilled lamb, sausages, chicken and steak were certainly the order of the day, accompanied by many delicious wines from the Mendoza region such as Malbec and Trapiche." Turning towards their Spanish guests, he added, "At first, we didn't realize that Argentina was one of the world's major wine producers and that Mendoza was the first region outside of France that the prestigious French Champagne house Chandon selected for the production of its high-quality sparkling wines due to the area's chalky soils and semi-desert climate."

"We haven't visited Argentina yet but we must add it to our travel list," declared Juan, looking affectionately at Carolina.

"And Carolina, don't forget to tour the Evita Peron Museum in Buenos Aires," suggested Shannon, knowing of the Spanish woman's interest in style and clothing. "There is a most amazing collection of her iconic outfits there."

"How I would enjoy visiting that museum!" exclaimed Carolina. "Of course, Esmeralda has already spoken very favourably of Buenos Aires, having visited it on several occasions to perform in flamenco shows in various venues there. Speaking of dances, I understand, Charles and Shannon, that you became proficient tango dancers during your stay in Buenos Aires."

"I'm not so sure about dancing the tango proficiently but it was fun trying. However, it is very different from the Irish folk dancing that was part of my early life in Newfoundland," answered Shannon.

"I'm sorry to interrupt but is anyone hungry?" David asked as I set the last platters of food on the table.

Once seated at the table, David asked Francisco about his current work.

"I have decided to pursue my work as an emergency physician in Seville for the near future. However, like Maximo, I am considering a six-month contract with *Médecins sans frontières* next year as I feel the need to contribute my skills and knowledge to regions which are so deprived of medical help."

"And you, Maximo? "asked Diego. "What are your career plans?"

"I will most probably begin working for Canada's National Microbiology Laboratory in Winnipeg later this fall. The scientists there are concentrating their work on the development of a vaccine to prevent Ebola, as well as on the creation of a mobile laboratory that will facilitate testing in the remote areas of West and Central Africa where Ebola strikes."

"How is the virus transmitted?" asked Alicia.

"The disease is transmitted via wild animals such as bats and then spreads in the human population through direct contact with the blood or bodily fluids of infected people and with surfaces such as bedding and clothing contaminated with these fluids. Consequently, it is very dangerous for the medical personnel treating the patients who must wear protective clothing from head to toe. Sadly, Ebola kills about half of those who become infected."

"What a very valuable initiative!" commented Francisco who was proud of his friend's achievements.

"Carolina, how is little Carlos doing?" asked Paula who had learned all about Sophie's "adopted" family in Spain.

"Very well, indeed. And your children?"

"They are all active and happy but, of course, keep me very busy as I struggle with my hectic schedule as a television reporter."

"And how is Miguel, Alicia?"

"He is very well for his age. Do you know that he will turn one hundred in two years and continues to take an active interest in the winery? He is also very pleased that Eduardo and Alejandra are getting married and has made them promise to provide him with a video recording of the ceremony."

As the meal was ending, David and I thanked our guests for travelling to Toronto on the occasion of our daughter's and Eduardo's wedding. "You don't know how much this means to us."

Meanwhile, Alexandra and Eduardo had eyes only for each other. It was difficult to believe that they would actually be wed in two more days.

Our daughter's wedding day! It seems that it was only yesterday when I was rocking her in my arms, soothing her tears when she had a scraped knee or comforting her when she faced life's little disappointments. Now, she was about to walk up the aisle with her father and marry a man who would take her thousands of kilometres away to a land that I had always loved but which was now separating me from her. The old adage "Be careful what you wish for!" came to mind…

The morning had flown by so quickly, taken up by hair and make-up appointments, and now we were seated in the church, dressed in all our finery to witness this memorable moment in Alexandra's and Eduardo's lives. I looked across the aisle and saw Alicia dabbing her eyes and Diego putting a comforting arm around her. I reminded myself that it was the cycle of life and that my parents had undoubtedly experienced the same emotions the day I married David.

The old church organ stirred into life and the first notes of the Bridal March sounded. Loud whispers followed as Alexandra, looking so beautiful in her Spanish wedding gown and veil, slowly made her way on David's arm to the front of the church where Eduardo was waiting. I could just make out his words "*Eres tan bonita, cariña,*" (You are so lovely, my darling) when she reached him. The couple smiled as the priest greeted them and soon after they promised to "love and honour each other" for the rest of their lives, they were pronounced man and wife.

After the ceremony, Alexandra and Eduardo thought of Miguel and asked Maximo for a Skype connection and soon the happy couple posed with their parents so that a faraway nonagenarian could enjoy the moment with them just as they experienced it themselves. Eduardo reminded

David and me, "Do not feel that you have lost a daughter, only that you have gained a son and all his loving family." In the midst of the celebrations, I could not but feel that he was speaking the truth.

The next day, we wished the newlyweds "Bon Voyage" as they left on their honeymoon trip to the Rockies and the wineries of British Columbia and California. Cries of "Try not to work too hard when visiting the wineries!" followed the happy couple as they boarded their plane.

After showing our Spanish guests many of Toronto's highlights, I asked them if they would enjoy a visit to the city's unique Elgin and Winter Garden Theatres. The double-decker building featured the Elgin, constructed as a formal, gilded theatre resplendent with red velvet and cherubs, and the Winter Garden sitting seven stories above it, a botanical fantasy reminiscent of a garden with evocative hand-painted murals and a ceiling of real beech branches with small lanterns twinkling over pillars resembling tree trunks. The Elgin and Winter Garden Theatres are the last surviving Edwardian stacked theatres in the world.

Two days later, David and I accompanied our guests to the Canadian Museum of History in Gatineau to view the *Empress of Ireland* exhibit which we had promised to show them. Titled "Canada's Titanic: The Empress of Ireland", the exhibit evoked both the splendour and tragedy of the lovely but doomed ocean liner on the one hundredth anniversary of its sinking on May 29, 1914. After colliding with another ship in the fog east of Rimouski, the *Empress* sank in fewer than fifteen minutes, taking with it 1,012 passengers and crew.

"What a fascinating exhibit!" remarked Carolina who, other than hearing about her grandmother's and great-uncle's trip on the *Empress of Ireland* to Canada, had little knowledge of the liner nor of its sad history. As such, the many artifacts displayed, as well as the artfully recreated cabins and lounges, helped to tell the riveting story of the ill-fated voyage that changed the course of so many lives. The ship's bell and compass and samples of the china used to serve its many passengers provided a glimpse of its sad history but, a century later, I was struck by the personal items such as a hand mirror, a pocket watch and a shoe which helped to create the emotional connection between the tragedy and visitors learning about it through the exhibit.

"We thank you so much for introducing us to this aspect of the lives of Maria Cristina and Eduardo. Their journey across the Atlantic on the *Empress* must have been a most enjoyable one," affirmed Diego. "I will tell Miguel all about this exhibit when we return to Spain. He will undoubtedly wish to hear more about the life of the mother he barely knew and of his beloved uncle Eduardo."

"We have reserved a table at Zoe's (named after the wife of Canada's Prime Minister Sir Wilfrid Laurier) at the Château Laurier for high tea," I informed our guests. It seemed to be an appropriate way to end an afternoon devoted to the history of a famous ocean liner. "Did you know that Charles Melville Hays, President of the Grand Trunk Railway, was actually travelling to Ottawa in April 1912 to officially open this hotel when he perished at sea on the *RMS Titanic*?"

David and I bade a fond farewell to our guests, wishing them a good trip to the Niagara Region where they planned to enjoy the triple attractions of wine, theatre and nature. "You may not be aware of this but, for many years, Niagara Falls was the honeymoon capital of Canada. You can always recreate this feeling while you are there!" teased my husband as we left the Château Laurier.

"We will do our best!" promised Alicia and Diego, as well as Carolina and Juan.

"And we look forward to seeing you soon at the *Villa Sol y Iris* for Eduardo and Alejandra's second wedding reception," added Alicia and Diego.

Six weeks later David and I were back in Canada once again, unpacking our suitcases after attending our daughter's second wedding reception in Spain. I could still picture Miguel's wide smile as he opened the massive but familiar door at the *Villa Sol y Iris*, welcoming us with great enthusiasm. "*¡Que bueno de verlos otra vez, amigos míos!*" (How good to see you again, my friends!)

A well-tanned Alexandra and Eduardo soon arrived to greet us. "You both look so happy," I observed. "It is indeed wonderful to see you again," David added as we hugged the newlyweds who were eager to describe their wedding trip to British Columbia and California. Diego and Alicia soon joined us in a very animated conversation about their trip to the Niagara Region and the wines that they had tried while they were exploring the area.

After the highlights of their trips had been shared with us, we turned to Miguel who told us how happy he was to have been able to share the joy of Eduardo and Alexandra's wedding day from afar. He had also been active in planning certain aspects of the reception that was held at the winery for close members of the family such as Alonzo and Rocio, Allegra and Martín, Rafael and Eva, as well as Maria and Esmeralda who had been unable to attend the wedding in Toronto. In addition to serving his vineyard's best Cava, Miguel decided to highlight Eduardo and Alexandra's marriage by personally selecting some of the music for their reception, including the lovely "Noches de boda" (Wedding Nights) by Joaquín Sabina, one of Spain's great songwriters.

As Miguel invited the newlyweds to begin the first dance, he spoke movingly of his attachment to the couple. "Eduardo, you epitomize many of the qualities not only of your father but also of your great-great uncle, my uncle Eduardo. I know that if he were here today, he would be so proud of you and of your choice of a bride and lifetime companion. Alejandra, while I never knew the joy of having my own daughter, I can truly say without, I hope, offending your own father that nobody could have filled that role any better than you. May you and Eduardo enjoy a long and rich life together as I did with Teresa and may your love grow stronger with each year of your marriage!" There were few dry eyes watching the couple as they kissed Miguel and their parents before beginning the first dance in the beautifully decorated courtyard.

As Alexandra and Eduardo waltzed around the courtyard, the new bride whispered to the groom, "Like Dom Pérignon, 'I am tasting stars!' Is it the Champagne or you, my love?", she asked playfully.

Unknowingly echoing the words of his great-great-uncle to his wife's great-grandmother so many years earlier in another country across the ocean, Eduardo gallantly replied, "You may be tasting stars but I see them in your azure eyes and wonder at the magic of it all."

As we closed our suitcases on yet another successful trip, I remarked to David, "Isn't it strange how the discovery I made in my grandmother's attic so many years ago eventually led to my writing to Margarita in Spain where Alexandra met and married Eduardo's namesake? Now, that is quite a story although I still find it unusual that I wasn't able to find one single letter that Eduardo wrote to my grandmother. Surely, they must have corresponded to express the love they felt for each other after Eduardo's departure for Spain. After all, he had promised to return for Maggie the next year."

"Perhaps they are somewhere close to you but you just haven't found them yet," David suggested somewhat enigmatically.

Chapter 40

Toronto, August 2015—February 2016

Toronto, August 2015

Dear Carolina,

It is difficult to believe that more than a year has already elapsed since we last saw each other at Villa Sol y Iris for Alexandra and Eduardo's second wedding reception. In the intervening period, we were saddened by the loss of my father whose gentle and kind presence was always a source of great delight to us.

At Canada's National Microbiology Lab, Maximo has been working with a team that has developed a very promising vaccine to treat Ebola. I shudder whenever I think of him working with such dangerous pathogens. Of course, he has agreed to travel to Africa to administer the vaccine where it is needed. I pray every day for his health and well-being. How is Francisco's work with Médecins sans frontières *working out?*

One good consequence of Maximo's work in Winnipeg has been his new relationship with Charlotte, a lovely physician, whom he is now dating on a regular basis. We had dinner with them last month and were very impressed with her.

Alexandra continues to enjoy life at the winery but will not be able to sample any of its products for the next months as she is pregnant and due to have twins early next year! What good news! Over the past few months, she has been calling me frequently to compare her twin pregnancy with mine when I was carrying Nicholas and Charles. I am happy to hear that she is doing very well and to date has not experienced any significant problems. Actually, the twins should be born before our 40th wedding anniversary trip to Spain next spring and we expect that the babies' christenings will take place during our visit.

There will be a third grandchild born in 2016 as Charles's wife Shannon is expecting for next February.

We are happy that we are able to see Nicholas and Charles, along with their families on a regular basis. At least, we have two children living in the same city now!

I look forward to hearing from you soon and hope that you and Juan are well. Where is Esmeralda performing these days? Is Alonzo's wife enjoying her work at the boutique?

Sophie

Seville, October 2015

Dear Sofía,

I was sorry to hear about your father's passing. You must miss him very much.

What wonderful news about Charles and Shannon, as well as Alejandra and Eduardo! I saw Miguel last week and he is so looking forward to the birth of the twins. Imagine: three new grandchildren for you next year!

Francisco will soon be finished his work with Médecins sans frontières. *He is currently in Brazil, dealing with the devastating effects of the Zika virus. The virus is transmitted by the same mosquito that carries dengue and yellow fever and it is particularly nefarious when it infects pregnant women as it can cause infants to be born with microcephaly and other problems such as severe motor and vision impairment. Juan and I are proud of Francisco's contribution to the management of the Zika virus pandemic that began in 2015 and that affected many countries, especially those in Latin America and the Caribbean, but so relieved that he will be returning to Seville soon. I am certain that you remember seeing the sad reports on television about the babies afflicted with the Zika virus and the difficult future that they face. As well, many women are being abandoned by the babies' fathers, left alone to take care of these unfortunate infants.*

Before leaving for Brazil, Francisco proposed to his girlfriend Liliana and they are to be married next April. We are very happy for them both and hope that you and David will be able to attend the wedding in Seville. I believe that your anniversary cruise will end in time for you to join us. Apparently, Maximo will serve as best man.

We will have much to celebrate next year in addition to the wedding. Miguel turns one hundred and Eduardo and Alejandra have confirmed that they will celebrate Miguel's milestone birthday and the babies' christenings while you are in Spain to allow you and David to attend both events. Also, how lovely that you will also celebrate your fortieth wedding anniversary in Spain where you enjoyed your honeymoon!

Alonzo and Rocio are expecting a second baby next February. Our families are definitely growing! Rocio enjoys her work at the boutique very much and I am pleased to have a lighter work schedule.

Esmeralda is still touring, this time in South America. How we wish that she would settle down but, of course, it is her life to lead as she wishes.

I am counting the days until we meet again at Villa Sol y Iris *next May. It will be such an exciting year!*

Abrazos,
Carolina

Toronto, February 2016

Dear Carolina,

Our Christmas celebrations were most enjoyable although we missed not having Alexandra and Eduardo with us, as well as Charles and Shannon who flew to Newfoundland to spend the holidays with Shannon's parents. Charlotte and Maximo flew in from Winnipeg for a few days and his girlfriend proved to be very popular with Nicholas, Paula and their three children, as well as with our extended family. We all thought that Charlotte was a wonderful match for our son and I, of course, did not hesitate to inform him of our opinions!

Charles and Shannon returned to Toronto in time spend New Year's Day with us. Eight weeks later, they welcomed the arrival of their first child, a daughter. Now that their baby has been born and is in good health, I am nervously awaiting news of Alexandra's delivery. I keep reminding myself (as does David) that, as the twins will be almost full-term at birth, they should be in good health.

To distract myself, I am concentrating on the many plans that we have made for our 40th wedding anniversary cruise and holiday in Spain. We plan to retrace part of our honeymoon journey, as well as to explore some new territory. Of course, we are also excited about attending the twins' christenings and Miguel's 100th birthday celebration. How history repeats itself! It does not seem that long ago that we were at Eduardo's same celebration…

We are looking forward to seeing you and Juan very soon.

Sophie

•

One snowy day as I was sorting through various pieces of correspondence, my eyes fell upon the bundle of Maria Cristina's letters, Eduardo's short note to her, the train and opera ticket stubs and the studio portraits of Eduardo and my grandmother that I had discovered in her attic almost fifty years earlier. As I was handling the photos, I noticed that there was an unusual thickness between them and their cardboard backing. I carefully slit the side of the frame and to my amazement discovered letters carefully hidden behind each photo, safe from prying eyes all these years. What would these letters reveal?

The first letter from Eduardo was written on board the *SS France* on his return journey to England and I could easily imagine the emotions my grandmother must have felt upon reading it:

> *"Tonight, as I walk down the promenade deck, my eyes seek the shimmering stars scattered across a velvet blue sky. Placid yet scintillating, they remind me of your lovely, calm nature and your sparkling eyes. I wonder, Maggie, if you, too, are gazing at the same stars as I am and thinking of this astral connection which brings us together despite the vast expanse of ocean which separates us. Although I have known you for only a short time, I find that the weeks that we have been together have revealed how much we share in common and how deeply our love binds us in so many ways. I wish that it was already next spring when we will be together once again.*
>
> *Each morning, when I wake up, I dream of the day when you will be beside me again and, every evening as I fall asleep, I imagine that I am holding you in my arms, never to let you go."*

A few days later, Eduardo wrote:

> *"Today, as I contemplated the pewter-coloured waters of the ocean and the threatening sky overhead, all seemed so dull and forlorn. Then, like sunshine bursting through the clouds, my thoughts turned to you and the entire melancholy scene before me was suffused with light and joy. How I love you, my sweet!"*

Yet another letter began with:

> *"As the kilometres are swallowed by the ship and day fades into night, the distance and time remaining before I see you again disappear. The thought of your smile uplifts me; remembering your charm and special qualities brings me joy and thinking of your love sustains me. I look*

forward not to the end of this sailing, but to the beginning of our journey together as man and wife shortly after my arrival in Winnipeg next May."

In October, after describing all the plans that he had made for his return trip to Canada and their subsequent wedding voyage to Europe and honeymoon in southern Spain, Eduardo wrote once again of his great love for Maggie:

"It seems so long ago since I last saw you, but you are always in my thoughts, particularly when I admire the photo which you gave me shortly before my departure for Spain. Although I am far away from the pleasure of your company, your presence in my heart and mind fills me with such joy that you become the light of my day."

On a cold November day, Eduardo spoke once again of how uplifting his love for Maggie was:

"Today, as the sun shone its weak autumn rays over Madrid, I thought of the warmth of your words, your generous spirit, your lovely blue eyes and, of course, the promise of your love. Just a few more months and we shall be together again!"

In yet another letter, Eduardo revealed the extent of his feelings for Maggie:

"How the words you wrote in your last letter warmed my heart and spirit! I love you, mi amor, more than you will ever know and feel so confident that we are destined for a long, happy life together."

David began gently teasing me as he saw the tears streaming down my face. "I gather that you have finally found the missing love letters from the young Eduardo that you have been seeking for so long and that they have moved you a great deal. Am I right, my love?"

I could only nod as I set down the love letters relating to the romance that had fascinated me for so long. What sort of details would I learn from the other letters hidden behind my grandmother's photo?

The first letter, sent in late November 2013, was markedly different in tone from the previous ones full of love and passion. It merely described Eduardo's latest activities and what was happening in Madrid at the time. I could imagine the disappointment and bewilderment my grandmother had felt when she read this letter. The second letter, sent in early December, stated that all wedding plans were now on hold and that Maggie should refrain from speaking of them with her family at Christmas. And now the last letter... This letter, sent a few weeks later, described the situation which led to the end of their great romance.

December 29, 1913

Querida Margarita,

By the time that you receive this letter, I shall be married. I know that this news will undoubtedly come as a shock to you and I know that it is completely my fault. I never wished to hurt you nor did I ever plan for this to happen, please believe me.

Eduardo then escribed the circumstances that led to his marriage to Victoria, ending his letter with one last wish for Maggie:

I do not ask for your forgiveness as I don't deserve it. I only ask that you believe me when I say that every word of love that I ever spoke or wrote to you was true, every gesture sincere and every sentiment authentic. Oh, my darling Margarita, I only hope that you will meet and marry a much better man than I will ever be!

Te amaré para siempre,
(I will love you forever.)
Eduardo

P.S. I have asked Maria Cristina never to refer to Victoria and to mention me as little as possible in her letters to you. Do not blame her for following my wishes. I hope that this small measure will allow you to forget me quickly and resume your life as happily as possible.

As I dabbed away my tears, the telephone rang: it was Alicia informing us that Eduardo had just left for the hospital with Alexandra and would be calling us soon to keep us abreast of all the latest developments. I thanked her for her thoughtfulness in calling as I began to think back of how I felt when I gave birth to our sons, Nicholas and Charles.

"David! David!" I called. "That was Alicia informing us that Alexandra has just left for the hospital. Oh, how I wish I was there with her!"

"Don't worry, my sweet. You know that Alexandra is in good hands. I am sure that we will be hearing from her or Eduardo very soon."

In the middle of the night, the telephone rang once again but, this time, it was Eduardo announcing the safe arrival of Miguel Diego David and Teresa Alicia Maria Cristina. We shared the parents' joy as they welcomed their two children into this world.

The next day, I was busy calling relatives and friends to let them know about the safe arrival of the twins. In my absence, Alicia generously promised to do her best to help Alexandra adjust to life with her two babies. "Dear Sofía, please know that I will look after your daughter and the infants to the best of my ability. However, I know that you will wish to care for them yourself as soon as you can and Diego and I look forward to seeing you soon."

"How is Miguel reacting to the news?" I asked.

"He is so excited that he can barely contain himself, rushing about the winery and telling everyone that he is now a great-grand-father to twins. You probably know that Miguel is very close to Alejandra and he could not be prouder of her if he were her own father!"

To add to the excitement, I also received a call from the publisher of the travel magazine for which I wrote on an ad hoc basis. Would I be interested in preparing articles on my next cruise and land trip to Spain for his magazine? He liked the idea of running a series of articles on the Mediterranean by the same writer rather than the usual single pieces, as well as the notion of featuring reviews on return visits to well-loved cities. I jumped at the opportunity and agreed to begin working on a series of articles on the Mediterranean that would be published over several months.

Chapter 41

Along Spain's Coastline, March 2016

Before leaving for Spain, I read a great deal about the country that had beckoned to me for so long, like the legendary sirens from Greek mythology luring sailors with their enchanting voices. Of course, there were many others who, like me, had succumbed to its charms including Ernest Hemingway who declared that, "Spain is the country I loved more than any other except my own." His interest in Spain provided not only the setting but also the inspiration for several of his books such as *For Whom the Bell Tolls*, *The Sun Also Rises* and *Death in the Afternoon.*

Does any other culture display the flamboyance of Spain? I hoped to convince my readers that they would be hard pressed to find a destination with as much to offer as the country which had cast its spell upon me since the early days of my childhood.

Fortunately, David and I had meticulously planned our 40th wedding anniversary trip to Europe eight months prior to our departure as, later on, we were so excited by the birth of our twin grand-children that we might have overlooked some aspects of our cruise which featured ports of call to such appealing destinations as Tangiers, Madeira, Monte Carlo, Malta, Sicily and Palma de Mallorca. We also planned to travel by train to some of the memorable Spanish cities that we had visited on our honeymoon, given that travel by rail in Spain had much improved since, as a student, I had first taken the dirty, hot, slow and malodorous trains run by RENFE. I recalled one particularly unpleasant overnight trip by train when the temperature in the cars must have been close to 40 degrees Celsius with no breeze whatsoever to refresh the fetid air. The cars were so crowded that many passengers were forced to spend hours on their feet, fighting for a little space on which to stand. At one point, one poor soul was stranded in the foul-smelling W.C. for at least a quarter of an hour, knocking furiously against the door which was piled high with suitcases that tired and discouraged passengers had placed against the restroom door, preventing the user's exit!

I flew to Spain two weeks before our cruise was to set sail from Barcelona in order to have more time with our daughter and grandchildren. David joined me some ten days later. We planned to stay for baby Miguel's and Teresa's christenings, as well as for the elder Miguel's one hundredth birthday celebration.

Things were well organized when I arrived and, for that, I was most appreciative of Alicia's many efforts. She and Diego were very kind to Alexandra who was so far away from her Canadian family at this important juncture in her life.

The babies' christening ceremony was very lovely and David and I were delighted to serve as baby Miguel's godparents and Alicia and Diego in the same capacity for little Teresa. Much Cava was drunk at the reception following the baptism but not as much as at the birthday celebration for Miguel two days later!

Eduardo asked Juan if he would kindly take a photograph of the four generations present for the occasion: Miguel, Diego, himself and the newly born babies.

Alexandra had developed a warm relationship with Miguel who obviously considered her to be a special member of the family and she certainly did her utmost, along with Eduardo, to ensure that his one hundredth birthday celebration would not soon be forgotten. She and Eduardo worked on video tributes featuring highlights from Miguel's life that were projected continuously during the reception and Alexandra designed special name cards for the occasion. A shortened version of *Carmen*, his favourite opera, was presented on the small stage in the courtyard and Esmeralda was persuaded to showcase her talents as a flamenco dancer for the guests, old and young, who gathered to pay tribute to Miguel and recognize his devotion to his family and his dedication not only to the Martínez enterprise but also to the larger community in which he lived.

At one point in the afternoon, Diego asked for everyone's silence and then proceeded to thank the audience for attending his father's special event. "I am so happy to note the many people who have come from close and afar to attend this event, including, of course, my sisters María and Allegra, who is accompanied by her husband Martín and their children, our family from Seville, Rafael and Eva, Carolina and Juan, as well as their children including Francisco who has just returned from his work with MSF in Africa and who is accompanied by his fiancée Liliana. My father has always been a family man and to see so many of you here today is a source of great pride and happiness for him. Of course, my son, Eduardo, scored extra points with my father by welcoming twins to this world with a little help from Alejandra whose parents are also here from across the ocean, along with their son Maximo and his friend Charlotte. Alicia and I would also like to thank all the Martínez personnel who have worked so hard over the years to ensure the success of this winery. My great-uncle, Eduardo, would be so pleased if he were here today to witness the outstanding international reputation enjoyed today by the small, local winery that he transformed into a large, successful enterprise. Let us raise a glass in his honour!

"Alicia and I, as well as Eduardo and Alejandra, have been working for over two years to create a special vintage wine to highlight my father's one hundredth birthday. I want to thank you, papá, for deciding not to leave us before you could taste it! We have named this Gran Reserva Cava *Miguel*, the first Martínez Cava named after a man, and ask that you all raise your glass in honour of a warm, caring man who is a loving father, grandfather and great-grandfather, as well as a special "uncle" to many other family members and a good friend to all. To Miguel!"

Miguel then rose to speak, thanking his many guests for sharing his milestone birthday with him. "I would like to thank my dear son Diego and his wonderful wife Alicia, as well as my granddaughters María and Allegra and grandson Eduardo and his wife Alejandra, for organizing this special event. You have all contributed so much to my life. With my son and family members, I also have been working on a special wine but this one is to highlight my hope for the future with the arrival of the newest additions to the family and my appreciation of the constant love that you have given me. This new *Cava Reserva* is a first for *Las Cavas Martínez*, a rosé bursting with strawberry and red current notes that was Alejandra's suggestion. I have named it *Esperanza* (Hope) and it's my wish that you will all appreciate its promise for the future. Ah, here comes my birthday cake! Enjoy!"

Alexandra had designed a huge birthday cake in the shape of a Cava bottle and bearing photos of the vineyard and its proprietors over the years. One hundred candles were carefully lit on the cake which was carried to the stage on a decorated board supported by family members. Miguel cut the first slice, tasted it with a rather quizzical look and then asked Alexandra, "Was Cava added to the ingredients of this cake? It is so light in texture, almost as if it were fashioned of angels' kisses." When she responded in the affirmative, he declared that it was the secret ingredient that made the cake so delicious.

Alexandra had also arranged for individual cakes shaped and decorated in the same style as the large birthday cake to be given to all the guests upon their departure.

After the guests had left, a very moved Miguel thanked his family once again for creating such a memorable occasion for him. He kissed his great-grandson and great-granddaughter and retired for the evening, tired but happy.

While Charlotte was talking to David, I noticed Maximo deep in conversation with Esmeralda. I hoped that the former two sweethearts had reached a reconciliation that would pave the way to new, positive feelings about their past relationship.

On the eve of their departure, family members gathered for dinner once again at *Villa Sol y Iris*. Miguel was pleased to enjoy another evening in their company, sensing perhaps that there would be very few more such gatherings for him. As usual, he was interested in the current activities of the family and in hearing about the different winemaking techniques used around the world.

"Alicia and Diego have told me how much they enjoyed their trip to the Niagara Region two years ago. I was particularly keen to learn more about the sparkling wine produced in this area and they provided me with many details. This was supplemented by Eduardo and Alejandra's report on the wines produced in the Okanagan Valley and in California. If only I were younger, I would get on a plane and see them for myself! Sofía and David, how do you find the wines of the New World as compared to those of Europe?"

While we shared our opinions with Miguel, Carolina and Juan joined their family and friends in describing their impressions of the various wines that they had tasted in the Niagara Region. "What fascinated us the most was trying the Icewines that are produced there, especially as they are so rare in Europe with the exception of a few German ones."

Esmeralda added that she had also tried the sparkling wines of Chile and Argentina while touring those countries and had enjoyed them.

Juan asked, "Why not sell some of these wines in our wine boutique, Alonzo? I think that they would do very well."

"You are right, papá. I will purchase some next month and see how popular they are, especially among younger Sevillians who are always eager to try something new."

"Speaking of boutiques," Carolina mentioned, "Rocío hopes to purchase mine within two years, once she finds the right partner."

"I am thinking of some new lines that I could introduce in addition to the ones that we already carry," Rocío added.

"Liliana, I haven't had the pleasure of speaking to you yet. I was wondering how you met Francisco?" asked Miguel.

Liliana then proceeded to explain that she was a nurse at the hospital where Francisco worked and that they had spent many long hours together during grueling shifts in Emergency.

"Francisco and Maximo, you must tell me about your work with *Médecins sans frontières* during the past few years and your current endeavours. I so admire you for your courage and willingness to take on the challenges of such work. And Charlotte, I hear that you are an obstetrician. That must be rewarding work as well."

Miguel then engaged in a long conversation with the three physicians who discussed the difficulties of treating contagious diseases such as Ebola and Zika especially in underdeveloped countries and learned more about Charlotte's demanding work with mothers undergoing difficult pregnancies.

After Miguel had spoken to each of his guests, he declared, "All this talk has made me thirsty," he declared. "Let's enjoy a glass of the *Gran Reserva Cava Margarita* that my uncle Eduardo introduced on the occasion of his ninetieth birthday, the Cava he created to honour the Canadian woman he so dearly loved many, many years ago. There are still a few precious bottles left in our cellar and I think that we should enjoy them today. To Eduardo!" he said as the flutes of Cava were served. "May the Martínez bodega that you founded continue to prosper!" A second glass was poured and Miguel said, "And now, let us drink to Francisco's and Liliana's happiness as we prepare to celebrate their upcoming wedding. May they be as happy in their marriage as all the other couples here tonight and as I was with my own beloved wife, Teresa! May I also offer my special wishes to Sofía and David who are celebrating their 40th wedding anniversary this month in Spain where they honeymooned. So many happy occasions to celebrate."

"I will say goodnight to all as I must attend to the twins now," explained Alexandra. "It has been wonderful seeing you all here for the christenings and Miguel's birthday. Please stay as long as you like. Eduardo will be pleased to give our new guests a tour of the cellars if they are interested."

Maximo walked towards me to wish me goodnight, taking the time to mention that he had had a good conversation with Esmeralda and that they were now parting on excellent terms. As I walked towards the residence, I could see him smiling at Charlotte and giving her an affectionate kiss. The future looked promising for the happy couple.

The next day, David and I left for Barcelona where we would begin our 40th wedding anniversary cruise through the Mediterranean Basin. Before embarking on our ship, we spent a weekend with Maximo and Charlotte in Barcelona. It was a golden opportunity to learn more about the woman who had apparently charmed our son and of whom we were already very fond.

I began writing the draft of a future magazine article based on our most recent stay in Catalan's capital.

> *Our experience in Barcelona was focused on Gaudí, the city's most famous Modernista artist who developed unusual approaches to architectural structures, incorporating various shapes from the natural world into chimneys, windows, balconies, benches, etc. Appropriately enough, we stayed at the Hotel Gaudí where the huge sun terrace on the top floor allowed us to enjoy exclusive views of the unique and extremely colourful chimneys embedded with broken pottery pieces covering the roof of Palau Güell, a mansion across the street designed by Gaudí for his patron, Count Eusibe Güell. From our vantage point, we could see tourists walking on what appeared to be a children's very imaginative playground enlivened with huge cones, towers with curved triangular windows, giant ceramic plants and trees mounted on pedestals with their own staircases, etc. Our terrace also provided us with panoramic vistas of Barcelona ranging from the pedestrian sight of laundry flapping in the wind to that of magnificent church spires reaching towards the heavens.*
>
> *The next day, we started with a tour of Parque Güell, an upscale housing development designed by Gaudí, that was never realized. Nevertheless, several public areas were completed including a large plaza surrounded by an impressive undulating bench of mosaics in green, blue, yellow and orange, as well as drainage pipes disguised as trees for a planned market square. A huge chimney on a gingerbread gatehouse decorated with upturned coffee mugs and a charming mosaic*

fountain whose dragon spouts a stream of water add a whimsical note to the setting.

In the next part of our tour, the guide pointed out the many facets of the exterior of Gaudí's soaring Sagrada Familia Basilica (Holy Family Basilica*) with its three grand façades designed to tell the stories of the New Testament. Begun in 1883, this magnificent house of worship remains unfinished with plans for its completion set for 2026, the one hundredth anniversary of Gaudí's death.*

Our tour ended with a walk down Passeig de Gracia where a number of famous Modernista residences are located, all of which make extensive use of ceramics, wrought iron and fanciful sculptures. One of Gaudi's landmark residences is located here: his Casa Batlló, a building with sinuous curves in iron and stone and rounded balconies. As the sun had set by the end of our tour, we were treated to the lovely sight of this building, glistening in silver and blue under its well-designed lighting which enhanced the curved stained-glass windows. After our tour, we walked to the Plaza Real close to our hotel and enjoyed a delicious paella dinner in the square amidst the palm trees and the large central fountain, all illuminated by lovely carriage lamps designed by Gaudí.

We said good-bye to Maximo and Charlotte in Barcelona before embarking on the next phase of our anniversary tour, a cruise of the Mediterranean region.

The Canary Islands

From Barcelona, we sailed to Tangiers, Morocco before arriving in the Canary Islands. I continued to work on my articles on the Spanish ports of call that we would see on our cruise as we arrived in Las Palmas de Gran Canaria.

Las Palmas is the capital of the third largest of the seven main islands forming the archipelago of the Canary Islands. Stretching from 100 to 150 kilometres away from Africa, these islands were conquered by

Spain in the fifteenth century. Our tour included a visit of the Jardín Botánico Canario *where we observed many plants indigenous to the islands of the archipelago. The most unusual one was the dragon tree whose red sap (dragon's blood) has earned it the name by which it is known. Romans used the sap and fruit of the dragon tree to create a medicinal powder, as well as to dye paints and varnishes.*

Following lunch in Las Palmas, we explored its oldest district, La Vegueta, which is known for its labyrinthine cobblestoned streets lined with historic houses embellished with wooden balconies. Among these, one finds the Casa de Colón, *the palace of the first governors of the island. Tradition has it that Christopher Columbus stayed there in 1492 during a break in his voyage to the New World while one of his three ships was being repaired.*

We ended our pedestrian tour with a walk down the lovely Santa Ana Square, a striking example of colonial Spanish architecture that boasts of a huge fountain with a canopy crowned by pineapples. Of interest to cinephiles, Hotel Madrid on the square was used in filming the movie Allied; *the café scene took place just a few metres outside the hotel.*

Our next stop was in Santa Cruz de Tenerife on the largest and most popular of the archipelago's islands. The first tourists arrived there in the late nineteenth century seeking sun and fresh air but the real boom began in the 1960s with beach-seeking crowds from northern Europe hoping for an escape from dreary grey skies. Given that the Easter period was approaching, we observed several shops selling First Communion attire. I was impressed by the pristine white sailor outfits worn by boys and the miniature wedding dresses and veils for girls, still popular in Spain today with first communicants and their families.

We then proceeded to La Orotava, home to many of Tenerife's noble families. After the Spanish conquered the Canary Islands, Andalusians emigrated to this area that features many exquisitely carved wooden balconies, the most famous of which are found at the Casa de los Balcones. *Local products such as intricate embroidery, lace, pottery and dolls dressed in regional costumes can be purchased at this site.*

Palma De Mallorca

After a side trip to Elche, famous for its date palms, we stopped in Palma de Mallorca where we took a bus that travelled past almond trees and olive and citrus groves to Sóller. An old Mediterranean town northwest of Palma built on the proceeds of the orange and lemon trade, Sóller *is a delight to visit. Upon our arrival, we strolled through its narrow, cobblestone streets lined with townhouses bearing the popular green Mallorcan shutters. In the main square, dominated by the Church of San Bartolomé, attractive cafés beckon tourists and locals alike to enter for a coffee or fresh orange juice (*"Suc de taronja de Sóller" *in the Mallorquin language, a dialect of Catalan}. The return trip to Palma, via an antique narrow-gauge train to Palma, is well worth the cost of the ride as it not only features vintage carriages with mahogany panels and brass fittings but offers a scenic journey through the mountains.*

In Palma, we enjoyed a leisurely walk through the historic quarter of the city, stopping to admire the cathedral and the lovely gardens of the Palace of Almudaina so reminiscent of those of a miniature Alhambra. The Palace, formerly an alcazar built by Muslim rulers in the thirteenth century, is today the official summer residence of Spain's Royal Family. Readers may remember the photos taken of King Juan Carlos and Queen Sofía hosting The Prince and Princess of Wales who vacationed at this palace with the young Princes William and Harry. We continued our pedestrian tour of central Palma with a visit down the tree-lined streets with their high-end boutiques selling designer shoes, purses and jewelry. Our guide pointed out a hotel designed by Gaudi during his stay in Palma; the windows and balconies of the building feature many of the elements of the artist's trademark style. On our way back to the ship, after enjoying a cup of coffee on a sunlit terrace on a warm spring afternoon, we noted the profusion of serrano hams, red peppers and garlic bulbs hanging from the ceilings of shops selling vast quantities of black and green olives and artichokes and could readily imagine the tapas that would be served with a good fino later that day…

Valencia

Valencia, the home of paella, was the last port that we visited on our cruise. While there, we decided to explore a lesser known but interesting museum called Museu Faller. *This museum preserves two of the massive figures created every year, originally from papier mâché and later from polyester and foam, from the hundreds that are consumed by fire in a pyrotechnical extravaganza held to mark the Feast of St. Joseph on March 19.*

The Festival of Las Fallas is one more of the many festivals in Spain which are part of the life cycle of the country. During the festival, elaborate and sometimes bawdy figures are created which satirize a wide array of political and popular subjects. Other figures can be very touching such as those of parents singing or playing with their children. Some are representative of the country's cultural traditions such as dancers and guitar players while others are historical or evocative of religion, trades or professions. The grand finale of the Las Fallas Festival is the torching of all the figures but two in a blazing inferno, accompanied by the sound of a million firecrackers exploding. The "pardoned" characters are preserved in the Faller Museum and illustrate the changing tastes of society over the years.

The next day, we docked in Barcelona from where we flew to Malaga to begin our own special journey of memories and of new experiences.

Chapter 42

ANDALUSIA, APRIL 2016

MALAGA

Ah, to return to the lovely parador on the mountain top overlooking the Mediterranean, the bougainvillea-draped stone building where we had spent the first few days of our honeymoon forty years earlier!

David and I were pleased to note that the *Parador de Gibralfaro* with its views of the turquoise ocean, the bullring and the revitalized port area was essentially much as we remembered it. We enjoyed dinner on the outdoor terrace, admiring the twinkling lights of Malaga and the stars overhead. While we were not served fourteen *entremeses variados* as had been the case in 1976, we did savour a delicious meal in the same dining room with its striking view of the sea. Parador staff obliged by taking an anniversary photograph of us in our lovely surroundings.

We spent a sunny afternoon in Malaga, strolling past its attractive palm-shaded parks, refreshing fountains and colourful horse-drawn carriages. Glimpses of the azure sea teased us from street corners where vendors sold bags of almonds from carts parked beneath the shade of orange trees. We climbed up the hill to revisit the old Alcazaba from Moorish times that we had toured on our honeymoon, admiring its gardens as well as the lovely vistas which it provided of the city and the ocean.

We ended our afternoon by touring the *Castillo de Gibralfaro* which we reached by taking a winding trail from the parador before relaxing under the warm Spanish sun with a pre-prandial drink on our balcony and newly created memories to cherish.

Ronda

Our return trip to Ronda did not resemble the harrowing one that we experienced during our honeymoon. It began with a very smooth, fast train ride from Malaga. The sleek modern car was markedly different from the old carriages with compartments in which we had travelled previously in Spain and vastly different from the bus which we took to Ronda from Marbella in 1976. The efficient train system was a complete contrast to what we remembered as we whizzed by endless olive groves to our destination with electronic boards overhead advising us of the time remaining before our arrival. Gone were the narrow roads hugging the mountains and the deep gorges along the way. We were so puzzled by the complete lack of dizzying heights that we felt compelled to ask upon our arrival if we were truly in Ronda! Of course, we forgot that, in 1976, we had taken a completely different route to our destination that, from Marbella, required travelling through the mountains.

Ronda was a great favourite with the nineteenth-century Romantic writers who explored various parts of Europe as part of their Grand Tour of the continent. An attractive ceramic mural featuring the dramatic scenery of Ronda as well as a bust of Hemingway stand proudly in the city which honours the writer who was so enamored of Spain.

Later that evening, comfortably installed in our room at the parador, I wrote the article that would subsequently be published on our experiences in Ronda.

When our taxi stopped in front of the parador in Ronda, we were awestruck by the atmospheric building that would provide us with accommodation for our stay there. Housed in the former town hall, the building is located in a prime spot in the very centre of Ronda with spectacular views of the Tagus River. From our balcony, we gazed down the steep ravine splitting the city in two and saw the famous hanging houses dangling precariously from the cliffside. Our spacious room was very Castilian in style with dark furniture and classic wrought-iron decorative features.

As it was still early in the afternoon, we walked to the Old Town, negotiating with more difficulty than forty years earlier the long, winding paths and steps to reach the historic Baños arabes *(Arab Baths), one of Ronda's main attractions. As the video there explains, the Moors would heat the water that would be channeled as steam under the floor. Water would then be splashed on the floor, creating a steamy atmosphere. As was the case with the Romans, people would move among the cold, warm and hot chambers, pausing to chat with their neighbours or to enjoy a massage provided by trained slaves.*

Visiting the Arab Baths was an interesting experience but the steep climb back up to the centre under a hot sun was tiring. To cool off, we decided to visit the impressive Palacio de Mondragón, *the residence of a Moorish ruler and one that even welcomed Isabella and Ferdinand to experience its charming serenity. With its balconied inner courtyard and attractive gardens refreshed by the sound and coolness of fountains, the* Palacio de Mondragón *offers a welcome respite to the tired tourist. It also features a museum on its upper floor detailing the history of Ronda.*

We crossed the Puente Nuevo once again that evening to dine at a delightful cliffside restaurant facing the parador directly across the gorge. Under a starlit sky, the lights illuminating the parador on the other side of the Tagus made the building appear magical from our table just inches from the edge of the ravine. Walking back to the parador at night down the narrow cobblestone streets lit by old-fashioned lamps, hearing the clop-clop-clop of horses with their carriage loads of enchanted tourists and the gurgling of fountains as well as smelling the white jasmine flowers exuding their fragrance under the moonlight all contributed to another very special experience.

The next day began with a walk along a promenade where I spotted a man painting fans. When I enquired about his work, he explained that he was a retired pharmacist who had always dreamt of becoming an artist and that, in retirement, he was finally pursuing his dream in miniature by creating fans decorated with his original designs. The fans were so lovely that I couldn't resist buying three of them, which I still use occasionally on hot summer days, rekindling memories of my student days in Madrid.

We decided to revisit Ronda's bullring, built in 1785 and distinguished not only for its architectural features but also for being the oldest one in Spain. I vividly remembered walking through the sandy Plaza de Toros *on our honeymoon and taking pictures of David as a would-be matador rushing towards my pretend cape in the deserted bullring. This was far from the case in 2016 as people congregated in the plaza and lined up for tickets to visit the* Museo de Tauromaquia *which portrays the history of bullfighting in Ronda with displays of* trajes de luces *(matadors' "suits of light") and swords, as well as a chapel* where *matadors pray before entering the ring and a small operating room where, in case of injury, they are initially treated before being transported to a hospital.*

Cordoba

Another quick ride on the train and we found ourselves in Cordoba where a millennium ago, Christians, Jews and Muslims lived together in harmony. We had booked a lovely hotel in the old quarter of the city and were pleased not only with the amenities that it offered but also with the sense of history that it projected. In addition to its lovely Andalusian courtyards, the *Eurostars Patios de Córdoba* also contained archaeological remains from Roman times that were discovered on the land it occupied and conserved within its property. As guests made their way to the basement breakfast room, they walked over a protected area covered by glass, allowing them to glimpse at history. Throughout the hotel, there were the illustrated words of some of Cordoba's most illustrious denizens. Our room had a drawing on the wall of a matador's cape and hat and paid tribute to Manuel Rodriguez, a famous bullfighter, while colourful illustrations testifying to the glory of Andalusia, its flamenco dancers, matadors, horses and carriages, etc. were proudly displayed in the public rooms. As David and I were commenting on the hotel's many attractions, there was a knock on the door and we were presented with a bottle of Cava and two flutes, reinforcing our already positive opinion of the hotel.

There was much to describe in Cordoba and, after dinner, I prepared the first draft of my article on the city:

> *As Cordoba's most famous attraction, the Mesquita, was only a short walk from our hotel, we made our way there, walking by the old Roman bridge over the Rio Guadalquivir. We enjoyed our return visit to the Mesquita and its lovely* Patio de los Naranjos, *a large courtyard featuring orange trees. Inside the eighth-century red and white striped mosque, the sixteenth-century baroque cathedral* boasted *intricately carved choir stalls and ornate ceilings with gilded cherubs.*
>
> *Upon our return to the hotel, we stopped to look at an excavation project bringing to life a classic amphitheater unearthed in the middle of a busy intersection as cars whizzed by unconcernedly.*
>
> *During our first evening in Cordoba, we savoured a tapas meal at a restaurant recommended by our hotel. We were served one of our best meals in Spain at this atmospheric taberna. We decided to* tapear, *that is, to try a variety of small plates:* gazpacho, ensalada cordobés, setas a la plancha *(huge grilled mushrooms) and* calamares con patatas fritas with a copa de vino. *Delicious! As I was unsure of the quantities involved, I ordered a good variety of tapas and was surprised to hear the waiter cut me off with "¡Basta!" (That's enough!). Of course, he was right as I would have ordered too much food for the two of us. It was a very atmospheric restaurant with huge barrels of wine, pots of flowers, ceramics and an ornate wrought-iron door to admire as we enjoyed our meal.*
>
> *Cordoba is famous for its patios and, every May, the City bursts into bloom with a special festival known as* Las cruces de Mayo *(The*

Festival of the May Crosses), followed by patio contests which encourage residents to compete with each other in producing a visual floral feast. The Romans, and later the Moors, created these oases to provide relief from Cordoba's hot, dry climate. Over the years, Cordovans have maintained the tradition and, today, many of their beautiful patios can be glimpsed through the heavy iron gates that partially shield them from the curious eyes of the public. However, during the Festival, the doors are opened, inviting passersby to admire the patios with their profusion of colourful flowers, stone mosaics, bubbling fountains and ceramic decorations, as well as appreciate the classic fragrances of the scents associated with Cordoba: jasmine and orange blossoms.

Many of the patios are located in the old Jewish quarter of the city, the Juderia, and we explored its narrow streets with pleasure, enjoying both the relief from the hot sun and the perfume of its flowers. We stopped at a store specializing in exotic spices and were amazed to see the mounds of prized golden-red saffron threads, burnt-orange turmeric, deep yellow curry and brownish-red chile powders which filled its aisles. We also entered a leather shop where we admired the quality of the belts and other items of clothing produced on the premises before making our way to El Zoco, a Jewish market selling artisanal products.

We ended our day with a bottle of Cava in the quiet of the dimly lit courtyard of our hotel. What a special day, a harbinger of what was to follow in Seville!

Seville

David and I returned once again to the enchanting city of Seville for five days during our fortieth wedding anniversary trip. Could our most recent trip match previous ones? Indeed, our expectations were exceeded, given that our visit coincided with the Holy Week celebrations in this city renowned for its religious processions.

Trying to describe the many wonders of Seville is a daunting task, but it was also a pleasure to write about the exciting five days that we spent there. I hoped that my readers would enjoy learning about the experiences that I shared with them.

> *Being in Seville during Holy Week, which is such an important period in the religious calendar, it seemed only appropriate to stay in a hotel that had once been home to an eighteenth-century religious institution and that, today, maintains the serenity and quiet beauty of its origins. We selected the* Sacristia de Santa Ana, *a small hotel with a patio featuring a terra cotta floor and a marble fountain in its centre, a scene from old Andalusia…*
>
> *Hotel Sacristia de Santa Ana lies in the heart of Seville facing a large square offering many options for dinner. As the shopping district is only a short walk away, we decided to explore the area right away and, attracted by the splendid flamenco dresses featured in the windows of the Corte Inglés store along our way, I urged my husband to enter the building. I found myself in flamenco heaven, surrounded by a sea of colourful dresses with so many flounces that they appeared to almost dance from their hangers! Tempted, I checked the price tags of a few, which dampened my initial enthusiasm somewhat (over $500 a dress) and so voluminous that an entire large suitcase would be required to carry just one! I was also amazed to observe the quantity of adorable flamenco dresses designed for little girls to wear. Looking grimly over the miniature flamenco dresses, David and I noticed the hooded "Nazareno" (penitent) attire for sale as well. It contrasted soberly with the rest of the cheerful attire greeting customers.*
>
> *When my husband became bored with my fanciful window-shopping, we checked out the store's models of religious floats made for Holy Week by children participating in school contests. What proof of ingenuity and talent the young students had displayed in fashioning these miniature religious floats replicating those seen in Holy Week processions! We marveled at the number of everyday household items from toothbrushes to candy to small birthday cake candles that had been used to recreate such detailed models.*

We returned to the magnificent Cathedral of Seville, admiring its elaborate choir stalls with the huge spinnable book holder placed in the centre holding a gargantuan hymnal that choir members could see at a distance in an age when books were scarce and very expensive. Columbus's remains, transported to Seville from Cuba in 1902, are buried beneath a huge monument in the cathedral.

Next on our agenda was a return visit to the Alcázar whose splendid gardens had deeply impressed us during our honeymoon with their intricate carvings, perfumed oranges trees and exquisite English, French, Italian and Moorish sections. It is the oldest European royal residence still in use: The King and Queen of Spain still stay at this palace when in Seville just as Isabella and Ferdinand did when they welcomed Columbus here after his historic voyage to the New World in 1492.

All along the major streets of old Seville, we noticed buildings with balconies draped in red cloth in preparation for the Holy Week processions. Many drivers with their carriages congregated on the Plaza del Rey in front of the cathedral, waiting for passengers. As we walked back to our hotel along Sierpes Street, known for its elegant boutiques, I noticed several boutiques selling a wide array of fans bearing images of court scenes, of sharply dressed matadors and of flamenco dancers in their brightly coloured dresses wearing high combs and mantillas.

The next day, David and I attended Francisco's wedding to Liliana and met Maximo and Charlotte at the cathedral, as well as Alexandra and Eduardo who had travelled from Barcelona for the occasion. After the lovely ceremony, we had the opportunity during the reception to exchange a few words with the bride and groom, as well as with Carolina and Juan with whom we made plans to meet later in the week. During the music selection which followed the dinner, David and I danced like newlyweds to the popular new song *Robarte un beso* (Stealing a Kiss from You) by Colombians Carlos Vives and Sebastián Yatra. We noticed that Eduardo and Alexandra only had eyes for each other as they swept by us, softly whispering the words of the song to each other.

"And my dear Sophie, how about whispering the words to me in English?" asked David playfully as we danced across the room.

"Why not? It is a very appealing song that mentions the special thrill experienced in the presence of the person who lights up one's life. "

David commented, "Having begun to understand a few of the Spanish words in the song, I can enjoy it even more now as I hold you in my arms. Let's dance to a few more slows before stealing a kiss ourselves…"

"What is it, Mom?" asked Alexandra when she returned to our table with Eduardo. "You look so wistful and yet so starry-eyed tonight. Has Dad been whispering sweet nothings into your ear?"

"At least as many as Eduardo has whispered into yours!" joked David.

"I was just thinking of the time that Eduardo danced with my grandmother on their clandestine date at the Royal Alex when he returned to Winnipeg on business. I remember that he told me he danced with her to the music of *Bésame Mucho* and here we are today in Seville many years later dancing to another Spanish song about kissing. Isn't it rather amazing, like life reaching full circle?"

"Well, of course, everyone knows that we Spaniards are great lovers!" laughed Eduardo as he swept Alexandra away for another dance.

All too soon, the evening ended and we bade goodbye to our son and Charlotte who were returning to Winnipeg and to our daughter and her husband who were flying back the next day to be with their twins.

Our days in Seville allowed David and me to experience some very special events which I described in one of my articles:

> *"During our third evening in Seville, we enjoyed "We Love Tapas", a combined birthday gift for the two of us from our family. This very original gift consisted of tapa hopping with a lively and knowledgeable Sevillian guide who escorted us to local tavernas in Seville not usually visited by tourists.* La Casa Morales *was our first stop where*

we enjoyed a glass of fine Manzanilla sherry, accompanied by Ibérico ham (made from black pigs fed a diet of acorns, chestnuts and olives).

Our second stop, the Taverna La Fresquita, *was a very small bar where people eat and drink standing up, facing solid walls of religious articles and photos with rosaries hanging from the ceiling. This very odd mix of the religious and the profane is extremely popular with locals who bring their own chairs and sit outside the bar on the street to join their neighbours and friends. We then proceeded to our third stop, walking through Santa Cruz with our guide until we arrived at the* Casa Roman *with its iconic hams hanging from the ceiling. We drank sangria and wine and we enjoyed the marinated mushrooms and fried cod and pigs' cheeks which were a specialty of the house!*

As we concluded our tapas tour in the last hour of the day, we heard music, faint at first and gradually becoming louder. Our guide indicated that something special was about to happen. We looked down a narrow street and caught a first glimpse of dozens of brightly burning candles slowly moving forward into the night. Then, the music and light coalesced as our eyes fixed upon an early Holy Week procession winding its way through the cobblestone streets. A hush fell upon the crowd gathered along the street and all talking ceased as Nazarenos *(penitents) in pointed hooded purple robes, some wearing sandals with others barefoot as a form of penance, carried a huge cross across the square. Next in the procession was a float of a sorrowful Christ illuminated by a multitude of candles and decorated by myriads of flowers. Floats such as these can weigh up to three tons and are carried by thirty to fifty men who are hidden beneath, with only their feet occasionally betraying their presence. More penitents followed with the procession concluding with a float of the Virgin Mary wearing a glittering halo crown. What an unforgettable experience!*

The next day, we visited Plaza de España and *were fortunate enough to see an impromptu flamenco dancer entertaining those who had gathered at the site. On the walk back to our hotel, I peered inside several bakeries that displayed pastries in the shape and colour of* Nazareno *penitents with their pointed hoods, as well as elaborate and edible religious floats far too beautiful to eat. David and I found it difficult to believe that such a pronounced and ubiquitous religious theme could still exist in a world so often devoid of religious beliefs.*

The day concluded with an excellent flamenco tablao at the Casa del Flamenco. *After the flamenco performance, we passed by a building with a ceramic plaque in white and blue attesting to the fact that we were in the area of the old prison where, in the opera* **Carmen**, *Don José jailed Carmen after the argument in the Tobacco Factory. It seemed so fitting to have this whimsical testimonial in a city where so much of what we visited could have served as dramatic props in an opera!*

We then joined Carolina and Juan for dinner at their home. "It seems that our visits are becoming more frequent. David and I are so happy to have this opportunity to be with you once again," I said as we sat on their lovely palm-shaded patio, drinking a glass of sherry. "Francisco and Liliana's wedding was so lovely and we found it interesting to witness the different customs that each country has developed for ceremonies like weddings. This was our first Spanish wedding."

After a delicious meal, we embraced our friends and expressed our hope that we would see them again very soon.

"David, it is truly amazing to note how much material I have here in Seville to write my articles. I only hope that I am doing justice in my descriptions to all the events and experiences that have been part of our stay here. Let's hope that my editor likes what I have to say!"

"Sophie, I never cease to be astonished by your constant enthusiasm, a trait which is readily apparent in all your articles. I'm sure that your editor will love them even if he has to curb your effervescence a little…" David teased.

"Thank you for your encouragement. I think that I will add the last section to my piece on Seville right now," I concluded, a glass of Cava in hand as I returned to the almost-finished article on my tablet.

The next day, I went for a stroll in the square by our hotel and noticed a man making churros in a huge vat of oil. However, they weren't the usual elongated ones that I knew but huge spirals of fairly thick dough that were cut into portions as required. I asked for a serving, which was of course much too large for one person, and dipped the pieces in sugar for a delicious treat that reminded me of my student days in Madrid.

We spent a quiet, relaxing afternoon before watching the Palm Sunday procession taking place near our hotel. Some 1200 participants, penitents dressed in white robes with blue conical hats and masked faces walked slowly down the street. They carried huge tapers, which would be lit at night, and were accompanied by musicians. During the processions, we noted a curious mix of the sacred and the profane. On the one hand, a carnival-like atmosphere prevailed with cotton candy, balloons, couples kissing and people eating and drinking while, on the other hand, we saw a well-dressed teenage boy reverently touching the float of the dying Christ and making the sign of the cross. What was remarkable was the smart attire worn by nearly all: no jeans, shorts, crop tops, etc. Teenagers were dressed in what used to be called one's "Sunday Best" and there were many families gathered together with their young sons dressed in miniature suits and their little girls in the prettiest of frocks, a spirit of formality which has long been abandoned in North America. Once again, we were amazed by the solemn spectacle of it all: the religious procession with the beautiful floats, the devotion of the penitents and the rapt attention of those gathered to witness the event.

Cuenca

After spending the night at the very atmospheric *Hacienda del Cardenal*, a cardinal's former summer residence in Toledo, we boarded the train for Cuenca. Travelling through the dry lands of La Mancha, I was reminded that the arid region along the route rather surprisingly gives birth to the crocus flower so important to Spanish cuisine and an essential if expensive ingredient in paella. Known as the "red gold of La Mancha," Spain's much prized saffron originates from this Castilian plateau.

I began the next segment of my articles on Spain with a brief description of Cuenca.

> *"Perched on the edge of gorges with its* casas colgadas *(hanging houses) overlooking a deep chasm, this small mountaintop city reminded David and me of a grey, rather melancholy Ronda. With some trepidation, we crossed the swaying suspension bridge which links the parador where we were staying to the Old Quarter across the gorge. We walked down the narrow, winding and gloomy streets, entering a little old-fashioned pharmacy which sold drugs exclusively (no shampoo or magazines!) and readily imagined that we had stepped into an old apothecary's shop from another century.*
>
> *We spent the night at the Parador de Cuenca which sits on a high rocky outcrop sandwiched between the deep gorge of the Huecar River and sheer rocky cliffs. A former sixteenth-century convent, its many pillar candles scattered throughout the building and the long colonnaded walkway surrounding the glass-enclosed cloister provide visitors with a sense of monastic life although the former chapel is now ironically a bar! Our lovely room had a panoramic view of the mountains and valleys surrounding the city.*

Madrid

We arrived in Madrid, the last destination of our fortieth wedding anniversary trip, on a sunny late afternoon. My last article on this trip provided a capsule description of our brief time in a city that we knew well.

> *Our hotel façade was painted over with a colourful shawl – so very original and, of course, so very Spanish! Our balcony at The Hotel Mayorazgo was huge and our room boasted a painted scene on the wall with the famous statue of Felipe III riding a horse in the Plaza Mayor, the site of my humourous experience with Iago so many years earlier.*
>
> *We visited the* Real Palacio de Madrid, *the former residence of Spanish kings and queens but still used today for official events and ceremonies. In the opulent Throne Room, one can see the abdication*

document signed by Juan Carlos in 2014, as well as the proclamation made by his son, the new King Felipe VI.

David and I had the pleasure of returning to one of our favourite honeymoon venues.

"We enjoyed dinner at the Sobrino de Botín where we had dined forty years earlier. As I had reserved a table and told the restaurant that it was a special occasion, we were wished a happy anniversary and offered a complimentary glass of Cava. A friendly American woman seated next to our table offered to take an anniversary photo of the two of us. Returning to our hotel proved to be difficult as the Holy Thursday processions attracted so many crowds that it was virtually impossible to make our way through them (some fifty rows deep in places). As we were unable to walk or to take a taxi to our hotel due to the densely crowded streets near the Plaza Mayor, we pushed our way to a subway station and were relieved when we finally reached the safety of our hotel.

We spent the last day of our trip, strolling down the *Gran Via,* admiring my favourite statue of *Cibeles* at Madrid's former central post office and doing a little shopping before packing and enjoying a seafood paella dinner to close the chapter on another memorable trip to Spain.

Chapter 43

Winnipeg, January 2018—Toronto, December 2019

January 2018

Dear Carolina,

Once again, Christmas came with good news: Maximo and Charlotte are engaged to be married. We couldn't be happier. The couple plans to be married in Winnipeg in September and, of course, we hope that you and Juan will be able to attend. Apparently, Francisco has already agreed to be Maximo's best man.

Eduardo and Alexandra are planning to fly down to Winnipeg for the wedding without Teresa and Miguel, given that Diego and Alicia have generously offered to take care of the twins. This will allow the couple to enjoy Winnipeg on their own and then to travel to the Niagara Region before spending a few days with us in Toronto.

Alexandra sends us photos of the twins practically every week and, as we communicate regularly by Skype, we can follow their progress quite readily. Obviously, it is not the same as holding them in our arms but it is much better than not seeing them at all. They are already two years old!

Eduardo and Alexandra continue to work diligently at the winery. While Eduardo's passion for the vineyard is easy to understand, we remain amazed that Alexandra enjoys it so much. It is almost as if she had been born to that life!

Charles and Shannon are busy with their careers and young daughter but are looking forward to the arrival of their second child this summer. Nicholas and Paula are juggling their professional lives with the responsibility of raising three children. We have the families over for dinner several times every month and enjoy our time with all of them very much.

And how is life in Seville? How are Juan and the family?

Sophie

Seville, March 2018

Dear Sofía,

The good news here is that Esmeralda has decided to curtail some of her dancing to allow her to teach the many different styles of flamenco here in Seville. This means that she will be spending much less time travelling in the future. She has also decided to co-purchase my boutique with Rocío and will provide her with a new line of flamenco clothing and shoes. Eventually, when she tires of dancing, Esmeralda will help Rocío with the daily operations of the boutique.

As suggested by Juan, Alonzo is now selling some sparkling wines from around the world in his wine store, in addition to Seville's quintessential favourite: sherry. Juan likes to stop at the wine boutique for a short visit on his way to the library or to a café to meet a friend.

Francisco and Liliana are, of course, very busy at the hospital. They live close to us and we see them often to our great delight. Wonderful news: they have just announced that they are expecting their first child in late September!

Juan and I are pleased to accept your invitation to attend Maximo and Charlotte's wedding in Winnipeg next September. In addition to wishing to share this special moment in the life of your family, I was wondering if it might be possible to see the places that my grandmother Maria Cristina mentioned so often in the letters that you photocopied for me. Hopefully, you could be my guide!

Juan and I are very much looking forward to seeing you and David once again,

Um gran abrazo de
Carolina

P.S. We will be visiting Diego and Alicia over the Easter holidays and, of course, will have the opportunity of spending time with Eduardo and Alejandra, along with little Teresa and Miguel. As a result, you will undoubtedly receive more photos to add to your growing collection!

SEPTEMBER 2018

David and I are now in Winnipeg for Maximo and Charlotte's wedding. The day could not be lovelier: a warm Manitoba fall day with a bright and cloudless azure sky. The bride and groom are exchanging their wedding vows and they look so very happy that I dare not allow a tear to slide down my cheek. Francisco is handing the ring to Maximo who confidently places it on Charlotte's fourth finger. She, in return, places a matching gold band on his finger and the two seal their love with a kiss. This is the fourth time that I have witnessed the marriage of one of our children and I never fail to be moved by the ceremony. I take David's hand and turn around behind us to see the smiling faces of Nicholas and Paula, Charles and Shannon and Alexandra and Eduardo and I bask in the joy of the moment.

Carolina and Juan also look very happy as they join their son, his best man's duties now over for the time being. Liliana could not accompany them to the wedding as her due date is in three weeks. Francisco made her promise to delay the birth until he returned to Seville, he laughingly tells David and me.

On the way to the wedding reception at Assiniboine Park, I tell Carolina that she has already seen at least one of the landmark buildings that Maria Cristina and Eduardo would have known during their 1913 visit to Winnipeg. "The cathedral where Maximo and Charlotte were just married was the fourth church constructed on that site but it has greatly changed since my grandmother knew it as most of the interior was destroyed by fire in 1968. A smaller version was built later within the remaining stone walls. Moving south down the same side of the street, you can observe the old oak building built by the first Grey Nuns who came to the Red River colony to offer care to the sick, to teach the children and to look after its orphans. Today, it is a museum housing many important articles relating to the Métis leader, Louis Riel, as well as to the history of the Grey Nuns in Winnipeg.

"From what I read in my grandmother's letters, the hospital where Maggie worked is close by; is it not?" asked Carolina.

"Yes, indeed. Across the street from the museum is the former nursing school where my grandmother studied. St. Boniface Hospital, the first hospital in Western Canada, is next to the old school and is the hospital where both Maggie and her daughter Maeve worked as nurses."

"If memory serves me correctly, I believe that there were several serious polio epidemics in Manitoba during the last century," commented Francisco.

"Yes, during the first half of the 20th century, some 10,000 Canadians contracted polio; of them, almost 6000 were Manitobans. Initial attempts to treat them by using a nasal spray and serums proved to be largely unsuccessful although subsequent patient management techniques such as hot packs and the manipulation of muscles and joints proved to be helpful. I do remember visiting an older cousin who, in her youth, was placed in an iron lung to help her breathe while one of my friends had to wear a brace on her leg due to partial paralysis."

"How sad! Fortunately, the Salk and Sabin vaccines virtually conquered poliomyelitis," observed Francisco.

"Yes, I remember lining up at school to receive the Sabin oral vaccine which was placed on a sugar cube that dissolved on our tongue," I added.

"We will now head to Assiniboine Park for the wedding reception," David announced. "It will be held in the atrium of the Pavilion, a newer version of the original one destroyed by fire. You may recall that your relatives had tea with Sophie's grandmother in that building during the summer of 1913. On our way there, we will pass by St. Mary's Academy where Maria Cristina taught for one term before returning to Spain."

We were able to spend a little time with the bride and groom after photographs were taken at Assiniboine Park and then we enjoyed an evening of dining and dancing as they made their way from guest to guest. We kissed the happy couple goodbye as they left on their honeymoon.

Returning to the hotel, the rest of us gathered over coffee to plan our next day's activities as Carolina and Alexandra were especially eager to retrace our relatives' steps in Winnipeg. Thanks to Maria Cristina's detailed letters, we had an excellent record of most of the places that they had visited.

"Tomorrow, we will cross the Red River and stroll through The Forks at the confluence of the Red and Assiniboine Rivers, which is a lovely area now but, when I was a child, it was an ugly, abandoned and dilapidated old railroad yard that was a visual blight on the city," I recalled for the benefit of our guests.

"However," added David, "the area where machinists and blacksmiths repaired and maintained vast quantities of railway equipment, locomotives and cars was undoubtedly a hive of activity when Maria Cristina and Edward were living in Winnipeg."

"That's my husband, ever the history professor," I laughed.

"After lunch at The Forks, which today boasts numerous restaurants and boutiques, we will travel down Broadway Avenue and walk past the historic Fort Garry Hotel where Maria Cristina and Maggie said their farewells and then view the Legislative Building which was still under construction when they saw it in 1913. They also attended a garden party at the Lieutenant Governor's Residence which we will pass by on our tour."

David added, "Sophie and I had our wedding photographs taken in the beautiful gardens of that residence. After a stop there, we will show you where the former Eaton's store was located, the store that Maria Cristina and Maggie so enjoyed visiting before Christmas, admiring its special windows full of holiday displays."

"Would you like to visit the old Walker Theatre where Maria Cristina, Eduardo and Maggy saw *Carmen*?" I asked. David told our guests about the history of the theatre with its Italian marble, gilt trim, crystal chandeliers and curving balconies. He added, "The Walker closed during the Great Depression and was converted into a cinema in 1945. As it was transformed into the Odeon theatre, many of the original surfaces were masked and a false ceiling was added to close off the upper balcony."

"I remember lining up outside often for more than an hour, even in the winter, to attend a movie at the Odeon when I was a university student in Winnipeg," I mentioned. "However, after its purchase by an arts group, the building's original architectural features were restored and, in 2002, it was renamed in honour of Burton Cummings, a popular local musician and songwriter."

"Was he not the lead singer with the rock band, *The Guess Who*?" asked Francisco.

"You are right, Francisco. You must be hanging out with too many Canadians!" laughed David.

"If you aren't too tired, we could also drive by the Old Exchange District, a turn-of-the-century warehousing area associated with the grain trade, financing and later the garment industry in Winnipeg. There we will find the building that was the site of the former R.J. Whitla and Company clothing store where Maggie, Maria Cristina and Eduardo bought summer attire."

"Did you know that Winnipeg is often used as a stand-in for movies about Chicago and other mid-western cities?" asked David. "As a matter of fact, the city's Exchange District with its unique turn-of-the-century architecture has been featured in a number of Hollywood movies such as *The Assassination of Jesse James*, a western starring Brad Pitt. In *Capote* which focuses on the American novelist's writing of *In Cold Blood*, portions of the Exchange District were transformed to recreate Kansas City in the 1870s."

"And don't forget the 2003 movie *Shall We Dance?* starring Richard Gere and Jennifer Lopez," I added, remembering how I had enjoyed this film that featured scenes filmed in Winnipeg, including those of the couple dancing in the University of Manitoba's Taché Hall.

Also, Winnipeg, due to its cold climate, is frequently used as the backdrop for movies about Christmas," concluded David. "Movies are shot not only in the Exchange District but often in such locations as The Forks, the Fort Garry Hotel and stately homes in such upscale areas as River Heights."

"Moving from cinema to beaches, how do you all feel about travelling to Winnipeg Beach the day after tomorrow? It has a lovely stretch of sandy beach where we could have a picnic and go for a walk," I suggested.

"That would be lovely and it would allow us to visit the town where Eduardo and Maggie were engaged just before Eduardo's return to Europe," said Alexandra who was as intrigued as I was about their romance.

Two days later, we woke up to another bright, sunny Manitoba morning and began the day by driving by the spot where the Royal Alexandra Hotel had once kept company with its neighbour, the former Canadian Pacific Railway Station. "The Royal Alex was torn down in 1971 but this is where the grand hotel once stood. My parents actually spent their wedding night at that hotel and took the train the next day for their honeymoon trip to the States," I told our visitors. "It was very common during the first half of the 20th century for newlyweds here to take the train to their honeymoon destination."

"Was Winnipeg Beach not the resort served by the Moonlight Express, the train that Eduardo and Maggie took the day of their engagement?" asked Alexandra.

"Yes, indeed, it was and, very early Sunday morning, it would arrive at the station adjoining the hotel," I answered.

"It makes me wonder where my great-grandmother spent the night upon returning with Eduardo in the early hours of the morning after a romantic day and evening at Winnipeg Beach… The hotel was so close to the station and there probably wasn't a streetcar running at that time for Maggie to take home," observed Alexandra.

"Well, I'm afraid that will remain one unanswered aspect of their romance, Alejandra," said his namesake.

We arrived in the resort town of Winnipeg Beach which, of course, did not resemble the picture that our visitors had formed of it. Gone were the Dance Pavilion that had welcomed so many wishing to display their virtuoso moves to an admiring public, the Empress Hotel and its fancy venues, the honkytonk midway with its barkers and tinkling organ music, the giant wooden roller coaster eliciting screams and thrills and even the original boardwalk where Maggy and Eduardo had once strolled so many years ago… All had faded into the mists of time.

During dinner that evening, David and I had a lively exchange with our visitors about Winnipeg and its links with our families before bidding farewell to our Spanish friends. Francisco had enjoyed his trip to the provincial capital, his first to Canada, as well as the opportunity to serve as best man to his good friend but was eager to return to Seville and Liliana who would be giving birth to their first child any day. Carolina and Juan were also eager to welcome their new grandchild but happy that they had been able to retrace some of their family ties. Promises to visit Spain within two years were made as we wished them "Buen viaje!" (Bon voyage!).

December 2019

Dear Carolina,

Once again, it is that wonderful time of the year when our thoughts turn especially to our loved ones. Nicholas and Charles and their families will, as usual, celebrate Christmas Day with us. It will be lovely to have our youngest grandchild (Charles and Shannon's second daughter) join their cousins here for the occasion.

We are so pleased that Maximo and Charlotte will travel from Winnipeg to join our family for the festive season. Maximo is very worried, however, about the ever-increasing information that he is receiving concerning the development of a new, highly infectious virus which has started to infect people in China and is likely to make its way across Europe and then the Americas. It is called Corona Virus (Covid 19) and could potentially prove to be very deadly.

On a happier note, we are looking forward to welcoming our newest grandchild early next year. Alexandra and Eduardo will certainly have their hands full with the twins and the new baby, in addition to their work at the winery. Thus, we plan to spend at least a month at Villa Sol y Iris *next March to help Alexandra with the baby and to become better acquainted with the twins. David and I hope to see you there or, perhaps later, on the island of Ibiza where we have reserved a condo for three weeks by the ocean, smelling the salty tang of the sea and the fragrance of the wild rosemary that grows on the island, as well as walking on its sandy beaches and admiring the scenic views. You are welcome to stay with us as we will have plenty of room for the two of you. Of course, this is all contingent upon Covid being controlled and, consequently, we will have to carefully monitor the situation.*

How is your family? I look forward to hearing your latest news.

Alicia tells me that Miguel is most excited about celebrating Christmas with the twins of whom he is very fond. He is also, apparently, preparing a cup of tea every day for Alexandra to allow her to kick up her feet and relax a little in mid-afternoon while the twins have their nap. Isn't it wonderful that a man who is 103 still takes such a strong interest in his family and in life?

Well, I have much baking and shopping to do if I am to be ready for Christmas. All the best to you, dear friend. I hope to see you soon.

Sophie

Chapter 44

Villa Sol y Iris, February-March 2020

February 20, 2020

Dear Sofía,

As you know, we are in mourning now for Miguel who died last week. It has been a difficult time for us all. Diego, Alicia and their children are grieving for a very kind and decent man who lived a good and long life. While not a blood relative, Alejandra also suffers greatly for there was a deep connection between her and Miguel. Every day, they would spend time together at breakfast and rare was the time that she did not stop to wish him a good night as she put the twins to bed. Miguel also insisted on joining her for a cup of tea in the afternoon and would prepare it himself. Fortunately, Alejandra has the new baby as well as young Teresa and Miguel to keep her busy. Moreover, business at the winery never stops for anyone and, according to Eduardo, the past year has been the busiest one yet.

How fortunate that Miguel so enjoyed his last Christmas with us all! He took the time to speak at length not only to Juan and me and my brother Rafael and his wife but also to Alonzo and Rocío, as well as to

Francisco and Liliana and Esmeralda and her new friend Fernando. I sometimes wonder if he didn't have a premonition that the end was near as he was so intent on being involved in the preparations for the holiday and in participating in all the activities of the season. He was very particular about choosing the right gifts for the twins and for our grandchildren, as well as for the rest of the family. Moreover, he looked forward to the birth of Alejandra and Eduardo's new baby and was so relieved when he heard of Alejandra's safe delivery.

I am glad that you and David will be arriving at Villa Sol y Iris *very soon. Diego, Alicia, Eduardo and Alejandra could use the additional emotional support at this time. Moreover, you must be excited about having the opportunity to spend time with your new granddaughter and the twins. Juan and I are eager to see you at the christening and then later in Ibiza. Covid has resulted in a heavy toll of sickness and deaths in Spain but we are praying that this will only be temporary and that all will be well very soon.*

Un gran abrazo de tu amiga Carolina

March 2020

David and I arrived at *Villa Sol y Iris* as March made its appearance and could hear the twins chattering behind the door before Alexandra and Eduardo opened it. There was the whole family, Alexandra with the baby in her arms and Eduardo holding Teresa and Miguel by the hand. Although they were now four years old, we had only seen them once in person and that was for their christening. It was one of the great disadvantages of living an ocean away from Alexandra despite the fact that we communicated with her and her family on a regular basis. David and I could see the recognition in the twins as they suddenly connected the images of us on the screen with the persons before them. "*¡Abuela! ¡Abuelo!*"(Grandmother! Grandfather!), they cried excitedly in their youthful exuberance as they danced around us. After greeting them, we turned to our newest grandchild cradled in our daughter's arms. "Meet Sofía Carolina Margarita," she proudly stated. "Eduardo and I thought it was most appropriate to name her after her grandmother, godmother and great-great-grandmother. What do you think, Mom?" After assuring her that I was very touched, I added, "We will have to make plans as of now to visit you at least once a year."

I then pulled a box out of my carry-on and gave it to Alexandra, saying, "When I was a little girl, I used to drink tea from this set with my grandmother and aunt and, later, when you were a little girl, we shared many happy moments together drinking from those same cups, which were a gift from Maria Cristina to your great-grandmother who eventually gave them to me. Now I would like you to have this Spanish tea set to start a new tradition with your own daughters."

Alexandra was very moved as she opened the box and slowly looked at the dishes, remembering how she had enjoyed playing with the tea set as a young child. "Thank you so much, Mom," she said as she gave me a huge hug.

After allowing us sufficient time to get reacquainted with our family, Diego and Alicia joined us for a few minutes. "Would you like to freshen up before dinner? You must be tired after your long flight," Alicia remarked. "And we want you to enjoy Alicia's specialty for dinner tonight," added Diego.

Just like the adults, little Teresa and Miguel devoured Alicia's delicious paella with gusto. They then showed us their latest toys received at Christmas, repeating several times that they were gifts from their "Bisabuelo"(great-grandfather). They had not forgotten Miguel who had played so often with them and read them stories at night.

We asked the twins if they would like us to read to them, an offer which they happily accepted. When they were fast asleep, David and I returned to the dining room for coffee with our hosts and asked about Miguel's final days. "He was truly well until the end. The day before he died, he told us he was very tired and would retire early. He never woke up. He died the way that he lived, quietly but rejoicing in the life that he had created for himself and his family," said Diego.

"There were so many people at his funeral that we had to open the doors of the church so that latecomers could hear the service outside," commented Eduardo.

"Carolina and Juan, Rafael and Eva and their families were all here, as were María who travelled from Ireland and Allegra and Martín from Madrid to join us on this sad occasion."

"It appears, Alicia and Diego, that you have a regular hotel here and such a pleasant one with great food, wine and accommodation. We hope that we are not imposing upon you but so appreciate your constant kindness," said David.

Two days later, we were celebrating little Sofía Carolina Margarita's christening with her parents and paternal grandparents, as well as with Carolina and Juan who flew in from Seville for the occasion. "Mom and Dad, Eduardo and I feel that it is very appropriate for Carolina and Juan, who have been so close to you over the past four decades despite the geographical distance that separates you, to act as Sofía's godparents."

"And Juan and I are so pleased to be part of this long-standing union of our families," replied Carolina.

"Thank you, Alejandra and Eduardo, for this honour," added Juan.

As David and I expressed our happiness with the arrangements made, Alicia and Diego served the last bottle of the *Margarita Cava* that Eduardo had inaugurated at his ninetieth birthday celebration in 1980. Could it really have been four decades ago since that first visit? "To Sofía and her future!" wished Alicia. "To Sofía!", we said as we raised our glasses to her happiness.

"And now, I am pleased to serve a glass of the *Miguel Cava* that I developed for my father's one hundredth birthday," declared Diego with pride. "To Miguel!" "To Miguel!" we chanted in memory of this beloved figure whom we would all miss very much.

"How is the family, Carolina?" I asked.

"Everything is working out very well. Alonzo and Rocío, as well as Francisco and Liliana, are enjoying their growing families. And, finally, it appears that Esmeralda is in a good, stable relationship with Fernando whom she met last year in Seville. As they have so much in common, I foresee a happy future for the two of them, maybe even marriage."

"A common mother's hope!" teased Juan before proceeding to speak of Alonzo's successful wine shop, Francisco's and Liliana's burgeoning careers in emergency medicine and Esmeralda's happiness not only with teaching flamenco but also with running Carolina's former boutique with Rocío.

"And we are so pleased to receive the indispensable assistance and guidance that we receive from Eduardo and Alejandra in managing our winery!" added Diego with great pride.

Alicia mentioned that she and Diego had recently met María's new boyfriend Patrick who had travelled to the Villa to spend Christmas with them. "Life is working out so well for Allegra and María, both personally and professionally. We are so pleased for them."

At that moment, the telephone rang and Alicia answered it. "It's Martín calling from Madrid," she whispered before continuing with her conversation in another room. Her initial happiness upon receiving the call soon turned to dismay and then sadness as she ended the conversation. She returned to the living room, greatly disturbed. "Diego, I have just heard from Martín who informs me that Allegra has contracted Covid from one of her critically ill patients in the ICU and is very sick. She felt unwell two days ago, was hospitalized yesterday and, this morning, was transferred to the ICU unit where she works. She is so ill that she will be placed on a ventilator within the next hour and doctors fear for her life. Oh, Diego, how can this be? Our sweet daughter who was just here for Miguel's funeral!"

"No, it can't be, Alicia. My heart is torn apart by this news. How is poor Martín bearing up?" I asked.

"He is devastated, especially as the current Covid protocol does not allow him to even visit Allegra. Our course, the children are also very upset that their mother is not with them. What shall we do?"

"Unfortunately, we can only pray, Alicia, and hope for the best."

David and I, as well as Carolina and Juan, tried to encourage Diego and Alicia but there was little that we could do to allay their fears. Alexandra and Eduardo offered to manage the winery should they wish to travel to

Madrid, but Alicia gently declined. "No, Martín has asked us to wait until he receives more news from the hospital. He will also be calling María to let her know about her sister's condition."

Of course, the question of Covid was on our minds for the rest of the day as we learned about the very high numbers of people who had contracted the virus in Europe. Deaths were increasing on a daily basis in Spain, Italy and France and people were being advised to stay at home.

Early next morning, the phone rang and Alicia rushed to answer it. "It is Maximo calling for you, David and Sofía."

I felt a vague unease as we reached for the phone. Why would Maximo be calling us at this time? Was there a family emergency at home?

"Mom, Dad, I am calling you as the Prime Minister has just announced that all Canadians should return home immediately due to the serious nature of the situation caused by Covid. Soon, borders will close overseas and it will be very difficult for you to fly back to Canada. You must try to change your tickets to return home as soon as possible, hopefully within the next two or three days. We are all worried about you and want to see you back in Toronto. Nicholas and Charles have called me repeatedly to check on the Covid situation and have asked me to advise you to return now as there will be a major lockdown in Canada and people are already beginning to self-isolate. It is likely that a quarantine will soon be imposed for returning travellers."

"Yes, of course, we will return as quickly as possible, Maximo. Please tell the others that we are fine. How are they and their families? And how are you and Charlotte?" I asked.

"Nicholas and Charles and their families are all doing well. I, of course, am very busy with my work as is Charlotte but we have no complaints. We are healthy and so happy."

When we ended our conversation with Maximo, I explained the situation to Alexandra and Eduardo and David and I agreed that we would cancel our trip to Ibiza and reschedule our flight back to Toronto as soon as possible.

"How sad that you have to leave so soon after your arrival but we understand, of course, why this is necessary," said Eduardo.

"We were hoping to offer your parents a little moral support during our stay at least until they hear more about Allegra. On the other hand, it might be better if they were not burdened with guests at this difficult time. Alexandra, have Alicia and Diego heard anything more about Allegra?"

"Martín called this morning to report that she is still the same and doctors are unsure whether she will recover or not."

"What a sad situation! We can only hope that she will improve over the next day or two," said David, expressing a sentiment that we all were hesitant to voice, given the seriousness of Allegra's condition.

Very quickly, we realized how serious the situation was becoming, not only in Europe but also in North America. We advised Carolina and Juan that we would, of course, be cancelling our trip with them to Ibiza and returning home to Canada.

"Of course, we understand, given the current conditions. Perhaps, if things improve, we will be able to meet together next year?" suggested Carolina.

"It is, of course, our fervent hope, dear friend!"

We were able to reschedule our flights for two days later, allowing us to spend a little more time with Alexandra and Eduardo and the grandchildren before bidding them goodbye.

On the eve of our departure, Alexandra gave me a large envelope that Miguel had asked her to hand over to me in person after baby Sofía's christening. "Mom, this is an envelope that Miguel gave me shortly before his death. It apparently contains several letters written by your grandmother to Eduardo once he left Winnipeg. I believe that you have been looking for these letters for years, especially once you found Eduardo's letters to Maggie behind the photo frames. There are also two letters written by Eduardo, one to you that he never mailed, and one last letter that he wrote to Maggie. Eduardo told Miguel that he had kept this last letter for many years and had planned to destroy it but changed his mind after meeting you. In reviewing his final will, Miguel was reminded of these letters that Eduardo had asked him to give you at the right time. He was planning to do so after the christening but asked me, if ever anything happened to him before then, to make sure that you received them. Miguel told me that his uncle was very fond of you just as I was very fond of Miguel," she said, a few tears running down her cheek.

I placed the envelope in my carry-on bag and decided to savour the moment of reading its contents once I was quietly seated on the plane. In the meantime, I had much packing to do and many tearful farewells to bid.

To our relief, on the morning of our departure, Alicia came running to us with a huge smile, a precursor of her good news, "Doctors say that Allegra is doing much better now and will survive her illness!"

"What good news to hear just as we leave! We are overjoyed for you and Diego," I said as we hugged each other and danced across the floor to the amazement of the twins who were watching us.

David and I bade farewell to our hosts and Carolina and Juan before embracing Alexandra and Eduardo. We hugged the twins and kissed my little namesake goodbye as she slept contentedly in her mother's arms. Waving goodbye to the family as we left Villa Sol y Iris, we promised to return as soon as it was safe to travel once again. "¡Y vayan con Dios!" wished Alexandra as we stepped into the taxi taking us to the airport.

Epilogue

Somewhere over the Atlantic Ocean—March 2020

Barcelona Airport was a frenzied scene as Covid panic seized the world. Everywhere, harried clerks attempted to calm frazzled vacationers with exhausted children as well as impatient officials desperately seeking to make new flight arrangements before the airports closed down. Masses of frustrated travellers gathered in crowded halls, pushing their way to the departure gates in a hurry to reach home. As yet, the vast majority of the population had no real idea of what awaited them: deaths increasing by the thousands, hospitals overflowing with Covid-related cases and medical personnel searching for elusive personal protective equipment. Soon, virologists would be working on a new vaccine; doctors would be trying various treatments on their patients such as the use of ultraviolet light and the administration of old drugs such as steroids used in new ways; scientists would be developing different ways of disinfecting surfaces in large areas and of analyzing waste waters to measure infection rates in specific communities while public health officials would be elaborating policies on masking, distancing, self-isolation, quarantines and lockdowns and small businesses would be devising methods of staying afloat amidst a sea of obstacles.

When David and I were finally in our seats for the overnight flight to Toronto, I reached for my bag and retrieved the special package that I had been wanting to open for the past day. I slit the envelope and began reading the letters that my grandmother had written to Eduardo more than a century earlier. The first one, sent on the day of Eduardo's departure by train from Winnipeg to New York, began with,

> "*I thought that I would join you in spirit by writing to you. Every hour since your departure this morning summons yet another thought of you. When your train left the station today, it took my world away with it. How will I ever live through the next eight months without you?*"

In another letter, Maggie wrote,

> *"Although I realize that you won't be reading this letter for several weeks, I feel compelled to write to you now to tell you how much I love you and miss you. You are my first thought in the morning and my last one at night. Nothing is the way it was before you left, like a sunny day which suddenly turns cloudy and grey without warning."*

In yet another letter, Maggie reminded Eduardo that her "*heart was heavy with longing and love*" for him and how she was "*counting the days before his return to Manitoba.*" She added,

> "*The love that I feel for you is beyond compare. I love you more today than yesterday and less than I will tomorrow. I cannot wait to be in your arms once again and to feel your lips on mine. Oh, for that special day when I will become your wife!*"

After carefully folding Maggie's touching letters and returning them to the envelope, I reached for the letter that Eduardo had written to me but never mailed, dated June 1980 shortly after my first visit to Villa Sol y Iris.

> *Querida Sofía,*
>
> *It was such a pleasure meeting you and your husband this past weekend. In many ways, you remind me of your grandmother Maggie and it is for that reason that I would like you to read the attached letter that I*

sent to her in 1971, not knowing that she had died earlier that year. I was devastated when I saw that the letter was returned to me with the note "Return to sender. Addressee deceased". Somehow, as all lovers tend to do, we think that our great love stories will never die but, of course, even if they live on forever like those of Romeo and Juliet and Antony and Cleopatra, the lovers are unfortunately mortal.

Please do not feel sorry for me as you read this letter. I have known great happiness as well as sorrow. In the springtime of my life, I enjoyed a sunny youth with my parents and beloved sister Maria Cristina while, in the summer of my life, I experienced the passion of my great love for your grandmother as well as the pain of its loss. Not having been blessed with children, I also felt a deep affection for my nephew Miguel who became like a surrogate son to me and my niece Margarita a surrogate daughter. Felipe, his second wife Lucia and the children spent most of their holidays with me at Villa Sol y Iris *for many years and I enjoyed their company more than I ever imagined I would. During this period, I was also introduced to another passion, winemaking, and it gave me a new lease on life. During the autumn of my life, Ariana became my wife for fifteen wonderful years and Miguel's son, Diego, was born. He followed me everywhere on the property, seeking constantly to learn more and more about its operations. Then, in the winter of my life, Diego's son Eduardo was born and I was overjoyed. To add to my happiness, I met you, dear Sofía, and, like an old romantic fool, dreamed that perhaps one day your daughter and Diego's son might marry, finally uniting the two families that truly were meant to be together from the first time that I set eyes on my beloved Maggie.*

Be happy!
Eduardo

Wiping away a tear, with David's comforting arm around me, I began reading Eduardo's letter to Maggie, dated March 25, 1971, just a few weeks after her death. To my surprise, I read that, after so many years, he was still thinking of her and hoping to fly to Winnipeg to join her as she was now a widow, thus releasing him from his commitment not to contact her.

Querida Margarita,

I am sure that you are wondering why I am writing to you at this late stage in our lives.

After my dear wife Ariana died in a car accident in 1967, I allowed myself to begin thinking about you once again. As you may suspect, my old friend Pierre, the concierge at the Royal Alex Hotel, would from time to time provide me with a few details about you, how you were doing, what milestones and special events you were celebrating, etc. From the limited information that I received over the years, it appeared that you and Thomas were well and happy and the busy parents of five children. While Victoria and I were not fortunate enough to have children, Felipe, Maria Cristina's husband, and his family spent much time with me at my Villa in Catalonia and brought me incredible joy.

For my part, becoming a winemaker as opposed to a wine merchant was a tremendously good move and, while I did not appreciate my parents' choice of Victoria for my wife, I was most grateful for their wedding gift of my uncle's vineyard, which has been a great source of satisfaction to me over the years.

In the Christmas card which Pierre sent to me in 1949 after Victoria had died, he added a newspaper notice which included a reference to your son Michael's upcoming wedding and, as you know so well, this led to our memorable meeting in Winnipeg in 1950, a few days which, along with those that we enjoyed together in 1913, were among the sweetest of my life.

Then, in late 1969, Pierre informed me that The Royal Alex, "our hotel", would soon be torn down. He also told me that Thomas died last year. I kept my promise never to contact you again during his lifetime but I believe that his death has released me from my commitment. It is for this reason that I am writing to you now. Would you be willing to see me this summer? While I am no longer young, I am in good health and would so enjoy seeing you again. When I think of you now, I am often reminded of William Butler Yeats's poem, When You Are Old. *(I don't suppose that you knew that I took several Irish culture and literature courses in my semi-retirement; did you?) Yeats wrote this poem in remembrance of the woman he had once loved and lost, a woman who, like him, eventually married another. However, his love for her never really died. As the poem is beautiful but ends sadly, I have taken the liberty of changing the last stanza to reflect a different and happier outcome, one that I hope will be ours very soon… I know, I can almost hear you exclaim, "Oh,* Eduardo, you have always been such a hopeless romantic!"

When You Are Old

When you are old and grey and full of sleep,
And nodding by the fire, take down this book,
And slowly read, and dream of the soft look
Your eyes had once, and of their shadows deep;

How many loved your moments of glad grace,
And loved your beauty with love false or true,
But one man loved the pilgrim soul in you,
And loved the sorrows of your changing face;

And bending down beside the glowing bars,
Murmur, a little sadly, how Love fled
And paced upon the mountains overhead
And hid his face amid a crowd of stars.

Here is my version of the third stanza:

And bending down beside the glowing bars,
Smile, wondering how love found us again
After Time erased our youth and our pain.
Now we walk hand in hand amid the stars.

I will be counting the days until I receive your reply, dearest Maggie. I know that I am perhaps asking for too much after all that has happened but, even as an old man, I still dream and think of you. To quote Yeats once again, "I have spread my dreams under your feet; Tread softly because you tread on my dreams."

With my undying love,
Tu Eduardo para siempre
(Your Eduardo forever)

What a magnificent love story! It is now time for me to finally conclude my narrative about Maggie and Eduardo's great romance, a love that defied time and distance and that eventually united their families with the marriage of my daughter to his great-great-nephew.

About the Author

Originally from Manitoba, Rosemary graduated with a B.A. (English, French and Spanish) from the University of Manitoba before moving to Kingston, Ontario where she earned an M.A. in English literature from Queen's University. After working in France and studying in Spain, she spent almost 30 years as Chief of Correspondence and Protocol Advisor at Rideau Hall. In 2011, Queen Elizabeth appointed Rosemary to the Royal Victorian Order in recognition of her service to the monarchy.

Upon retirement, her deep interest in travel and culture led Rosemary to write three children's books, published as *Les voyages de Caroline* (2016), *Le Monde de Rosemarie* (2017) and *Aloha, Hola et Salut de Caroline* (2020).

Passionate about the life and culture of southern Europe, especially Spain, Rosemary enjoys preparing Mediterranean meals for her family and friends. She lives in Ottawa with her husband where they enjoy the company of their children and grandchildren.

Printed in Canada